STAR TREK®

CONSTELLATIONS

STAR TREK®

CONSTELLATIONS

Edited by Marco Palmieri

Based upon *Star Trek*
created by Gene Roddenberry

SF
Sta

POCKET BOOKS
New York London Toronto Sydney Meekrab

151229

 POCKET BOOKS, a division of Simon & Schuster, Inc.
1230 Avenue of the Americas, New York, NY 10020

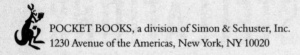
ISBN-13: 978-0-7434-9254-6
ISBN-10:   0-7434-9254-4

This Pocket Books trade paperback edition September 2006

10 9 8 7 6 5 4 3 2 1

POCKET and colophon are registered trademarks of Simon & Schuster, Inc.

Cover art by Jerry Vanderstelt

Manufactured in the United States of America

For information regarding special discounts for bulk purchases, please contact
Simon & Schuster Special Sales at 1-800-456-6798 or business@simonandschuster.com.

Space . . . the final frontier.

These are the voyages of the Starship Enterprise. Its five-year mission: to explore strange new worlds . . . to seek out new life and new civilizations . . . to boldly go where no man has gone before.

CONTENTS

INTRODUCTION
by David Gerrold

THE CONTINUING VOYAGES . . .

In 1966, the world was a lot simpler.

It was a time of innocence and promise. By today's standards, we had barely begun to climb the ladder of possibility.

We didn't have the Internet, we didn't have video games or e-mail, we didn't have laptop computers, and we didn't have phones in our pockets. Telephones were still connected to the wall by a wire, and many of them still had rotary dials. The integrated circuit didn't exist yet. If you wanted music, you listened to an AM station on a tinny transistor radio.

There were only a few places called McDonald's and the number of burgers they'd sold was about 15 million. Gasoline was 35 cents per gallon. You could still drive across country on Route 66. Lyndon Baines Johnson was president. The Beatles hadn't recorded *Sgt. Pepper's Lonely Hearts Club Band* yet. Martin Luther King hadn't yet stood on the steps of the Lincoln Memorial and declared, "I have a dream!" The United States was discovering that Vietnam was more than just a "police action." The baby boomers were in college and getting restless.

The most popular car in America was the Ford Mustang, with nearly a million copies on the road. In the movie theaters, Hal 9000 hadn't yet locked Dave out of the pod bay, it was still safe to go in the water, Don Corleone hadn't made any offers you couldn't refuse, and even the Force would not be with us for another eleven years.

Oh, and one more thing—there were no footsteps on the moon. That particular dream was still three years away.

Then, on September 8, 1966, NBC broadcast the first episode of a new television series, called *Star Trek*.

That moment was a cusp. It was the first pebble rattling down the slope before the rest of the avalanche starts. It was, in a sense, the moment the future arrived in America's living room.

Star Trek's vision was so far beyond the lives of ordinary Americans that it may very well have been incomprehensible to many of them. It was a vision of a different way of being.

It was startling.

Part of it was the details. The clothes. The hair. Those ears. Doors that slid open as you approached. Handheld communicators that flipped open. Wall-sized viewscreens. Medical scanners and displays. Information stored on credit-card-sized blocks or silvery discs. Beams of light that could be used to heat things or cut through them. Computers that could store an unlimited amount of information, sounds and pictures and video. All of these things, and more, suggested that in the future, life would be *different*.

It was the beginning of the beginning. The vocabulary of science fiction was about to enter the mainstream.

Today, we take it for granted that supermarket doors slide open as we approach, that we can flip open a telephone and call anywhere in the world, that television is a 60-inch high-definition display, that we can look at our unborn children with ultrasound scanners, and that we can carry a library of music and movies and photos in a unit smaller than a candy bar. We use hand-lasers for pointing—or for teasing the cat; we use industrial lasers to cut wood and metal and plastic. And if I were to discuss all the things we now use computers for, I wouldn't have room to talk about *Star Trek,* or the stories in this book.

But after we step past the technological predictions, there was something else about *Star Trek,* something far more important than flip-phones and HDTV and laptop connections to the Internet.

Star Trek represented a different way of being human—because it represented a different way of thinking about humanity. We'd come out of World War II, shocked and horrified to discover the level of brutality that human beings were capable of. In direct reaction, new schools of philosophical thought came into being—new political movements took root all over the world. Many of them had as a central part of their vision, "We can do better, we have to do better. We cannot continue doing the same things we did before."

A veteran of the war, as well as a veteran of the urban war in the streets, Gene Roddenberry spoke the vision very succinctly: "We are going to show people that the way things are is not necessarily the way they have to be."

In that simple subversive statement, Roddenberry was declaring that *Star Trek* was about possibilities. Not simply the possibilities of technology—but the possibilities of humanity.

Science fiction, even before *Star Trek,* has always been about the questions "Who are we? What are we doing here? What does it mean to be a human being?" *Star Trek,* the television show, visualized those questions in almost every episode. Sometimes silly, sometimes startling, sometimes melodramatic, sometimes tragic—but always, somehow asking, "What if things were like this instead? What would that be like?"

That's the real legacy of *Star Trek* (and all the best science fiction, for that matter)—it invites you to think. It encourages you to ask questions. It stretches the event horizon of your imagination.

And the proof of that simple assertion can be found in this book of thirteen new stories set in the universe of the original *Star Trek* series. The authors here have not spent much time postulating or predicting startling new technologies that will change our lives in the future. Instead, they've stayed focused on the larger vision of *Star Trek.* The stories you are about to read are all about human beings taking on the challenges of their own humanity.

"First, Do No Harm," by Dayton Ward and Kevin Dilmore, examines one of the most difficult dilemmas of the original series: the Prime Directive. The Prime Directive is a dispassionate rule; detached from specific circumstances, it is only a guideline, not a limit. Sometimes circumstances are so compelling that to stand back and let terrible events occur unchecked is the greater evil. So where does duty lie?

Indeed, one of the continuing themes of *Star Trek* is that the real strength of our heroes is their ability to learn their limits—so they can transcend them. Robert Greenberger explores this in depth as he takes us down to the surface of another new world with "The Landing Party." This time, the focus is on the responsibilities of command—not just the responsibilities of Captain Kirk, but also the responsibilities of Lieutenant Sulu as well.

Likewise, Howard Weinstein, who has considerable experience in the *Star Trek* universe, takes on Pavel Chekov in "Official Record." As always, there are lessons to be learned—and again, there are uncomfortable parallels to present events. What do you do when duty isn't enough?

In "Fracture," Jeff Bond takes us out into deep space for some spectacular scenery—and a surprising encounter with the Tholians. Encounters with alien races will also be confrontations with the difficult questions of belief and being. Sometimes the best answer is that there are no best answers, only possibilities.

Stuart Moore brings us back to the *Star Trek* universe in "Chaotic Response," an examination of Spock's unique commitment to logic. Half human, half Vulcan, Spock lives in two worlds; he is native to none. Here, tested to the breaking point, his only salvation is to use his logical abilities to understand his emotional components. It is the same choice that every sentient being has to make—how to assimilate rationality with the drives and desires of one's inherently animal nature.

In "As Others See Us," Christopher L. Bennett gives us a very different perspective on the same situation. Don't make hasty judgments. Things are not always as they seem. There will always be surprises. There's a lesson to be learned here—but who needs to learn it is the real surprise.

"See No Evil," by Jill Sherwin, gives us a welcome (and long overdue) look at Lieutenant Uhura and her importance to the workings of the *Enterprise*. Taking place shortly after Uhura's encounter with Nomad (and subsequent memory loss), Sherwin relates not only Uhura's recovery and resumption of duties, but also her resumption of confidence. Along the way, she shows us a surprisingly insightful side of Scotty as well.

Dave Galanter goes for a more traditional story of action and suspense in "The Leader." It's a clearly recognizable adventure, taken directly from the basic elements of *Star Trek*. Yes, there is a disabled shuttlecraft and a Klingon threat and the inevitable colonists in danger; but ultimately the story is about the nature of leadership. It's about the quality of character that justifies authority, both human and Klingon.

Taking a situation that evokes some of the best moments of the original series, William Leisner examines the question of "Ambition." But unlike the original series, he leaves Kirk and Spock behind, so he can show us that the other members of the crew, with their own unique personalities, can also meet the challenges of an encounter with a very unusual alien life-form.

In "Devices and Desires," Kevin Lauderdale rummages around in Starfleet's attic, taking the time to examine some of the lost treasures that the *Enterprise* and other starships have discovered. The problem is that you usually find a lot more in an attic than the dusty past.

Then, Jeffrey Lang turns his attention to one of *Star Trek*'s most beloved characters, Dr. Leonard "Bones" McCoy, in "Where Everybody Knows Your Name." As the *Enterprise* approaches the end of her five-year mission, Dr. McCoy and Mr. Scott step off the ship for an adventure of their own, involving a misguided Klingon and several Denebian slime devils—proving once again that you're only as old as the liquor you drink.

And finally, Allyn Gibson takes a giant step out of the box to tell a story that is both unique and powerful. It's about a different kind of mission, and the result is a very different look at who we are. "Make-Believe" is one of the most insightful stories in the book, because it isn't just about *Star Trek*. It's about *all of us*. Like a great bell, long after you have put this book away, this story will continue to echo in your head.

As you read through these tales, you will notice that the mission of the original *Enterprise* has been fleshed out and expanded in ways that the television series could never achieve, partly due to the limitations of budget and partly due to the conventions of television, but primarily because all of these authors have done their job and taken their tales into undiscovered countries—where none have gone before. They have given us the opportunity to look deeper into the souls of our heroes—so that we can discover ourselves.

And that is the real mission of *Star Trek*—to seek out new vistas of imagination and discovery.

Because after all is said and done, what remains is this simple truth:

Space is not the final frontier. The final frontier is the human soul. Space is where we will meet the challenge.

—David Gerrold

First, Do No Harm

Dayton Ward & Kevin Dilmore

Dayton Ward

Dayton Ward has been a fan of *Star Trek* since conception (his, not the show's). His professional writing career began with stories selected for each of Pocket Books' first three *Star Trek: Strange New Worlds* anthologies. In addition to his various writing projects with Kevin Dilmore, Dayton is the author of the *Star Trek* novel *In the Name of Honor* and the science fiction novels *The Last World War* and *The Genesis Protocol* as well as short stories that have appeared in *Kansas City Voices* magazine and the *Star Trek: New Frontier* anthology *No Limits*. Though he currently lives in Kansas City with his wife, Michi, Dayton is a Florida native and still maintains a torrid long-distance romance with his beloved Tampa Bay Buccaneers. Be sure to visit Dayton's official website at http://www.daytonward.com.

Kevin Dilmore

For more than eight years, Kevin Dilmore was a contributing writer to *Star Trek Communicator*, penning news stories and personality profiles for the bimonthly publication of the Official *Star Trek* Fan Club. On the storytelling side of things, his story "The Road to Edos" was published as part of the *Star Trek: New Frontier* anthology *No Limits*. With Dayton Ward, his work includes stories for the anthology *Star Trek: Tales of the Dominion War*, the *Star Trek: The Next Generation* novels *A Time to Sow* and *A Time to Harvest*, the *Star Trek Vanguard* novel *Summon the Thunder*, and ten installments of the original e-book series *Star Trek: S.C.E.* and *Star Trek: Corps of Engineers*. A graduate of the University of Kansas, Kevin lives in Prairie Village, Kansas, with his wife, Michelle, and their three daughters, and works as a writer for Hallmark Cards in Kansas City, Missouri.

Blood was *everywhere*.

Revati Jendra knelt before the young male's motionless form, fighting to bring her breathing back under control after the harried sprint from her clinic to the village's small ironworks. Coughing as she inhaled some of the building's sooty, metallic-tasting air, she pried open the injured adolescent's eyes to see that his large, black pupils remained sensitive even to the dim, orange-hued light within the metal shop. That was a good sign, at least a somewhat better sign than the pale pink blood staining his chalk-white hair and widening into a disturbingly large pool where his head rested on the bare, dirty floor of the shop.

"He just fell, *Beloren*," said a voice from the crowd, addressing her, as nearly all of the villagers did, by the Grennai term for "healer." It was a name to which she'd grown accustomed during the year or so she had lived and worked among them. "He started shaking and then just let go of the ladder."

A growing crowd of concerned friends and co-workers—all of them, Jendra thought, appearing too young to be working in such a place—began to encircle her as she lowered her ear to the injured male's lips, listening and feeling for even the faintest breath.

If only they weren't hovering over me, this could go so much more damned quickly.

Spasms abruptly wracked the young man's body, and Jendra reached down to support his head with one hand while rolling him to one side in case he started to vomit. "I need help to move him," she called out to no one in particular as he continued to tremble. "We have to take him to the white home right away." Though possessing only rudimentary facilities, the Grennai hospital and its staff would probably be able to see this young man through most of his injuries. As his seizure started to fade, however, Jendra began to suspect that the man's fall had been no mere accident.

In a practiced move, she reached into the pocket of her frayed, homespun overcoat and retrieved a small, light-colored cloth. Hoping her actions appeared to the onlookers as trying to staunch the flow of blood from her patient's wound, Jendra activated the small Starfleet medical scanner concealed within the cloth. Pressing it against the dark skin of the man's head and watching as it turned pink with his blood, she manipulated the hidden, silenced device in order to determine the extent of his injuries. While his neck and spine were undamaged, the scan had detected a small tumor within the man's brain, and Jendra recognized it as the likely culprit behind the man's seizures.

"Step aside," said a strong, deep voice, that of Crimar, the ironworks supervisor. Jendra looked up to see the burly Grennai and one of his workers carrying a makeshift stretcher. Sweat matted their stark white hair to their heads and soot stained their rough, woven clothing. "We will carry him, *Beloren.*"

"Just a moment, Crimar," she said as she searched through her worn, leather medicine satchel. While she knew the bag did not contain what she needed to eliminate the tumor, which under Grennai medical standards would be undetectable and eventually fatal, Jendra was sure she could cure the young man given a little time and privacy. Unable to administer a hypospray in the midst of the onlookers, Jendra opted for an oral dose of trianoline. She slipped the small strip into his mouth, where it dissolved instantly on contact with his tongue. Within moments, the medication would begin to relieve some of the trauma the fall had inflicted upon his brain.

After taking an additional few moments to wrap the man's head in a thick bandage, Jendra pointed to one of the workers and had him kneel next to her. She handed him another wad of cloth, instructing him to hold it against the victim's wound.

"Keep pressing here until you get to the *beloren* at the white home," Jendra ordered as she rose and waved to Crimar. "Take him now. I'll follow after you." She stepped back, allowing the supervisor to direct two workers to load their comrade onto the stretcher.

After directing the rest of the workforce to return to their respective tasks, Crimar turned to Jendra. "Thank you for coming so quickly, *Beloren*," he said. Though normally she found his accent as he spoke in his native language to be fluid and almost musical, on this occasion his tone was flat and emotionless. "But he has lost much blood. Surely he will die?"

"Not if I can help it," Jendra replied, the resolve in her voice abruptly shattered beneath the force of a ragged cough that hunched her aging, slender form. Seeing the look of concern in Crimar's wide eyes, she offered a weak smile as she wiped her mouth. "I'm fine, my friend. It's merely the soot in here. Maybe you could tidy up for me the next time I pay a visit?"

A wide smile creased Crimar's dark features. "I hope that is not for some time, *Beloren*."

Jendra patted his shoulder as she suppressed what would have been another coughing fit, then gathered her meager medical bag and headed for her home. As she walked down the village's main thoroughfare with its dual row of one- and two-story wooden frame buildings, she hoped she would not have any patients awaiting her return. Still, she knew that as the villagers became more accustomed to her presence, they would come in a steady stream even for the most minor of ailments. That seemed to be the way of the Grennai as she moved from settlement to settlement, this one her fifth since her return to this planet more than a year earlier.

While her personal mission of medical duty on this decidedly primitive world—catalogued in Starfleet databases only as NGC 667—had not gone precisely as she originally planned, Jendra managed to allow herself some small measure of satisfaction in her accomplishments this afternoon as well as what she would do for her latest patient at the first opportunity. Thanks to her, with an admitted assist from her borrowed Starfleet-issue medical equipment, one young man's life would change for the better.

The least I can do for these kind people, and we should be doing a damn sight more.

Hoping to catch a little rest before following up with her patient, Jendra opened the door to the clinic that doubled as her home. Moving shadows in the hallway leading to her examination room caught her by surprise, though, and she stopped. Hushed voices—she could not make out any words—carried from the far room.

Making her way down the hall, minding her steps so as not to clatter her hard-soled shoes against the wooden floor, Jendra peered into the exam room and saw three cloaked figures searching through her belongings. They seemed to know exactly what they were looking for and were gathering specific items atop her worktable: two Starfleet medical tricorders, a communicator, assorted surgical instruments, a hyrospray kit, and other equipment that was at extreme odds with the room's comparably primitive trappings.

Her temper flaring at the violation, Jendra burst into the room, hoping to catch the intruders off guard. "Just what the hell do you think you're doing here?" she shouted.

Three Grennai males looked up at her with matching expressions of alarm, though none of them moved from where they stood. Instead, one of the men regarded her, his features changing from shock to what Jendra read as annoyance. In a firm voice, he said, "I've been waiting to ask you *exactly* the same question, Dr. Jendra."

The words were in Federation Standard, rather than the language native to Grennai in this region. Jendra's jaw dropped as she fumbled for her own response. She remained silent as one of the other men stepped forward, his hand reaching up to move his hood back from his head, and Jendra was startled to realize that she recognized his face.

"Revati, we need to talk."

Despite the darkened skin, white hair, and obviously prosthetic ears, there was no mistaking the voice of Dr. Leonard McCoy.

McCoy watched as Revati Jendra—cosmetically altered just as he was to resemble the indigenous Grennai—regarded him with an expression first of shock, then confusion before comprehension dawned and a wide smile creased her aged features.

"Leonard?" Jendra exclaimed, stepping forward to clasp both of his hands in hers. Smiling, she said, "I never thought I'd see you again, least of all here."

"You're not exactly the easiest person to track down," McCoy replied, relief at seeing her seeping into his voice. "I've been worried about you. A lot of people have."

Her smile fading, Jendra cast her head downward. "I can imagine." She cleared her throat before returning her gaze to meet his, and McCoy saw a hint of regret in her eyes. "Not a chance this is happy co-incidence, I suppose."

"You suppose correctly, Doctor."

Even with his normal features disguised beneath the darkened skin tone and the artificial hair and ears, there was no hiding or suppressing James Kirk's command presence. McCoy saw the familiar set to his captain's jaw as he stepped forward to confront Jendra. "We're here to take you back with us."

She glanced at McCoy before offering a warm, knowing smile the doctor would have recognized regardless of the situation at hand. "You must be Captain Kirk," she said. Looking at McCoy's other companion, she added, "And Mr. Spock. Leonard has spoken very highly of you both." She held out her hand in greeting.

As if unprepared for Jendra's lack of initial resistance, the captain paused before nodding. "Thank you," he offered, his tone less rigid now. As Kirk and Jendra shook hands, McCoy noticed the slight yet obvious relaxing of his friend's stance and, yes, even the first hints of that now-familiar glint in the man's eye. For Jim Kirk, turning on the charm for a woman—any woman—seemed a reflex as natural as breathing.

"I'm sorry we have to meet under these circumstances, Doctor," Kirk said after a moment, his tone all business once again, "but I'm afraid Starfleet can't allow you to remain here."

Pulling herself up as if to meet Kirk eye-to-eye, Jendra replied, "The nature of my work here is humanitarian, Captain. I want us to be clear about that."

"Then *clearly*," Kirk snapped, biting down on the word, "you must be aware that your presence here is a violation of the Prime Directive and poses a risk to these people and their natural course of development. Your knowledge, your equipment, all of it is centuries ahead of these people and their level of technology."

McCoy saw the anger in Jendra's eyes, but she held her tone in check as she glared at Kirk. "I'm well versed in the Prime Directive." She held her hands out and away from her body. "As you can see, I've taken steps to prevent any cultural contamination. I'm also no stranger to the Grennai and how they live."

"Indeed," Spock said, moving to stand beside Kirk. "Three years ago, you were assigned as a medical officer to the initial Starfleet cultural observation detachment on this planet."

Jendra nodded. "That's right, Mr. Spock. We were tasked with covert study of the Grennai's preindustrial development, which we believed very closely mirrored that of your own people on Vulcan. We were here for nearly a year, during which we spent a great deal of time among the Grennai. So, you see, I've become quite adept at blending into the indigenous population."

"Your mission was terminated prematurely," Kirk said, "due to issues stemming from atmospheric irradiation and planetary conditions deemed potentially harmful to the research team. According to your own report, the planet was deemed unsafe to anyone but the local population."

"It is safe," Jendra corrected. "The rings of radiation encircling the planet constantly bombard the atmosphere, yes, but the indigenous population is immune to the radiation's effects."

Spock nodded. "*Enterprise* science teams have been studying the phenomenon since our arrival."

"Then you also know that it was part of the reason for our research here," Jendra said. "Trying to learn about the Grennai's natural immunity. Outsiders can only be exposed for short periods without protection. My team and I received regular inoculations of a hyronalin derivative to protect ourselves. I'm able to synthesize a version of that compound with the equipment I have and with raw ingredients I collect as I need them."

McCoy said, "After you returned to Earth, you were involved in some kind of research for a while, but then I get a message from you saying you're leaving Starfleet, and you just disappear." The words came out harsher than he had intended, and he swallowed the sudden lump in his throat. Looking around the crude examination room and its array of equally primitive medical and surgical implements—for all intents and purposes a medieval torture chamber when compared to his own sickbay aboard the *Enterprise*—he shook his head. "It was Starfleet Command that eventually suggested you might have come back here, but why?"

Looking away for a moment as if considering the weight of her response, Jendra finally sighed. "I have my reasons, Leonard."

The answer was vague, but her eyes spoke volumes, McCoy thought, reminding him of what he remembered most about the time they had spent together as colleagues—her drive to heal, the strength she drew from confidence in her abilities, her sense of doing right by her patients regardless of any personal toll it might exact upon her—all of that shone through her expression with startling clarity.

What the hell have you gotten yourself into, Revati?

In response to her words, Kirk stepped forward. "I'm sorry, Doctor, but you'll have to explain your reasons to Starfleet Command."

Jendra smiled once more, a tired, resigned smile. "I can imagine they're quite upset with me, but that doesn't change anything. I can't go. Not now."

Casting a glance toward McCoy that the doctor understood as the first hint of true irritation with the current proceedings, Kirk said, "It's not a request. You can come voluntarily, or I can carry you out of here."

"Such a tactic might prove unwise, Captain," Spock said, his tone and demeanor unflappable and—to McCoy, anyway—almost comical in its seriousness. "We would almost certainly attract attention during our attempt to return to the shuttlecraft."

At that, Jendra's eyebrows rose. "Shuttlecraft? Oh, that's right. I'd almost forgotten what the radiation bands do to transporters and communications." Shaking her head, she made a *tsk-tsk* sound through pursed lips. "A shame, that."

McCoy saw Kirk open his mouth to reply, no doubt with the intention of playing some kind of bluff, but Spock beat him to it.

"Our chief engineer has been researching the problem since our arrival," the Vulcan said, "but at last report he had not succeeded in recalibrating the transporter's annular confinement beam to work within this planet's atmosphere. I calculate the odds of his completing that task before we can return to the *Columbus* at seven thous—"

"*Thank* you, Mr. Spock," Kirk snapped.

Sighing, McCoy shook his head. "Spock, one of these days we need to have a long talk about that nasty habit of yours."

Spock's right eyebrow, artificially whitened and thickened in keeping with typical Grennai facial features, arched in the manner that always characterized his curiosity or skepticism. "What habit is that, Doctor?"

"Your mouth runneth over."

"That's enough," Kirk said, his tone and the expression on his face clear indications that he was in no mood for his friends' latest round of verbal jousting. To Jendra, who was still smiling as she observed the exchange, he said, "You seem to think this is funny, Doctor. I assure you it isn't. My orders are to return you to Starfleet Command, in restraints if necessary."

No sooner did the words leave his mouth than McCoy heard the sound of the door at the front of the building being thrown open, followed as quickly by a series of rapid, almost frantic footsteps on the hardwood floor. He felt his pulse quicken as he heard pain-wracked sobs from what could only be a child, all but drowned out by a louder, more adult voice echoing down the passageway.

"*Beloren! Beloren, kono nata!*"

Whatever enjoyment Jendra might have been feeling at Kirk's expense vanished. "This'll have to wait, Captain." Waving her arms toward the worktable and the array of Starfleet medical equipment lying atop it, she hissed, "Hide that, *now!*" Without waiting for a response, she grabbed her worn satchel and hurried from the room.

Leaving Kirk and Spock to tend to the sanitizing of the room—which involved both men stuffing various articles into the pockets of their robes or the large bag Spock wore slung over his shoulder—McCoy followed after his friend. He found her kneeling beside the body of a young Grennai female, a child, whose clothing was stained with what his gut told him was far too much blood. Standing nearby was a Grennai woman, obviously the girl's mother, whose clothes also sported blood. He reached for her in an attempt to help.

She only waved him away, her expression pained as tears ran down her cheeks. "It is not my blood," she said, his universal translator filtering the native Grennai language into Federation Standard. "Please, help my *tundato!*"

"I'm trying to do just that," Jendra snapped, also in the local dialect, and McCoy looked down to see her hand clamped around the girl's right arm just above the elbow. To him, she said, "Help me get her to the examination room." It took only seconds to transfer the young patient to an exam table at the rear of the clinic, after which Jendra waved him out of her way as she set to work. Kirk and Spock hung nearby, watching intently.

McCoy could see a large gash in the girl's arm and pale blood running liberally from the wound. Jendra reached for a nearby clay pitcher with her free hand and began to pour water over the blood-covered wound. The girl screamed as the water hit her olive skin.

"Looks like a vein was hit," Jendra said before whispering something McCoy could not hear to the still-squirming child. Looking at the mother, she asked, "What happened?"

"We were working in the fields near our home," the woman replied. "Litari was clearing brush when she slipped in the mud and fell on the blade." Holding a hand to her mouth, she trembled for a moment. "Can you help her?"

Rather than answering the question, Jendra said, "Leonard, bring me the tray on the middle shelf." She nodded toward a set of wooden shelves to her right.

Glancing toward Kirk and Spock before doing as instructed, McCoy moved the tray near Jendra's left hand. "What can I do?" he asked.

"The dish with the green paste," Jendra replied. "Take some and rub it on her upper lip, just under her nose." As she continued to work at cleaning the struggling girl's wound, she added, "Don't inhale it yourself."

"Bones," McCoy heard Kirk say, the captain's tone one of caution, but he ignored it. Instead, he reached for what appeared to be nothing more than an earthen petri dish and—without thinking or even checking to see that his hands were clean—dipped his right forefinger into the viscous, emerald-colored substance it contained. Leaning forward, he applied the paste beneath the girl's nostrils even as Jendra kept working.

Almost immediately, the child's movements grew weaker and she began to relax. Less than ten seconds after he had applied the ointment, the girl's breathing slowed and she went limp on the examination table.

"I'll be damned," McCoy breathed.

Reaching for what he saw was a rudimentary version of a hemostat, Jendra looked up from her work. "It would be better if the mother waited outside." Her gaze locked with his for an instant before she glanced in the direction of her ever-present satchel, the meaning behind her words now quite plain.

She needs her equipment, and doesn't want to use it in front of the mother.

"We should all make room for the . . . *beloren*," Spock said, taking the initiative and stepping toward the girl's mother.

When the woman did not budge from where she stood, Jendra looked to her and offered an encouraging smile. "Don't worry, Walirta. She's going to be fine."

Walirta allowed Spock to escort her from the examination room, with Kirk following after them. McCoy reached for the door, intending to give Jendra and her patient some privacy, and before exiting the room nodded encouragement to his friend.

"I'll be outside if you need me," he offered, and in that instant saw the determination in her eyes. Jendra's calling as a healer of body and spirit had led her to this place and to these people, and no person or regulation was going to hold sway over her.

But what are you trying to prove here? What do you think you can change?

Closing the door, he turned to find Kirk waiting for him, his jaw set in an expression of determination that the doctor knew too well.

"She's committed herself to this place, Jim," he said, "and to these people. I don't think I can convince her to leave, at least not until I know more." Frowning, he added, "Assuming I can get it out of her."

Looking over his shoulder as though to ensure Spock had taken the Grennai woman out of earshot, Kirk said, "Bones, she's appointed herself their caretaker. She's using her advanced medical knowledge and equipment to treat them in clear violation of the Prime Directive. It's not that I don't sympathize with her desire to help, but . . ." He shook his head, his brow furrowing as he pondered the situation. "It's as if she feels responsible for them somehow, as though she can save them, but why? From what?"

McCoy had to admit that the same questions were troubling him, as well.

"What do you mean, *classified?*"

Feeling his temper flare as he listened to the open communicator channel, Kirk rose from his chair and began to pace the small room at the front of Dr. Jendra's clinic.

From the communicator in his hand, the voice of Ensign Pavel Chekov replied, *"I am sorry, Captain, but all attempts to access the mission logs of the NGC-667 survey team are being rejected. Starfleet Command has flagged them off-limits except to authorized personnel."* Static eroded the quality of the transmission, despite the signal-enhancing effects of channeling the connection through the larger and more powerful communications system of the shuttlecraft *Columbus,* which sat concealed in a wooded valley three kilometers distant.

It had taken a bit of digging by the resourceful ensign—with Spock helping him to create an A7 computer specialist's rating and access key—just to discover that there was more to Jendra's mission to NGC 667 than was recorded in the official file Kirk had already reviewed prior to the *Enterprise*'s arrival in the system. Still, even the Vulcan's formidable prowess with Starfleet computer technology had proven insufficient to penetrate the security apparently surrounding the information Kirk now sought.

"Captain," came another voice from the communicator, this one belonging to Lieutenant Hikaru Sulu, *"Lieutenant Uhura has just informed me that she's received a subspace message from Admiral Komack. He wants to talk to you as soon as possible, and Uhura says the admiral doesn't sound very happy."*

From where he sat near the window at the front of the room that overlooked the village's main street, McCoy said, "Komack upset? That's a surprise."

"Not now, Bones," Kirk snapped. To his communicator, he said, "Stall the admiral, Mr. Sulu. What's the status on transporters?"

The *Enterprise* helmsman replied, *"Mr. Scott reports he's made some progress, but he's still running safety tests. He thinks he can certify it safe for bio-matter within three hours, sir."*

It was not the best news, the captain thought, but it would have to do. "Keep me informed, Lieutenant. Kirk out." As he closed the communicator and returned it to an inside pocket of his robe, Kirk shook his head. "I knew something about this wasn't right." He looked to McCoy. "She came back here for a reason, Bones, and it has something to do with whatever Starfleet has classified about her first mission here."

"She's a doctor, Jim," McCoy replied. "It's what she does." He waved through the window. "Can't say I blame her. Lord knows how many primitive cultures we've visited where I wished I could stay longer, help them in some lasting way."

Clasping his hands behind his back, Spock said, "Even with the advanced technology and pharmaceuticals at her disposal, one physician cannot hope to make a lasting impact on any society by treating random incidents of illness and injury. The risk Dr. Jendra poses toward adversely affecting this culture's development should any of her advanced equipment be discovered is exponentially greater than any help she might offer. Logic suggests that—"

"Logic is probably the last thing on her mind!" McCoy barked. "Can't you drop that damned Vulcan stoicism and just try to connect with someone's feelings for once?"

"Actually, he's right, Leonard."

Kirk whirled toward the voice behind him to see Jendra standing in the doorway, regarding him with an expression mixed of equal parts amusement and resignation.

"I heard you in contact with your ship," Jendra said as she entered the room. "You should take better care to conceal such conversations as well as your equipment. Wouldn't want to disrupt the indigenous culture, after all."

Kirk ignored the gentle verbal jab. "How's the girl?" he asked, hoping to soften the doctor's demeanor.

"She'll be okay," Jendra replied, following that with a small cough. Clearing her throat, she reached up to rub the bridge of her nose. "I had to repair the severed vein, but don't worry, I did so in a manner that's undetectable to the Grennai *beloren*. I've had her taken to the local hospital." Releasing a sigh, she regarded Kirk with tired eyes. "So, ready to haul me away in irons?"

"Revati," McCoy said, "please. Jim's not the enemy."

A raspy, humorless chuckle pushed past Jendra's lips. "Doesn't look to be my friend, either."

"This isn't personal, Doctor," Kirk said, once again feeling his irritation growing. "I have my orders, and my duty, just as you once did."

He saw the tightening of her jaw line as she regarded him in silence for a moment, and he thought he almost could sense the struggle taking place within her. What secrets did she harbor? What burden did she carry? Why was she so driven?

"Maybe that's the problem," Jendra said after a moment, her gaze hardening. "It's not personal for you."

Kirk shook his head. "I don't understand." Even as he spoke the words, however, something told him that her passion and focus went far beyond even the absolute commitment typically displayed by the most dedicated physicians.

She'll accept help, his instincts told him. *Let her ask for it.*

"What hasn't Starfleet told us?" he asked. "What happened during your mission that made you come back here?"

Crossing the room to the chair next to McCoy, Jendra coughed again as she sat down and spent a moment fussing with the hem of her woven shirt before drawing a deep breath. "Our primary task was to learn about the Grennai's inherent immunity to the planet's radiation in the hope of learning ways to perfect protection against similar hazards."

She indicated her face and clothing with a wave of her hand. "Our disguises allowed us to interact with the indigenous population, but our actions were in keeping with the Prime Directive. We did *not* interfere with these people's societal development." Her features clouding into what Kirk recognized as an expression of guilt, she cast a glance toward the floor before sighing and shaking her head. "At first, anyway."

McCoy leaned forward until he could take her left hand in both of his. "Revati, what happened?"

"It was Roberts," Jendra replied.

Kirk knew the name only from the report he had read during the transit to NGC 667, but that was why he had Spock. A single glance was all that the first officer required, and he nodded in reply.

"Prior to his retirement," the Vulcan said, "Dr. Campbell Roberts had a noteworthy career spent almost entirely within the xeno-sociology field. He participated in the concealed observation and study of more than two dozen developing cultures, including a solo endeavor where he spent over a year embedded within a tribe of primitive humanoids who had not yet discovered fire. It was revolutionary research—something never before attempted by any pre–first contact team."

"That's what I call dedication," McCoy remarked.

Jendra nodded. "He had a reputation as a bit of an eccentric, of course, particularly after that mission, but no one could ever argue with his work or most of his recommendations. When our passive research and observation of the Grennai failed to turn up anything useful about their apparent immunity to the radiation, it was Campbell who made the decision to take additional measures. He began collecting tissue and blood samples, first from the bodies of dead Grennai but later from living specimens."

"I take that to mean he didn't do so within the guise of a local doctor?" Kirk asked after she paused again.

"Correct," Jendra replied. "He and his assistants enacted a program where they would select a promising candidate, tranquilize them while they were sleeping, then move them to one of our secure locations where the patient could be subjected to a full battery of tests, all noninvasive except for the collection of samples. The patients would be returned to their homes unharmed and none the wiser."

Kirk said nothing, but instead watched as McCoy's expression turned to one of horror and disbelief.

"Revati," the doctor said, his voice low and solemn. "He abducted innocent people for medical testing without their knowledge?"

Coughing again, Jendra reached up to wipe her forehead before replying, "Yes, and I helped him." Before McCoy could respond to that she pressed forward. "I didn't accept his reasoning at first, but after a while I became convinced it was the only way to learn about the long-term effects on their physiology, to track how the radiation worked in concert with the Grennai's normal growth and aging cycle. We gathered samples from children as well as adults, even babies, but at no time was anyone in any danger. At least, that's what we thought."

She stopped to clear her throat, and Kirk could see that recalling the mission was evoking what could only be pain the doctor had been only partially successful at suppressing.

Then she collapsed.

McCoy caught her as she fell forward from her chair, with Kirk and Spock both lunging across the room to offer assistance. The captain saw that Jendra was unconscious, her body limp in McCoy's arms as he lowered her to the floor.

"What's wrong with her?" Kirk asked.

"How the hell should I know?" the doctor growled as he reached into his robe for his tricorder. Kirk and Spock watched in silence as their friend conducted a brief, hurried examination, with the captain's attention moving from the door to the window overlooking the street and back again as the whine of McCoy's medical scanner echoed in the room. It lasted only a few seconds, after which the physician looked up and locked eyes with Kirk.

"She's dying, Jim."

After helping to move Jendra to a bed in another room of the doctor's home, Kirk and Spock could only wait while McCoy conducted a more thorough examination of his friend. The captain considered a return to the shuttlecraft *Columbus* but decided against it as darkness fell over the village, opting instead for a check-in call to Lieutenant Sulu. The status report was not promising, with Scotty still hard at work attempting to recalibrate the transporters while Admiral Komack continued his efforts to strangle Kirk via the subspace connection linking Starfleet Command with the *Enterprise*.

Another entertaining after-action report for the admiral, Kirk mused. *It's a wonder he doesn't bust me down to second officer on a garbage scow.*

"She's got three, maybe four months at most," the doctor said thirty minutes later after inviting his friends into the room where Jendra lay in bed, asleep and resting. "If she stays here, that is."

"The radiation?" Kirk asked. "I thought she was inoculating herself to protect against that, like we are."

It was Spock who replied. "I took the liberty of examining her supply of medications, Captain, but I found no quantities of the hyronalin derivative developed for use here."

"Revati told me the synthesizer she brought with her broke down and she wasn't able to fix it," McCoy said. "She'd manufactured a reserve to get her through in case she ran into trouble procuring the raw materials to make more, but she went through the last of that a month or so ago, and once her immunity started to fail . . ." Shaking his head, he let the sentence fade on his lips.

Kirk frowned, turning to regard the still-sleeping Jendra. "The condition can't be reversed?"

"I might be able to do something for her on the *Enterprise*," the doctor replied, "but her best chance is a Starbase medical facility."

"I'm not going."

Her voice was feeble as Jendra struggled to sit up in her bed, coughing as she did so. McCoy moved to help her and she allowed the assistance, and in a moment was sitting with her back against the headboard, still dressed in her heavy shirt but covered from the waist down by a thick woven blanket.

"Revati," McCoy began.

Shaking her head, Jendra held up a hand. "I can't leave these people, Leonard. Not now, not after what we did to them."

"Did to them," Kirk repeated. "You mean there's more to what you were telling us, don't you?"

Looking to McCoy, Jendra offered a weak smile. "You said he wasn't stupid."

"I also said he wasn't your enemy," McCoy replied. "Tell us, Revati. Tell us everything."

"It was one of our team members, Dr. Quentin Melander," Jendra said. She paused to cough once more before continuing. "He had been exposed to a strain of Ametan rubeola some years ago on another mission. According to his most recent physical, the virus was dormant in his system, held in remission thanks to a regular vaccination schedule. What no one counted on was the virus mutating once he came into contact with the atmosphere here."

"Dear God," McCoy whispered. "No."

Her expression one of sadness, Jendra nodded. "The radiation exposure altered the virus so that he became contagious." Kirk saw her eyes watering, and a single tear fell down her right cheek. "Not to us, though. Just the Grennai."

"Ametan rubeola causes dehydration, pneumonia, encephalitis," Spock said. "Left unchecked, it can decimate populations, particularly those with a level of medical knowledge and technology similar to this one."

"Children are especially susceptible to it," McCoy added. "I've seen it run through thousands of people in a month, Jim."

"The mutation accelerated even that timetable," Jendra said. "Melander died within seventy-two hours, and his exposure to just two members of the village we were observing was enough to wipe out its entire population—two hundred thirty-eight people—in less than two weeks."

"What did Starfleet do?" Kirk asked, though he felt his gut already trying to scream the answer at him.

"Starfleet Medical evaluated the situation," Jendra said, "and determined the virus in its mutated form would be immune to available vaccines. Projections for developing a new treatment were poor—far beyond the projected life expectancy of anyone exposed to the virus. Our team was evacuated from the planet, and all signs of our presence were removed. We left the Grennai to their fate."

Spock said, "According to public news sources, Dr. Roberts retired from Starfleet due to health reasons and withdrew from public life. If memory serves, he still publishes for the *Starfleet Medical Journal,* though on an infrequent basis."

Releasing a humorless laugh that was all but lost in a renewed coughing fit, Jendra replied, "Campbell was convicted of violating the

Prime Directive and sent to a penal colony. The rest of us were given suspended sentences and official reprimands in our files—all classified, of course, along with pretty much everything pertaining to the mission. It was all buried." She shook her head, turning to look at a spot in the corner of the room as though to avoid making eye contact with her visitors. "In some ways I wish they would have sent us with Campbell. Instead, we were left with our own conscience to act as judge, jury, and deliverer of punishment."

"Well," Kirk said. "At least now it makes sense why Starfleet 'guessed' you might be here." As he digested the new revelations, he nevertheless found himself drifting away from disdain for what Jendra and her colleagues had done. While he could not argue that their actions were in clear, unquestioned violation of regulations—including the one upon which every Starfleet officer's oath of service was based, General Order One, the Prime Directive—the captain could see that Jendra's intentions, along with those even of Campbell Roberts, had been noble if misguided.

During his own Starfleet career, Kirk had already violated the letter of the law on occasion while at the same time struggling to uphold its spirit. Had his actions always been successful? Not at all. Several failures continued to loom in his mind, harsh lessons and hard-won wisdom he hoped would guide him toward making better decisions in the future, while at the same time allowing him to retain the humanity that had driven him to make those early choices—and mistakes—in the first place.

Because of that, he felt for Revati Jendra.

The question now was, where did he—and she—go from here?

"I don't understand," Kirk said. "Obviously there was no planetwide epidemic." He waved toward the window opposite Jendra's bed, beyond which was the darkness of early evening. "You didn't wipe out the entire population."

"Only by luck," Jendra replied. "When I came back with a new vaccine, I discovered that the contamination had spread, but only marginally."

"The Grennai's current level of societal development," Spock said, "including the limited means of travel over great distances, would have done much to offer rudimentary protection against widespread outbreak across the planet."

"Correct," Jendra said. "I was able to track the spread of the contagion from village to village, but by then the cases of infection were very widespread and infrequent. I've not seen any indications of a renewed outbreak in months, but I still move from province to province, working as a local healer—a *beloren*—and as part of my routine examinations of the villagers I very carefully administer a preventive vaccine to them in the form of tablets or powders. I tell them it's vitamins or protections against some local malady." Sighing, she looked down at her hands lying listlessly in her lap. "It's not much, but it's better than doing nothing."

"And that's what you've been doing here all along?" McCoy asked.

Sitting up straighter in her bed, Jendra replied, "That's right. We got very lucky here, Leonard. Despite that good fortune, several hundred Grennai still died who would be alive if not for our meddling."

She looked to Kirk. "It was a violation of the Prime Directive, Captain, to say nothing of my oath as a physician. There's a penance to be paid for that, and so here I am. I'll treat these people and care for them as best I can until the day I die. You can't take me away. Not now."

"For God's sake, Revati," McCoy said, moving to sit beside her on the bed. "We've been friends for twenty years. Why didn't you tell me? I might've been able to help."

"If she had, Doctor," Spock replied, "you would be as culpable in the continued violation of the Prime Directive as Dr. Jendra. Starfleet would almost certainly find you guilty of being an accessory in some manner."

"Guilty of what?" McCoy snapped. "Helping to correct a mistake Starfleet made in the first place? If I have to be guilty of anything, it might as well be that."

"Bones," Kirk started to say, but stopped when his attention was caught by a faint orange glow flickering from somewhere outside the window. An instant later a dull thump reverberated through the room's wooden walls and floorboards, followed by the momentary rattling of the window's panes and a few loose objects scattered on the bureau across from Jendra's bed.

"What the hell was that?" McCoy asked, rising from where he sat next to Jendra.

Having already retrieved his tricorder from beneath the folds of his robe, Spock activated the device, its high-pitched whine echoing within the small room. "There has been an explosion from within a large structure near the village's northern perimeter."

"The ironworks," Jendra said, her eyes widening in concern.

From outside the building, Kirk heard a horn blowing, instinct telling him it was an alert signal for the rest of the village. "Spock?"

Still studying his tricorder, the Vulcan replied, "I'm detecting a fire inside the building, Captain, spreading rapidly."

"We have to go," Jendra cried as she struggled to rise from the bed. "There may be people hurt."

"Revati," McCoy said, holding out a hand to steady her, "you're in no condition to go running down there."

"They'll need me, damn it!" Jendra shouted, appearing to gather strength as she moved from the bed toward the door. Stopping at the threshold, she turned to regard the three *Enterprise* officers. "And I could use some help, too."

Despite the rules and regulations, Kirk knew there was only one choice to make.

Komack's going to have my hide.

Even before they reached the massive, two-story structure housing the iron smelting factory as well as—according to Jendra—the village's trio of blacksmiths and also the dozen or so kilns used for brick-making, Kirk could see flames licking from inside the structure's highest windows. As he, Spock, McCoy, and Jendra drew closer, the captain noted the large gathering of people near the building's main entrance. He counted eight people lying scattered on the ground, two of them coughing and five unmoving as others hovered over them. The eighth was writhing and screaming, both of his legs scorched black. The unmistakable odor of burnt flesh assailed Kirk's nostrils, and it was a physical effort to keep from retching.

Without saying a word, Jendra moved to the burn victim. Several of the villagers saw her approach and stood aside to allow her passage, and Kirk heard a steady chorus of *"Beloren!"* as she knelt beside her newest patient.

"I'm going to see what I can do," McCoy said. It wasn't a request for permission, Kirk noted, not that he would have expected anything less from the doctor. Though worried about the potential for their exposure as outsiders here among the Grennai, the captain trusted his friend to use sound judgment even while doing everything in his power to heal those in need.

"Captain," Spock said in a low voice, and Kirk turned to see the Vulcan surreptitiously consulting the tricorder he held concealed by his robe. "I count six life-forms inside the structure, surrounded by fire. They appear to be trapped."

Looking around, Kirk took in the scene of Grennai villagers scrambling to maneuver various kinds of crude fire-fighting equipment into position, chief among them a device that he recognized as a form of hand-operated water pump set atop a wagon and drawn by a quartet of sizable, long-haired quadrupedal animals that looked to be a cross between horses and water buffalo. Members of the wagon team were already unloading spools of hose made from either canvas or leather.

There was no way, Kirk decided, that the villagers would be able to get the fire under control in time to save the trapped workers.

"Damn," he hissed through gritted teeth as he retrieved his communicator and flipped it open. "Kirk to *Enterprise!*"

"Enterprise. *Lieutenant Sulu here, sir,*" came his helmsman's prompt reply.

"Sulu, tell me Scotty's got the transporters working."

"Not yet, sir." Kirk heard the regret in the lieutenant's voice. *"They're still not safe for biomatter transport."*

There was nothing to be done about that now. "Have sickbay stand by for possible emergency triage to treat burn victims, and start prepping a shuttlecraft with the appropriate equipment and supplies."

Closing the communicator, the captain caught sight of McCoy looking over at him from where he knelt beside Jendra. The hint of an understanding and appreciative smile teased the corners of his mouth.

"Shut up," Kirk said to his friend before turning to Spock. "Where are the trapped people?"

The Vulcan pointed toward his left. "Toward the rear of the structure on the ground floor. Life-signs are weak."

"Let's go, then," Kirk said before taking off at a run down the length of the ironworks. Flames billowed from open windows on the second floor, licking at the structure's exterior wood trim. Kirk spied a dark sliver farther along the wall and was buoyed to see that it was a door, standing open and offering unimpeded access to the building.

"Come on, Spock!" Kirk yelled as he plunged through the doorway, the heat from the fire playing across his exposed skin the instant he was inside. Smoke stung his eyes and he reached up to cover his mouth with part of his hood. Inside the building, the only illumination was that offered by the blaze eating at the flammable materials around him. With Spock indicating the correct direction, the captain moved across the floor of the ironworks, dodging between equipment, tools, and burning debris that had fallen from the ceiling, all while trying to ignore the nagging feeling that the entire building was about to fall down around his ears.

"Help!" a voice called out from somewhere to his left, and Kirk turned to see a male Grennai waving in his direction, the man's frantic plea and the emotion behind it channeled through Kirk's universal translator. As he drew closer, the captain saw the panic in the man's eyes. "We're trapped in here! Help us!"

"Don't worry," Kirk said, hoping to ease the man's fears, "we're going to get you out of here." He placed his hands on the Grennai's shoulders. "Where are the others?"

"This way!" the man replied, leading Kirk and Spock deeper into the building to where a group of five other Grennai were lying beneath a set of stairs in the rear corner of the room. A quick check revealed that all of the workers were unconscious, having succumbed to either the heat or smoke inhalation.

The fire was close, Kirk knew, working its way across the structure's wooden framework. Smoke thickened the air, making it difficult to see and even harder to breathe. As he pressed a fold of his robe over his mouth, the captain was sure he heard dull groans and creaks of protest as the burning building continued to deteriorate around them.

Something cracked and snapped above and behind Kirk an instant before he felt a hand on his back pushing him forward. Struggling to keep his balance, he turned in time to see Spock narrowly avoiding a large, burning timber as it fell from the ceiling and plummeted to the cobblestone floor. Embers and ash swirled around the massive piece of wood as it came to rest less than a meter from the Vulcan's feet.

"You all right?" Kirk called out.

Spock nodded. "We do not have much time."

"We must hurry!" the Grennai cried, his voice cracking under the obvious strain.

Nodding in agreement, Kirk replied, "No time to get them all out the way we came." Reaching inside his robe, he retrieved the compact phaser from his pocket, showing it to Spock while also shielding it from the other man.

Spock exchanged a look of understanding with Kirk before stepping closer to the man. "Sir, a fragment of burning ash has landed on your clothing. Let me help you." His hand clamped down at the junction of the Grennai's neck and shoulder, and the man's eyes opened wide in surprise as his body fell limp.

"What are the odds I'll ever learn to do that?" Kirk asked as Spock lowered the man's unconscious form to the ground.

"They continue to defy my efforts at computation, Captain."

Moving closer to the wall, Kirk checked the power setting on his phaser before taking aim and firing the weapon. Harsh blue-white energy lanced from the phaser and struck the wall, washing over the crude earthen bricks and expanding outward in a near-perfect circle. Masonry dissolved beneath the glare of the phaser blast, revealing open ground outside the building. Kirk ceased firing, and smoke immediately began to filter through the newly created hole.

He set to work assisting Spock to move the stricken victims from their place of fleeting shelter to safety outside the structure. Once outside and safely away from the scene, the Starfleet officers could only stand by, administering preliminary first aid to their unconscious charges and watching as the building was slowly yet inexorably claimed by the intensifying blaze.

"Captain," Spock said after a time, "you do realize that Dr. McCoy will almost certainly find no end of humor and irony in your actions?" There was a subtle yet still wry expression gracing the Vulcan's features.

Kirk offered a stern look to his first officer. "Then we'll have to be sure not to tell him, won't we?"

I think I might actually be getting too old for this.

Jendra's entire body—her lungs and sides in particular—ached from the exertion of hiking through the thick forest and uneven terrain in the predawn darkness, and she was appreciative of the moderate pace McCoy had set. Grunting with new effort, she hitched her modest pack a bit higher onto her back, once again feeling its straps digging into her shoulders even through her thick shirt.

"You all right?" McCoy asked, looking over at her with an expression of concern.

She nodded. "I'm fine." He had offered to carry the pack more than once, but she had refused, insisting instead on carrying what remained of her personal belongings. With the *Enterprise*'s engineer having successfully recalibrated the ship's transporters, Captain Kirk had assured her that the bulk of her possessions, including what remained of the Starfleet equipment and supplies she originally had brought with her to NGC 667, would be transferred aboard. All that remained was to get her up to the starship, and she was damned if she was going to have someone else carry the rest of her things—or carry her, for that matter.

Other than the periodic offers to assist her, McCoy had said almost nothing during their hike from the village. She sensed his discomfort, and though she had said nothing to the effect herself, Jendra was thankful for the silence. Despite the way she had faced off against Captain Kirk, she had felt constantly on guard, required to justify actions that before the *Enterprise* officers' arrival she was certain were unquestionably the right thing to do, from a moral perspective if not a legal one. She knew that—on some level, at least—McCoy agreed with her, but Jendra nevertheless was grateful for a respite from having to defend herself.

"There she is," McCoy said after a moment, pointing to his right. A glint of artificial light flickered through the trees, and as they drew closer Jendra could make out the straight, smooth lines of the shuttle-craft *Columbus*. Sitting in the center of a small glade barely large enough to accommodate it, the vessel's flat gray-white hull and bright red striping contrasted sharply with the muted browns and greens of the surrounding forest.

She and McCoy emerged from the woods near the shuttle's left side, and as they approached, Kirk stepped through the craft's open hatch and down onto the ground. All traces of his Grennai disguise—the white hair, prosthetic ears, and artificial skin pigmentation—were gone, and he was now wearing his standard Starfleet captain's uniform.

"Hello, Doctor," Kirk said, offering a smile that, while guarded, still retained much of the charm Jendra had observed earlier.

If I were thirty years younger . . . I think I'd still be more interested in his first officer.

"Captain," she said, nodding her head in greeting as she slid the pack from her shoulders and set it on the ground at her feet.

"How are your patients faring?" the captain asked.

Pausing to wipe perspiration from her brow, Jendra replied, "We lost five, all told, but three others are still missing. More than a dozen wounded, but they should recover in time." Feeling the resignation creep into her voice, she added, "They've not found the foreman, Crimar. He was the most knowledgeable metalworker among them, and he was a friend to me. It's quite a setback for us . . . that is, for the whole village."

She had been surprised by Kirk's decision to let her remain at the village and oversee the treatment of the fire victims. He could have had her transported to his ship without another word on the subject, of course. That he had not done so spoke volumes about the man's character, so far as she was concerned.

Leonard was right about him, I think.

"You know these people," Kirk said after a moment. "Will they be able to rebuild the ironworks in short order? Get back on their feet?"

Jendra shrugged. "The building's a total loss. Collapsed in on itself during the fire. They'll have to start from scratch, but if I know them, they'll be just fine. I never thanked you for your help, Captain. You saved a lot of lives. It would have been easy just to stand back and let things happen without . . . interfering."

The smile on Kirk's face faded, and he seemed to take on a wistful expression for the briefest of moments before shaking his head. "Easy? Not really, no." When he spoke the words, Jendra saw for the first time that this man had encountered similar dilemmas in the past and been forced to make difficult decisions in the face of such crises. She could not be sure, but she sensed that he might even harbor guilt over the results of at least some of those choices.

More to him than meets the eye, I'll grant that.

She caught movement behind the captain and looked up to see Spock exiting the shuttlecraft. Like Kirk, the Vulcan also was dressed in Starfleet garb, all vestiges of his Grennai persona gone. "I take it the local look didn't agree with you gentlemen?" she asked.

"The need for us to interact with the indigenous population has ended," Spock said. "There was also the matter of my . . . compromised disguise."

"One of his ears melted at the fire," Kirk deadpanned, his expression remaining fixed and neutral.

"Damn shame, too," McCoy said. "I thought it was an improvement. Spock, you were almost likable."

Jendra started to laugh but was interrupted by a coughing fit so severe that it felt as though her lungs were tearing. McCoy moved to her side, maneuvering her so that she could sit on the steps leading into the shuttlecraft. After taking a moment to catch her breath, she looked up to Kirk, sighing. "All right, let's get this over with, Captain. I'm only here because I'm too damned tired to outrun or outfox you. What's done is done, I suppose I'm ready to atone for my actions, and I want to do it while I'm still breathing." She had given her word to Kirk that she would not attempt to flee the village, in return for his allowing her to tend to the victims of the fire. Despite momentary temptation, she had every intention of keeping her promise, no matter how difficult it was to do so.

Kirk regarded her in silence for several heartbeats, and Jendra thought she saw conflict behind the captain's bright, hazel eyes. His jaw line tightened, and he inhaled a deep breath before drawing himself to his full height and squaring his shoulders.

"No."

Confused by the abrupt statement, Jendra blinked several times. "No, what?"

"While waiting for you this morning," Kirk said, "I completed my after-action report for Starfleet Command. I haven't yet transmitted it, but it says that you died earlier this morning from complications due to injuries you suffered while rescuing Grennai villagers from the fire."

"Jim?" McCoy said, and Jendra was sure that her friend's expression of uncertainty mirrored her own. She found herself fumbling for something to say.

Finally, she managed to whisper, "I don't understand."

"My report will also state that your body was interred in accordance with local Grennai customs," Kirk continued, "and that your presence didn't introduce any obvious or permanent cultural contamination. Our mission here was concluded without further incident." Looking down at her, he smiled again. "It's not often that someone gets the opportunity to correct a mistake, Doctor. I wasn't sure about this until just a little while ago, but I think you should have that opportunity."

Her eyes darted from Kirk's face to McCoy's, and she saw a knowing smile spreading across her friend's features.

"I'll be damned," McCoy said, shaking his head before looking at Spock. "You're going along with this, too?"

The Vulcan nodded. "While I do not condone violation of the Prime Directive, Doctor, this situation is somewhat unique. Dr. Jendra's efforts, limited though they may be, do serve a noble purpose. It seems logical to allow her to continue."

"And you're okay with lying?" McCoy asked.

His right eyebrow arching, Spock replied, "It is not a lie to protect the truth from those who would act against it without concern for mitigating circumstances, Doctor. In this matter, I believe Starfleet to be wrong, both then and now."

"My God," McCoy said in mock astonishment. "I need a drink."

Now unable to stifle a joyous laugh even as she felt her eyes watering, Jendra reached out until she could grasp Kirk's hands in her own. "Thank you, Captain. I don't know what to say."

"It's my pleasure, Doctor." Casting a quick glance toward the approaching sunrise, he said, "It's almost daybreak, and we need to be going." He offered a look at McCoy. "But we've still got a few minutes, Bones."

The captain and Spock offered their farewells and good luck wishes before climbing into the shuttlecraft, leaving McCoy alone with her even as she wiped tears from her face. Ever the gentleman, he produced a handkerchief for her.

"Leonard," she said, "I don't believe it."

"I probably shouldn't, either," McCoy replied, "but I know better. This isn't the first time I've seen Jim wring a second chance out of a bad situation." He reached into his robe and withdrew a small pouch and offered it to her. "A parting gift, I suppose. It's not much, but you might be able to do some good with it." She saw tears welling up in his eyes as he pulled her close, his voice trembling as he planted a soft kiss on her weathered forehead. "Take care of yourself, Revati."

Jendra stepped back from the shuttlecraft as McCoy climbed aboard, turning to wave once more to her before the hatch was closed. A moment later, she felt the rush of wind whipping her clothes and her hair as the vessel's thrusters lifted it into the air and pushed it into the slowly brightening sky.

As the echo of the departing shuttle's engines faded, Jendra looked down at the pouch in her hand and opened its protective flap, only to find several vials of tablets. The labels on the vials identified the medicine as the hyronalin derivative she had lacked for these many weeks. While the medication would not reverse her condition, it certainly would allow her much more time among the Grennai than she might have hoped for.

Given the extra time, she might even find a substitute remedy, she decided.

Clutching the medication to her chest, Revati Jendra closed her eyes and offered silent thanks for the fortune that had been visited upon her.

Leonard, my friend, your captain is hardly the only giver of second chances.

The Landing Party

Robert Greenberger

Robert Greenberger

In 1968 he snuck downstairs and saw his father watching a TV show where three colorful people were disappearing into thin air. That was his first glimpse of *Star Trek,* and it must have made an indelible impression because he has written about or for the series ever since. Articles for the school newspaper led to fanzine articles, and from there he wound up editing the *Star Trek* comic book for DC Comics. He began writing for the *Star Trek* fiction line in 1990 with the first of several collaborations. Since then, he has written four solo novels and a handful of short stories.

Additionally, Bob has worked in the comic book business, logging twenty years with DC Comics and one year with Marvel. His various titles included Senior Editor and Director–Publishing Operations.

He has written some original short fiction and over a dozen young adult nonfiction books on a wide variety of subjects.

A lifelong New York Mets fan, he currently makes his home in Connecticut with his wife, Deb. His daughter, Kate, has fled home for Washington, D.C., and his son, Robbie, is attending college clear across the state. Learn more at www.bobgreenberger.com.

Kirk wasn't sure what they called the device in McCoy's hand, but it seemed to be doing the job, quickly sealing closed the wound on Sulu's left shoulder. The lieutenant, lying limp on the diagnostic bed, barely twitched in reaction to the device's softly humming activity. Anxiously, Kirk stole glances at the monitor above the bed, reassuring himself the helmsman's condition was as stable as the deep thump of the heart monitor suggested. He'd been standing in place for several minutes, watching in silence, knowing he needed to let the doctor do his job without interruption. For an idle moment, he was impressed by how quickly his new chief medical officer had stepped into the role. McCoy was older than Kirk, but not as old as Mark Piper, who was about to retire and had rotated off the *Enterprise* just weeks before.

He'd been in command just over a year and still felt everyone was treating him like he was fresh out of the Academy. Surrounding himself with the older medic and even his first officer, Spock, made him self-conscious of his youth, which he had always seen as an advantage. Turning his attention back to Sulu, Kirk reminded himself that the lieutenant's youth and strength were likewise assets at this critical time.

McCoy accepted another device from Nurse Chapel, and the captain remained transfixed. He ignored Spock's presence, which he felt behind him. Kirk couldn't help but feel a flash of guilt, wondering whether, if Spock had been more persuasive, Sulu wouldn't be lying on that bed. Had Kirk rushed to judgment, relying too much on his own instincts and too little on Spock's logic? Still, another part of him recognized that if it wasn't Sulu, it would be a different crewman on that bed, being put back together. What happened wasn't Sulu's fault.

"That should do it," McCoy suddenly said out loud. His instructions to Chapel had been low-voiced, demanding things Kirk couldn't make out. But this remark was clearly intended for his guests.

"What's the prognosis?"

"Well, Captain," McCoy said, wiping his hands on a sterile cloth, Sulu's blood turning the shiny blue fabric a dull purple, "while the lieutenant here has a lot of injuries, none of them are life-threatening. I've stitched him up, knit a few bones, and treated the rest. He needs forty-eight hours bed rest in sickbay and then maybe another day in his quarters before he's fit for duty."

"So noted. Thank you, Doctor," Kirk said.

"I'm not done," McCoy interrupted. Kirk gave him a quizzical look.

"He was barely conscious when they brought him in here," the doctor continued. "He managed to explain what had happened to him, and maybe it was the shock of the injuries, maybe not, but I'm certain this rattled him. A lot."

"Rattled?"

"Jim, you sent him down there ill-prepared for that place and it shook him to his core. When I got him, he was scared to death. He's likely got psychological injuries, and those may be harder to heal than the physical ones."

Kirk was thankful that the doctor stopped the harangue, but then saw that McCoy was staring at him. He could only imagine what expression he was projecting. Sucking in a lungful of air, he tried to calm his feelings.

"Look," McCoy said, "I don't know this kid yet. In fact, I'm still learning about the entire crew, so I don't have an informed opinion, just adding up my observations. When he awakens, I'll talk to him and make a better evaluation."

"Thank you," Kirk said quietly, flicking his eyes once more to Sulu's body. He was reassured by the steady breathing.

"Now get out of here, I have an autopsy to perform."

As the captain and first officer left, McCoy and Chapel gathered up their tools and cleaned up around the bed where Sulu lay still. He didn't want to open his eyes, didn't want to answer questions. Too many parts of his body were sore, too many parts felt numb from anesthetic, and besides, they were discussing him. He heard the conversation, every word, and had to agree with the doctor: He wasn't prepared for that planet. In fact, he wasn't sure he was prepared for his new career and was coming to regret his decision. Because of that lack of preparation, someone died. Maybe it should have been him.

On the way to the turbolift, Kirk brooded. Everything about this landing party bothered him. He'd lost crew before, although he had to admit, he never imagined he'd lose as many since taking command. While he normally disliked comparing himself with the captains who had preceded him, he knew his mortality rate was higher than Chris Pike's, and that angered him.

"Computer, deck five," Kirk ordered as the doors closed. "Mr. Spock, keep the ship in orbit another twenty-four hours. I want to make sure that planet is secure before we leave. I'm leaving you in command," he said as his hand twisted the turbolift's control wand.

Spock merely nodded, keeping his comments to himself, which was just fine with the captain.

The turbolift slowed to a stop, went horizontal for a few moments, and then resumed its vertical path. As the doors opened seconds later, Kirk stepped out, feeling his first officer's eyes on his back.

Eschewing the center seat for the moment, Spock sat in silent contemplation at his usual bridge station, his arms folded across his chest. He had ample time to begin his review of the tricorder records that had been taken on the surface below, the first logical step to understanding what had transpired.

With a few deft flicks of the controls to his left, Spock summoned the audiovisual transcripts from the three tricorders belonging to the landing party. Their contents had been automatically uploaded to the computer library banks as soon as the party returned to the ship. Three screens above Spock's station flickered to life as the recordings began to play. As he adjusted the controls, modifying the playback speeds for his preference, Spock allowed his mind to review the recent past.

Weeks ago, following a disastrous mission to the edge of the galaxy, three key personnel were lost in the line of duty: the ship's helmsman, the senior navigator, and the ship's psychiatrist. At a command staff meeting, Kirk reviewed the various staff openings that needed addressing. Piper's retirement had already been in the works, but now Alden at communications had requested a transfer to be with his fiancée, and engineering had an opening. Spock, as first officer, was reviewing internal candidates for consideration before Kirk turned to Starfleet Command for fresh personnel. Kirk had made it clear, when he took command, that he always wanted to start looking internally, letting the crew know that advancement was possible during his tenure as captain.

The command staff had determined the need to bring on at least a new engineer and communications officer, but decided on promoting Janice Rand to replace Smith as the captain's yeoman. Kirk and Smith had not established a good working rapport, so Spock suggested a more experienced person in the role. Helm remained an open question as the meeting ended.

A day later, Spock was finishing a meal when Kirk approached him in the mess, a smile on his face.

"We may have solved our problem at helm," Kirk said. "After yesterday's meeting, Hikaru Sulu came to see me. He wants to move from astrophysics to the helm. I looked at his record. The kid has terrific scores."

"Indeed he does," Spock said. In his mind, the move did not make sense to him or for the lieutenant.

"I know that tone, Spock," Kirk said, taking a seat. "You disapprove."

While Spock was still learning to "read" the captain, James T. Kirk had more rapidly learned to read the Vulcan. Uncertain if the mess hall was the best place for the conversation, he hesitated.

"Go ahead, Spock," Kirk encouraged.

"Lieutenant Sulu has the makings of an exceptional scientist. His scores alone show an innate spatial sense that has been borne out by his work aboard the ship. The science staff responds well to him, and he is an excellent section leader. The lieutenant has what you might consider an unquenchable curiosity in a wide variety of subjects. He has taken, recently, to spending his off-hours in the botany lab, getting to know the various plants we have under observation."

"So, you discount his ability to move to the command track?"

"On the contrary, if the lieutenant put his mind to it, he could make an excellent commander. However, I see him best serving this ship and Starfleet in the sciences."

"You said it yourself, Spock," Kirk countered, his expression showing he relished the debate. "He's interested in a great many things. Did you know he tested as a crack shot? Between that and his physical reports, he'd excel in security, too. Why trap him in one department? If we move him to the bridge, that would put him on the command track and his interests would be sated. We'd certainly get a better officer out of the deal."

"On the other hand, sir, he might also be what you humans call a jack-of-all-trades and master of none. By working with him in my department, we can get a specialist in a more focused number of fields, the yield being that we'd all benefit from his knowledge."

"But, Spock, he's got a terrific feel for space, which would make him a gifted helmsman. His simulator scores were among the top in his class."

Spock cocked an eyebrow at Kirk, choosing to let the captain have the officer rather than create disharmony between them. "I see you have done your research and have given this a good deal of thought. Arguing with you further would not change your mind."

"You give in too easily," Kirk said, still smiling.

"Not at all, I merely know when an argument is no longer productive. You wish to make the transfer."

"Yes, I do. Helm is an important position and a strong part of the command staff. I want the crew to know that opportunities like this can happen. I'm not just picking a raw kid out of the lower decks. He's already a section head so this is a logical step in his career, sideways as it seems to you."

"I'll process the change orders and begin searching for a new astrophysicist."

Kirk nodded and stood, clearly enjoying the victory. As the captain strode out of the mess, Spock remained at the table. This captain was nothing like Christopher Pike, the only other captain he had served with. Pike was more cerebral, relying as much on experience as on the Starfleet guidelines. Kirk, though, seemed to count more on his intuition, seemingly ignoring logic in favor of what he referred to as his gut. While familiar with the human idiom, he remained perplexed why humans would still follow such irrational hunches over empirical evidence. Still, Kirk had proven a more than able commander, and studying him was endlessly fascinating.

Given the *Enterprise*'s schedule, it was determined the ship could do without an astrophysicist for a short while, so Sulu was given an almost immediate transfer to the bridge. Spock, in his role of first officer, made certain the lieutenant was aware of bridge rules and operations. He even made Sulu go through simulations to test him on the helm during crisis scenarios. The captain had been correct; the lieutenant was a gifted pilot and passed with the highest marks yet recorded on the starship. Sulu smiled easily, his broad grin exposing white teeth, and he did so often, even during simulated crisis missions. He was clearly relishing the opportunity, and Spock recognized that the new helmsman was more like Kirk than he imagined. Perhaps it was self-recognition that informed the captain's gut that Sulu would excel in his new post.

Still, as part of the command track, Sulu would need experience taking the lead in various circumstances. He had already commanded the bridge for two gamma shifts without incident. Now he needed more seasoning with planetary experience, something astrophysics seldom offered.

The *Enterprise* had encountered a star system with one Class-M planet, previously uncharted. Kirk had ordered the ship inside the system, and they had surveyed six outer planets before settling into orbit around the only one capable of supporting life. Sensors indicated the planet was devoid of any life-form more complex than lower flora and fauna. However, they had also detected ruins of a civilization, so something sentient had lived here once. The captain deemed the planet worthy of further exploration and cataloguing, and he also decided it was an ideal scenario to let Sulu lead his first landing party to the surface for initial fieldwork. Spock couldn't argue with the reasoning and, in fact, supported the decision.

"Mr. Sulu," Kirk said, standing to the helm's side, "we'll beam three of you down and let you begin surveying. Sciences is all excited about some anomalous readings that turned up while surveying the asteroid belt. I've decided to give in to Mr. Spock and let them go take some samples and do the spectrographic analysis. We should be gone a total of twenty hours so you'll spend the night below. At that point, I'll expect an analysis and recommendations for how best to proceed studying this dead culture."

"Aye, sir," Sulu said with a smile. His body language told Spock how anxious he was to get started. The Vulcan privately expressed the desire for the lieutenant to contain his emotions, but had grown to know the man well enough to know that would be a fruitless conversation.

Spock had finished adjusting the controls, and on the left screen, he saw the recording taken by geologist Vanani Manprasad, with sociologist Christopher Lindstrom's playback on the center screen. Sulu's occupied the one to the far right.

Sulu's screen was filled with complex constructs, clearly some control panels for a facility. Spock took close-up readings and determined that the metallic composition of the technology included fairly ordinary composites seen on other worlds. That in itself might provide a clue to the culture's origins, but that was for another time. Turning his attention to Lindstrom's screen, he saw the readings indicating the size and shape of the facility. Adjusting his earpiece, Spock heard Lindstrom's observation that the scale indicated the people were larger than the human norm. Spock concluded the facility the party landed at was some form of engineering control center. Based on the conduits leading in and out of the building, and the centralized way the conduits converged many meters below, this was a substation linked to a larger facility some distance away.

Lindstrom's fieldwork was up to its usual high standards. Sulu's screen showed Manprasad, tinier than the two men, with jet-black hair pulled back in a ponytail, reaching out to take samples of the building itself.

Spock folded his arms, his eyes scanning the three screens as the routine examination of the dead planet continued. His mind, efficiently processing the information, was also looking for clues and ways to prevent what was sure to come.

Sulu didn't realize he had passed out again until he opened his eyes and saw McCoy waving a scanner over his face. He had only met the new CMO once before and they didn't really know one another, but the helmsman felt at ease under his gaze.

"Will I live?" he croaked.

"If you listen to your doctor, you'll be back on the bridge in a few days."

"Days?" He heard the alarm in his voice. He worried that his absence would somehow hurt his reputation or future at the helm.

McCoy cocked an eyebrow at him and nodded. He checked the monitor above Sulu and then placed a reassuring hand on his patient's right shoulder, apparently the one part of him not sore. "Don't worry about it. It could have been much worse."

Instantly, Sulu flashed back to what happened and realized it could have been him that was being autopsied. Finally, realizing McCoy wasn't leaving his side, Sulu gingerly propped himself up on his elbows, despite the discomfort of doing so.

"Worse? This was my first landing party, my first time in charge, and what happens? I lose a crewman! How much worse could it get?"

"Son, I've lost patients on the table and in the field," McCoy said quietly. "It's part of the mission out here. Just when you think everything is safe and sound, something happens to pull the rug out from under you."

"I guess you're right," Sulu said uncertainly. "But what sort of commander will I make if I can't even survey a dead planet," he continued, trying to keep a whine from his voice. He felt the strain of the past day catching up to him and wanted to keep in control of his feelings. Idly, he wondered how Spock managed.

"Commanders aren't decided based on one experience, you know," McCoy said, adjusting a readout on the display. Dissatisfied with the number, he reached out and pulled at Sulu's lower left eyelid, peering in closely at the eye. "You know, there's more to being a commander than leading landing parties or steering starships. You want to know when we'll know if you're a good commander?" More satisfied, he stepped back.

"Yeah," Sulu replied.

"When someone adds a braid to your sleeve, gives you a handshake, and sends you into the unknown, backed by a few hundred of your fellow officers all stuck in the same tin can."

"Like that'll happen," Sulu muttered and turned his head away from the doctor. McCoy knew enough to walk away without prolonging the conversation. The young man lay on the bed, uncomfortable and alone with his thoughts. He reviewed his conversation with Kirk once more, heard the enthusiasm in his own voice as he described how he desired new challenges, the kind he'd never find in the lab. Still, no one ever died reading sensor scans, running equations, or looking through a telescope.

Sulu lost track of time and had no idea how long McCoy had left him alone. Even Chapel and the rest of the staff gave him some distance. He craved another voice, maybe a friendly nonjudgmental one. A short while later, he heard the sickbay doors whoosh open, followed by the sound of boot heels.

"You awake, Sulu?"

His eyes snapped open, and involuntarily, he broke into a smile. Turning his head, he saw Janice Rand, the newly appointed captain's yeoman. The handsome blond woman had her hair done in the complicated style she had recently adopted. When she had received her new posting, all Rand would do was fuss over how to make herself more presentable, worthy of being a captain's personal assistant. Sulu recalled how merciless he was toward her as she fretted over hairstyles and even debated how much makeup was tolerable. She had worked herself up into knots trying to earn the captain's confidence and nearly was late for her very first shift.

And then, when he found himself upgraded right after her, it was Rand who was suddenly counseling Sulu on the habits of the alpha shift bridge staff. An already good friendship deepened as a result, and whenever possible, Rand and Sulu would commiserate on goings-on throughout the ship.

"How're you feeling?"

"Like hell," he admitted.

"You going to live?"

"So the doc tells me."

"Well, that's something, isn't it?"

Sulu was silent, then finally said, "I suppose."

"I heard about what happened," she said softly, her expression sad. "I'm so sorry, Hikaru."

He just stared ahead, not meeting her eyes.

"Want to talk about it?"

He continued to stare ahead and refused to reply. She patiently waited him out, and Sulu finally realized she wasn't leaving. More than that, he needed to talk about it, relive it with someone so he could prepare for the inquest. He knew there'd be a hearing as soon as McCoy cleared him for duty. After asking for some water, he told her what happened.

The landing party materialized on the planet's surface and immediately began a more intensive local scan. The tricorders registered nothing unusual, and the atmospheric conditions matched their expectations. Sulu glanced at the grayish sky, filled with thick clouds, and was thankful the air was warm.

He studied the exterior of the structure they had selected as the target site. The building had a single, very large entranceway. The color scheme was monochromatic browns and beiges, with not much in the way of signage or decoration but plenty of vines creeping up the sides. In fact, he concluded, it looked fairly utilitarian. Taking point, he started for the doorway but paused to watch as Manprasad approached the exterior and ran a slender hand across the surface. Opening a compartment of the tricorder, she took some scrapings and stored them in one of the sample discs. She actually sniffed the wall, and Sulu was afraid she was going to taste it next, but realized she was just doing her job, using all her tactile senses.

"No energy signatures at all," Sulu confirmed for the others. "What do you make of this?"

"I estimate it is at least five centuries old," Manprasad said. "It's all metallic, with paint, or what's left of the paint. Can't say yet when it was abandoned."

"That's fine, we have all day," Sulu said cheerfully. "Set your tricorders for passive scans so we don't miss a thing." He actually liked being on the surface, with a different feel to the ground beneath his boots, and a mystery to explore. As first-time landing parties go, this one was very promising. "Lindstrom, ready to go inside?"

Christopher Lindstrom, with his short blond hair and broad face, nodded once, also obviously pleased to be part of the team. Manprasad was already in motion without replying, her enthusiasm matching Sulu's own.

"I appreciate being a part of this," Manprasad added as they walked toward the entrance. "When I heard we were orbiting, I was certain D'Amato would go as section chief."

"Yeah, lucky they decided to send the junior guy so no one more senior should go to intimidate me," Sulu said happily. "Besides, he's done this a dozen times. How often have you done this?"

"This makes three," she replied. "After all, I'm pretty junior, too."

"You two are making me feel old," Lindstrom quipped. "I've done eight planetary surveys since Kirk took command."

"Enjoy the fieldwork?" Manprasad asked.

"You bet," he said. "Seeing a society up close is the only way to do it right. And the more I see for myself, the better my analysis gets."

"Any guesses?" Sulu asked.

"You're getting way ahead of yourself. Ask me that again in the morning. Let's get inside."

Sulu nodded in agreement. As they reached the threshold, he paused for a moment, using his own senses to make certain there were no signs, no visible booby traps, things too low-tech for the tricorders or ship sensors to detect. They had noted that the entranceway had no doors, just an open aperture to admit them. Dirt trailed inside, and weeds of varying sizes and shades of green and gray were growing haphazardly within. Seeing nothing more threatening than a vine, he took a big step through the entrance and walked inside the structure.

The others followed, pausing behind him and forming a triangular pattern as they made certain nothing had been triggered. All they heard was a breeze behind them, outside. With a gesture, Sulu indicated their equipment and personal belongings be left near the entrance. All three dropped their backpacks and stepped forward. Slowly and deliberately, he let his eyes pan the room.

The setting seemed familiar enough to draw a few preliminary conclusions: It was a control room of some sort. A high ring of elaborate consoles and viewscreens dominated the chamber's central space, the surfaces dull and thick with dust, loose dirt, dead leaves, and other detritus that had undoubtedly been blown in from outside over the course of centuries. It was clear that the place had been abandoned for some time. Tricorder scans revealed a series of smaller rooms beyond this chamber, accessible by corridors at left and right.

Lindstrom scanned the room. "I have one guess already," he told Sulu.

"What's that?"

"They were larger than us. Over two meters, easy. Look at the scale." Lindstrom gestured at the large chair in front of the controls.

"Good point." Sulu took another step and heard Manprasad's tricorder at work to his left. In front of him was a main panel. He'd have to climb up the oversized chair to get a better look at it.

"Sulu!"

"What is it, Manprasad?"

"Some sort of energy buildup!"

All three looked at their tricorders, which stopped passive scanning when given a different command, and sure enough, there was a gradual increase of energy, the exact nature of which the device was unable to determine. With a twist of the controls, Sulu tried to figure out where the energy was coming from, but it was elusive, and he didn't like it one bit.

"Everybody out!"

As Lindstrom got to the door, though, he rebounded as a bright orange electric field crackled to life.

"What the hell is that?" Sulu demanded.

"Security barrier," Lindstrom said, a touch of anger in his voice. "That's fairly obvious. I wonder how we missed that."

"Wish we'd brought an engineer with us," Sulu said, his eyes returning to his tricorder.

"What, and spoil this unique opportunity for a bunch of junior officers?"

"Shut it," Sulu snapped. He reached behind his back and pulled his communicator off the utility belt he wore under his duty shirt. As it flipped open, all he heard was static. The energy buildup clearly was interfering with the communicator's signal, and with each passing moment, the starship was that much farther away. They were on their own.

Decisively, he stepped toward the main console, straining on tiptoe to get a look at the dust-covered controls. Nothing looked intuitive so he gambled, stabbing at one large, circular blue button. He felt it depress, but nothing occurred. Trying each button and control seemed like a waste of time since the panel's lights were out, its small screens dark. *Okay,* he thought, *time for something else.*

"Manprasad, check those smaller rooms off to the rear, see if there's any working technology there. Lindstrom, go left, I'll go right. Let's see if we can find some way to turn this off." He heard confirming ayes and was satisfied that they were respecting his position as leader. Now he had to make sure they still felt that way once they were safely away from the building.

The first thing Sulu did was take more detailed readings of the force field. While the energy disrupted his communicator, it didn't prevent the tricorder from performing as expected. That told him something, but he wasn't sure what yet. According to his scans, the energy was charged plasma at a very high temperature. He didn't dare touch it for fear of severe burns.

From deep in the building, he heard Manprasad call out, "Hey, this room just woke up!"

"Anything beyond lights?" Sulu called back.

"Nothing. I'm looking around," she replied.

"Be careful," he added.

"No kidding, Sulu, I have it covered," Manprasad said. Sulu turned his attention to Lindstrom, who was on the far side of the large central room. Looking up, Sulu saw what fascinated the sociologist: some alien writing on the upper portion of the wall.

"Anything interesting?" the helmsman asked.

"I really like the way the loops intertwine, but only in certain places. That may be a clue to how the language is constructed."

"Let me guess, you need more time before you can hazard a guess as to what it's saying?"

"Something set this far back and this high, even for being this size, it's probably something standard, not a warning, if that's what you want to hear," Lindstrom said.

"I'll take anything to reassure us—" Sulu's words were cut off as Manprasad's shriek pierced the air. In one fluid motion, he swung his tricorder behind him. His left hand was already grasping his phaser as he hurried toward the smaller room.

Sulu skidded to a stop when he saw the same energy fill the doorway, felt the rising heat that barred him from reaching the geologist. He could, however, see seven metallic arms snake out of secret places in the wall, ceiling, and floor. They reflected the orange light as they writhed, curling around her wrists and ankles. Manprasad stopped screaming, but he could hear her heavy breathing as she struggled against the tightening tendrils. At the end of each one were five pincer-like devices that she was trying to pry loose, but with each passing second, she was losing the struggle.

"Lindstrom! Where are you?"

Sulu heard a gurgle and the scratch of boot heels skidding in the dirt covering the slick floor. He took a few steps for a better view and saw that Lindstrom was doing his level best to avoid getting himself ensnared by another set of these obvious security devices. Without the energy field as a factor, Sulu took a calculated risk, leveled his phaser, checked the setting, and fired a quick burst. The crimson beam lashed across the room and struck the nearest tendril's base, causing some sparks but mainly being deflected in another direction. He placed the pistol back on his belt and reached around for his tricorder, desperately needing to know what they were dealing with.

"Manprasad! Are you okay?"

"I wouldn't call it okay," she shouted back. "I can't move! I'm totally immobilized."

"We'll get you free," he said to reassure her, even though he didn't actually believe his words. Some commander he was, lying to his team. "Lindstrom, where are you?"

"Back near the exit," the sociologist called.

"Reach into our gear and set the emergency beacon. We need help!" Sulu disliked the volume and tone of his voice, and vowed to modulate it lower next time in order to sound the part of the commander even if he didn't feel it.

Sulu quickly swiveled his head around from one side to the other, searching for more of the tendrils. The ones that had tried for Lindstrom had retracted back into their wall pockets, sealed behind what had looked like wall decorations.

His thoughts were interrupted by the sound of panels opening, and sure enough, a set of coordinated tendrils reached for him from the floor, tearing through what appeared to be a small bush. Sulu ran forward, cracking an elbow against a console. Still free, he leapt away from the security system, closer to the sociologist. As he got farther away, the tendrils stopped at their limit, paused, and then began to retract.

Sulu watched briefly as Lindstrom reached their gear and started assembling the tripod to hold the beacon. Satisfied that he was in good shape, Sulu returned his attention to Manprasad. Carefully, he approached her room, now more like a prison cell. She was suspended several feet off the ground, spread-eagle. She gave a shake to once more test the strength of the metal confines. They didn't even quiver.

"They hurt?"

"Damn uncomfortable," she said, and gave him a small, reassuring smile. He should be the one reassuring her.

"There were more out here, but we seemed to avoid them."

"Lucky you."

"Any clue what these smaller rooms are?"

She gave him a look indicating she thought he was mad, asking about something so mundane. "I only stepped into this one, but I'd say it's a monitoring post for a specific set of systems. Other than lights, nothing else went live."

"Got it. Once we figure out more about this place, we'll likely find a way to free you."

"Well, I'll be right here."

He chuckled at that and then turned his attention to a sound over his head. A series of panels were retracting inside the ceiling, and several platforms, each stuffed with technological items, descended into the main chamber.

"Lindstrom, watch out!" he shouted as several of the devices swiveled, clearly homing in on the life-signs. One stopped moving, a dull orange light appearing at its tip. A moment later, it fired a beam of coherent light at the sociologist. He ducked and then twisted his body, avoiding a second blast.

Sulu tried to ignore Lindstrom's gymnastics, being otherwise occupied by the platform nearest his position. Sure enough, two cylindrical elements had locked on to him, cool blue light growing in intensity along the length of each one. He looked for safe cover and threw his body forward, tucking into a somersault and scrambling beneath the main console. As he moved, twin beams of light crisscrossed once, twice, and sizzled as they struck the floor where'd he'd just been standing, scoring it.

The scientist in him wanted to understand the principles behind the light, but the man shoved those thoughts to the rear and concentrated on survival. With his phaser once more in hand, he took aim at the platform's base and fired a more concentrated burst. His energy beam reached the ceiling and seemed to be having some effect on the base.

"Lindstrom! You okay?"

There was no reply, and Sulu worried that his crewmate was unconscious or worse. A moment later, he heard the scream and his breath caught in his throat.

On the bridge, Spock removed his earpiece as the tricorder playback reached the point of Lindstrom's cry. He cross-referenced the three tricorder downloads, but there were no visuals for what had occurred to Lindstrom. He mused that the lack of that particular datum may have been for the best.

Kirk was completing a report regarding the landing party, reluctantly preparing notes for the inquest that needed to follow. The door buzzer sounded. Kirk looked up and invited his visitor inside.

McCoy ambled into the captain's cabin carrying a tray containing two glasses and a delicately curved dark green bottle. Kirk smirked despite himself. "Are those the sort of prescriptions I can expect from you?"

"If you're lucky," McCoy answered. As he filled each thick, squat glass about one third of the way with an amber liquor, the doctor said, "They're both going to be fine, Jim."

"But you said Sulu might have psychological injuries."

Kirk accepted his glass as McCoy settled into the high-backed chair opposite the desk. He saluted the captain with his own glass and took a healthy swallow. Kirk followed suit and enjoyed the burning sensation of the liquor.

"He does, and we'll see how deep they are. He's talking to Rand right now, and maybe talking to her will be better than talking to me."

"She's a yeoman, trained to keep things on schedule, not a psychiatrist."

"True, but she's been one of his closer friends on the ship."

"I didn't know that," Kirk admitted. He grasped the glass in his right hand, tipping it back and forth, watching the liquid move.

"My understanding is that they both signed aboard around the same time, so they were sort of thrown together. It's better when crew rotate aboard a ship in groups as opposed to solo."

"Speaking from experience?"

"Of course," McCoy said, raising his eyebrows at the captain. "I beam aboard right after you return from the galactic edge and everyone's preoccupied with the deaths of Mitchell, Dehner, and Kelso. It was days before someone thought to give me a ship's tour."

"Sorry," Kirk said, feeling somewhat guilty about the oversight. They had all been preoccupied, and he had never stopped to consider how a newcomer would react. He made a note to improve crew indoctrination, a matter to discuss with Spock. He mused whether or not the first officer would see the "logic" in the extra attention, but it mattered to the captain.

"How's your other patient?"

McCoy took another sip, placed his glass down, and thought about it. "On the mend. Lindstrom will be fit for duty in a couple of days. Of the two, Sulu seems to have gotten the worst of the hell they went through down there. I'm guessing you want Sulu back at the helm as soon as I release him."

"It's to get him back on track," Kirk admitted.

"I know the theory," the doctor agreed. "Still, I told you seventy-two hours based on his physical condition. I'll adjust that once I see how clear his head is."

"I'm counting on it. I have a lot of faith in his ability to bounce back and get this job done."

"How much of that is your faith in Sulu and how much is it to prove to Spock you were right?"

Kirk gave the doctor a sharp look, eyebrows drawn down in a frown. His debate with Spock may have been in the mess, but he had been fairly certain no one was paying that much attention, and he knew McCoy wasn't present; otherwise he'd have joined in the conversation. For the first year of his command, Kirk had relied pretty much on Spock for counsel and advice as befitted a first officer with more years in the service than the newly minted captain. However, since McCoy had beamed aboard, he found that the duo had somehow morphed into a trio, and it gave him some fresher perspectives. In fact, he thought McCoy's probing questions hidden within snide comments were actually helping Spock adjust to a primarily human crew. After eleven years with a similar crew under Pike, Spock still seemed overly uncomfortable but stubbornly refused to ask for help. McCoy might be just what Spock had been waiting for.

"And just how did you know about that conversation?" Kirk asked bluntly.

"There are only four hundred and thirty of us aboard this boat, Jim," McCoy said, and sipped again at his drink. *Okay,* Kirk concluded, *someone overheard and gossiped.* The perils of having that conversation in public.

"You win. But what if Spock's right? Is Sulu really better off being a scientist?"

"Didn't he go to you with the idea of switching to command?"

"Yes. Sat where you are now," Kirk admitted.

"Okay, so he asked for the post. You gave it to him. How's he handling the ship?"

"Actually, better than Kelso," Kirk said, finishing the glass. "He has such a feel for the mechanics of space flight."

"And you've left him in charge of the bridge a few times, right?"

A nod and then a gesture for a refill.

"He do fine with it?" McCoy poured two fingers' worth and sealed the bottle. He handed the glass back to the captain.

"According to Spock's reports," Kirk said.

"Not everyone is born to wear that gold shirt," McCoy said casually. "Some rise to the occasion when there's no choice. Others are better followers, and sometimes they don't learn that until after they've tasted command. Now you, you were born to it. I knew that the day we met."

"Really?"

"Absolutely. And Spock's a follower, the best second-in-command you'll ever find. That green-blooded physiology of his makes him damn efficient, able to remember every rule and regulation they think of back at HQ. But he has no feel for leading a crew and may never make a good captain."

Kirk grinned at the doctor. "You've given this a lot of thought, haven't you? What about you? Were you born to be the chief medical officer?"

"Hell, no," McCoy said with a laugh. "I'm just an old country doctor who stood on the wrong line."

"Some doctors would make terrific captains," Kirk observed.

"The sick ones, maybe," McCoy said over the lip of his glass. "No, tending to a single crew is fine by me. Gives me time to do research. I'm not after the center seat, Jim."

"Glad to hear that," Kirk replied, grinning broadly. Then he flashed back to the image of Sulu lying on the diagnostic bed, McCoy working feverishly to repair the damage from his reckless decision. The doctor evidently spotted the sudden change in attitude.

"So, what are you worried about?"

"Maybe Sulu wasn't ready and I pushed him too hard."

McCoy thought about that for a moment, studied his glass, and then slapped it down on the desk. "Bull! If he came to you and asked, then he thought he was ready. You agreed. He's been fine right up to now, so don't start second-guessing yourself. If, in a month, he's still shaky and can't steer the ship, then fine, stick him back in Spock's department. But right now, there's no need to get so damn morose."

"I think that's enough, Doctor," Kirk said, letting an edge slip into his voice.

"We agree on something, then," McCoy said, gathering his things back onto the tray. "I'll be with my patients if you need me." Without waiting for a reply, the doctor walked out of the cabin, leaving Kirk smarting from the tart tone. Piper never talked to him like this. And maybe he needed to hear some dissenting voices now and then.

Spock had completed a spectral analysis from the tricorder readings and had concluded that various directed energy weapons had been brought to bear against Lindstrom, which resulted in the scream. He had clearly passed out from the onslaught, and the science officer thought it fortunate that the sociologist was not immediately killed. Spock speculated that the weapons may have had adjustable settings, similar to the phasers, and they were modulated not to kill but merely to incapacitate intruders. Still, a part of him was impressed by the sheer variety of security devices in place to safeguard the building, and he began to revise his estimate of its purpose.

He glanced from screen to screen, noting that Manprasad remained totally immobilized in her small chamber. Lindstrom was unconscious. That left Sulu the only mobile member of the landing party. His athletic skills, which were clearly exceptional, allowed him to avoid attacks deftly. Fascinated, the Vulcan watched as Sulu clambered over a console and twisted to avoid several energy discharges. The agile human was in constant motion as he probed the room, obviously searching for some means of deactivating the security system while firing his phaser at the weapons whenever feasible. Several off-target shots blew holes in the ceiling, opening the structure to this world's gray sky. A glance at the far left screen showed that the local barometric pressure was dropping rapidly. Spock anticipated that rain would soon follow.

Rand was still seated by the bed when Sulu opened his eyes, and he blinked a few times in surprise. She merely grinned at him and handed over a cup of water before shutting off the library monitor.

"Reading anything good?" His voice sounded thick and sleepy, which felt about right.

"Actually just the online scuttlebutt. Never you mind about that. You want to finish the story?"

Sulu thought about it, unhappy with rehashing the pain, but the arguments that had gotten him started remained valid. He delayed a bit longer, sipping at his water, partly hoping Rand would get bored and slip away, but she remained in her chair. After taking a deep breath, he picked up his narrative.

Sulu stared at the ceiling for a moment, not daring to take any longer. So far, his shots hadn't stopped the weapons and only managed to bring a chill to the air. He saw that more weapons were targeting him, so he was in motion again, the sweat on his back now feeling clammy.

Once more he attempted to reach Manprasad and free her. As he got closer, he took his eyes off the weapons and looked past the orange haze of the force field. The tendrils were at last lowering her to the ground, but then his eyes went wide in shock. He saw a thick purplish gas start to fill the room. Given what the building had thrown at the party already, he feared the worst.

He fired a few quick shots at the nearest weapons platform and then ducked two return volleys from his automated opponent. Sulu rolled under a console, took aim by holding the phaser with both hands, and squeezed the trigger. He was hoping that a concentration of phaser fire might overload and short out the force field. It was about the only trick he had yet to try, and he was running out of ideas.

Above the whine of the phaser, which would start to overheat in another thirty seconds, Sulu heard a different sound, something buzzing. Since the force field hadn't even changed hue, let alone shorted out, he took his aching finger from the trigger and holstered the phaser. He reached for his tricorder and took a fresh set of readings, revealing a new energy signature. He also learned something new: An electric current seemed to extend several kilometers beneath them. The structure was the tip of what could be a very complex iceberg, he concluded. But the information was of little value in his present circumstances.

Swiveling his head, he spotted something flit out of sight, but the buzz grew louder. Then he saw it, a robotic flying weapon, not unlike an insect. That is, if the insect was entirely metallic, painted puce, and had sparking stingers protruding out the sides. It had headed up in the air and then down, launching itself toward him. Sure enough, twin yellow bolts fired. One missed him as he rolled to the side, but the other glanced off his hip, and it stung something fierce. He wanted to let out a grunt but swallowed instead.

The weapon came toward him again in a direct run, but then he caught the whine of a second device. It was coming from behind. Sulu curled himself into a tight ball and tried to roll himself back under the nearest console, but he felt another sting right above his kidney. He let out an anguished sound between gritted teeth.

The robots met up in formation and began swooping down toward his level. He had to ignore the burning pain he felt and act quickly. His left hand gripped his tricorder and he swung, backhanding the machines as they came in range. Sure enough, one of them was struck and it went buzzing off, away from him. The other veered from the tricorder, circling around to renew its attack. Another shot, and this one hit his left shoulder.

For a moment, his scream drowned out the buzzing.

His left arm numb, Sulu drew his phaser with his right hand and fired. One robot dematerialized in a burst of light.

The other was nowhere to be found. The exhausted helmsman carefully walked around the area but heard nothing. He assumed that when one robot went off-line the security system summoned the other back as a protective measure. At every little sound he reacted, snapping his head around, looking for the next source of attack.

Shaking with anger, Sulu decided finesse had not worked thus far so it was time for a more direct approach. Once more he approached Manprasad's room, paused to make sure she hadn't woken up or moved, and this time he aimed and fired a tight beam to the left of the doorway. With no energy field to absorb the phaser beam, the wall smoked and crumbled. He poured it on, knowing he risked an overload but determined not to waver.

As the wall crumbled, debris mixing with the dirt on the floor, Sulu wondered what the building had to throw at him next. He stole a look above him and saw that the weapons platforms had gone still. Had the entire system seized somehow?

When there was finally a hole in the wall, he stepped back, trying to avoid the escaping gas. The air was tinged with a sweet smell and he began to cough, then vomited. His finger still triggered the phaser, the hole enlarging and the gas escaping, dragged to the sky by air currents from the openings he had previously punched through the ceiling.

When the hole was large enough, he holstered his weapon, waved at the air before him and waited a moment to stop coughing. Ready, he carefully approached the hole, still warm from the phaser fire. The energy shield from the door continued to heat the air in the vicinity, making him sweat further. He sucked in a lungful of air, exhaled, and approached the hole. Dissipating heat radiated from it, but he felt an overwhelming need to check his crewmate so, ignoring the still too-high temperature, he pulled his battered body into the small room. He felt his uniform shirt rip on a jagged edge, and he bumped his injured shoulder against a different part of the wall. The pain forced him to stop halfway through the inches-thick hole and take deep breaths, the heat burning his legs through his trousers.

Finally, he was through the wall and into the chamber.

Only then did it dawn on him that if that little made him sick to his stomach, what would a roomful of gas have done to Manprasad? He scrambled over to her inert form on the floor, released when the tendrils retracted, and shook her right arm. No reaction. He searched for a pulse. Feeling none, he leaned over her head, praying to detect a breath.

After a few more seconds, it was clear she was dead.

Rand leaned over and grasped Sulu's hand, squeezing it between both of hers. They sat in silence.

On the bridge, Spock had noted the toxic nature of the gas, cataloguing its recorded properties and forwarding them to sickbay, presuming it would help McCoy with the autopsy. He made himself a note to add the information to Manprasad's service record. The science officer hadn't known her well; in fact, he hadn't gotten to know D'Amato and the other scientists in his department. True, he knew their records and capabilities, but Kirk had made him keenly aware that under his command, getting to know the people, outside the context of their vocations, was important.

Spock returned his attention to the trio of screens, strangely comforted when the rain arrived as expected. It came down hard and fast and, according to the readings taken from Lindstrom's tricorder, quite cool.

He paused the playbacks for a moment and called up a schematic of the facility. From what he could tell, its oversized structures had provided places to hide during the attacks, but now that same advantage became a liability, as the ceiling was entirely beyond their reach and it was the only exterior wall the phasers had managed to pierce.

He didn't see any way for them to get out, given what the tricorders managed to detect next. With a flip of a control, Spock resumed the playback and saw that the damage Sulu had caused was quite effective in shutting down the defensive systems.

However, the weakened ceiling had started to give way and at least two of the weapons platforms had come crashing down, shattering upon impact with the hard floor. Wires sparked and equipment smoldered. Soon the entire slick surface would carry the current from the weapons and Sulu and Lindstrom would be electrocuted, if Lindstrom wasn't dead already.

"Any good gossip about someone other than me?" Sulu really didn't feel like discussing any more of what happened, what, yesterday? It seemed so long ago. He pleaded at Rand with his eyes and she seemed willing to change the subject.

"You know Angie Martine?"

"The phaser chief?"

"That's the one. She and Tomlinson set a date for the wedding."

"Well, good for them," Sulu said, his mood darkening again. "You know, Vinani was engaged."

Rand shook her head, face softening in sympathy. "No, I didn't know her other than to say hi in the rec rooms."

"Yeah, me either." He lapsed into silence again, his diversion lasting only a minute or two. Clearly, not long enough.

"Hikaru, you have to finish," Rand prompted.

He looked at her, giving his friend a weak grin. She returned it sympathetically. "You just want to see how I survived, right?"

"Well, I know you did, but I think you need to do this for yourself. You can't bottle it up, and you need to get comfortable with the telling."

He frowned. "Not too comfortable."

"No, not too comfortable."

Sulu recognized he had a responsibility to his team before himself. He cradled Manprasad's corpse and carried it from her death chamber to the main part of the building. There was the one wide bench and he carefully placed her on it, wincing in pain from his shoulder and back. He realized he might have cracked a rib or two along the way. He watched as the rain began to soak her hair and smudged uniform.

Then he turned and sought a place for Lindstrom's body but didn't see a second bench, just the oversized chair by the main console. He couldn't believe both members of his team were dead. If he wasn't careful, he'd kill himself, going for the trifecta in incompetence. Maybe simply surrendering to his failure was the answer.

As he approached Lindstrom's limp form, the man's duty shirt a deep, soaked blue, Sulu adjusted the tricorder for base human life-sign readings. Sulu wasn't a trained field medic so he'd have to be very careful. But the sociologist was alive, and that changed Sulu's attitude from resignation to determination. He hobbled over to the sodden, muddy gear to locate the emergency medical kit. First, he activated the emergency beacon and then moved back to his patient. The bandages were soaked, but he managed to wrap the visible injuries, treating them with an ointment and following the directions he found inside the kit.

The instructions said not to move the body, but the rain continued to pour in and Sulu saw that it was starting to collect on the surface. He could leave Lindstrom on the muddy floor and play it safe, or risk further injury and move up off the ground and avoid drowning his patient.

Gritting his teeth against the pain, Sulu hefted Lindstrom in his arms and heard a moan escape the man's lips. Okay, that had to be a good sign, he hoped. Making certain each step was secure, he moved Lindstrom closer to the chair, ignoring the rain that ran across his face, listening carefully for any discharge of power.

The walk probably took him two minutes, but it felt like an eternity given the dead weight, his fatigue, and his injuries. Still, Sulu placed Lindstrom in the oversized seat, tucking his legs under him to be safe, immobilizing him as well as possible.

By the time Sulu was done, he realized the floor was not only soaked but the water was definitely rising, bits of destroyed robot and wall floating. The energy shield that blocked the main entrance kept the water in, hissing and turning some of it to steam, so there was no drain system evident.

With alarm, Sulu heard a sparking sound and a different kind of hiss. Some of the advanced technology he had destroyed might not have been able to follow its programming but was clearly still drawing power. With the exposed energy about to be submerged, possibly electrifying the dirty water, Sulu recognized that he couldn't stay on the ground much longer. He'd need somewhere to wait until the storm stopped or rescue arrived. He cursed himself for not grabbing a handful of wrapped rations when he was at the gear. Now was not the time to go back, he concluded.

He looked around the entire room and realized there was but one place for him to place his own battered body.

Sulu was halfway across the room before he registered that he was now limping, which seemed to urge him to move more quickly despite the wince each step brought. Finally, he was at his destination and stared down, unhappy about his option. Still, survival was essential. He had to survive to help Lindstrom; he couldn't lose a second shipmate.

Once more he carefully moved Manprasad's body to the side of the bench. Then, he struggled to get himself onto the bench and find a position that brought him the least discomfort. He lay on his side, knees bent, back to her corpse. He tried not to think of the pressure against his back, tried to remember that Vinani was gone and wouldn't mind. As his eyes drooped, he felt his teeth begin to chatter in the chill as the rain continued to pour down and the sky grew darker.

The next time Sulu woke up, he felt markedly better. Not great, but he was aware that the doctor's ministrations had worked. Nurse Chapel was nearby and noticed him moving. She flashed him a smile and walked over, checking the diagnostic board over the bed.

"You're doing well, Lieutenant," she said happily.

"Thanks."

"Can I get you anything?"

"Well, I'm finally hungry," he began as the sickbay doors swooshed open. He looked past the nurse to see Rand walking in, carrying a tray.

"I have only a few minutes before I'm due on the bridge," Rand said, placing the tray on his lap. "But I wanted to make certain you had a good meal. Who knows what they'd give you here."

She took the lid off the plate and Sulu inhaled deeply, noting there was no pain associated with breathing, which was a great sign of improvement. Some form of seared, spiced meat awaited him, along with some purple potato-type side dish and a large slice of chocolate cake.

"That's not on his diet card," McCoy snapped as he joined them from his office. Sulu wanted to protest, but he spotted a gleam in the doctor's eye. He was beginning to like the CMO.

"You feeling better, Hikaru? You certainly look it."

"Yeah, I do," he said, stuffing a forkful of meat into his mouth. He then broke into a happy smile, the first he felt like giving in quite some time. Maybe he'd keep on living.

"Good, but I'm telling you, this is the last coddling you get from me," Rand said. "Can't spoil you like I have to spoil some other officers on this ship."

As she sat beside him and he ate, Sulu still brooded about what happened. It was a feeling that wasn't going away anytime soon, no matter how much better he felt physically. "You still think I'm bridge material?"

"Where'd that come from?" Rand asked in surprise.

"I was given a taste of command and botched it entirely. Manprasad lost her life on a routine survey. Who's going to trust me next time?"

"I will," she said seriously. "No one's perfect, you know that. It's a dangerous galaxy and we're never going to know what lurks on every planet. Look at poor Mitchell. He was just the latest, not the last."

"No," he said bitterly, Manprasad's pretty face swimming in his mind.

"I'm also willing to bet you right now that Lindstrom wouldn't hesitate to team with you again. He knows the risks and he knows you helped save his life."

"I hope you're right, Janice," Sulu said between forkfuls. He started to talk again, but Kirk and Spock entered sickbay. Sulu grew solemn at their arrival, more so when Rand grabbed his now-empty tray and took it with her, nodding just once in recognition of her superior officers.

"How are you, Mr. Sulu?"

"I'd be lying if I said fine, sir. I'm pretty sore," he admitted.

"And what about emotionally? This was quite an ordeal. It would have been for anyone down there," the captain said as kindly as possible.

Sulu thought for a moment and then said, "Ordeal is the right word, I think."

Before Kirk could reply, Spock interrupted. "I believe you are feeling guilty over the events on the planet's surface," he began. "Having reviewed the tricorder downloads, I believe you have nothing to feel guilty about, Lieutenant."

Sulu was nonplussed, uncertain what to say when McCoy piped up, his voice brimming with sarcasm. "He always this charming, Jim?"

"He has his moments," Kirk said with a sly smile. He turned to his first officer and said, "Now that you've carefully brought up the topic, you want to tell them what you told me?"

"The tricorder analysis has allowed me to determine that the facility had a passive sensor system that was in a form of stand-by mode until the threshold was crossed by sapient life-forms."

"The landing party," McCoy interjected.

"A keen observation," Spock said drily, earning him a dirty look from the doctor. Sulu suppressed a smirk, not wanting to derail the explanation. He had dreaded waiting days until the hearing before getting a sense of his culpability in the mess he had made of the survey.

"If I may," Spock said, not taking his eyes off the doctor. When McCoy said nothing, he continued. "The artificial intelligence running security for the facility was quite sophisticated. Sulu, Manprasad, and Lindstrom entered the building, triggering the security protocols, which were designed to constantly upgrade themselves in response to how well the threat handled each level of security activated. Regardless of what the landing party did, the computer would compensate and increase the level of defense, up to and including the lethal gas."

"Manprasad was immobilized. Why would the gas be released under those circumstances?" Sulu asked.

"Ensign Manprasad continued to struggle, testing the device that held her in place. The computer adjusted to render her unconscious, but the gas was designed for the natives, not a far smaller person. Its concentration is what killed her."

"Shouldn't there have been gas released in the main room?"

"The smaller rooms seemed to work on separate circuits. I may be able to confirm that should the captain permit me to beam down and study the building more thoroughly."

"But why did it suddenly shut down after it killed Manprasad?" Sulu asked, a hard feeling forming in the pit of his stomach. He wondered if the feeling would fade with time or haunt him for the rest of his career.

"Actually, her death had no effect on the computer's actions," Spock corrected. "Its advanced age coupled with your phaser counterattack helped short-circuit the system. In that, you are to be commended for not giving up."

Ignoring the rare compliment, Sulu asked, "How does that explain why the force fields remained in place?"

"Again, I suspect there was a separate circuit for the doorways, just as there was one for the main room and one each for the smaller rooms," Spock explained. "Just because one was taken off-line did not necessarily mean the others would have followed. Had you tried to use the other rooms, you would most likely have been killed yourself."

"Any clue who these people were?" Sulu asked, trying to avoid further discussion of his actions.

"From what we learned based on your recordings plus additional surveying from orbit, we can surmise that they were not native. They were trying to colonize this world, but the attempt failed and the facilities on each continent were abandoned."

"Their work doesn't match anything we have on file?"

"No, but we continue to find new worlds and our catalogue grows, so someday they may be identified," Spock said, sounding more optimistic than normal.

The captain turned to Sulu, looking him directly in the eye and giving him a warm, comforting smile. "Your actions, from what Spock tells me, did everything possible to protect the team. That's all any commander can ask of his crew. Something you'll learn in the years to come."

Sulu sat, not returning the smile, but alone with the image of Manprasad's body, which had undergone rigor mortis by the time the security team, led by Commander Giotto, arrived. They were gentle, draping the body in a blanket before taking it off the bench and beaming back to the *Enterprise.* McCoy himself beamed down to examine the other two, and Sulu had directed the doctor to start with Lindstrom. It turned out the lieutenant had a concussion and some bruising but would be fine in a few days. Only then did Sulu allow McCoy to treat him.

He hadn't noticed that Kirk had already turned to Spock, saying over his shoulder, "You'll learn, Spock, that following your gut, your instinct, may sometimes be the difference between life and death."

"Indeed."

The single word carried with it much that was unsaid, the flat tone indicating neither agreement nor disapproval. Still, Sulu had logged enough bridge hours to sense that the first officer remained unconvinced of the captain's conclusion but was open to further discussion. And he imagined there would be plenty of that.

He wanted to be there to watch that debate and learn from it. Right then, he knew he didn't want to run away from his failure, hiding back in astrophysics. No, he wanted to be on the bridge, exploring with Kirk and Spock, learning what was among the stars.

"Sulu, we still need to hold the hearing, whenever the good doctor says you're fit. However, from what we just heard, I would think you have nothing to worry about, and the helm will be waiting for you if you still want it."

All eyes turned to Sulu, who smiled in return, but he wasn't given an opportunity to reply. Instead, McCoy stepped to the bed and started waving his arms at his superior officers as if they were birds on his tree.

"That's enough of that. He still needs rest and some treatment. If he listens to his doctor, I can throw him out of sickbay tomorrow."

Sulu leaned back, hearing Kirk and Spock leave sickbay. They were returning to the bridge, and he knew in his heart he'd be following them there just as soon as possible.

Official Record

Howard Weinstein

Howard Weinstein

Howard Weinstein's writing career now spans four decades. Fortunately, he started young (at age 19), with the sale of an episode, "The Pirates of Orion," of the animated *Star Trek* series in 1974. Since then, his varied credits include six *Star Trek* novels; three *V* novels; sixty issues of the *Star Trek* comics for DC, Marvel, and Wildstorm Comics; and assorted other literary and nonfiction flotsam.

More recently, Howard's short story "Safe Harbors" appeared in the *Tales of the Dominion War* anthology in 2004. Marking *Star Trek*'s fortieth anniversary in 2006, Howard is involved in three special projects: an essay in BenBella Books' *Boarding the Enterprise* on the meaning and legacy of *Star Trek*; "Official Record" in this anthology; and "The Blood-Dimmed Tide," one of the stories in the *Mere Anarchy* e-book series.

Outside of *Star Trek,* his recent books include *Puppy Kisses Are Good for the Soul & Other Important Lessons You & Your Dog Can Teach Each Other,* an account of his fifteen-year relationship with his wonderful Welsh corgi, Mail Order Annie; and another true labor of love for this lifelong baseball fan, a biography of his childhood hero, New York Yankees star Mickey Mantle.

Howard's other main occupation these days is Day-One Dog Training. He calls himself a "doggie social worker" and enjoys using Annie's valuable lessons to help dogs and humans have the best possible life together.

Until a week ago, Ensign Pavel Chekov had been quite certain of his future. That is, until the explosion that was, indisputably, all his fault.

Now he was certain only of his past. And it sure as hell wasn't supposed to lead to *this*.

From his first day of school, this only child had displayed an exceptional sense of purpose. While other children tended to skip from one dream to another as casually as they changed play clothes, Pavel had always impressed his teachers—and startled his parents—with an unswerving determination to serve on a starship and explore the cosmos.

Even as he grew up and his world widened, and opportunities and distractions multiplied, his course and confidence never wavered. While friends sweated out their university applications, Pavel never doubted he'd be accepted to Starfleet Academy. Once there, unfazed by homesickness and unbeguiled by San Francisco's myriad old-city charms, he'd led his peers in academic achievement and graduated at the top of his class.

Now, fresh out of the Academy, a baby-faced but uncommonly sober twenty-two, he was the newest and youngest crew member aboard the *U.S.S. Enterprise*. Living his dream . . . until a week ago.

Until the explosion.

All new crew members were required to serve duty rotations in all departments. There was no better process for rookies to learn their way around a vessel from stem to stern, to test their skills at varied tasks, to see firsthand how a starship and her crew relied upon crucial cooperation and communication for their success and very survival in the unforgiving environment of space. And this system gave commanding officers a chance to evaluate performance prior to making permanent assignments.

That's how Chekov, who already knew he wanted to pursue interests in navigation and science, ended up doing power-conduit and antimatter injector maintenance, on the night shift, in a cramped Jefferies tube, in the bowels of the *Enterprise*. And how he missed one little live circuit during a theoretically routine plasma purge.

Fortunately, Chekov's mistake caused no injury beyond his own mortification. And though the power disruption triggered a minor red-alert panic on three decks (not to mention a barrage of largely indecipherable maledictions from Chief Engineer Scott), the fire-suppression system worked perfectly, no bulkheads ruptured, and auxiliary power kicked in as designed. Yet the reprimand for what amounted to fatigue-induced carelessness still shook Chekov loose from his moorings for the first time in his entire life.

"It's just one black mark," Sulu told him with a grin. "It had to happen sometime."

"Why?" Chekov muttered. "Why did it have to happen *any* time? I'm not supposed to make mistakes the dumbest Academy washout would not make."

Sulu peered over the rim of his steaming mug of tea, then took a deliberate sip. "Did you really expect to be perfect forever?"

"I had hopes, yes," Chekov said, without a shred of irony or apparent awareness that Sulu was looking at him as if he were crazy.

"Well, in case you hadn't heard this before, nobody's perfect."

Chekov had no answer beyond yet another in an unending series of soul-searching sighs. Other than his normal duty shifts, this venture to the mess deck with pals Sulu and Uhura was the first time he'd been out of his quarters since the explosion. And after a week of solitary stewing, his entire conversation revolved around increasingly melodramatic pronouncements of self-recrimination:

"It was all my fault." And:

"It never should have happened." And:

"I've never done anything so stupid in my entire life. Only an idiot could be so stupid." And:

"The captain will *never* trust me again." And:

"How long can I avoid Mr. Scott?" And:

"I've finally found out what I'm good at: *incompetence.*" And:

"The next mistake I make will probably destroy the entire ship." And:

"This will haunt me for life." And:

"My career is ruined. I should just quit Starfleet and work with something soft and noncombustible."

Uhura reached across the table and patted Chekov on the cheek. "Poor kid." Then she stood and picked up her tray. "Sorry, boys, but I have to go back on duty."

They watched her leave, and Chekov sighed again. "You should probably go, too. You don't want to be associated with Starfleet's biggest loser. Besides, I have to finish my next groundbreaking assignment from Mr. Spock—preparing a briefing on this planet we're on approach to, Tenkara. Exciting, hnnh? That is why I worked my ass off at Starfleet Academy, so I could go into space and spend the rest of my life in front of a library computer, where I cannot do any damage worse than deleting a database."

Captain Kirk strode into the briefing room. First Officer Spock was already seated at the conference table, while Dr. McCoy extracted a fresh mug of coffee from the food synthesizer slot. "Well, Jim?" the doctor said impatiently. "Did you decide?"

Kirk took his usual seat. "It was a bonehead screwup. I expect better out of kids with his Academy record."

"Oh, and you never made any mistakes?" McCoy parried as he sat at the end of the table. "I happen to *know*—"

"We're not talking about me, Bones. You still think I was too harsh on him."

"Nobody's perfect. Nobody got hurt. It could've been worse."

"Tell that to Scotty."

"Jim, the point is, this boy's really down on himself. Every time he's on duty, he's as nervous as a long-tailed cat in a room full of rocking chairs. Now, I'm not sayin' you pat him on the head and say, 'Good dog.'"

"Doctor," Spock interrupted, "your metaphorical presentation loses cogency when you mix species."

McCoy paused for a half second as he flashed a withering glance in Spock's direction. "All I'm sayin' is, if you think he's got any future at all in Starfleet, now's the time to get him out of this funk."

Before Kirk could respond, the briefing room door opened and Chekov entered—and froze. Kirk felt a twinge of sympathy for his young officer, who'd been expecting to deliver his report to Spock for review and referral to the captain. Instead, Chekov found himself facing a roomful of senior officers. Kirk had a pretty good idea what Chekov must have been thinking at that moment: *Not only are my captain and first officer here to judge my competence, but the ship's CMO is here to judge my sanity, too.*

And that, in fact, was correct. They were together to evaluate the young man, but there was something else brewing, about which Chekov had not a hint. No matter. Kirk waved him in. Chekov swallowed, and Kirk knew the kid's mouth must be feeling as dry as Vulcan. As Chekov edged into the seat across from Kirk and Spock, McCoy kindly slid a cup of water within his reach. Chekov took a careful sip.

"Ensign," Spock prompted, "your report, please."

Chekov slid the data card into the computer, started speaking from memory, and delivered a flawless recitation on Tenkara, complete with graph, chart, and photographic backup on the viewscreen. Tenkara was one of the few planets in its sector with abundant (though not easily extracted) natural resources, including some exceedingly rare and treasured dilithium deposits and a wide variety of minerals and ores needed by other inhabited worlds nearby. When the Tenkaran government initially asked for help developing those resources, the Federation saw an opportunity to build regional stability and block Klingon expansion, and provided civilian technical assistance to get Tenkara's backward mining industry up to modern standards.

After two years, some Tenkarans started to resent the presence of outsiders, and dissident native miners began sabotaging operations. The government begged for a low-profile, short-term Starfleet security presence, just to get things stabilized. Despite its reluctance to get drawn into civil conflicts, the Federation Council decided that Tenkara's strategic

importance warranted a measured effort to get things under control—
and to send a message to the Klingons.

That small Starfleet detachment had been on Tenkara for the past
year, with limited success. But the diplomats and brass still believed the
potential strategic benefits outweighed any misgivings and rumblings
about corruption within the Tenkaran government. So the Starfleet
force remained in place, trying to do the increasingly difficult and un-
popular job of maintaining the planet's critical mining and processing
operations while training the local military to take over all security tasks
as expeditiously as possible.

Tenkara's development status corresponded roughly with that of
mid-nineteenth-century Earth. And as with many less-developed planets that had been exposed to interaction with far more advanced civilizations, Tenkaran society was a potentially volatile mix of traditional
tribal culture and modern technology—and weapons. In short, the government's uncertain claim to power and pursuit of stability depended
on its capacity to project strength and authority sufficient to override
age-old clan allegiances and hostilities. As a result, the government's
desperate desire to avoid appearing dependent on the Federation led in
turn to tight limits on Starfleet's presence there, in both size and scope
of operations.

"Ensign," Spock said, "do you agree with current Federation policy?"

The question plainly caught Chekov off guard. "Well, sir . . ." He
licked his lips. "Benefits rarely come without risks. Given a period of
some stability and prosperity, it's quite possible the Tenkarans who now
oppose Federation involvement will end up appreciating their planet's
enhanced position of importance in the sector, the advantages of economic development, and their eventual ability to run their own affairs.
Logically speaking, that is."

"Good lord," McCoy snorted, "he hasn't even been on board for
three months and he already sounds like Spock."

"Ensign Chekov is merely making a rational evaluation," Spock said.

"Is everybody forgetting? Without dilithium in the mix," McCoy argued, "the Federation wouldn't be here, and neither would we."

"Doctor," Spock countered, "you fail to grasp the strategic logic of preventing Klingon incursion into a sector where no planet has the strength to resist them."

"So *you* think it's logical for us to be galactic policemen!"

"Captain," Chekov blurted, "the Tenkarans have managed to create a global council to manage interplanetary trade and resource wealth for the good of the entire planet. Such profit-sharing arrangements are rare in mistrustful tribal cultures, and do tend to promote unity."

Kirk glanced pointedly from Spock to McCoy. "A salient point, Ensign. Thank you. So, it's 'in for a penny, in for a pound.'"

"Which," McCoy added, "is a good way to lose the penny *and* the pound."

"The fact is," Kirk said, "they do have dilithium . . . and we have our orders. If this goes well, then we build a region full of allies able to deter Klingon invasion—and they might even appreciate our effort."

McCoy rolled his eyes. "Fat chance. No good deed goes unpunished."

"All right, gentlemen," Kirk said as he stood, "our mission to Tenkara is simple: deliver a shipment of medical supplies to the Starfleet outpost and a Tenkaran clinic in the capital. The government council has requested that we keep our visit as low-key as possible. To meet that request, the *Enterprise* will spend the next two days doing resource surveys of nearby solar systems. We'll be sending Dr. McCoy and these supplies via shuttlecraft. Mr. Chekov, you will be pilot and mission commander."

Chekov blinked as Kirk's last few words rattled around inside his head. "E-excuse me, sir?"

"Did I not make myself clear, Ensign?"

"Uhh, no, sir. I—I mean, yes, sir. It's just that . . . I thought . . . after what happened . . ."

McCoy guided Chekov toward the door. "Don't look a gift-captain in the mouth, Ensign," McCoy murmured in Chekov's ear. "Just say, 'Yes, sir.'"

"Y-y-yes, sir," Chekov said uncertainly to McCoy, then immediately repeated the same words, with gusto, to Kirk. "Yes, sir! Thank you, Captain. I won't let you down, sir!"

As Chekov marched out with a grin on his face, Kirk couldn't help smiling a bit himself. McCoy was probably right . . . the kid needed a confidence boost, and this mission seemed idiot-proof. *What could possibly go wrong?*

The unfortunate answer to Kirk's rhetorical thought would come, but not right away.

En route, Chekov and McCoy reviewed the record of Captain Irene Kwan, commander of the Starfleet detachment. About Kirk's age, she was a fifteen-year veteran of combat missions ranging from skirmishes to wars, and she'd earned the nickname "Ice" for her tranquil grace under pressure. In view of that reputation for sturdy and stoic composure, her increasingly emphatic warnings to her superiors that this mission would fail without more personnel and fewer restrictions demanded to be taken seriously. Unlike some officers who scrupulously avoided uttering a discouraging word, Kwan consistently delivered in his reports what she believed to be the unvarnished truth. And McCoy and Chekov both wondered: *Is Starfleet listening?*

It was midmorning local time when the shuttlecraft banked over a rolling landscape resembling the dusty frontier of the American Southwest or Australian outback. From their altitude over the largely treeless plain, they saw the main mining and ore processing facility twenty miles outside the capital city of Kurpol, a patchwork of irrigated farm fields, and a sparse web of narrow roads leading to the city. The capital itself sat in a verdant valley beside a broad river that flowed down from distant mountains. It was large enough to have distinct districts, including a bustling riverfront port, mansions in the scenic foothills, and slums to the south. Scattered factories smudged the sky with billows from their smokestacks. The downtown commerce district included stone and brick buildings between two and six stories tall. In a central plaza, a soaring white temple gleamed in the sun.

Starfleet's outpost squatted on a vacant bluff on Kurpol's outskirts. McCoy watched through the window as Chekov brought the loaded shuttle in for a feather-soft landing within the garrison's secure confines. Captain Kwan was there to greet them as they opened the hatch.

"Welcome to Fort Fed," she said with a nod and a smile. Tall and lean, with short black hair falling across her brow, Kwan gave them each a firm handshake as they climbed out.

"Fort Fed?" McCoy said.

"That's because it's the only place we're totally safe," Kwan explained. "We tend to get shot at with increasing frequency every time we're out on patrol. But the rules of engagement limit our ability to take offensive measures and go after the dissidents before they go after targets—or after us. On top of that, the Tenkaran security ministry leaks like the *Titanic*. The dissidents seem to know where we're going before we do. So we're pretty much stuck in defensive mode."

"Which must be great for morale," McCoy said.

"In the short run, we can manage it. But I've been telling Starfleet Command for months—this situation is not sustainable."

While her people unloaded the medical cargo, Kwan took McCoy and Chekov on a brief tour of the drab, bare-bones compound, which consisted of six modular buildings housing barracks, offices, mess hall, sickbay, and brig, surrounded by a perimeter stockade force field. Along the way, they were joined by Kwan's exec officer, Lieutenant Commander Joe Wilder, a towering mountain of an officer in his late twenties. As he trotted up to them, his shaved head and fierce eyes instantly radiated his self-image: *soldier.* Instead of the colorful uniforms found aboard a starship, he and everyone in Kwan's company wore drab utilitarian fatigues. After introductions, as the tour continued, McCoy noted with some concern that all of Kwan's people looked tired and stressed.

"That's the nature of this mission," Kwan shrugged. "We're either cooped up here most of the time, or we're out there doing a job some people don't want us doing."

"It's a gritty life," Wilder added, "compared to flying above it all like you starshippers get to do."

Chekov's face twitched; he knew that some planet-based Starfleet personnel like Wilder tended to use *starshipper* as an insult, and he didn't like it one little bit. Before he could think of a comeback, a female lieutenant approached them. "Captain, supplies are loaded in the truck and ready to deliver to the clinic."

Kwan nodded. "Commander Wilder, get the convoy saddled up."

"Aye, Captain." Wilder jogged off.

"Doesn't he ever just *walk* anywhere?" Chekov muttered to McCoy.

The convoy wasn't much—just a pair of bulky armored transport vehicles, one carrying the medical supplies, the other carrying McCoy, Chekov, Kwan, Wilder, and eight combat-ready personnel, complete with body armor, helmets, personal electronics, and phaser rifles. Chekov felt naked with just a tiny hand phaser hiding on his hip, tucked under the hem of his tunic.

"Is all this really necessary?" McCoy asked as the two TVAs rolled down the switchback road leading from Fort Fed down to the city.

"Preparation, Doctor," Wilder said. "Like the book says, 'Prepare, and take the enemy unprepared.'"

"The book?" McCoy looked confused.

"Sun Tzu's *The Art of War*," Chekov replied with intentional haste, beating Wilder to the punch.

Wilder looked down at Chekov, both literally and figuratively. "Surprised you know that, Ensign. Being a starshipper an' all."

"We went to the same academy," Chekov said.

"I'd say we learned different things."

"Then you'd be wrong . . . sir."

"Boys," Kwan chided. "Ensign, you'll have to forgive Commander Wilder. He forgets that starships are how we grunts get places. And 'the book' tends to be his bible."

They rode the rest of the way in silence, more or less. When they arrived at the clinic, on a narrow cobblestone street of shops and apartments, the hatch swung open and they were immediately assaulted by the pungent musk of livestock and manure. "The stockyards are two blocks away," Kwan explained as they clambered out.

"Remind me not to buy real estate here," McCoy said.

A motorized trolley rumbled by and belched an ear-splitting backfire from its exhaust pipe. Chekov and McCoy both flinched and ducked, Chekov's hand went to his phaser—and Wilder said, laughing: "You'll know when someone's shooting at us."

The clinic's director, Dr. Davaar, came out to greet them. Tenkarans were generally smaller than Terrans, but even by native standards, Davaar was reed-thin and barely up to Chekov's chin. He bowed to McCoy and Chekov as Kwan introduced them, and his nonstop chatter overflowed with gratitude for Federation assistance and supplies. "In just a few short years, yes? You've advanced our medical practice by decades," Davaar said with a clap of his hands. As Kwan's troopers moved the crates into the clinic, Davaar gestured for his visitors to follow.

Before they could enter, another explosion erupted and Chekov knew instantly from the ground-shaking roar and pulsing heat that this was no trolley backfire. Roiling, acrid smoke filled the street, and mayhem broke out around him at impossible speed while he felt himself frozen in time and space. Kwan shouted orders and her troopers rushed out of the clinic. Wilder set them in a defensive perimeter on the far side of their transport vehicles. Pedestrians screamed and scrambled for safety. Two more blasts boomed in quick succession, one farther down the street and one right near the clinic. Choked and blinded by smoke and heat, Chekov tripped and fell to his knees. He rubbed his stinging eyes, then wiped them with his sleeve. Through blurred vision, he could see only a cloud of chaos. Amid the shouts and clatter, he heard three short shrieks of phaser fire. He steadied himself, grabbed his own phaser, jumped to his feet, and bumped into Kwan, who squinted into the clearing smoke, trying to figure out what was going on. Wilder trotted back from across the street, with an unconscious Tenkaran man slung over his shoulder.

"Captain, whoever they were, they all got away, except this one," Wilder said. "No damage, either, other than some broken windows. We suffered no wounded or injured."

"What the hell were they doing?" Kwan looked around at residents stepping gingerly out of doorways where they'd scurried for shelter, and cautious clinic personnel scanning the scene to see if anyone needed help. "I don't get it. Chekov, go get McCoy out of the clinic. I think we'd better get you two back to Fort Fed."

Davaar came up to them. "Captain, Dr. McCoy isn't in the clinic, yes? Isn't he with you?"

Kwan cursed through gritted teeth. She ordered half her troops to finish unloading the remaining supplies in a hurry, while she sent Wilder, Chekov, and the others on a sweep of the block, hoping to find McCoy in some safe haven. When they came up empty, Kwan's entire squad withdrew. As the TVAs rumbled back up to the outpost, grim reality set in: McCoy was gone, and the cuffed prisoner riding with them seemed to be their only lead.

Back at the outpost, Chekov felt very much like a child trespassing on adult turf as he trailed Kwan and Wilder to the brig where the prisoner had been taken directly. "Just so you know," Kwan told Chekov, "it is my intent to retrieve McCoy safe and sound. But this was the first time we've been engaged by the dissidents without provocation, on a public city street and not on a military maneuver. They've upped the ante: McCoy was the target, and we don't know why."

Chekov had no idea how he was supposed to act, what he was supposed to do, or what anyone expected of him. On the one hand, he was an ensign of twenty-two, with barely two months of starship duty under his belt. On the other hand, Captain Kirk did say he was "commander" of this mission . . . but what did that mean? Was Kirk going to hold him responsible for McCoy's disappearance? And what about here and now? Was Kirk's designation a card worth playing? If he tried, would Kwan just laugh in his face? For the moment, Chekov opted to observe and listen. Improvisation was not his strongest attribute, but he was starting to realize it was a skill he'd better develop if he planned on staying in Starfleet.

When they reached the cell, the Tenkaran prisoner was under guard, bound hand and foot, and seated on a hard chair. Still groggy from being stunned by phaser fire, he'd gathered his wits sufficiently to stand up to Kwan's questioning and reveal nothing beyond his name and profession: "Apek. Free miner."

For two hours, Kwan tried every interrogation technique—ranging from affable appeals to harsh threats, and back again. Chekov was no expert, but he detected an intentional rhythm and modulation in Kwan's approach. Even when she grabbed Apek by the collar and throat and looked like she was about to snap his neck, she was in total command of the room and herself. Unfortunately, nothing rattled the prisoner out of his professed ignorance of the attack at the clinic, McCoy's abduction, or any dissident missions of sabotage against mining facilities. Then, suddenly, Apek refused to speak at all. Kwan's fury flared and, for a second, Chekov was sure she was going to slug him. Instead, she turned and stalked out. "Wilder, Chekov, with me," she growled.

The Fort Fed compound was dark and moonlit when they strode back to the commander's sparsely furnished office.

"Captain," Wilder said, "we can't let this go unanswered. I don't know if they've even read the book, but they're using it on us: Attack the enemy where he's unprepared . . . appear where you're unexpected. Today it was smoke and noise to distract us, next time it could be real ordnance with real shrapnel slicing off real limbs. Picture that street littered with bodies torn apart, including ours. They crossed a line. Whoever's responsible, we have to go get 'em and destroy 'em."

Chekov finally spoke up, in a tentative voice. "Doesn't Sun Tzu also say, 'Whoever is first in the field and waits for his enemy will be fresh for the fight'? How do you get the upper hand when you're already behind?"

"Boys," Kwan said, "you can argue Sun Tzu till the cows come home. Sometimes you gotta make your own rules and improvise."

Improvise . . . the word made Chekov wince.

"Captain, permission to speak freely," Wilder said, a statement rather than a request.

"When have you not? Sure, go ahead, Commander."

"The gloves come off. This detainee is our only source of intel. This situation warrants use of aggressive, extreme tactics."

Chekov stared in disbelief. "You're talking about . . . *torture?*"

"Grow up, Ensign." Wilder sneered. "There's a whole catalog of coercive strategies."

Chekov glanced at Kwan and noticed with a flicker of horror that she actually seemed to be considering the idea. "*Captain!* Torture violates everything Starfleet stands for! It violates Federation law and every civilized code of conduct! And in practical terms, it almost never gets prisoners to give up truthful information!"

"If they won't let us take the battle to the enemy out there," Wilder argued, "then we have to do it here, where we're in control. How do you know they're not torturing McCoy right now?"

"I don't," Chekov shot back. "But that's still no justification—"

"Morality's a relative thing when you're in the trenches."

"That's enough," Kwan said, her voice barely above a whisper. "Morality should never be a relative thing, Commander. They caught us napping down in that street. If they'd wanted to kill us, they could've done it then and there. They took McCoy for a reason, and that makes me believe he's alive. And we're gonna find him, without selling out who and what we are. Is that clear, Commander?"

Wilder hung his head, just a little. "Aye, Captain. Clear."

To Chekov's great relief, extreme interrogation was not an option, after all. Despite the late hour, Kwan decided to get the leader of the planetary council, Prime Minister Obrom, out of bed and demand permission to round up suspected dissidents and sympathizers for questioning, in hopes of shaking out some useful intelligence on who took McCoy and why, and where he was being held. If Wilder had doubts, he kept them to himself for the moment. Kwan left the outpost and drove down to the council chamber in the city.

Chekov sat alone in the mess hall, picking listlessly at a chicken salad platter and wondering if coffee might not be the best beverage right now, considering how late it was and how jangled his nerves were. On the other hand, since he was too wired to fall asleep anyway, the caffeine might be helpful. Kwan had been gone almost two hours—was that a good sign or a bad one?—and he prayed she'd produce a miracle to end this whole nightmare.

He kept thinking he should contact the *Enterprise,* just to report the situation. But he knew what would happen—Kirk would turn the ship around and speed back to Tenkara, because Chekov clearly was unqualified to be entrusted with a trash detail, much less a shuttle mission and the safety of a fellow crew member. Chekov didn't know if he could bear the disgrace. But maybe that would be best: just admit failure and let others clean up this mess. At least then he would be stripped of all responsibility for what might ultimately happen to McCoy. Not that he really had any responsibility, or authority for that matter. Nobody listened to him, nobody cared what he had to say. Not that he even had anything to contribute, beyond colossal incompetence. As he took an indifferent sip of lukewarm coffee, he knew the taste of shattered dreams.

A distant howl of what could only be blinding pain jolted him out of his misery. One gruesome scream became a series, and Chekov bolted toward the sounds coming across the courtyard from the next building, from the brig. Not knowing what he'd find, he instinctively grabbed his phaser and confirmed the stun setting. When he reached the cell where the prisoner had been, it was empty. The inhuman shrieks led him to a storage room at the end of the corridor. Two burly young guards stood at the entry, one with dark hair, the other a blond Asian, their backs turned toward what was going on inside. The prisoner Apek hung upside down, wrists and ankles shackled to structural support beams. Wilder held a modified surgical laser tool and he used it to deliver burning shocks to the prisoner's body. Chekov also saw a barrel filled with water and an unzipped body bag; he didn't even want to guess how Wilder planned to use those, and he stood momentarily immobilized and speechless.

"He is violating direct orders from Captain Kwan," Chekov finally said to the guards. Their sullen expressions and unwillingness to look Chekov directly in the eye made their distress clear, but they said nothing and held their ground.

"They have their direct orders," Wilder called. "Nothing they see here leaves here. If they or you report this, I *will* deny it, and I *will* see that your Starfleet careers are ruined."

Chekov shook his head. "How can you do this? Kwan told you—"

"Kwan is a great commander. Like the book says, she stands for wisdom, sincerity, benevolence, courage . . . that's why she can't do what I can do. We are going to get McCoy back, but we don't have the luxury of being delicate."

Chekov took a step forward. The guards shifted to block his way. "This is wrong."

"I decide what's right and wrong, Ensign. You can stay, watch, and learn about real life. Or you can get the hell out."

With a deep breath, Chekov nodded. "All right. I'll watch, and learn."

The guards edged out of his way and Chekov entered the torture chamber. Then, though he had a feeling he'd probably end up regretting it, he quickly drew his phaser and shot Wilder, who crumpled to the floor. A second later, before Chekov could brace himself, both guards fired their phasers and *he* collapsed in a heap.

Chekov woke to find himself on a brig cell cot, locked in by a force field, still feeling the vaguely nauseating aftereffects of getting stunned by phaser fire. The rest of the building was quiet now. Whatever Wilder had intended to do was apparently finished. Beneath the revulsion he still felt toward Wilder, Chekov detected something else—an irritating internal voice nagging him with questions he did not want to answer: *Was Wilder justified? Was this the only way to rescue McCoy? If I were in Wilder's boots, would I be capable of . . . that?*

He heard approaching footsteps and rolled to a sitting position in time to see a grim Kwan turn off the force field. Without a word, Kwan turned and walked off. Chekov followed her back to her office where Wilder already sat. Even though his head was spinning, Chekov remained standing as Kwan looked from one to the other, then sat at her desk.

"Where to begin," she muttered. "My meeting with Minister Obrom was . . . unsatisfactory. He's a bureaucrat who excels at finding reasons to avoid action, no matter what the provocation. He rejected my demands. The notion, as he put it, of Starfleet personnel spiriting Tenkarans off to a dungeon, well, that simply would not do. He was more concerned about being perceived as a puppet controlled by an occupation army than he was about the total withdrawal of Federation and Starfleet support if anything happens to McCoy. Or the potential for the overthrow of his non-puppet government, once we're not here to prop it up."

"I told you," Wilder said.

"Shut up, Commander," Kwan snapped. "He did agree to have the uniquely inefficient Tenkaran police bring in suspects for questioning. As you can imagine, I was not happy about that. Then I come back to find a severely beaten detainee in my brig, courtesy of you, Mr. Wilder, who became a barbarian in my absence. And you, Mr. Chekov, had the good sense to try and stop him . . . but failed to do so in an effective manner."

"When do you get to the part where I succeeded?" Wilder asked.

Chekov's eyes widened. Wilder smirked at him. Kwan sighed. "So," she said, "we do have what we believe to be actionable intel, including a location and tactical data on what kind of resistance we're likely to face. Ensign, if you're in command, do you or do you *not* use this information, no matter how it was obtained, to rescue our missing man."

Chekov frowned, but he honestly didn't know what to say. "There . . . are . . . arguments for both, Captain."

"In debating class, yes. In the real world, no. We have no idea if this intel is sound or bogus. But we have nothing else to go on, and no way to know if time is running out. So we will mount a covert rescue mission using the information extracted from the detainee. We depart at oh-six-hundred hours."

Wilder jumped up. "Thank you, Captain. I'll get the squad saddled up."

"No, you won't. You're not going."

"But, Captain," Wilder argued, "I'm the one—"

"—who violated direct orders and Starfleet regulations," Kwan said, cutting him off with a disdainful look. Yet, somehow, her voice remained level. "There will be an inquiry later. You'll wait here for the other shoe to drop. Only five of us know what happened to the detainee—you two, two guards, and me. For now, until I figure out what to do, it's going to stay that way. Is that clear?"

Wilder nodded. Chekov squared his shoulders. "Request permission to go with you, Captain."

"Denied. I need people I can trust, and neither of you fits the bill. You both stay here." Kwan shook her head. "And stay out of trouble until we get back."

•   •   •

Before dawn, Kwan and thirty combat troops boarded the company's ungainly armored personnel flyer. Chekov and Wilder watched as it lifted off from the center of the compound, headed for an abandoned mining facility in rugged volcanic mountains. And then they waited, unable even to monitor telemetry or communications, since Kwan wanted absolute signal silence to avoid even the slightest chance that their approach would be detected.

When the APF returned, limping in for an unsteady landing four hours later, Chekov's stomach knotted as soon as he saw the scorch marks pocking its hull. The engines powered down and sighed into silence. Chekov glanced over to catch Wilder chewing his lip in a rare moment of anxiety. Then the hatches hissed and opened, but instead of triumphant troops returning from a rescue, bloodied soldiers climbed out bearing stretchers. The company medic, a sturdy, dark-haired woman named D'Abruzzo, jumped down to the ground and shouted for all medical personnel to report to sickbay. No one stopped for explanations, and Chekov saw no sign of McCoy or Kwan.

Once the wounded had been moved to sickbay, D'Abruzzo caught sight of Chekov and Wilder and came over to them, her face grim and her jaw tight. Chekov tried to squelch that terrible sinking feeling in his gut. "They knew we were coming," D'Abruzzo said. "They were ready for us. Eight wounded, two dead. Captain Kwan . . . she died on the way back."

Wilder didn't react. Maybe he couldn't. "What about McCoy?" Chekov said.

D'Abruzzo shook her head. "We never got close. If he was there, which I doubt, no way we could've gotten to him. Sorry. I've got patients to take care of." Then she headed for sickbay.

Chekov gave Wilder a contemptuous look. "It looks as if you're in command now . . . *sir.*"

Still, Wilder said nothing and his face revealed nothing. Chekov shook his head in disgust and turned away. He'd done his medic's rotation on the *Enterprise* just last month, so he went to sickbay to see if he could help, and to keep himself busy. He didn't want to think about what was going to happen here next, with Kwan dead—

nor did he want to think about facing Kirk when the *Enterprise* returned.

D'Abruzzo turned out to be a skilled and efficient medic; under her direction, the wounded were stabilized and getting necessary treatment swiftly. Fortunately, none of their injuries exceeded the capacities of the outpost's sickbay. After two hours of nonstop work, D'Abruzzo finally collapsed on a corner cot. Chekov brought her a fresh cup of coffee. She took it with a nod of thanks.

"What happened out there?" he asked.

She shrugged. "I don't know if it was an intentional trap, or they just got lucky. But we were sitting ducks. The intel had to be bogus. Do you know where it came from?"

Chekov looked away. "Uhh, no, not really."

D'Abruzzo brushed her sweat-dampened hair off her forehead and exhaled a long, weary breath. "The captain was wounded, but she kept giving orders. She's why we got away without more casualties. Man, she was the best. I thought if I could just get her back here . . ." Her voice trailed off and she tried to swallow the lump in her throat. "Posthumous medals disgust me . . . as if a ribbon could ever make up for a life. But she damn well better get one."

Chekov patted the medic's shoulder and left sickbay. He found Wilder in the commander's office, sitting at the desk with a blank expression on his face. His eyes were red. It took him a few seconds, but he finally looked up at Chekov.

"Whatever you've got to say, Ensign, it doesn't even matter," Wilder said, his voice as hollow as his stare. "I sold out what we believe, what we're supposed to stand for . . . for nothing. Kwan's dead . . . because of me. This whole disaster . . . my fault."

Chekov really wanted to unload all his pent-up frustration and hatred at Wilder and blame him for everything. But he hesitated. Wilder looked crushed, defeated, and Chekov had his own ethical standards to uphold—he didn't want to kick a man who was already down, despicable as that man might be. So all he said was: "It was Kwan's decision to go, not yours. The commander is ultimately responsible. That was her. Now it's you. What are you going to do?"

Wilder took deep breaths, as if trying to resurrect his shattered soul. "I need to make this right. I need a chance to make sure Kwan didn't die for nothing. I need to keep this going, for her, in her memory, the way *she* tried to teach me . . . not my way."

A chill ran down Chekov's spine. "What are you talking about?"

"What happened in that brig room . . . it stays there. Kwan said it— only five of us knew. Now it's four. And I outrank you and the guards. What I said stands. If any of you tell anybody, I *will* bury you."

"You're crazy," Chekov whispered. "What makes you think I won't report everything that really happened?"

Wilder stood up and loomed over Chekov, toe to toe, jaw muscles twitching and fists clenched at his sides. "There's no record of what happened, so you have no proof. Whose word are they going to take—a decorated combat commander or a rookie starshipper flyboy?"

Chekov gulped. More than anything else, he wanted to stand up to Kwan, but he wasn't sure how, or whether it would do any good. And not for the first time on this mission, he found himself wishing he could be *anyplace* else in the universe. At this point, he just wished the *Enterprise* was already here to take him away. He needed some time to weigh his options, so he simply backed away from Wilder and left the office. *Let him think he's won . . . for now.*

Back outside, Chekov hunched his shoulders and hiked the perimeter of the compound under the afternoon sun. How could so much go so wrong in a day's time? Four words kept rattling around in his mind: *It's not my fault.* And, objectively, it wasn't. None of it, up until now. But commanders take responsibility for what happens on their watch, and he was the commander of this mission, in name at least. In practical terms, he had no idea what that meant, how much damage these events— largely out of his control—would inflict on his already tarnished reputation. Would he be court-martialed for dereliction of duty? Or would Starfleet simply send him packing with a general discharge, or worse?

It's not my fault. There it was again. How would a court-martial panel assess all this? The attack on the clinic certainly wasn't something *he* could have foreseen. McCoy's abduction? Well, *that* happened under Kwan's command. He tried to stop Wilder from torturing the prisoner, even to the point of shooting a senior officer (for good cause). *He* didn't make the decision to use questionable intelligence—the unfortunate Captain Kwan did that. *None of that was my fault.*

Letting Wilder get away with a cover-up? Now, that would be my fault.

But who would know? That, after all, was the whole point of a cover-up. But did he want to live the rest of life hiding that kind of secret—that kind of personal failure? There was no other way to describe it. Before Chekov could travel any further down this depressing hypothetical road, he heard shouts coming from the front gate of the compound and he ran toward the commotion. He got there just as Wilder did—and Chekov was nothing short of shocked to see McCoy ambling toward them, escorted by two armed and armored perimeter guards.

Chekov broke out in a huge grin, surged forward, and wrapped the dusty but uninjured McCoy in a bear hug. "Doctor! I am *so glad* to see you!"

"Well, I'm glad to be seen," McCoy said as he wrapped an arm around Chekov's shoulder.

Chekov stepped back for a look. "Are you all right, sir?"

"I'm a mite parched, but other than that," McCoy said as he patted his own torso, "I'm in one piece."

Wilder stood in their path. "Chekov's right, Doctor. We're thrilled to have you back. Do you need our medic to check you out?"

"No, Commander, I'm fine. Really. A sandwich and a tall, cool drink, I'll be good as new."

Wilder nodded. "Good. Let's get you what you need, and then let's debrief you."

"What happened to you?" Chekov asked as they walked toward the mess hall.

McCoy shrugged. "They needed a doctor and wanted to make a point. But other than being blindfolded going to and from wherever the hell they took me, they treated me fine. But where's Captain Kwan? I've got some new information she's gonna want to hear." At the mention of Kwan's name, McCoy could tell from the faces around him that something was very wrong. His eyes narrowed. "Where's Captain Kwan?"

Wilder's mouth twitched. "She . . . she was killed in action, Doctor."

McCoy stopped in his tracks. "What? What the hell happened?"

With a hand on McCoy's back, Wilder got them moving again. "We'll cover that in the debriefing, sir." McCoy didn't notice the glances exchanged between Wilder and Chekov, with which Chekov made it clear he wasn't going away and Wilder made it clear his threat remained operational. With that provisional understanding—or stand-off—in place, and McCoy oblivious to the entire subtext, neither man was ready to blink.

Kwan's death cast a pall over the relief at McCoy's safe return, and McCoy was visibly heartbroken to learn that she'd been killed leading the misguided mission to rescue him. What he didn't learn were the circumstances that spawned the rescue mission, because Chekov wasn't yet ready to challenge Wilder.

Now that McCoy was out of danger, Chekov was surprised and re-lieved to find himself no longer in the grip of paralyzing stress. Like a ship released from its docking clamps, he felt free to maneuver again, propelled by a reserve of clarity and purpose he thought he'd lost for-ever. The conflict was actually stunningly elemental: Wilder had staked his future on a lie, while Chekov was trying to stake *his* on truth.

In order to prevail against an opponent desperately determined to keep his shameful misdeeds hidden, Chekov knew he had to be equally determined to find just the right strategy. He needed the discipline to hold his fire, resist impulse, and pursue alternatives without commit-ment until there was no doubt his final choice was the best choice. Had he simply blurted out his account, he was reasonably sure McCoy would have believed him. But McCoy hadn't witnessed the torture; his confidence wouldn't constitute proof. It would still have been Chekov's word against Wilder's. So revelation at this moment would not advance Chekov toward his goal. For now, he would have to plan, watch, and wait.

For the first time since the explosion on the *Enterprise,* that pervasive feeling of spinning his wheels in sand was being replaced by a sem-blance of control and purpose. And, possibly for the first time in his life, the word *improvise* didn't scare him.

McCoy told them everything he knew. He'd been taken to a mountain stronghold where a group of rebellious miners had holed up. He was asked to treat their leader, named Rivaj, who'd been severely wounded during a recent ambush by Tenkaran forces, which also killed their only healer and destroyed their makeshift medical facility.

"Why you?" asked Wilder. "Why not get a healer from another tribe?"

"Near as I can figure," McCoy said, "even with that new council, clan rivalries still run deep. They don't trust anyone from outside their own tribe. It struck me as odd that they'd trust somebody from another planet, and somebody they'd just kidnapped, to boot. But they figured I didn't have any rooting interest and they promised they'd release me as soon as I was done treating Rivaj. Meanwhile, I figured I'd try to learn more about what makes these dissidents tick."

"Did you?" Chekov asked.

"I think so. A lot of these tribes are convinced the central government is riddled with corruption, and they believe the Federation turns a blind eye so we've got an excuse to annex Tenkara and its resources. I told Rivaj he had to be delirious to believe that, that we don't annex other worlds, but the Klingons sure do. If it's us or the Klingons, they'd rather have us. Then Rivaj said something that made me think. He said we're *addicted* to dilithium, that we'll do anything to get it, that without it, we wouldn't be able to dominate the quadrant. He's dead sure the only reason we're here is because the Federation covets their minerals."

"Did you change his mind?" Chekov asked.

"I told him he could believe what he wanted, that I was just going to fix his wounds because that's what doctors do, and what *he* did after that was up to him. I think he found my attitude refreshing." McCoy allowed himself a satisfied smile. Then he took out a data disc and set it on the table. "But before they released me, Rivaj gave me what he said was evidence that Tenkaran officials were conspiring to hide the true extent of their dilithium reserves. I'm sure the Federation is going to want to look this over and see if there's anything to it."

Wilder reached for the disc, but Chekov grabbed it first. Before Wilder could respond, D'Abruzzo's voice barked from the comm speaker: *"Dr. McCoy, we need your help in sickbay!"*

Wilder keyed the intercom. "Wilder here. What is it?"

"The prisoner, sir. He's gone into cardiac arrest. He needs surgery, and this is out of my league."

"Prisoner?" said McCoy. "Tenkaran?"

"He was captured when they kidnapped you," Chekov said.

"He resisted arrest," Wilder said quickly, before Chekov could say anything else. "He got hurt in the pursuit and scuffle."

"Prep him. I'm on my way!" McCoy bolted for the door.

Wilder and Chekov loitered in the corridor near the operating room, neither seemingly willing to let the other out of his sight. The surgery took about an hour, and when it was done and Apek was out of danger, McCoy came out wearing a forbidding frown. "That man was brutalized," he said flatly as he stripped off his blood-stained surgical gown. "I'm startin' to put two and two together here, and I don't like how it adds up. He must've been the source of the bad information Kwan used for that rescue mission. She must've been desperate enough to beat it out of him. There's no other way he could've got those injuries. Unless I find out otherwise, that's what my report's going to say."

"You have to be wrong about that, Doctor," Wilder said. "Starfleet doesn't condone prisoner abuse. Captain Kwan would never do that. The detainee's injuries had to have happened at the time of his capture."

McCoy bristled. "Commander, I know extended torture when I see it." He leaned back against the wall and shook his head. "Ironic, isn't it? After a career like hers, her last act is a breech of conduct and she ends up dying for it. That's how her official record ends, in disgrace." McCoy turned sadly and went back into sickbay to see if D'Abruzzo needed any more help.

Wilder's chin dropped and Chekov seized the moment, his voice soft but urgent. "Once Dr. McCoy files his report, what you did will be on the record—on *Kwan's* record. Doesn't she deserve better than that? I'm giving you one last chance to tell what really happened and clear her name."

Wilder straightened up to his full height and glared down at Chekov. "Don't threaten me, Ensign. As long as you don't have any proof—and you never will—it's still my word against yours. You don't have the guts to challenge me." Then he turned his back on Chekov and walked away.

Outside, Chekov found the two brig security officers aimlessly throwing rocks into the perimeter force field just to see the power flares. They weren't much older than he was, so he hoped he had some idea of how they felt about what they'd witnessed. Robinson, the dark-haired one with the wide eyes, paused with a rock in his hand when Chekov came up to them. "How's the prisoner?" Robinson asked.

"He'll live, no thanks to Commander Wilder. Robinson, you know what he did was wrong."

The other guard, the sandy-haired Asian named Bjorklund, sifted the dirt for more good throwing rocks. "There's nothing we can do, Chekov." And that, apparently, was all he had to say.

"You're a starshipper, you're leaving, but we're stuck here," Robinson said. "Wilder's our CO, and we don't know that's gonna change. You gotta understand."

"I do. And if it was any *one* of us against Wilder, you'd be right. But *three* of us know what happened. We know what time Kwan went to see the prime minister, and we know what time she came back."

"But that's circumstantial," Robinson said. "It doesn't prove Kwan didn't beat on the detainee, or that she didn't order someone else to do it."

"It's one more piece of the puzzle, and one more fact that puts pressure on Wilder."

Robinson kicked at the ground. "Without *proof,* we've got nothing."

"That's what I thought, that we're subordinate officers, questioning a commander's integrity. No way can we claim he's lying without being able to prove it." Chekov's eyes narrowed. "But that's not *good* enough! If we let this go, not only does Wilder get away with it, but we have to live with knowing we let him."

"I've wanted to be in Starfleet since before I could *say* 'Starfleet,' and now you're telling me to risk throwing it all away for something we can't prove?"

Chekov ran a hand through his thick mop of hair, trying to conjure a persuasive answer. But there wasn't one. This wasn't that kind of argument. Either these guys got it, or they didn't. And Chekov had a sinking feeling they didn't. "I'm not telling you anything, Robinson. But I know what I have to do."

"Throw away your career?" said Robinson as he hurled another rock.

"Starfleet is what we *do,* it's not who we *are.* Whether I wear this uniform or not, I have to look at myself every day and know that my integrity was stronger than my fear. We're young, and we're learning something we need to learn—that there won't always be proof when you need it. Wilder lied. We know it. If we don't stand up, then a liar gets to define the truth. And I can't let that happen." Then Chekov turned and walked away without looking back, feeling very much alone.

When he got to the main courtyard, he saw McCoy standing with Wilder at the shuttle, ready for departure. "Let's go, Chekov."

"Thanks for your help, Doctor," Wilder said as McCoy climbed up and through the hatch. "Sorry for what you went through."

"No harm, Commander. Once the Federation goes over the information I got from Rivaj and the dissidents, maybe it'll eventually make your job easier. Sorry about your captain." McCoy ducked inside the shuttle cabin.

Chekov paused with one foot up on the ladder and looked Wilder square in the eye. "This isn't over, Commander. I will report what I know to Captain Kirk and Starfleet."

"It won't matter," Wilder said in a dead voice. "You can't win this one."

His expression revealed what Chekov suspected—that Wilder was going to be one tortured soul. By contrast, Chekov felt at ease about how he'd handled things. He'd done his best to get the guards to step forward; he'd given Wilder every chance to do the right thing. In the end, he realized he couldn't control their choices, just his own. His report would tell everything that really happened, and whatever the consequences, he would have no regrets. He was just about to step in and shut the hatch behind him when a voice called from across the compound: "Chekov—wait!"

Chekov and Wilder both turned to see Robinson walking slowly toward them, with Bjorklund trailing a few yards behind. Chekov glanced at Wilder, whose face remained impassive.

"As you were, men," Wilder said, without much force.

Robinson averted his eyes. "Sorry, sir," he mumbled. "We need to see Dr. McCoy."

Chekov stepped aside and McCoy peered out through the open hatch. "What's going on?" he asked, glancing from one man to the next, searching for a hint.

"Ummm, Doctor," Robinson said, "you're the ranking officer here. Me and Bjorklund, we need to report to you about . . . an incident."

Chekov gave Wilder a probing look. "Unless Commander Wilder wants to tell you himself."

Wilder stared right back at him. "Without loyalty, there'd be no discipline in the service."

"Correction, sir," Chekov said, "without respect for the truth, discipline and service mean nothing."

Wilder turned to his young guards. "You boys sure about this?"

"What the hell are y'all talking about?" McCoy growled impatiently.

Chekov cleared his throat and waited for Wilder to speak first. When he didn't, Chekov said, "The prisoner—"

"—was tortured," Wilder interrupted, "and I was responsible." Standing ramrod straight, he confessed everything. Robinson and Bjorklund reluctantly confirmed the account, and Chekov added his corroboration.

"Captain Kwan died because of me," Wilder said to McCoy, his shoulders finally sagging under his burden. "Leaving this stain on her record, on top of that . . . I can't do that. But I just want you to know, I did what I thought I had to do to save you, Doctor. I'm ready to face whatever punishment Starfleet chooses."

Under these extraordinary circumstances, nobody—least of all the flustered McCoy—seemed quite sure what to do next. So, for several awkward seconds, nobody did anything.

"Doctor," Chekov prompted, "I think you should secure his weapons and place him under arrest for violation of Starfleet's code of conduct. And we should take him back to the *Enterprise*."

McCoy nodded. "Well . . . all right then, Chekov. Do it."

En route to rendezvous, Chekov and McCoy transmitted advance reports to Kirk, who relayed them to Starfleet Command. By the time the shuttle docked and Wilder was escorted to the brig, Kirk had Starfleet orders to transport him to the nearest starbase for court-martial. A new officer team would be dispatched to assume command of the outpost on Tenkara. In addition, the information given to McCoy by the dissident miners was already under review by regional Federation officials overseeing the Tenkaran project.

Once Kirk had read their full reports, he and Spock met with McCoy and Chekov in the captain's office. "Your assessment is pretty blunt, Ensign," Kirk said warily as he skimmed the file on his computer screen. "I quote: 'The mission on Tenkara is being compromised by the Federation's dysfunctional relationship with what may be a corrupt local government, and by counterproductive tactical restrictions placed on Starfleet personnel stationed there.' Do you want to . . . reconsider . . . before I send it to Starfleet?"

"I may only be an ensign, sir, but I know what I saw there," Chekov said without hesitation. "No, sir. My report stands."

Kirk smiled. "Good. There's an old saying: 'Truth fears no trial.' If you believe it, and you can back it up, say it—no matter who doesn't like it. From what Dr. McCoy's told me, you showed both brains and backbone on this mission. You've set yourself a pretty high standard. I'll expect you to live up to it."

"Thank you, sir. I'll try."

"All right, Ensign. Dismissed."

Chekov turned to leave, then stopped and turned back with a sigh. "Captain, ever since the . . . the explosion . . ."

Kirk nodded and finished the sentence for him. "You've been afraid of making mistakes."

Chekov seemed relieved that Kirk said what he couldn't. "Yes, sir."

"I'm afraid mistakes are in our DNA. *Trying* to be perfect is all well and good, as long as you understand it's an unattainable goal."

"*Expecting* to be perfect," McCoy said, "now, *that's* a fool's errand."

"Mistakes are inevitable," Spock added, "especially for humans." He ignored McCoy's dirty look.

"Mr. Chekov," Kirk said lightly, with a humorous glance at Spock, "we're *all* going to make mistakes as long as we're breathing."

Chekov sighed again. "A lifetime of mistakes . . . that's what I have to look forward to?"

"Think of it as . . . a lifetime of *lessons*. Mistakes are how we learn to do better."

"I know I did the right thing," Chekov said, "so why don't I *feel* better about it?"

Kirk smiled again. "Sticking your neck out in defense of the truth can be . . . unsettling."

"Ensign," Spock said, "your decision to report misconduct by a senior officer was entirely logical."

McCoy gave Chekov's shoulder an avuncular squeeze. "Just remember what the Bible says: The truth shall make you free." He paused for effect: "But first, it'll make you *damned miserable.*"

Spock's eyebrow arched. "Doctor, I am thoroughly conversant with Earth's New Testament. The common biblical quotation does not include your addendum."

"Well, it *should* have," McCoy shot back.

"Ahh . . . King James," Kirk said drily, "as revised by Leonard McCoy."

Fracture

Jeff Bond

Jeff Bond

Jeff Bond is Executive Editor of *CFQ (Cinefantastique)* magazine and covers film music for *The Hollywood Reporter* and *Film Score Monthly* magazine. He is the author of *The Music of Star Trek* and is coauthoring an upcoming book on makeup artist Rick Baker. He briefly glimpsed a few minutes of *Star Trek* during its original third season in 1968 and began watching the first syndication package of the show around 1970 in his hometown of Defiance, Ohio, where he eventually drove his family crazy by watching and rewatching every episode of the series dozens of times. He studied creative writing at Bowling Green State University and held down exciting jobs at the Holiday Inn and Kinko's before moving to Hollywood. There the knowledge and experience he had gained by ignoring his mother's advice to go outside and get some exercise instead of watching TV could finally bear fruit, and he has been able to interview many of his childhood heroes, like Charlton Heston, William Shatner, John Williams, Jerry Goldsmith, Sigourney Weaver, Richard Matheson, and others. His beautiful and understanding wife, Brooke, continues to put up with his hobbies, which include filling his garage full of spaceship models and action figures, listening to loud movie soundtracks, and becoming speechless with excitement at meeting old character actors like William Windom and Morgan Woodward. Jeff and Brooke currently reside in Burbank, California, with their cat, Burbank.

CAPTAIN'S PERSONAL LOG, Stardate 6453.4:

Now entering the Veletus system after a voyage of 12 days to resupply Deep Space Station M-33, currently under the command of Commodore Julius "Falcon" Merrill. I must admit to some excitement at the chance to meet the commodore, one of the most renowned commanders in the history of Starfleet.

Although our trip here was uneventful, the commodore's reports have mentioned intermittent encroachment by Tholian vessels into this sector, and we anticipate providing at least some tactical support to the station. But I—

James Kirk's thoughts hit a wall as the door to his cabin buzzed. "Computer, pause recording," he commanded as he hit the intercom button on his desk. "Come," he said, unlocking the sliding cabin door.

He wasn't surprised to see Leonard McCoy grinning at him from the open doorway. "No dress uniform today, Jim?" the doctor asked as he entered the cabin. Kirk stood up from his desk and cast a sideways glance at the *Enterprise* chief surgeon.

"No, but if you're eager to get into one I can arrange it," Kirk said. He sighted a familiar-looking cylindrical container in the doctor's hand. "What's that?" he asked suspiciously.

"Altairian rice wine," McCoy said. "I believe it's the commodore's favorite. For some reason there's a case of this stuff in the cargo bay."

Kirk shook his head ruefully. "I swear I'm going to put Chief Stillwell on report. Is everyone on the ship in on this?"

"Jim, you've earned your crew's respect. Let's just say there are quite a few of them who take an interest when they find out who it is out there that *you* look up to."

Kirk felt uncomfortably transparent. "Falcon Merrill was a childhood hero of mine," he said disapprovingly. "When I became a captain myself I put away childish things."

"Yeah, keep telling yourself that," McCoy said. "The fact is I grew up reading about Merrill, too. Five starship commands and two diplomatic appointments; not too many people have a career like that."

Kirk's intercom whistled: *"Bridge to captain."* Kirk thumbed open the channel.

"Kirk here."

"Approaching Space Station M-33, Captain," Spock's voice came.

"On my way."

They were halfway insystem when Kirk and McCoy exited the turbolift. Kirk slowed slightly as he stared at the image of Veletus V, the system's lone gas giant dominating the main viewer. The planet was a looming sphere of banded gray and green, but an immense, triangular smear of crimson blocked more than a third of its surface from view. The orbiting cloud was far larger than Kirk had imagined it would be. "The Ifukube Veil," Kirk said as he stepped down and settled into his command chair.

"Affirmative, Captain," Spock said from his science station. "Named after twenty-second-century astronomer Kenji Ifukube, the cloud is composed of ionized hydrogen and other trace elements, held in orbit around Veletus V by a combination of the planet's magnetic fields and the gravitational loci of its five moons."

"Wouldn't something like that normally take the form of rings, Mr. Spock?"

"Over millions of years, yes," Spock said. "The Veil was formed far more recently, although we have not yet determined precisely how."

As the image grew with their approach, Kirk could see the shape of Deep Space Station M-33 in the screen's lower right-hand corner: a collection of glinting metal cones connected by concentric rings. Even after two years sections of the station remained under construction. Indicators on the screen pointed out a series of dozens of satellite substations surrounding the Ifukube Veil and the gas giant itself: remote drones of the space station designed to monitor the condition of the hydrogen cloud and the complex gravitational forces around the planet.

As Kirk stepped down toward his command chair, his eyes still fixed on the screen, he saw a flash of light like an electrical discharge crawl across a small section of the hydrogen cloud, illuminating it from within.

"Fascinating," Spock said, dividing his attention between the screen and his hooded science station viewer. "Extraordinarily active."

"Aye," Montgomery Scott agreed from his engineering station. "There's enough charged hydrogen in that cloud to power a fleet of starships."

"Message from M-33, Captain," Uhura announced. "I have Commodore Merrill for you."

Kirk glanced at McCoy, who'd stepped down to stand next to the captain's chair. "You want the honor, Bones?"

"It's all yours," the doctor said. Kirk punched his command chair intercom.

"This is James Kirk of the *Enterprise;* it's a pleasure to speak to you, Commodore."

"*Well, if it isn't the* Enterprise." Julius Merrill's unmistakable voice, familiar from dozens of recorded speeches, filtered through the chair speaker. "*Nice to hear from you. We were damn near running out of toilet paper out here.*"

Kirk smiled. "I hope we can provide better supplies than that," he said.

"Captain," Sulu interrupted. "We're picking up two Tholian vessels converging at the edge of the system, moving at extreme speed."

"Excuse me, Commodore," Kirk said. "Course, Mr. Sulu?"

"Sir, they're changing course now, heading directly toward the fifth planet and M-33."

"Their speed is approximately warp seven, Captain," Spock said, peering into the hooded viewer on his sciences console. "At that rate they will be in weapons range of the station in two minutes."

"Contact those ships, Uhura. Warn them off."

"Trying, sir," Uhura said.

"Sound red alert," Kirk snapped. "Mr. Sulu, plot an intercept course and get us between those ships and the station; increase speed to warp seven-point-five."

"Aye, sir."

"Spock, why didn't we sight those vessels earlier?" Kirk demanded, swiveling to look at his science officer. "I'm assuming the Tholians don't possess cloaking technology."

Spock straightened and turned toward Kirk. "Vessels were too small to register on our sensors until they reached the edge of the system, Captain," the Vulcan explained. "Their configurations indicate Tholian design; however, they are far smaller than any Tholian vessels we have previously encountered."

"Kirk, don't intercept those ships!"

Kirk tore his attention from the tactical display on the screen ahead of him as Merrill's voice registered.

"Excuse me, Commodore? Their course certainly seems to indicate a hostile intent."

"I said, don't intercept them," Merrill barked. *"My people can handle this."*

"Sir, with respect, the *Enterprise* is far better equipped—"

"Just follow my orders, Captain. Back off now, and keep your distance until this is over."

Kirk frowned, his nerves on fire at the sight of the Tholian vessels careening into the star system. It made no sense for Merrill to refuse his help . . . but it made even less to argue tactics with a man of the commodore's experience.

"No reply from the Tholian vessels, Captain," Uhura said. "They may be unable to respond."

"Unable?" Kirk asked.

"The Tholians designed diplomatic language specifically for our translator technology, Captain," Uhura explained. "Only vessels designated for border patrol and diplomatic duties use it. Our ability to translate Tholian standard languages is limited."

"Mr. Sulu," Kirk said quietly. "Come about; program a parallel course to the incoming vessels at seven-hundred-thousand kilometers."

Sulu glanced back at Kirk for a second but didn't question the order. Kirk watched the Tholian vessels close the distance to the gas giant, pointing like two arrowheads at M-33. The Tholian ships bulleted into the system in tight formation, curving away from the space station and toward the swath of red gases a thousand kilometers past it. Just as the ships were about to penetrate the Veil, energy surges flashed between the network of satellites fringing the cloud, forming a barrier that both tiny craft now crashed against. The *Enterprise* scanners focused in sharply on the Tholian vessels as tractor beams from the drone system damped their forward momentum. One of the vessels managed to wrench free of the tractor beams and penetrate the Veil, disappearing inside the cloud. The other ship hung suspended between two of the Veil satellites. Spock looked up from his science station. "The remaining Tholian vessel has been immobilized, Captain," he said.

The bridge crew watched as the drones shunted the alien ship between overlapping tractor swaths, efficiently maneuvering the vessel for kilometers at a pass until the M-33 station's own tractors could take over and draw the ship toward a spherical holding bay. Kirk shook his head, marveling a little at the tactical efficiency on display.

"All clear, Enterprise," Merrill's voice returned. *"You can come back on approach."*

"You made that look like a drill, Commodore," Kirk said.

"Captain, out here we've got nothing to do but drill. We're preparing to receive you; transporter coordinates transmitting now."

Kirk got out of his chair. He'd been expecting a bored old man eager to share stories, but the encroachment of the Tholian ship, no matter how elegantly handled, had thrown him. Now he wasn't quite sure what he was getting into. "Spock, Bones: with me."

The operations center of M-33 was big; it dwarfed the *Enterprise*'s bridge, but there were only three or four more officers inside the domed chamber than there were in Kirk's command; that and the high, vaulted ceiling gave the room a strange, denuded quality, like a forest clearing somewhere. Kirk's pupils dilated at the wash of red light from the Ifukube Veil flooding through a broad viewport that dominated half of the ops center. He could see the glint of the station's drones surrounding the gas cloud even from here, as well as the swollen curve of Veletus V behind it.

A tall, gaunt Andorian stepped forward from a group of officers as

Kirk, Spock, and McCoy glanced at their surroundings. "Captain Kirk," the blue-skinned alien said. "I am Commander Thavas. Welcome aboard M-33."

Kirk looked around expectantly, but Merrill was nowhere to be seen. "I thought Commodore Merrill might be here," Kirk said.

"The commodore is waiting for you in his office, Captain," Thavas replied. "If you will follow me."

Kirk spared a last glance at the operations center and noted Spock too studying the layout and the hum of activity as several screens showed the Tholian vessel being maneuvered into a holding bay. If this was an emergency, Kirk thought, the station's crew was doing a pretty good job hiding it.

They walked down a large, long corridor toward Merrill's office, past technicians still at work on pressure seals, evidently expanding this section of the station. Then they were ushered down a shallow flight of stairs to the entryway to Merrill's inner sanctum.

Thavas signaled and Merrill's no-nonsense voice issued a brief "Come" over the doorway intercom. The door slid aside and Kirk and his officers entered the ready room. The chamber, evidently one of the numerous spherical pressure chambers dotting the skin of the station, related to an "office" the same way M-33's ops center related to Kirk's bridge—it was huge, vaulted, and dark. Merrill himself stood silhouetted against the view of the gargantuan planet the station orbited, red light from the hydrogen gas cloud above lighting his shoulders like a mantel. Kirk wondered if the commodore planned all his meetings this way, with the surroundings designed to dazzle his visitors.

Merrill turned as the four officers entered his domain, and in the dim light Kirk felt a flush of recognition at that weathered profile, the still-thick head of wavy hair, and the athlete's build. Only when the commodore waved the lights up and strode toward them did Kirk have to adjust his Academy memories of what this man looked like and acknowledge that this was a human being in the ninth decade of his life. The recruiting poster smile blazing off a row of perfect teeth now sported a hint of a rictus to it, Kirk noted, as if Merrill were grinning through some vicious little internal ache. The brilliant blue eyes had paled a little since he'd last been holographed, but they fixed on Kirk with the focus of a man a third of his age.

"You must be Jim Kirk," Merrill said as he closed his fingers around Kirk's hand. Kirk's eyebrows rose as he felt the vigor in Merrill's grip and reflexively returned it.

"It's a great pleasure, Commodore Merrill," Kirk said, smiling, as he introduced his officers.

"Sorry about that business when you were on your way in," Merrill said affably.

"Your people certainly seemed prepared for it," Kirk acknowledged.

"Like I said, nothing to do out here but drill. For this crew that little trespass was a walk in the park."

"But surely of some political importance," Spock remarked. "Federation contact with the Tholian Assembly has been intermittent at best over the last century. M-33 lies approximately seven light-years from the Tholian border; navigational errors could not account for such an incursion."

Merrill leveled a look at Spock. When he turned to look at someone, Kirk thought, he was like an ancient artillery piece swiveling to aim at a target. "There probably wasn't an error," he said. "But we'll have the ship back in Tholian hands soon enough. You've contacted the Tholians, Thavas?"

"Affirmative, Commodore," the Andorian officer said. "A transfer vessel with escort is already en route; evidently Assembly forces were tracking these particular ships before they entered the system. They will arrive in less than two hours."

"Two hours?" Suddenly Merrill seemed surprised. "That's a new record. Let's have our supplies beamed aboard before then if possible. See to it, Commander."

The Andorian nodded and turned to leave, but Spock interjected. "With your permission, Commodore," he said, glancing at Kirk. "Captain, this is an unprecedented opportunity. If I may, I should like to observe the Tholian vessel before it is retrieved."

"Of course," Merrill said. "Thavas, please take Commander Spock down to the holding sphere."

Spock nodded politely and followed the Andorian out of the ready room.

"You don't mind if we sit and talk for a bit?" Merrill said, motioning Kirk and McCoy over to a pair of couches facing each other across a low, rectangular table. "I get visitors about once a year now and I sure as hell intend to take advantage of it."

Kirk glanced briefly at McCoy. Kirk actually pulled rank and pushed the *Enterprise* ahead of the *Akagi* on the list of supply vessels for just this opportunity, just for the chance to shoot the breeze with Julius Merrill. But now the incident with the Tholian ships made casual conversation seem strangely inappropriate.

"Of course, your hospitality's greatly appreciated," Kirk said slowly. "But I'm concerned about this incursion, sir. You're more than a week from Starfleet assistance out here, and—"

Merrill waved a hand dismissively. "I told you, we have the situation well under control. Ever try one of these?" As Kirk and McCoy settled onto one of the couches, Merrill opened a box of narrow, finger-sized cylinders: Deltan cigars, Kirk realized. McCoy's eyes flashed in a combination of envy and disapproval.

Kirk looked apologetic. This was going to be more challenging than he'd thought. "I can't say that I have." Kirk knew Merrill was an old man, but smoking was an activity that was positively prehistoric. He took the proffered smoke, which was strangely heavy in his palm, and waited while Merrill lit the cigar with an old fuel-based lighter. Even McCoy started slightly at the sight of the open flame: not something a starship crewman was used to seeing without hearing an alert klaxon.

Merrill watched while Kirk drew the smoke in cautiously, holding it in his lungs for a moment. It felt like a mix of hot magma and poison. Kirk struggled to keep from choking while the commodore let out a hearty laugh. "Easier to face a hundred angry Romulans than your first cigar. Let's see if you do better with cognac."

"That sounds more up my alley," Kirk groaned. "Even better if you have Saurian brandy."

"I might be able to scare up a bottle. I developed expensive tastes pretty young, in my early days on the frontier." Merrill headed over to a case of rare beverages and rummaged around inside, clinking old glass bottles. "You're not off the hook with that cigar yet. You pull the whole thing down, then you can tell me whether you approve or not. The finish is the best part."

Kirk clamped the toxic object between his teeth once again and glared at McCoy while the surgeon grinned at him smugly. "Be careful what you wish for, Jim," McCoy said under his breath.

"I'll be counting on you to cure whatever this does to me, Doctor," Kirk hissed back before Merrill turned around with a bottle in his hand.

"There we go," Merrill said as he poured three glasses and then raised his own as Kirk and McCoy took their drinks. "Enjoy life's little pleasures while you can; it'll all be gone soon enough." If it was a toast, it hung uncomfortably heavy in the air, Kirk thought. "Now, how is it we never met, son?" Merrill said, the vigor returning to his voice. "I've kept an eye on your career. You've got promise. A little sentimental for my taste, based on your logs, but I give that a pass."

"Sentimental?" Kirk said.

"That business on Gamma Trianguli VI for one thing," Merrill went on as if Kirk hadn't said anything. "Slaying an ancient god and getting everybody to love each other. I'll admit it makes an entertaining log entry, but sometimes you've got to leave well enough alone."

Kirk stole another glance at McCoy, but the surgeon was still clearly enjoying himself. "Well, I can't quite believe that after five starship commands you haven't run into a similar situation," he argued gamely.

"Well, now that you mention it, there was something," Merrill said as he settled into a plush chair that looked to be half a century old. "Now granted, this was about thirty years ago and the planet was pelagic . . ."

"Our station's xenobiology team will meet us in the holding chamber," Thavas said quietly as he and Spock exited a turbolift at a circular airlock station. "Environmental suits beyond this point." The Andorian pointed out a row of silver pressure suits and helmets lining one wall.

Spock pulled a suit off the wall and adjusted it to his measurements. In a few minutes he had the suit on and made the final adjustments to the helmet before fastening it into place.

Four suited technicians were visible ahead as Spock and Thavas entered the holding chamber. Spock felt a slight crackle as the heat and pressure of the chamber pressed in on his suit seals. Behind the four station personnel lay the Tholian ship, a wedge-shaped vessel similar to the gleaming webweavers Spock had encountered before, but far smaller, with a faceted central core bulging out from between its three triangular hull segments. As he approached he saw three similar vessels lined up behind the pair the technicians were examining: all three looked strangely desiccated, their hull surfaces shriveled and cracked. Spock's eyebrows rose appreciatively; it looked as if his earlier declaration of the scientific opportunity here might be an understatement.

One of the figures ahead of him turned as Spock and Thavas approached, and Spock saw the face of a surprisingly young human woman behind the environmental suit helmet. "This is M-33's chief xenobiologist, Dr. Casio Glasser. Doctor, may I present Commander Spock of the *Enterprise*."

"Commander Spock," the woman said. She seemed about to extend a hand almost excitedly and then seemed to think better of it, inclining her head slightly in the Vulcan way instead. "This is an honor."

"I was not aware this station had a full xenobiology staff," Spock said.

"Well, we didn't originally—I was just doing planetary science until the first incursion thirteen months ago; after that I got a little promotion."

"Indeed," Spock said, gesturing at the lineup of Tholian vessels. "You have an enviable opportunity to examine Tholian technology. I am curious as to why the Tholians would allow it."

Glasser shrugged, looking back at the ships. "Well, you're welcome to join us, but you won't learn much. We haven't gone very far beyond the basics."

"Why have these three additional vessels not been transferred off the station by the Tholians?"

"The pilots all died before the Tholian Assembly transfer ships made it here. Tholians seem to have no interest in their dead, or the dead pilots' ships. These vessels started to decay shortly after we brought them on board. We've tried to approximate what we know of Tholian atmospheric conditions in here on the off chance the pilots might survive after their ships break down, but it seems to make no difference."

Spock approached one of the breached ships, its hull splintered and cracked. An entire side of the arrowhead-shaped vessel had disintegrated, leaving the remains of its interior and its dead pilot open to inspection. "Remarkable," Spock said, activating his tricorder. The Tholian pilot was now a glinting, lifeless husk, shards of its crystalline body fraying away from a hollow center. A barrel-shaped torso, multiple supporting, segmented legs, and the remains of the familiar, helmet-like head Spock had once viewed on the *Enterprise*'s main screen: the details were all there, but shattered to the point where they were barely recognizable.

"Somewhat insectile, as you can see," Glasser said. "That seems to extend to their society as well; individuals seem to be bred for specific societal functions, like ants. Or a caste society on Earth."

Spock nodded. "I have heard the caste system mentioned in relation to the Tholians." He found it interesting how often human scientists relied on Earth-based analogies. "It would appear that very little of their internal structures survived whatever caused their deaths," Spock said. "Yet you say the majority of your captures have survived."

"Yes," Glasser acknowledged. "The survivors have stayed sealed in their ships and are pretty uncommunicative. It's funny; two of these died in captivity and the other was dead when we brought it in. The Tholians declined to retrieve any of them . . . it was almost as if they knew these particular pilots would die even before their ships started to decay."

"I fail to see why those facts would be considered cause for amusement," Spock said, training his tricorder on the newly captured Tholian vessel. Its energy output was steady and it was clearly maintaining its own intense internal heat and pressure, but there was very little more useful information available. "It is quite effectively shielded. I should like to tie my tricorder into the holding chamber's sensors if I may. You said you have had at least some limited communication with captured Tholians?"

"We're not that certain of our translations, and we only got a few words; nothing that made any sense."

"Our ship's chief communications officer has had some experience in Tholian translation, which may be helpful," Spock said. "With your permission, I would like to involve her in this research."

"Of course," Glasser said. Spock reached up to toggle the communicator control just underneath the foreplate of his helmet, cycling through command channels to beam outside the station's interior relays. "Spock to *Enterprise*."

"Enterprise; *Uhura here*."

"Lieutenant, contact M-33's executive officer, Commander Thavas, and arrange to be transported to the station. I will need your presence in the—"

A piercing whine suddenly erupted over Spock's helmet speakers, and he saw the four human researchers reflexively clutch at their own suit helmets as the sound flashed through their communicators. One of the scientists had the presence of mind to focus his tricorder on the transmission.

"It's coming from inside the Tholian ship!" he exclaimed.

"Dr. Glasser, I assume this transmission differs from your prior communication attempts with the Tholians," Spock said.

Glasser nodded as she adjusted the volume of her helmet speakers, wincing as she shook her head. "It's different all right," she said. "We had to tap into their comm grids to get anything before." She looked back at the ship and then at Spock. "This is directed at us. The pilot is definitely trying to communicate."

Uhura's voice overrode the shrieking sound in Spock's helmet. *"Mr. Spock, report on situation, please."*

"We are experiencing a form of Tholian communication, Lieutenant," Spock said. "Your presence is urgently required."

Kirk found the right pause in Merrill's storytelling and managed to gesture at the big viewport across the room, standing as he pointed to the Ifukube Veil and a few of its artificial satellites. "Those drones weren't put in place for defensive purposes originally, were they, Commodore?"

"No," Merrill said, getting off his own couch with a little grunt. "That all started as a way to study the Veil. We found we had to reinforce the satellites even for that purpose because the Veil's so active and unstable—we actually lost a few satellites from energy spikes. Blew them to pieces. Ultimately we think we can tap this thing for one hell of a lot of free energy. M-33 could become a lot more valuable to Starfleet than anyone thought it would."

"How so?"

"We're out on the edge of Federation space . . . but we could expand our borders from here, using the station as a launch point."

"Wouldn't the Tholians have something to say about that?" Kirk asked.

Merrill looked at him seriously for a moment, then his face lit up in that irrepressible grin. "They might, son. They might."

Kirk frowned. "Commodore . . . you're facing what appears to me to be potentially dangerous incursions by Tholian vessels. I'm afraid I don't quite understand your attitude."

Merrill nodded. "We were warned about this. I got diplomatic messages from the Tholians around the tenth month of our construction and setup here. The Assembly has no interest in this system, but there are factions within Tholian society that do for some reason. Outsiders, they're called. The Assembly says they're renegades and pirates, probably looking to set up a base here just like we are. They could use the Veil in the same way; most of the incursions have centered on the cloud, penetrating it or skimming it. I think they're trying to figure it out, do their own experimentation, and they've had their accidents and successes just like we have."

"That certainly doesn't sound like a promising situation for the station, however," Kirk argued. "It's clear this dispute, or whatever it is, has been growing over the past year."

"I won't argue with that, but we're still talking about mostly small, one-pilot ships. And the Tholian government has assured us that it recognizes our claim to the system." At that a communications panel at Merrill's desk beeped. "Excuse me," the commodore said, moving to answer the call. Kirk's communicator beeped a few seconds later, and the captain glanced at McCoy as he flipped the device open.

"Spock here, Captain. There has been a development with the captured Tholian vessel." It was obvious from Merrill's end of his conversation that they were dealing with the same subject matter.

"Let's have it."

Uhura's brow furrowed as she made minute adjustments to the universal translator, which was plugged into a dataport on her tricorder drawing on logic interfaces from both the *Enterprise*'s and M-33's central computers. She had found a communications node on one edge of the Tholian ship and had attached a transponder directly to it to feed the translator telemetry through.

This would be a lot easier without a bulky environmental suit getting in the way, she thought. She hadn't even had time to adjust her suit quite to the optimal temperature in her rush to get into the holding chamber. There was a pesky bead of sweat on her brow, and Spock's impassive face staring at her as she worked wasn't helping.

She'd skimmed the records of previous communications with the Tholians the station had captured. It was clear from what M-33's xenobiology staff had told her that most of the other Tholian individuals had been drones or scouts, unequipped for any kind of sophisticated communication with beings outside their species, or perhaps even outside their caste. The ideas she'd been able to glean from the logs were fragmentary, even contradictory. It was remarkable how different these language concepts were from Tholian diplomatic tongue.

Strangely, the language coming from this newest Tholian individual was much easier to grasp, and the currents of communication seemed to be flowing faster as Uhura worked and transmitted her own responses, as if the Tholian was learning humanoid language concepts at an incredible rate.

Dr. Glasser nodded as Uhura relayed her conclusions. The copper-haired xenobiologist looked at Spock through her helmet faceplate. "It's adapting. I think this one's a Mage, Mr. Spock. Either that or it's been in contact with one."

"Mage?" the Vulcan said.

"They're Tholians that are able to move freely between castes. They have the authority to modify individuals from caste to caste, changing their societal roles. And they're able to do the same thing to themselves, apparently, so that they can take on specialized skill sets for specific jobs."

"As I understand it, that would represent a rather important role in Tholian society," Spock said. "What would such an individual be doing here?"

"With a group of Outsiders? Good question." Glasser shook her head. "Commodore Merrill's always thought the Tholian faction was trying to set up a beachhead here. This could be a leader."

Uhura frowned as she correlated the data feeding in from both computers and watched translation concepts cross-connect on her tricorder's small readout screen. "Mr. Spock, there's one clear idea that's appeared more than once in this transmission. It works out as 'sanctuary.' I thought initially it may have referred to something in this area of space, but it may now mean this station specifically or us." She kept her eyes on the readouts while computer translations filtered through her speaker headphones. It was a riot of information, but she could still make sense out of some of the concepts. "Sir, the word has a political aspect to it." She turned to look at Spock. "It's related to 'asylum.'"

"Political asylum," Spock said gravely.

"Nonsense," Merrill said a quarter of an hour later, glaring at Kirk, Spock, and McCoy while Thavas, Glasser, and Uhura sat around a conference table. "None of the Outsiders has ever asked for asylum. They'd rather face whatever punishment their own people have in store for them than deal with us."

"I do not understand how you draw that conclusion, Commodore," Spock said calmly. "Prior communication with Tholian pilots has been far from conclusive."

"But their actions have been conclusive enough," Merrill snapped.

"It's clear they want access to the Veil, and they're willing to sneak past us or even attack us if necessary to get to it."

"But why, Commodore?" Kirk said, studying Merrill intently. "If they're really trying to harvest that cloud, they wouldn't be using one-man ships to do it."

"We don't know what they're doing," Merrill said angrily. "We know some of the pilots are scouts; odds are they're testing our defenses for a more sustained operation."

"Uhura, what do you make of the communication you've had with this pilot so far?" Kirk asked. "Has it made reference to the cloud or what they might want with it?"

"It made reference to something," Uhura said. "The language did seem to relate to the Veil, but the terms weren't . . . well, they didn't sound like references to fuel, economic, or strategic concepts. More abstract than that . . . I haven't worked it out yet."

"But you're certain this pilot was asking for asylum?" Kirk asked. Uhura glanced at Spock before replying.

"I'd say it's a very strong probability, sir."

"Probability!" Merrill snorted. "I have an agreement with the Tholian Assembly, and I'll be damned if I'm going to violate that agreement over a *probability*. Thavas, tell the captain what you told me about that signal."

"The transmission was directed outside the system in addition to the direct feed to your communications receivers," the Andorian said quietly. "It may have been an attempt to distract from its true purpose."

Kirk glanced from the Andorian to Merrill, who met his look defiantly. "I'd like to speak with the commodore alone, please," he said. "Mr. Spock, Lieutenant Uhura, continue your work in cooperation with the station's staff."

A few seconds later the briefing room was empty except for the two commanding officers. Kirk studied Merrill carefully. It was clear the commodore was already angry at having his authority questioned. He'd been in command at M-33 for more than a year, and his experience, not to mention his rank, outstripped Kirk's. What Kirk had to say now would have to be said carefully.

"Commodore, what exactly *is* this 'agreement' with the Tholians? There were very few details of anything like that in our briefing on the situation here."

"It's simple enough," Merrill said flatly. "We keep any Tholian Outsiders away from our station and the Veil, and hold any we capture for transfer back to the Tholian government."

"In exchange for what?"

Merrill paused almost imperceptibly before answering. "Tactical aid, of course. Keeping these pirates off our backs as much as they can and shuttling them out of the system when they do manage to break in."

"You keep referring to them as 'pirates' against any evidence I've yet to see regarding their goals."

"That's how they were defined to me by the Assembly."

"Then why would a pirate request political asylum?"

"We don't know that's the case, Kirk."

"Then let's just assume that it is for a moment," Kirk said calmly. "How would it affect your agreement if I honor the request?"

Merrill stood up, shaking his head. "Don't you see how remarkable it is that *any* kind of agreement exists between a Federation individual and the Assembly?" he argued. "We've been trying to understand the Tholians for over a century now. We've barely come away from that with comprehensible territorial boundaries made between us. Now we have a working agreement, cooperation—"

"You're not answering my question," Kirk interrupted. "How will the Tholians react if we grant an individual asylum?"

"I don't plan on finding out," the commodore said. "I don't know about you, but I keep my word."

"Your word? What about your oath to Starfleet?" Kirk dropped that bomb and sharpened his focus on Merrill. He saw a volcanic rage erupt out of those clear blue eyes as Merrill put his hands down on the table and glowered down at the sitting Kirk.

"Don't you lecture me about my oath, *Captain,*" the commodore said, twisting his mouth around Kirk's rank. "I took that oath before you were born!"

"I won't ignore a request for asylum," Kirk said slowly.

"You will if I order you to!" Merrill barked.

Kirk let the impasse stand for a moment as he stared Merrill down. At this point he was more than prepared to override Merrill's authority. But even as he glared down at Kirk, Merrill seemed to compose himself. "Kirk," he said, "let's be reasonable, son. You know what can come out of this, what this means. In a few more months, maybe a year, I can have an alliance with the Tholians. We can anchor this sector and expand the reach of the Federation to dominate the entire quadrant."

"Dominate?" Kirk said. He stared at Merrill harshly. Somehow the big, athletic man seemed diminished, the wear and tear on his aging face uglier than it had been when Kirk had first met him. He began to understand now how a man with the commodore's reputation and history could be shuttled out here to a command on the edge of nowhere.

"All right, that was a poor choice of words," Merrill muttered. "But you must at least see the opportunity—"

"Commodore, I'm asking you to signal the Tholians that we will be holding that pilot under rules of political asylum. Until I find out what's going on here, there will be no transfer."

"No," Merrill shook his head. "No, you're destroying a year of work. You're putting us back to square one!"

"If you don't signal the Tholians, the *Enterprise* will," Kirk finished.

"The transfer ships are practically on our doorstep, Kirk," Merrill argued. "They've come too far to go back empty-handed. The Tholians won't be happy."

"Commodore, I won't argue with you further. Under Starfleet regulations, General Order Twelve, paragraph—"

"*All right!*" Merrill stared down at the desk furiously as if there might be some alternate answer on the faux wood surface. "All right," he repeated quietly. "I'll comply. But for God's sake, let me send the communiqué."

Kirk's communicator beeped, providing a welcome end to the conversation. "I'm returning to the *Enterprise,* Commodore," Kirk said as he stood. "Please report whatever response you get from the Tholians immediately."

Kirk flipped his communicator open as he met McCoy outside the briefing room. *"Sulu here, Captain,"* the helmsman's voice sounded out of the communicator grid. *"Tholian transfer ships have arrived. And Tholian traffic outside the system is intensifying, sir. Multiple ship signatures at the edges of our sensors."*

Kirk looked at McCoy. "Have the transporter room lock on to my signal, Lieutenant. Two to beam up."

Kirk was tight-lipped as McCoy tagged along while he marched from the *Enterprise* transporter room to the turbolift. The silent treatment finally became too much as the lift started to rise. "Bones, was it you who told me a man should never meet his heroes?"

McCoy smiled sympathetically. "The idea's always a little bit better than the actual experience."

"He thinks he has a potential alliance with the Tholians," Kirk said. "For all I know he's right. But it just *feels* completely wrong."

"Merrill's been a starship commander and an ambassador, Jim," McCoy said. "He's seen every side of this kind of issue. You can't count out his point of view just because M-33 isn't the most prestigious assignment for the end of a career."

"That's just what I'm afraid may be motivating him, Bones: a final chance for glory. If he could come home having forged an alliance with the most inscrutable race the Federation has encountered in the past century . . ."

The bridge doors snapped open on that thought and Kirk entered to see the familiar view of the space station on the viewscreen—with several new additions. The Tholian courier vessels held position just off M-33's northern flank, hovering menacingly over the station.

"Captain," communications officer Palmer said as Kirk stepped down toward his command chair. "Message from Commodore Merrill. He says the Tholians are demanding immediate transfer of the captured vessel to their ships."

Kirk sat down, eyeing the viewscreen. "Let's talk to them directly, Lieutenant."

"Aye, sir. Hailing frequency open."

"This is Captain James Kirk of the Federation *Starship Enterprise*. We have received a request for political asylum from the Tholian vessel captured by station M-33. Until we determine the status of the Tholian pilot, we respectfully ask you to delay your transfer—"

"This is Commander Iskel of the Tholian Assembly," came the triple-toned voice of the lead transfer ship commander. *"Our agreement with the commander of this space station grants us immediate access to all Tholians who intrude on this area of space."*

"With all due respect, Commander, *you* and *your* vessels are currently intruding in Federation space. And our policy is to grant asylum to anyone who formally requests it."

"Our agreement was designed for your protection, Enterprise," the Tholian replied. *"The Assembly has no designs on this sector. But we also seek to prevent Tholian Outsiders from intruding here. Those who do so will be dealt with by us."*

"We appreciate your concern, Commander, but—"

"Enterprise, *we grant ten of your minutes to release the captives from the station; after that time we shall use force to retrieve them. End of communication."*

Kirk blinked as the line snapped off. "Well, that was the world's shortest negotiation," McCoy said.

"Captain, I'm reading a large group of Tholian vessels headed into the system," Sulu said from the helm. "Their approach is far off normal Tholian shipping lanes, Captain—I don't think they're Assembly vessels."

"Outsider ships. Tactical on viewer," Kirk ordered. He watched as a cluster of ten Tholian ship signatures registered on the screen. "That's an attack group," he said.

"At least five webweavers, Captain," Sulu reported. "They're slightly smaller than standard configuration, but with five of them they still have significant offensive capability even discounting the support ships."

Kirk felt an ugly weight settle into his gut. Every instinct told him to move the *Enterprise* and intercept the Outsider attack group before it reached the station . . . but he couldn't leave M-33 with four Tholian ships already threatening it. "Raise the commodore," he said. "Mr. Sulu, what's the complement of the station?"

"Two hundred twenty currently, sir."

"This is Merrill," the commodore's voice sounded. *"You're in it now, Kirk."*

"How much of a defense can M-33 put up against a Tholian attack group?" Kirk asked.

"Yeah, we're tracking them," Merrill said of the approaching ships. *"Not too damn much, Kirk. We haven't faced down anything of that strength yet. And I've got even better news: the Assembly's called in their own forces. In a few minutes we'll have a civil war on our hands."* Merrill's voice was thick with anger. *"Maybe next time you'll listen to me."*

"I still don't understand what this fight is about," Kirk said. "Even the transfer ship commander insisted the Tholians have no claim on this system."

"Looks like some of them do," Merrill said.

"Commodore, have your people stand by to evacuate. We can't mount a defense while we're chained here to this station."

"You're going to beam two hundred people aboard your ship? Do you know how much power that will draw?"

Engineer Scott turned from his station at that. "He's right, Captain. We'll have to recalibrate the cargo transporters for evacuation protocols, and they've been running nonstop since we got to the station."

"Commodore, I know you only have a couple of cargo transporters on board the station, but you can use those to move some of your personnel—and you should also be able to channel an energy feed to us to augment our power."

"We can do it, but we still won't have enough time to move everyone before those ships get here," Merrill insisted.

"We'll have even less time if we don't start immediately," Kirk said.

Uhura was matching more translator concepts when the evacuation order came. She and Spock were huddled against the hull of the Tholian ship, the Vulcan correlating her information while Glasser and her team continued to work over the vessel.

"Lieutenant," Spock said, "it is imperative that we be able to converse in specifics with the Tholian pilot as soon as possible."

"I understand, sir. I'm getting close. And it's . . . adapting even faster now."

"It may not be fast enough," Spock said. "We could be called upon to leave at any moment. I doubt the *Enterprise* can spare the energy to transport this entire vessel into its shuttlebay under current circumstances, and once we leave we may never reestablish communication with this particular Tholian."

Uhura looked up at Spock. "Well, can't you just mind-meld with this thing?" The Vulcan's left eyebrow rose disapprovingly.

"I have been attempting to do so, Lieutenant," Spock said. "But it is rather difficult to sense thoughts through a ship hull. At any rate, Tholian thoughts seem to be incompatible with Vulcan telepathic abilities."

"You . . . must . . . leave."

Uhura's eyes widened as the strange, triple-toned sound of the Tholian diplomatic language sounded over the translator speaker.

"We understand you," she said. "Explain your request."

"You occupy Cathedral Station. You block the Way. I am Mage Naskeel. I am sent as Speaker."

"Naskeel, please quantify your differences with the Tholian Assembly," Spock said. "Your people have been referred to as 'Outsiders.' We are unfamiliar with such a segment of Tholian society."

Uhura looked at the science officer in exasperation. "Mr. Spock, I'm just getting a workable language interface going here. Ironing out complex concepts is still going to take time."

"We have very little left, Lieutenant."

"We are the Children of the Lost Ones," the triple voice continued. *"We return now to Cathedral Station. You must release me, that I may serve."*

Uhura looked at Spock. "Serve what?"

Kirk stared helplessly at the tactical screen as the phalanx of Outsider ships penetrated the system. "Sixty station personnel now on board, sir," Sulu reported.

"Scotty, how are the transporters holding up?" Kirk asked.

"They're doing the job all right, but our energy reserves are plummeting."

"Will we have enough power to complete the evacuation?"

"Aye, but not much more."

"The Outsider ships will be in weapons range in fifteen minutes, Captain," Chekov said.

"Red alert. All hands to battle stations," Kirk said quietly. "Is Commodore Merrill aboard yet?"

"The commodore refuses to beam aboard until the rest of his crew is evacuated, sir," Palmer replied.

"What about our personnel?"

"A few cargo handlers, Mr. Spock, and Lieutenant Uhura remain on M-33," Palmer said. "Mr. Spock requested that he and Uhura be among the last transferred off the station."

Kirk shook his head in frustration as he watched the advancing line of ships. Now another group appeared at the far frontier of the star system, still an hour distant. "That's an Assembly tactical force, Captain," Chekov said. "Several quite large ships, particularly for Tholian designs."

"Scotty, estimate our energy reserves and best possible speed out of the system."

"Jim, you're gonna abandon the station?" McCoy said.

"Consider it a tactical withdrawal at this stage, Bones," Kirk said. "Hail the Outsider fleet, Lieutenant Palmer."

Kirk waited while Palmer worked at her controls, but after a few moments the woman shook her head. "They don't answer, Captain. But they're beaming something very much like a general attack warning ahead of them."

"We're at eighty evacuees on board now, sir," Sulu said.

"Lead Outsider ships accelerating, Captain!" Chekov reported. "At new speed they'll be in firing range in two minutes."

Kirk did the math in his head; there were still more than a hundred people on the station. "Contact Mr. Spock and arrange to have him and Lieutenant Uhura beamed aboard in the next group . . . along with Commodore Merrill and his command crew."

"Yes, sir." It took only a few seconds for the arguments to begin. "Mr. Spock requests more time, sir. And Commodore Merrill refuses—"

Kirk clicked his chair intercom. "Transporter control: isolate M-33's command crew and beam them aboard in the next wave, along with Spock, Uhura, and that xenobiology crew they're working with."

"Lead Outsider ships are firing, sir!" Chekov announced. "The station's deflector shields have come up."

"Raise ours, Mr. Chekov," Kirk said helplessly as the first few bolts of plasma fire from the Tholian Outsiders struck the edges of the station. The Assembly transfer ships broke formation and began to return fire, but it was clear the Outsider attack force heavily outmatched them. Kirk blinked as one of the transfer escorts suddenly vaporized under heavy fire. Then the *Enterprise* herself lurched under a plasma hit.

The Outsider attack group lay down a firestorm as it converged on the station, and Kirk watched as the force's five webships fanned out with a cat's cradle of energy webbing strung between them. While their support ships blasted away at the Assembly vessels and the *Enterprise,* the Outsider webships began to draw their gleaming snare around M-33.

"They're going to destroy the station," Kirk said. "Divert power back to weapons and target those ships."

Spock stepped away from Uhura and the Tholian ship and walked toward the row of dead Tholian vessels with a deliberateness that belied the growing desperation of their situation. Glasser looked up at the Vulcan from where she'd been examining one of the Outsider ship's seals and then stood to follow Spock, bracing herself for a second as the deck shuddered under her feet.

"Dr. Glasser, you have never determined why these three Tholian pilots died; is that not correct?"

"We assume something went wrong with their ships' life-support systems. But we've never nailed down a specific cause."

"Yet the Assembly's failure to retrieve them strongly suggests they were aware of the inevitability of their deaths," Spock said. "What have you learned of Tholian metabolic processes?"

"They generate their own very high internal temperature," Glasser said. "But we've never been able to determine much about their internal structure. It seems to disintegrate very rapidly after death."

"Disintegrate or dissipate?" Spock said.

"Sir?" Glasser asked curiously.

"I believe Federation science may have taken the Earth insect analogy too far where it regards the Tholians," he said. "I do not believe Tholian external bodies are exoskeletons in the traditional sense."

"Then what are they?"

Spock moved a few steps into the fragile remains of the dead Tholian vessel he was examining and knelt next to the shattered crystalline corpse of its Tholian pilot. "Prisms, in a respect," he said. "You found no chemical residues of a physical body after this necrotic disintegration," the Vulcan continued. "I submit that no physical internal structures were there to disintegrate."

Glasser's face slackened as she caught up with Spock's line of reasoning. "We assumed the Tholians died when their ship's life-support systems stopped functioning. You're saying it was the other way around!"

"Precisely," Spock said, showing Glasser his tricorder viewing screen. "These high energy readings from within the Tholian vessel are not simply the ship's power systems. Some of them must emanate from the Tholian pilot itself."

Glasser shook her head wonderingly. "We were ID'ing those signatures as the ship's power feeds. We just assumed those readings were too high for a living creature's body temperature." Glasser pulled up her own tricorder and began cycling through its records. "Look at this," she said, showing her readings to Spock. "That means these are the energy readouts from the pilots that died, taken during their last few hours of life."

Spock nodded as he analyzed the readings. "Fascinating. A specific level of radioactive decay across a uniform spectrum. Doctor, by examining these levels, one could predict down to the nanosecond the life span of any Tholian individual."

"They're like living atomic clocks," Glasser said. "That certainly explains Tholian punctuality."

"It may explain more than that," Spock said. "Why Tholian society is so rigidly organized, for one thing. And perhaps why this particular individual represents such a threat to the Assembly."

"Mr. Spock," Uhura's voice sounded. "You'd better hear this."

•   •   •

Kirk watched as the Tholian web tightened around M-33, its blazing filaments now igniting a violent glow as they pressed in on the station's weakening deflector shields. The *Enterprise* had slowed some of the Outsider ships' work by focused phaser fire, but with the ships and their web now in direct contact with the station, Kirk had to be judicious about how much fire he could lay down on their adversaries. He swore he could see the structure of the station crunching inward under the press of the energy web, and he winced as lights on several levels of the station went dark as power levels drained under the assault. Suddenly the deflector grid on the station flared brilliantly and the bubble of protective energy disappeared.

"They've lost their shields," Chekov said.

"Scotty, route power back to transporters and beam the rest of those people out of there!" Kirk ordered.

"Aye, sir, if there's any power left to route," Scott groaned.

"Beam up the station's command crew, then Spock, Uhura, and that xenobiology team—immediately."

"Captain, incoming communication," Palmer interrupted. "It's from the commander of the Assembly attack force."

Kirk shook his head and blew out a sigh of exasperation. "Down here, Lieutenant," he said as he hit his chair intercom. "This is Captain James Kirk—"

"Starship Enterprise—*by order of the Tholian Assembly you are to depart this system immediately.*"

Kirk closed his eyes for a moment and took a deep breath before replying. "Tholian commander," he began, "your government has officially recognized our claim to this system and you have no authority here; we are involved in the evacuation of our space station and require more time to complete that operation . . . however, we would appreciate any assistance your fleet can render."

"*Your claim on this region is currently irrelevant,* Enterprise," the Tholian's dissonant voice replied. "*This situation will be resolved by us. We will not be responsible for the consequences if you do not withdraw.*"

"I can assure you the Tholian government *will* be held responsible for any further actions taken against Federation personnel," Kirk argued.

"Captain, the station command crew and Mr. Spock's party have been beamed aboard," Scott announced. "But our transporters will need at least five more minutes' recharge before we can beam another group aboard."

"Get Merrill, Spock, and Uhura up to the bridge immediately," Kirk said.

"Jim, what about the rest of the station crew? There's still almost a hundred people over there!" McCoy demanded.

"I haven't forgotten them, Doctor," Kirk snapped. "Maybe you'd like to walk over and evacuate them by hand?"

"Well, there must be something we can do!" the doctor argued.

"We can't stand between two attack groups at our current power output," Kirk said. "I'd be leery of doing that even at full power. We have to withdraw, at least until we can get our main systems back online."

Kirk eyed the formation of Outsider ships as they continued to tighten their web around the now-defenseless station. Most of the structure beacons and viewport illumination on the station had gone black now, and support pylons were searing and buckling under the strain of the collapsing web. Kirk could almost hear the station's alloys screeching under the strain.

The bridge elevator doors slid aside at that moment, and Spock, Uhura, Glasser, and Merrill stepped onto the bridge. "Kirk, what's the meaning of beaming me off my station before it's evacuated?" Merrill demanded.

Kirk motioned Spock to take his station. "I need you and your command crew here. Every attempt to get the rest of the station evacuated is being made."

"I told you what you were dealing with," Merrill said, gesturing toward the viewscreen where the Tholian's energy web was already contracting around M-33. "They'll crush the station before the Assembly ships get here. And now that you've broken the transfer agreement, we can't even count on help from them!"

"What about that hydrogen field?" Kirk said. "Merrill, you've been planning to tap that power. Can we find a way to channel the energy to the *Enterprise*?"

"On a ship like this?" Merrill said. "Sure, if you're using it to kick-start a dead engine."

"What?" Kirk said, but he saw Scott nodding in understanding.

"Aye," the engineer said. "To use raw plasma like that you'd have to bypass the intermix and flush the new plasma directly into the warp coils. We'd have to drain the engines completely before trying it on battery power. But at the rate we're losing power we'll be down to batteries sooner rather than later."

"It's not as bad as all that," Merrill said. "We still retain some control over the Veil satellites; we can use them to channel the plasma we need for our own use. In fact, we can do a lot better than that from a tactical standpoint."

"Meaning what?" Kirk asked.

"Meaning we can ignite the rest of the field once we're through. If we draw the Outsiders in the right way, we could take a hell of a lot of 'em down from the blast—if not half of the gas giant with them."

Kirk frowned, trying to divide his attention between Scott and Merrill and the cascade of data from the tactical screen. "Doesn't that obviate your plan for using the Veil as a power source in the future?"

"To hell with that," Merrill said. "The only way to keep the Veil out of the Outsiders' hands right now is to destroy it. It's what the Assembly wants in the long run."

"Explain," Kirk said.

"I believe I can, Captain," Spock said suddenly. The Vulcan had been intently studying readings from his science station viewer but now stepped away from the station with an unaccustomed sense of urgency. "It is imperative that we not interfere with the Ifukube Veil in any way. The Veil is the point of contention between the opposing Tholian forces."

"What are you talking about?" Merrill demanded.

"Commodore, your personnel's study of the Tholians you have encountered has been extensive but incomplete. You have failed to note the connection between the Ifukube Veil and the Tholians."

"What connection?" Kirk asked.

"Tholians are indeed silicon-based life-forms, as we have long suspected. But examinations of their physical structure have not revealed any definable internal organs. I suspect that these internal structures are not corporeal or even igneous in nature, but rather focused energy, organized and refracted through the internal facets of the Tholians' crystalline exoskeleton."

"Mr. Spock," Uhura said as she conferred with Lieutenant Palmer at the communications station. "I still have telemetry from the translator node we attached to Naskeel's ship. It sounds like the holding chamber on the station is depressurizing."

"Maintain communication with the vessel if possible, Lieutenant," Spock said before turning back to Kirk. "Captain, the Tholian internal structure—its life force, if you will—consists of highly organized high-energy plasma."

Kirk's eyes widened as he turned to look back at the screen and the red glint of the Ifukube Veil. "Plasma . . . like the plasma contained within that hydrogen cloud?"

"Affirmative, Captain," Spock said. "In our communication with the Outsider captive it indicated that this system was the site of a sectarian massacre of almost inconceivable proportions that occurred millennia ago. Billions of Tholians were killed in the orbit of that gas giant, enough to leave a cloud of ionized hydrogen several thousand kilometers in diameter."

Kirk stared at the hydrogen cloud on the bridge screen. Its abstract shape now took on a blood-chilling new aspect. "And they're only now returning to the site of the incident?" Kirk asked.

"Only after thousands of years of Tholian society's attempt to eradicate the memory of the event," Spock said. "Their own regimented social order has aided in that goal. Racial memory of the massacre is part of the genetic makeup of a segment of the Tholian population—the Outsiders. But the Tholians can repurpose such deviant individuals and in effect program out the drives that might ultimately bring them here."

"But the reverse is also true," Glasser cut in. "That must be why the Assembly was so eager to capture the pilot we snagged. As a Tholian

Mage it can reprogram Tholian individuals itself and keep the insurrection alive, repurpose individuals so that they can break away from the Assembly. And Tholians who step outside their defined functions disrupt not only their own roles but those of countless connected Tholians around them—a domino effect."

Kirk looked at Merrill. "Then they're not pirates. They're . . . pilgrims. That's the rift developing in Tholian society. The need to explore this ancient tragedy and the Assembly's desire to sweep it under the rug."

Even Merrill now looked humbled. "No wonder they wouldn't communicate with us. We were about to tear apart a mass grave . . . stir up the blood of a billion massacre victims."

"Not blood, Commodore," Spock said. "Something far more vital. I've cross-correlated my sensor readings of the interior of the Tholian vessel with the *Enterprise* and station sensor readings of the cloud. Without the key of an individual Tholian's energy signature to compare it with, it would all add up to meaningless complexity. But it is now clear the cloud contains billions of distinct, individual energy signatures that correspond to the internal plasma configuration that exists within Tholian exoskeletons."

"Souls." McCoy, who had been silent up to this point, suddenly seemed to surprise even himself by speaking. "You're talking about *souls,* Spock."

"In the case of the Tholians, a scientific reality," Spock said. "The magnetic and gravitational forces present here have created an environment in which these entities can still survive even after the destruction of their physical bodies."

Merrill stared at the viewscreen and the crimson haze of the Veil just past the space station. "And we were going to drain that cloud . . . kill them all a second time."

"Merrill, can we deactivate those satellites from here?" Kirk said urgently. "Get them away from the Veil somehow?"

"I can deactivate them for sure; maneuvering all of them away from the cloud would take time."

"Have your people deactivate them at least!" Kirk said. "The Outsiders must see the station as a threat to their dead." Merrill pulled out his communicator and began talking to his first officer. On the viewscreen the Tholian web had all but sealed off the station; Kirk saw lights winking out on the external structure of M-33 as the station began to collapse under the strain.

"Captain, Assembly forces on intercept course. They'll be here in seconds," Sulu reported.

Attack beams and plasma volleys began to erupt on both sides of the station now, and glancing blows hammered the hull of the *Enterprise*. In the space around the starship and the helpless space station, two forces of delta-shaped, glinting vessels converged, and Kirk had to shield his eyes for a moment from the glare of weapons fire and detonations flashing on the forward viewscreen. The civil war had begun.

"Several Tholian vessels of unknown design are flanking the Assembly attack group," Spock said, "on course for the Veil."

"They're webships too," Sulu said as he sighted five of the new ships. They looked like a cluster of Tholian spearhead-type webships fused together around a diamond-shaped core, and each vessel was larger than the *Enterprise*. As the starship drifted, the five vessels and their escort ships brushed past the *Enterprise* and the M-33 station almost as if the two Federation constructs were beneath notice. Between them a blazing web of energy filaments stretched out to form a web that grew in size by the second as the vessels fanned out. The web stretched until it was a hundred kilometers wide, then five hundred, finally a thousand and more.

"They're going to snare the Veil," Merrill said, shaking his head. "They probably want to drag the thing out of here once and for all."

"Or destroy it," Spock said. "The Assembly is likely to repeat the same mistake it made millennia ago."

"Uhura, hail the Assembly attack force commander again."

"Yes, sir."

Kirk stood behind Sulu and Chekov and watched as Outsider ships broke away from their concentration on M-33 to go after the giant Assembly webships. Shields flared on the massive vessels as the smaller Outsider ships fired on them, but their trajectory toward the Veil was unaffected.

"The satellites are all shut down, Kirk," Merrill said, closing his communicator.

"The Assembly ships are closing on the Veil," Chekov announced. "Contact in six seconds."

On the screen the yawning web, stretched so thin it was now almost invisible, maneuvered to ensnare the crimson swath of ionized gas. Kirk frowned as something changed; he blinked, not quite certain he was seeing right.

"Extreme activity inside the cloud," Spock said, looking up from his viewer.

"It's moving!" Sulu exclaimed. Kirk had seen the shift, too, as tendrils seemed to snake out from some of the edges of the cloud while its center compacted. The red glow of the Veil seemed to intensify into some color Kirk couldn't describe. An arc of energy flickered out from one wispy tendril and licked the hull of one of the Tholian Assembly ships, and for a moment the energy filaments snaking out from the ship's body flickered and faded before flaring back to life.

The Veil was defending itself. Kirk held his breath for a moment, stunned by the enormity of what he was seeing. Were those ten billion souls inside the Veil awakening now, lashing out in anger at their murderers' descendants?

"Sir, the Assembly ships are slowing," Sulu said, turning back to look at Kirk. "I don't think they expected that either."

"What's happening, Spock?" Kirk asked.

"Unknown, Captain," the Vulcan replied. "But clearly some kind of mass consciousness is retained by the surviving energy signatures within the cloud."

"One of the Assembly vessels is answering our hail, Captain," Uhura announced. "And I'm picking up another broadcast—from the Outsider pilot the station captured. It's escaped the station and appears to be communicating with the Outsider forces."

"Can you translate what it's saying?"

"No, sir," Uhura said, nodding toward the viewscreen. "But I'm guessing it's a request for their forces to stand down, too."

"Patch me through to the Assembly ship," Kirk said. If there was a time to talk, it was now. "This is Captain Kirk of the *Enterprise*," he began. "We request negotiation and the cessation of hostilities, between all vessels in this star system."

The triple-toned voice of the Tholian Assembly commander came after a moment's pause. *"The Assembly's agreement was not with you,* Enterprise."

Merrill added his voice. "That's right. It was with me. I'm commander of the Federation station here."

"You were informed of the consequences of refusing transport of your prisoner to us. Now your interference has exacted its cost."

"Your agreement with Commodore Merrill was to keep your people away from this system?" Kirk asked. "Why? Why not claim this space for yourselves?"

"We reject this area," the Tholian voice said. *"We reject the Outsiders who keep its memory within themselves. We were content that your people eradicate it for your own uses."*

Kirk glanced at Merrill for a second. "We will not take part in the eradication of your history . . . or in the suppression of a part of your population."

"Your principles are unimportant, Enterprise. *Our survival is paramount. All in our society have their place and their function. The memory of this place endangers that. Those who remember forget their function and soon they join with the Outsiders. Their numbers grow, and they serve no purpose but disruption."*

"Then what will you do here? What will your ships do with the cloud?"

The pause this time was long. *"It was thought that we would remove the dead from this system and dispose of it in our own way. We have avoided this necessity for thousands of life spans, but you have made the choice for us."*

"Yet you've hesitated," Kirk said. "Why? Because you see that something still survives inside that cloud?"

"We know the dead exist there. The dead have no meaning to us, only to the Outsiders."

"Yet this cloud moves . . . it shows life. Understanding," Kirk argued.

This time it was Spock who raised his voice. "What you describe as 'dead' is in fact billions of Tholian consciousnesses . . . perhaps even a mass consciousness that mirrors your own society. Would that not be worthy of preservation . . . even study?"

"*There is no such function in our society,* Enterprise."

A sudden thought struck Kirk. "But there could be," he said. "What about the Outsiders?"

"*The Outsiders disrupt society—*"

"But what if they could be made to *serve* society?" Kirk demanded. "The Tholian pilot you pursued here is one who alters the functions of your people from caste to caste so that they may serve the Assembly better, correct? Couldn't individuals like him do the same with the Outsiders? Modify them to do what they seek to do—study, perhaps even merge with this . . . well of souls, and bring its knowledge, the knowledge of your own past, perhaps many things you do not yet understand, to be shared by the Assembly for its greater good?"

"*Our society is defined. There is no role for Outsiders. They disrupt—*"

"But they disrupt because they *have* no role!" Kirk argued. "And as long as the Outsiders have no role, as long as racial memory stretches back to this tragedy, the ranks of the Outsiders will grow and Tholian society will continue to fracture."

"Even a logically ordered society must grow and evolve," Spock said simply. "Tholians are among the most complex and unique life-forms in the galaxy. They should be capable of adapting to the inevitability of change as well as or better than other species."

Kirk looked at Spock and raised his eyebrows appreciatively. A little flattery couldn't hurt, and the Tholians seemed to have a formidable streak of arrogance in them.

"*The Mage Naskeel is an Outsider, a fugitive. Why should Naskeel agree to serve the Assembly?*" the Tholian commander asked after another long pause.

"I still have a transponder lock on Naskeel's ship, Captain," Uhura announced.

"We have established communication with Naskeel, Commander," Kirk said. "We would be happy to assist you as a mediator to help you reach an agreement with the Outsiders if you desire it." Kirk glanced at the crumpled remains of M-33 still visible on the main screen. He looked back to where Merrill stood at the back of the bridge, diminished and disassociated from what was happening. The next steps would be even more painful.

"Under the circumstances, Commander," Kirk began, "we would be willing to discuss relinquishing our claim on this area of space. Clearly the history of this region is Tholian, and perhaps it's a history better explored and understood than buried."

Silence.

"Quite generous, Enterprise," the Tholian voice came after a long moment. *"We will take your proposal under advisement and begin discussion with Mage Naskeel."*

Kirk stepped up to the rear level of the bridge where Merrill stood next to a watchful McCoy. "Commodore, I can't think of anyone more suited to negotiate between these two sides than you."

Merrill stared at Kirk numbly. "You mean someone suited to sell out the Federation? Is that what you mean?"

"You wanted an alliance with the Tholians. Rather than precipitating a civil war by helping the Assembly crush dissent, why not forge one by knitting their society back together?"

"There's something I still don't understand," McCoy said. "How do these Tholian 'Outsiders' relate to this cloud? What are they getting out of contact with it?"

"Perhaps a communion of sorts with their ancestors," Spock said. "Perhaps something more. It is clear that Tholians have a rigid internal life clock that allows them a relatively brief and explicitly defined life span."

"You mean they know the time of their own deaths," McCoy said.

"Precisely, Doctor. Clearly the Veil offers Tholians direct evidence that their lives, their 'souls' if you will, can potentially survive beyond their deaths. By entering into the cloud before their prescribed death time they may be able to merge with the ionized mass around them and achieve a kind of afterlife."

"We do the same thing, Commodore." Kirk smiled, putting his hand briefly on Merrill's shoulder. "But human beings really only do it by switching careers. You've reinvented yourself more times than I can count."

"Damned if I haven't," Merrill said wryly. "I was wrong, son." He stared ahead at the viewscreen, the remains of his station, and the stationary mass of Tholian ships. "I guess the sentimental approach has its advantages."

"I'll assign one of our shuttles to take you back to the station; we'll need to share resources if we're going to get M-33 and the *Enterprise* up and running again." Kirk extended his hand as Merrill and Glasser stepped toward the opening bridge elevator doors. "And I've got a bottle of Altairian rice wine for you somewhere around here."

"I could use one," Merrill said. "We'll be in contact soon."

Kirk nodded, smiling reassuringly as the doors closed behind the Commodore. The knot in his gut was finally beginning to unwind. "Lieutenant Uhura, continue to facilitate communications between the Mage ship and the Assembly Commander."

"Aye, sir," Uhura replied.

"All this talk about souls and the afterlife," McCoy said, staring accusingly at Spock. "I thought Vulcans only believed in science."

"The concept of a Tholian soul is a scientific one, Dr. McCoy," Spock replied.

"Well, what about the human soul?" McCoy said. "Or the Vulcan, for that matter?"

"Such beliefs are not unprecedented, Doctor. Even among Vulcans."

"Well, I wonder what human beings would have done if we'd had certain knowledge of something like that, of an afterlife." The physician looked back at the armada of Tholian ships on the bridge screen. "I hardly think it could have divided us any more than we were already."

"I harbor no doubts that human society could have found a way to do so regardless, Doctor."

McCoy glared at the Vulcan faintly. "Maybe all we needed was a common enemy," he said. "Unfortunately, the Vulcans arrived a few thousand years too late."

"In that, we are in complete agreement, Doctor," Spock said.

"Stand down, gentlemen," Kirk said as he settled back into his command chair. "One civil war at a time."

Chaotic Response

Stuart Moore

STUART MOORE

Stuart Moore has been a writer, a book editor, and an award-winning comics editor. His recent and upcoming comics work includes *Firestorm, Nightwing,* and *JSA Classified* (all for DC Comics), *Wolverine* (Marvel), and *Stargate Atlantis* (Avatar Press). For Games Workshop's revived Dark Future series, Stuart has written the original prose novel *American Meat* and its upcoming sequel, *Reality Bites.* Other recent comics include *Lone, The Escapist, Justice League Adventures, Para,* and *Western Tales of Terror.* Of his graphic novel *Giant Robot Warriors* (AiT/PlanetLar), Steven Grant of Comic Book Resources said, "Stuart Moore's turning into one of the best comics writers in America. Buy this."

At DC Comics, Stuart was a founding editor of the acclaimed Vertigo imprint, where he won the Will Eisner award for Best Editor 1996 and the Don Thompson Award for Favorite Editor 1999. From late 2000 through mid-2002 Stuart edited the bestselling Marvel Knights comics line, before turning to writing full-time. Upcoming works include a comics adaptation of the bestselling novel *Redwall* (Philomel/Penguin), the original graphic novel *Earthlight* (Tokyopop), and more *Firestorm.*

Stuart lives in Brooklyn, New York, with his wife—and two cats who really don't know the first thing about logic.

"Mr. Salak. Mr. Spock."

"Sir."

"Sir."

"Take your places and begin."

Spock rises from his chair, steps up to the raised podium. The room is bright, harshly lit, unlike the antiseptic classrooms he has experienced before. Multicolored lights flash and strobe at irregular intervals along the walls: green, yellow, violet. Subsonic pulses hum through the room, raising the pressure in his sensitive inner ear.

This place, he realizes, is designed specifically to test one's logic.

Spock positions himself on the podium, facing his adversary. The Teacher stands between them, on a higher level. Despite himself, Spock shifts nervously. The other students notice; a ripple of murmured disapproval runs through them.

"Quiet!" the Teacher says.

As though a switch has been thrown, the students go abruptly silent. The Teacher turns to Spock's opponent. "Mr. Salak?"

"Sir."

"Begin!"

Salak cocks his head, smirks slightly at Spock. "Logical thought is lacking in lower life-forms. All humans are lower life-forms. Therefore, logical thought is lacking in humans."

Again, the murmuring laughter. Spock feels the words like a knife in his gut. Salak has chosen an opening gambit that strikes directly to the heart of his opponent's being.

A green light flashes on the far wall, then a sharp yellow one—directly in Spock's eyes. The subsonic hum rises, becoming almost audible.

"Spock?" the Teacher asks harshly.

Spock clears his throat. "Fallacy."

"Explain."

"Fallacy of presumption."

"Specify. Quickly!"

"Fallacy of accident. The first statement is true in general, but not as a universal. Logical thought is lacking in many lower life-forms, but not all. Therefore the conclusion is invalid."

"Correct," the Teacher says.

A bright light pulses from red down to yellow. Salak flinches slightly. The boys murmur, eyebrows raised.

Spock tries not to take satisfaction in his opponent's discomfort.

"Mr. Spock. Begin!"

Spock opens his mouth . . .

. . . and his mind goes blank.

He glances up, sees Salak half concealing a smirk. Then he turns to the class—and sweeps his gaze along a dozen more pairs of eyes, all fixed intently on him.

They have combined forces against me, he realizes. *They're acting in concert telepathically to disrupt my thought processes. They want the half-human to fail at this crucial class exercise.*

The old anger and frustration rise within him. The feelings . . . the unwanted, alien sensations he has tried all his life to deny. If he fails this exercise, he will not be passed forward!

Spock closes his eyes, tries to banish the thoughts. *I am a Vulcan,* he thinks. *A Vulcan—*

Then the Teacher is at his elbow. "Mr. Spock." His tones are even, cold, yet somehow soothing. "These are deliberately adverse conditions for logic. Focus; recall your techniques of Chaotic Response Suppression."

Spock jumps; for some reason, the phrase—Chaotic Response Suppression—provokes an emotional response. Why? Is he thinking of something else . . . somewhere else entirely?

No. There is no time for this. Spock quickly calms himself, eyes still closed. The Teacher, he realizes, knows what the other boys have done, and is allowing him the opportunity to compensate. Any other student would have been eliminated for such hesitation.

"Half the secret of logical thought," the Teacher continues, "lies in cultivating a garden where it may bloom."

Spock concentrates, forcing himself to begin Phase One of Chaotic Response Suppression. In a millisecond, he calms his mind. Then he proceeds to Phase Two, sorting the stimuli assaulting him into categories and dismissing them one by one. The lights: He banishes them from his consciousness. The sounds: They are nothing to him. The pressure on his mind: mere noise. Deliberately, meticulously, he pushes each of these distractions to the corners of his mind.

Then he opens his mouth and begins to speak.

"Mr. Salak believes that only purebred Vulcans should be admitted to the Science Academy," Spock says evenly. "But we all know that Mr. Salak desires a spot in the Academy for himself—a purebred Vulcan. Therefore, admittance to the Academy should be open to all."

The Teacher frowns; briefly, Spock wonders if he has gone too far. But then the Teacher turns to Salak. "I will allow the proposition. Mr. Salak?"

Salak's eyes light up. "Fallacy of relevance."

"Specify."

"Ad hominem reasoning. The conclusion rests on the fact that a single person believes the opposite proposition. But the opinion of an individual is irrelevant to truth."

"Correct."

I made that one too easy, Spock realizes. *That is the trouble with this exercise: Every statement must contain a flaw, or else it is invalid as a test of the other student. But if the flaw is too obvious, the test is too simple. I have hurt my own cause.*

"I must caution both students," the Teacher says gravely. "Personal attacks have no place in these proceedings. Employ your Chaotic Response Suppression techniques rigorously; banish such petty motives from your mind. Logic is all that matters here. It is your birthright, your salvation, your heritage. As Vulcans . . . it is your duty."

Spock and Salak nod as one.

Spock looks down, attempts to focus his thoughts. But somehow, the lights seem to shine even brighter than before.

"Mr. Salak. Begin."

Salak fixes Spock with a hostile, laserlike stare. "Humans are illogical beings. Mr. Spock is part human. Therefore, Mr. Spock is an illogical being."

Spock's hand quivers, just slightly.

The Teacher glares at Salak. "Final warning, Mr. Salak."

Salak nods, looks down with feigned contrition.

"Mr. Spock?"

Spock stares his opponent straight in the eye. "Fallacy of ambiguity—division. The conclusion rests on an improper inference. The premise may be true of the human species as a whole, but that says nothing of its truth when applied to any individual member."

"Correct."

Spock realizes he is shaking. Salak knew just how to attack him, even at the risk of another rebuke from the Teacher.

Suddenly Spock knows: *I'm going to lose.*

"Mr. Spock. Final proposition."

Spock begins to speak. But again, his senses begin to overload. The lights, blinding now. The aching thrum in his ears. The sounds of the other boys' thoughts, more hostile than ever.

He forces himself to concentrate. Phase One, he thinks: Calm the mental . . . the mental . . .

It is no use. His techniques fail him; he cannot suppress the chaos. His mind is a disordered, unclean thing.

But he must say something.

"All . . . all Vulcans realize that the so-called 'purity' of the Science Academy is nothing but rank bigotry dressed up in the guise of academic standards . . ."

He pauses, eyes darting about nervously. Salak looks like a feral *sehlat;* the boys, like carrion birds awaiting their meal. The Teacher glares at Spock with open hostility.

". . . therefore . . . the Academy must change," he finishes.

The Teacher shakes his head, turns to Spock's opponent. "Mr. Salak?"

"Fallacy of relevance." His eyes widen hungrily as he stares Spock down. "Appeal . . . to *emotion.*"

The word strikes like a blow to Spock's head.

Emotion. The bane of his existence; the unwanted heritage of his human mother. And now, he thinks, I've dragged it into this test of pure, impartial logic.

With a sick, creeping dread, he glances at the Teacher. As he feared, the Teacher is nodding approvingly at Salak's rebuttal.

". . . the overblown language of the premise disguises the fact that it has no relevance to the conclusion . . ."

Spock tunes Salak out. He has lost; he knows this now. Worse, he has proven the other boys correct. He cannot compete with them. He is *less* than them.

The thrumming sound fills his mind; the lights leave painful after-images in his vision. He can no longer block any of it out. Chaotic Response Suppression has failed him. He will not pass this course; he will not attend the Vulcan Science Academy. Ever.

A thought passes through his mind like a communiqué from another world, a foreign star. *But I don't* want *to go to the—*

Then, in the midst of the brightest, whitest spot of light, a figure in blue and black begins to form. A slim, craggy man with an analyzer device strapped over his shoulder. As he approaches, the rest of the room—Salak, the Teacher, the students, even the blinding lights—seem to recede to the corners of Spock's awareness. As in a Chaotic Response technique, he thinks idly.

The man reaches out a quivering, human hand.

"Mr. Spock," McCoy says. "You annoying Vulcan. Take my hand already, will you?"

The phaser blast struck the *Enterprise,* and Kirk pitched forward out of his command chair. He lurched past Sulu, then caught himself on a handrail. He shook his head to clear it, then looked around hurriedly.

"Everybody all right?"

General noises of assent. The red-alert siren continued, a grim back-drop to the chaos all around. Kirk crossed back to his chair, glancing briefly at Sulu's helm console.

"I still have full helm control," Sulu confirmed.

"Damage reports coming in now," Uhura said. "Minor hull breaches, decks seventeen through nineteen."

"Aft shields down to . . . 32 percent." The navigator, a young woman named Sanchez, sounded nervous.

"Hangar deck temporarily depressurized," Uhura continued. "No casualties—"

"Just a second, Uhura." Kirk stabbed a button on his command chair. "Scotty, how're we doing down there?"

A brief pause, then the Scotsman's filtered voice filled the bridge. *"We took a pounding, Captain. I'm gonna need an hour or so to get warp drive back online."*

"Life support? Essential systems?"

Scotty sighed audibly. *"We should be okay as long as those Klingons keep their distance."*

"I don't think there's much chance of that, Mr. Scott." Kirk looked up at the viewscreen, which showed the two D7-class Klingon battle cruisers. They were still moving away . . . but they were starting to circle around.

"Mr. Spo—" Kirk turned to his right, then stopped. "Mr. Chekov. Can you analyze the Klingon ships' energy output?"

Chekov looked up from the science station, his face lit bright blue. "Sir?"

"Their coil emissions. I need to know if we did them any real damage."

"Ah." The young Russian turned back to his work. "One moment, Captain."

Ensign Chekov had only been a bridge officer for three weeks. For a brief moment, Kirk wondered if he'd promoted the young man too quickly.

"Captain," Scotty's voice said. *"I'm getting a nasty cascade reaction in the dilithium chamber. I'm gonna need to stop and reconfigure pretty soon."*

"You'll have to wait a bit, Scotty." Kirk rose, stepped forward, put a hand on Sulu's shoulder. He pointed up at the viewscreen. "They're coming around?"

"Aye, sir." Sulu consulted the astrogator. "Converging in a vee formation."

"How long till they're back in phaser range?"

Sulu frowned. "Ninety seconds or so."

Kirk strode back to his chair, pressed the comm button. "Kirk to sickbay."

"M'Benga here."

"Doctor, I could really use my science officer up here. Any progress?"

"None, sir. They're both still inside."

Kirk hesitated. "Keep me posted." He glanced up at the screen, which showed the two cruisers headed back toward the *Enterprise.* "Mr. Chekov?"

"Ah, sir . . . the lead ship shows coil emissions vithin normal tolerances. The other one . . ." He hesitated.

"Yes?"

Chekov looked up, shrugged helplessly. "It's . . . fluctuating."

"Captain," Uhura said. "Hangar deck just lost pressure again. Repair crews dispatched."

"Aft shields failing," Sanchez said. "Down to 22 percent."

Kirk waved them both off. He surveyed the bridge: Sanchez looked frightened, grimacing as she plotted possible sublight vectors. Sulu was frowning, making small course corrections calmly, deliberately. Uhura's hands were a blur as she coordinated damage control reports from a dozen departments. Finally, Kirk's gaze rested on Chekov, who seemed to be struggling with the science station controls.

Kirk thought: *I need Spock.*

"Back us off, Mr. Sulu," Kirk said. "See if you can buy us a minute or two."

"Aye, sir."

"And ready phasers." Then Kirk rose, moved to stand next to Chekov. "Mr. Chekov. That damaged ship—the trailing one. Give me precise coil emissions and shield strengths on its two nacelles."

Chekov looked up. "Sir?"

"Now."

"Aye, sir." He grimaced. "T-together or separately?"

"Aft shields down to 16 percent." Sanchez's voice was grim.

"Separately!" Kirk felt the pressure building. "Sulu—the ships are coming around in formation, right?"

"Yes, sir." Sulu looked down briefly. "Phaser range in forty seconds."

"Captain," said Scotty, *"I can't divert any more power to the aft shields—"*

"Understood, engineer." Kirk whirled toward Chekov. "Science officer—your report!"

Trembling, Chekov read off a series of numbers.

Kirk listened, then strode down toward helm control. "Mr. Sulu. Move us in toward the damaged ship. Heading: 185 mark 28."

Sulu glanced at the captain. "Mark 28. Aye, sir."

Ahead of them, the two ships nearly filled the viewscreen. Their front sections glowed bright against the stars.

Chekov said, "They are charging phasers—"

"I know." Kirk pointed at a display, spoke urgently to Sulu. "Lock our phasers on that nacelle there."

"Phasers locked."

"Enemy ship is firing!" Sanchez exclaimed.

The ship shook. Kirk staggered backward but kept his balance.

"Forward shields holding."

"So we just have to keep them from getting behind us . . . till we can pull this off." Kirk lowered his voice, practically hissing in Sulu's ear. "Do you have a lock?"

"Yes, sir."

"Steer us in a little closer." On the screen, the image tilted, and the one ship drew closer. "Just one minute more . . ."

"Captain—"

"Not *now,* Sanchez."

Kirk stood, watching the numbers fly by on Sulu's console. All around him, voices chattered: damage control, shield strength, phaser power, casualty reports. Spock would have sorted it all out, cut through all this mess—all these voices—and told him exactly what he needed to know.

But Spock wasn't here. Might never be here again.

And McCoy . . .

"Enemy ship firing again!" Sanchez said. Her voice was frantic.

"Captain?" Sulu prompted.

With a sick feeling, Kirk realized he'd waited too long.

The bridge shook. Kirk pitched forward, catching himself on the astrogator console next to Sulu. "Fire!" he yelled.

Sulu pressed the firing button.

Energy stabbed out from the *Enterprise,* sparking and flashing as it struck the enemy ship's left nacelle. On the viewscreen, the Klingon vessel lurched, tilted sideways.

"Captain," Chekov said, "the other ship is—"

"Maintain fire. Hold that lock!"

Kirk reached out a hand, thumbed the viewscreen magnification back a notch. Both ships were visible now. The *Enterprise* phasers continued their assault on the damaged cruiser, which was beginning to veer off course. The other ship glowed with energy; clearly it was about to fire again.

"Casualty reports coming in," Uhura said.

"We're almost through their shield," Sulu said. "But our phaser power is fading."

"Hold on," Kirk replied. "Ready photon torpedoes."

The blue energy-stream sliced into the Klingon ship's warp nacelle. Then, abruptly, the nacelle broke apart. The cruiser pitched, sparked, fires dissipating off into space from its exposed warp engine. It lurched, pitched sideways . . .

. . . and grazed the other Klingon ship's shields. Sparks flew into space, and the second ship's phasers fired wild, into the void.

"Photon torpedoes, fire," Kirk ordered.

Bright pulses of destruction shot out of the *Enterprise,* bombarding the twin ships. As Kirk watched, they struck the healthy Klingon cruiser, detonating harmlessly against its shields. The other one wasn't so lucky; explosions and fires dotted its surface.

"Five . . . six direct hits," Sanchez said.

"Damaged cruiser's shields are at near zero strength," Chekov said. "She is heading off."

Kirk whirled, sat down in his chair. "Uhura, open a channel to the remaining Klingon vessel."

"Channel open."

On the viewscreen, a dark, furrowed face in black and silver appeared, surrounded by the smoky, regimented bustle of a Klingon imperial bridge.

"This is Captain Kirk to the Klingon ship," Kirk said. "It's one on one now, Commander. Do you want to make the first move, or can we resolve this peacefully?"

The face stood, glaring, for a long moment. The Klingon said nothing.

Then the screen flickered, returned to forward view. The Klingon cruiser turned, began a slow arc away.

"They're moving off." Sulu smiled. "Taking refuge with the other ship, behind that large moon."

"The Klingons like to fight in close quarters. We were able to turn that against them—this time. But they'll be back." Kirk could sense the admiring gazes of his bridge crew, but he felt no sense of triumph. He shook his head.

"Uhura. Damage report?"

"Seven casualties on lower decks, sir. None fatal."

Kirk grimaced, pressed the comm button. "Engineer. Time to warp drive?"

"Should still be about an hour, sir. Repairs already under way."

Kirk rose, and once more his disapproving gaze swept across the bridge. "That was sloppy all around," he said. "The Klingons will probably be back before we can depart this area. Let's do better next time." He looked pointedly at Chekov, then strode to the lift.

"Sulu, you have the conn. Run continuous drills. If anything happens, call me immediately."

The lift doors hissed shut, and he was alone.

Kirk exhaled heavily. The turbolift hummed, waiting for his command.

"Sickbay," he said.

• • •

When Kirk was gone, the bridge crew seemed to exhale all at once. Sanchez looked over at Sulu expectantly. The helmsman shook his head, sighed.

Uhura raised an eyebrow. "Rough day."

Chekov stared into the science station viewer, his head in his hands. "I think my career is over."

Sulu stood up and crossed to the young ensign, put a hand on his shoulder. "My first week aboard, I accidentally pressed an active plasma torch against the matter/antimatter reaction chamber. Nearly blew up the ship." He smiled. "The chief engineer taught me a few . . . exotic Scottish expressions. But I got over it."

Chekov looked up, smiled back sadly.

Then Sulu straightened, looked around. "Okay, you all heard the captain," he said. "Battle stations."

"This is very odd," Spock says. "And yet . . . strangely logical."

He gazes around at his surroundings. A neatly trimmed mass of green vegetation rises to a height of twelve feet in all directions, with an opening dead ahead. Through the hole, Spock can make out another wall . . . and, past that, yet another.

They have been walking through this huge, sunny garden for an indefinite period of time, and Spock has determined that it forms a maze. The bushes, all meticulously squared off, seem to be leading them to some unpredictable destination.

A phrase comes to his mind, half remembered: . . . *lies in cultivating a garden where it may bloom.*

"Of course it's logical," McCoy replies. "We're inside your brain."

Spock looks at him sharply. He knows this man, but he cannot remember exactly how. When he looks at McCoy, he feels a strong sense of friendship . . . but also a guardedness. A vague memory of attacks, of challenges to his intellect.

"I should . . . return to the classroom," Spock says, fighting down a sudden stab of panic. "If I lose the challenge, I will not be passed forward into the Science Academy."

"Spock. Listen to me." McCoy grabs the Vulcan's shoulders, turns to face him directly. "You're not on Vulcan. You're on the *Enterprise*. You are first officer and science officer there—you have been for years. Do you remember?"

Spock shakes free, turns away. A mockingbird screeches, breaking his concentration.

"The Klingons captured you—subjected you to their mind-ripper," McCoy continues. "They tortured you mentally, and you retreated into your mind using Vulcan mental disciplines. You retreated *here*."

Again, the panic. A burst of images: fiery combat in space. Cruel, bearded men in metal mesh vests. A machine with arms like snakes, cold and metallic and unstoppable, violating his mind.

Then pain. And the questions:

Fleet strength. Federation expansion plans. Starship deployment.

No, Spock recalls thinking. *I will not answer.*

More pain. And the snake-machine, hissing and probing his innermost thoughts. Pain. Chaos. Pain. No escape, no solution. The only option: draw on his training.

On Chaotic Response Suppression.

". . . got you out," McCoy is saying. "And we grabbed the mind-ripper, too. I'm using it right now, Spock. You've got to listen to me."

Spock shakes his head, looks around. This McCoy . . . he knows he should trust him. But what if it's another attack . . . another manifestation of the snake?

"You're in too deep, Spock. Only you can get yourself out of this." And McCoy reaches for him . . .

The mockingbird screeches; the sky darkens. Thunder roars from the sky.

Spock looks up, knowing what he will see. The hedges have turned brown, gnarled—dying. As he watches, they stir, come to a sick semblance of life. They reach out toward him, like thorned claws.

"Spock!"

Then the maze is upon them, pricking their skin and coiling around their throats. McCoy grabs at the branches, his eyes wide. As Spock watches, they cut into the doctor's hands. McCoy winces, crying out in pain.

Spock stands stiff, still, trying to evoke Chaotic Response techniques.

"This is illogical," he says quietly to himself. "I will push it aside; I will not be distracted. Phase One—"

McCoy struggles to speak. "Of course it's . . . illogical, Spock." He pulls free of a branch. "Humans are illogical beings, right? But need I remind you—you are half human."

And Spock hears Salak's voice, taunting, echoing: *Mr. Spock is part human. Therefore . . . Mr. Spock is an illogical being.*

The branches pull them into the hedge, gathering and squeezing them tight, smothering them against the brown, dying mass of vegetation. Steel-like vines tighten around McCoy's throat, stronger than ever, and he makes a strangled sound. But Spock barely hears. His suppression techniques have failed; his mind is closed off. He cannot help himself. He cannot help his friends. Beyond any doubt, beyond any logical calculation, he knows: He will die here.

Then, just ahead of him, a section of the hedge begins to glow. It burns red-hot, sprouts tiny flames, and incinerates from the center outward. And in its wake—

"Spock! Bones!" Kirk yells. His phaser is still raised, ready to fire again.

"Jim." The word comes oddly to Spock's lips. It sounds strange, like a language he has not spoken for a long, long time.

Kirk wades through the snaking, coiling vegetation, firing off short bursts at the errant branches. Then he holsters his phaser and reaches out one hand each to Spock and McCoy, pulling the vines from their throats. McCoy gasps, staggers a bit.

Then Kirk fixes Spock with a steely gaze. "Mr. Spock. You have to break free of this. We need you." He pauses. "You must return to duty."

Spock recalls the Teacher's voice: *Logic is your duty.*

Kirk's eyes are like lasers . . . like alien snake-machines, crawling and snaking into his brain. Like manifestations of chaos itself.

"Chaotic . . . Response . . ."

Spock closes his eyes, willing the snakes, the vines, the bloody thorns away. He pushes them aside. The pain, he tells himself, is a foreign object, a snapshot in another man's album. An *other*.

His shipmates fade away; the garden fades away. All is pure, white light. And he is alone, with his failure and his fear and his pain and his logic.

Alone.

"Is he comin' around, Doc?"

"Yes, Mr. Scott. They both are."

Kirk's eyes snapped open. He took in, first, the bright lights of sickbay, then the concerned faces of Scotty and Dr. M'Benga, peering at him. M'Benga leaned down, placed a hand on his shoulder.

"Easy, Captain. Take it slow."

Kirk leaned back, turned his head to the left. There, on the next bed, lay Spock . . . completely unconscious. No signs of life beyond the steady thrumming of the diagnostic instruments above his head. And past Spock: the device. Black and silver, a mass of coiled, glowing metal and thick, barely insulated wiring.

The mind-ripper.

"Your vitals were fluctuating dangerously." M'Benga reached down and gently disconnected the leads from Kirk's forehead. "I took a chance . . . waited till you hit normal levels, briefly, then pulled you out. I had no choice."

Scotty turned to the ripper, shook his head. "Blasted Klingon engineering. It's a miracle that thing didn't rip your head apart, sir."

Kirk sat up slowly. "Feels like it did."

To his right, McCoy groaned, sat up. He ripped the leads off his own head.

"Bones," Kirk said softly.

"We blew it, Jim," McCoy said. "And you took a damn-fool chance going in there after me."

"I wasn't about to lose *two* of my senior officers." He pointed to Spock's prone body. "Any change?"

M'Benga consulted the diagnostic bed readings. "None," he said. "His brain activity spiked, a minute or two before we brought you out. Now it's dropped back down again."

Nurse Chapel hurried in. "Doctor." She stopped, glanced at McCoy. "Doctors. The casualties from the attack are stable. They're all resting quietly."

"Thank you, Nurse." McCoy grimaced, lurched to his feet. He staggered over to Spock's bed, studied the indicators. "Those are the same readings we got when we first rescued him."

"Yes," M'Benga agreed. He was an expert in Vulcan physiology, Kirk recalled. "Under normal circumstances, I'd say he was engaged in some kind of internal healing procedure. But the damage to Mr. Spock's brain is severe—I'm worried about the lack of progress."

Nurse Chapel cast a quick, worried glance over at Spock's unmoving body. "I'd better tend to the . . . wounded . . ." And she left hurriedly.

"Scotty," Kirk said. "What are you doing here?"

"I came to report, sir," the engineer replied. "Repairs are well under way—my lads are on the case. We'll be ready to leave the area in approximately thirty minutes."

"But."

"But. Mr. Chekov has picked up strong long-range energy signals from the Klingon ships. He suspects they may be back before then."

Kirk frowned.

"Sir," Scotty continued. "We need you on the bridge."

Kirk looked down at Spock. The Vulcan's body was completely still: no blinking, no muscle twitches, no facial movements. He barely breathed.

"I need *him* on the bridge," Kirk replied. "And you'll forgive me if I don't take Mr. Chekov's judgments as gospel."

Scotty hesitated. "He's a sharp lad, Chekov."

"But inexperienced."

A sharp pulse came from Spock's diagnostic bed. Kirk turned in alarm.

Shakily, McCoy crossed back to Kirk's bed. "Jim, Spock's readings are starting to deteriorate. I'm goin' back in there."

"No." Kirk reached for the mind-ripper's connecting leads. "I'll go."

McCoy glared at him. "That's not appropriate."

"It's necessary."

"You are the captain of a starship in an ongoing combat situation. It's not merely foolish for you to risk your life like this—it's irresponsible to those around you."

Scott stepped forward. "I must agree, Captain. The Klingons outnumber us, and there's no other Federation ships in the sector. We barely escaped with our lives before."

"And those Klingons are still pretty mad about us stealing their little toy here," McCoy continued. "What was it you said to Spock? 'You have duties.'"

Kirk put a hand on McCoy's shoulder. He turned to the others. "Gentlemen . . . give us a moment?"

Frowning, Scotty and M'Benga moved to the far corner of the room.

"I've got to save him, Bones."

McCoy grimaced. "Jim, he's my friend, too. I—"

"No—you don't understand." Kirk looked down. "Scotty's right— we barely beat the Klingons before. They have us outnumbered and outgunned. I managed to slap them down once, but they'll be back. And you've got wounded down here who shouldn't *be* wounded."

McCoy cocked his head. "You said yourself they outnumber us."

"That's not the point. If Spock had been up there, we'd have gotten out of that battle clean."

"You don't know that. And we've had scrapes that turned out much worse."

"I'm not kicking myself, Bones. I did my job. But next time . . . the Klingons are going to be better prepared."

McCoy frowned.

"Scotty's right—Chekov's a good junior officer. But he's not Spock." Kirk frowned, remembering. "During combat, there are a dozen voices chattering away all the time, on the bridge. The communications officer relays damage reports. Scotty provides updates on engine status. The helmsman monitors phasers and ship movements. The navigator handles shield strength. They're all background noise to me—because one man always feeds me the exact information I need at the exact moment I need it."

"Spock," McCoy said tonelessly.

"Normally, I can compensate for his absence. But the Klingons have us at a severe disadvantage. I'm a good captain, but I don't have Spock's ability to filter through a thousand bits of information, screen out superfluous data, and zero in on the most crucial point—all in a millisecond."

McCoy smiled wryly. "I suppose part of being 'a good captain' is knowing one's own limitations."

"Exactly. That's why it's not irresponsible for me to try and rescue Spock. It's actually the only responsible thing to do." Kirk paused. "It might mean life or death for the entire crew."

McCoy crossed to the mind-ripper, and together he and Kirk stared at it for a moment. It was an unknown, alien device; M'Benga barely understood its controls, and they all knew its use could prove fatal at any time. Kirk recalled the feel of its electric probes, reaching tendrils into his brain. He shivered.

"All right," McCoy said. "But I'm going back in with you."

Kirk frowned. "There's no sense in both of us—"

"I screwed up in there, Jim." McCoy turned to him, and there was honest pain in his face. "I tried to prod Spock out of his stupor—I reminded him he was half human. And it backfired. That's when his mind—garden, whatever it was—went all haywire."

Kirk glanced over at Spock's bed. M'Benga stood before it now, looking at the diagnostic readouts and shaking his head slowly.

"It's my fault he's dying," McCoy said.

"That's ridiculous."

"It's what I know." He sat back on his bed, looked distastefully at the machine's leads. "I've got to make this right. Understand that, Jim."

Kirk locked eyes with McCoy for just a moment. Then he nodded.

"Scotty. Come here a minute."

Scott walked over to him.

"Dr. McCoy and I are going in again. If all goes well, we shouldn't be long."

Scott frowned. "Sir."

"Here's what you need to do. Get that warp drive fixed as quick as you can. The second you do, get us out of here. If the Klingons attack, don't try to be a hero. Hide behind the moon, slingshot around the sun, do whatever you have to do to get away."

"Aye, sir."

"If you think you can negotiate with the Klingons, by all means try it. But I don't hold out much hope there."

McCoy raised an eyebrow. "They don't seem too big on the Organian Peace Treaty."

"We're a long way out, Doctor." Kirk turned back to Scotty. "Get the crew home safe."

"I'll do my best, sir."

"I know you will."

Kirk turned to look at Spock. In all the time Kirk had been awake, the Vulcan hadn't moved an inch. He looked paler than usual, like a corpse prepared for viewing. Not a comforting thought.

Kirk glanced at McCoy, who flashed him a tight smile. Then he looked over at the alien device that held all their lives in its cold, metal grasp.

"Dr. M'Benga," Kirk said. "Send us back in."

Kirk's first impression is of a rush of bright red and blue, hazy yet familiar. Then the fog clears, and he and McCoy are standing on the bridge of the *Enterprise*.

But not, he realizes quickly, *my* Enterprise.

The alert tones sound different: longer, less sharp, more dissonant. The bridge stations sport an older, gooseneck style of personal comm screens. Star charts display an entirely different sector of the galaxy.

And in the center chair . . .

McCoy nudges Kirk. "Is that—"

"Yes. Chris Pike."

Not only is it Christopher Pike, Kirk's predecessor, but a younger Pike than Kirk has ever seen before. Younger even than in the Talos IV record-tapes. Pike sits, frowning at a padd, oblivious to Kirk and McCoy's presence.

Kirk looks around. The bridge is fully staffed—and no one else seems to notice him or McCoy, either. A young helmsman turns to Captain Pike.

"Space warp engaged, Captain. On course to Delta Aurigae III."

"Mmm." Pike doesn't look up.

"Jim. Look."

Kirk follows McCoy's gaze to the science station. A young Spock—again, younger than Kirk has ever seen him—is engaged in deep-voiced conversation with a handsome, dark-haired woman.

"Number Five," Spock says. "That is what the crew calls you?"

"That's right." The woman smiles tightly. "Because I'm fifth in command. Sixth, actually, counting the Captain."

"That is logical." Spock hesitates; he's not used to being around humans, Kirk realizes. "And you do not object to this appellation?"

Number Five shrugs. "It reminds me how far I have to go."

Spock raises an eyebrow.

Kirk and McCoy move closer to them, fascinated. Spock, Kirk notices, is an ensign.

"This is the main science station," Number Five says. "Just remember: When the captain asks for something, give it to him fast and to the best of your ability. You're only stationed here temporarily, till we pick up Science Officer Yu at Delta Aurigae."

Spock nods, studies the controls.

"Bones," Kirk says softly. "I think we're seeing a memory . . . of Spock's first day aboard the *Enterprise*."

McCoy smiles. "You don't need to whisper, Jim. They can't hear us."

Suddenly the scene freezes, and the sounds stop. Pike stares, unmoving, at his padd; Number Five halts in mid-gesture. Only Spock moves, turning to face the two visitors.

"I can hear you, gentlemen."

"Mr. Spock." Kirk smiles, reaches toward the Vulcan. "Do you know us? Do you know who we are?"

Spock's eyebrows narrow. He frowns and flinches away, toward the science console. "Captain Kirk," he says slowly. "Dr. McCoy."

McCoy nods. "That's right."

"Spock," Kirk continues. "Do you realize what this is? Where we are?"

Spock glances around, and a brief flash of fear crosses his impassive features. He looks so young, Kirk thinks. Untouched, as yet, by the scars of the Psi 2000 virus, by the agonies of the Denevan parasites, and most of all, by the violation of the mind-ripper.

"The *Enterprise,*" Spock says. "The *United Starship Enterprise.*" His pronunciation is odd, accented. As though, Kirk realizes, he's never said the word *Enterprise* before.

"No," Kirk replies. "This isn't the *Enterprise.* It isn't real."

But Spock is moving away from them, pacing the bridge with powerful, nervous steps. "The *Enterprise,*" he repeats. "My first posting in Starfleet. And I don't know how to do this." He pauses, looks fearfully from Number Five to the unmoving, frowning Captain Pike. "Too many humans. Too much chaos—too much illogic."

"Spock—"

"Jim." McCoy touches his elbow. "Let me try something."

Kirk nods.

"Mr. Spock," McCoy says. "You say there is too much illogic here?"

Spock nods. His face is impassive now, but his movements are still jerky, frightened. "Illogic—yes. And more. Danger."

"Well, what you want to do is take it one step at a time." McCoy smiles now, the very picture of a friendly country doctor. "You've been trained in how to deal with illogic, right?"

Spock does not answer. He looks up at the ceiling, then down at the science console. "Danger," he repeats. "Danger from within."

"Now, never mind that," McCoy continues. "Just use your training, Spock. You mentioned a technique before—what was it? Chaotic Response—"

"No!" Spock turns to them, panicked now. "Danger from within. Now!"

Suddenly, across the bridge, the engineering console explodes. A junior lieutenant flies backward, screaming, and sparks rain down across the bridge. Pike stands quickly, and alert sirens begin to blare.

The bridge has come to life.

"Phaser control reports overload!" the helmsman says.

Number Five is already at the engineering station, fanning away smoke and squinting to read the remaining active controls. "Radiation leak," she says. "Contamination, deck five."

"Warp drive has cut out," the navigator reports.

"Science officer!" Pike turns urgently to face Spock. *"Report!"*

They still can't see us, Kirk realizes.

Alert klaxons blare. Number Five coughs, recoils as her hand touches a burning switch on the engineering station. Medics exit from the turbolift, kneel down to attend to the wounded lieutenant. And backed up against the science station, looking around with wide eyes, stands Ensign Spock.

Frozen with fear.

The deck shifted violently, and a few instruments clattered to the floor. M'Benga grabbed onto Kirk's diagnostic bed to steady himself, almost yanking one of the Klingon machine's connector leads off the captain's forehead. He swore.

The intercom bleeped. M'Benga crossed to the desk.

"Dr. M'Benga here. What's going on?"

"The Klingons are back for another round, Doctor." Scotty's voice sounded tense—understandably, M'Benga thought. "How are things down there?"

Another blast shook the ship. M'Benga gripped the edge of the desk, glanced over at his unmoving patients.

"Shaky."

"I could use the captain and Mr. Spock."

"Hang on." Grimacing, M'Benga ran to Kirk's bed, examined the diagnostic for a minute. He shook his head, then returned to the desk.

"Their synaptic movement has plateaued at a wildly accelerated level, Mr. Scott. I don't know what's going on in there, but I don't dare bring them out now. The shock would probably kill them."

Another impact, even greater than before. McCoy's unmoving form shifted, moved dangerously close to the edge of the bed.

Through the intercom, M'Benga could hear cross-chatter on the bridge. The new ensign's heavy Russian accent, alternating with Mr. Scott's clipped burr.

Then Scott's voice came through again. "It's your call, Doctor. But if they don't come out soon, we may not have a ship for them to come back to."

"Understood."

M'Benga cut the connection. He glared at the Klingon mind-ripper, glowing with dark, electric energy. *Even if I understood that thing,* he thought, *I wouldn't dare adjust its settings.* The amount of energy coursing through the three men's minds was recklessly high.

M'Benga's eyes swept from Kirk's unmoving form to Spock, whose hands were twitching now, just slightly. Then he walked over to McCoy, spoke softly.

"Physician, you better hurry up and heal yourself," M'Benga said. *"And* your friends."

Outside, in the cold of space, the Klingons circled around for the kill.

Spock's mind is a welter of chaos. Flashing red lights. Shouting people. Smoke, small fires. Illogical human minds, pelting and assaulting him with their panic and their flaring, emotional thoughts.

"Science officer!" Captain Pike says again. "I said, report!"

For just a moment, Spock sees two Klingon cruisers, arcing around toward him with phaser turrets glowing. *No,* he thinks. *That's not right. Not Klingons; this is a phaser control emergency. An internal problem with the newly refitted ship, a malfunction. That's how it happened before.*

Before . . . ?

The two men are still here, too. His friends.

"Jim," one says. "I think something's going on outside—on the *Enterprise.* Our *Enterprise,* I mean."

"We'd better deal with this problem first, Bones."

Stop, Spock thinks. *Go away. Leave me alone. I cannot deal with this; no Vulcan could. This is too much.*

Again the thought flashes through his mind: *I will die here.*

Then one of the men—Kirk—has him by the shoulders. "Spock,"

Kirk says. "Listen to me. We have to get out of here—all of us. Your mind has retreated into this fantasy. But we're staring right down the barrel of reality now—and it's charging full phasers, locked straight on us."

The man's eyes are probing, knowing. Spock turns away.

"Your logic training," Kirk continues. "Use it. Use it to get yourself out of this."

McCoy steps forward. "For God's sake, Spock . . . if you were ever a Vulcan, be a Vulcan now."

Captain Kirk's eyes stare imploringly. Past him, Captain Pike's glare is just as steady, and much more hostile. A yeoman hovers over Pike's shoulder, staring at Spock along with the rest of the bridge crew.

Once more, Spock hears Salak's taunts: *Mr. Spock is part human. Logical thought is lacking in humans.*

And then, the Teacher:

These are deliberately adverse conditions for logic.

Recall your techniques of Chaotic Response Suppression.

Focus.

Spock turns to the science station. "Contamination is limited to deck five; damage control reports four casualties," he says. "Recommend sealing off deck five, port side, including emergency battery room and officers' lounge. All personnel, decks four through six, should be issued rad treatment packs."

Pike stares at him and begins to nod slowly.

"Do it," he says to the yeoman. She nods and moves off.

The crew move about, carrying out their tasks. Spock ignores them. The smell of smoke, the clamor of alert sirens: all these, he pushes to the side of his consciousness. He closes his eyes.

"Spock—"

He holds up a hand, and Kirk falls silent.

"There are two phases of Chaotic Response Suppression," Spock says aloud. "Phase One is the calming of mental processes. This plants the garden where logic may bloom."

The bridge sounds fade around him. All is calm; all is logical. The garden is green once more, and he stands within it. Gathering strength from its pure, ordered serenity.

Kirk and McCoy are still with him in spirit. He can feel Kirk's mind, in particular, close to his. Lending him strength.

He continues speaking aloud, to focus himself. "Once the mind is calm," he says, "Phase Two may commence. The employment of logic; the cold weighing of variables, of priorities. The strict code of controlled, emotionless judgment that saved my people from destruction, millennia ago."

"Yes," Kirk says.

Spock studies the green, healthy vegetation, feels the calm air. The sun shines warm, but not hot, on his back. This is a good place . . . a peaceful place. A place of logic.

"When the mind has been trained to remain calm at all times, the student has achieved *Kolinahr* . . . the state of total, eternal logic."

"Ugh," McCoy says.

"I have not achieved that state. Perhaps I never will. And yet . . . at this moment, my mind is calm."

Kirk nods. "Stay with it, Spock."

Spock looks around. He is alone here, and yet . . .

"All else has receded," Spock continues, "yet you persist. The two of you remain in my mind."

"Like bad pennies." He can feel McCoy's wry smile.

"Therefore . . . logic suggests . . ."

Spock hesitates. Kirk's consciousness hovers nearby, merged partially with his own. Supportive, but not intrusive. Watching, carefully, the process that will hopefully save all three of their lives.

Something shakes, violently. Pike's *Enterprise?* Kirk's? Spock's own mind?

". . . that only you two, out of all of this . . ."

"Spit it out, you blasted Vulcan!"

". . . are real."

Then Kirk and McCoy are there, shining mental constructs standing tall and proud in Spock's garden of logic. They reach out and take Spock's strong hands in their own.

"I understand," Kirk says.

Together they look to the sky, as they have always done, as they will always do. And together they rise, up and out, toward the bright star above and the unknown reality beyond.

Kirk's eyes flew open. He sat up, immediately alert.

To his right, McCoy groaned, rubbed his head. Kirk turned to the left, saw Spock lying still, his eyes wide open. Those eyes looked tired, but Kirk could see that they were taking in every detail of the scene, every piece of information available.

And so am I, he realized.

"Was that . . . a mind-meld?" McCoy asked.

"Of sorts," Spock replied. The Vulcan struggled to rise, then slumped back on the diagnostic bed.

Dr. M'Benga eyed them each briefly, then moved to the Vulcan. "You'd better take it easy, Mr. Spock. You've been through a lot."

"Indeed," Spock murmured.

Kirk's mind was spinning. Yes, the Klingon machine had merged their minds together. Spock had drawn strength from him and McCoy, enough to reassert his Vulcan disciplines and pull them all out of his mindscape.

And Kirk? Had he also taken something from the merge . . . ?

"Captain. Doctor." Spock's voice was raspy, his head almost perfectly still on the bed. "My thanks."

McCoy sat up, pulled the leads off his head. "It was worth it, Spock. Now you owe me one."

Kirk looked at his first officer, weak and unmoving on the bed. He recalled the way Pike had barked at the Vulcan, the trauma it had induced in Spock's mindscape.

Maybe I have been a little hard on Mr. Chekov, Kirk thought.

The ship shook with a harsh impact. Kirk looked up in alarm. He recognized the distinctive vibration of a phaser attack.

As if on cue, the intercom blipped.

"Any progress, Doctor?" Scotty's voice said.

Kirk tested himself, swung his legs around, and climbed to his feet. He crossed to McCoy's desk, pressed the intercom button. "Kirk here, Scotty. I'm on my way."

"Glad to hear it, Captain."

McCoy stood with M'Benga now, over Spock's body. Kirk hesitated, remembering his own words to McCoy a short time ago. He moved to their side.

"Mr. Spock," Kirk said slowly. "I could really use your help."

Spock nodded, tried to rise. "Just . . . one moment, Captain . . ."

He slipped, fell back onto the bed. McCoy and M'Benga grabbed him together, rolled him onto his back. Spock lay still.

"I'd advise against it," M'Benga said.

"Absolutely not, Jim. Not possible."

"Bones . . ."

I need Spock, he started to say. *I need his guidance, his ability to sort and evaluate information. I need his talent for—*

*—*Chaotic Response Suppression.

The moment the phrase popped into Kirk's mind, he saw the whole process laid out before him. Phase One: Calm the mental processes. Allow the garden to bloom. Push all external stimuli to the side. Phase Two: Employ logic. Evaluate all variables dispassionately, emotionlessly—

Kirk had never realized before just how rigorous Vulcan logic training really was. Spock had studied all his life—years, decades—to train his mind to this peak. And now . . .

Now, he realized, *I've absorbed it all from him in a matter of minutes.*

Those skills would fade, he knew. That was the nature of a mindmeld. Like a dream, the particulars would melt away, while the core memory of the experience remained.

But right now, Kirk possessed all the mental discipline of a Vulcan.

He closed his eyes, cleared his mind, and employed Chaotic Response Suppression. He saw the possible scenarios on the bridge, all the various ways the battle against the Klingons might play out. He inserted himself, with his new abilities, into the scenarios, one by one. All in the space of a millisecond.

And something else, too. His own human intuition—the unquantifiable, illogical talent that made him a starship captain—became part of the process. He could not only see the various scenarios, not only sort the necessary data. He could also pick and choose among those scenarios, zeroing in on the actual outcomes of each possible action. He could see which way the Klingons would jump if prodded. How far he could push the engines beyond their specs. How each of his officers would respond under pressure. How much pounding his ship could take, and how much the Klingon cruisers would withstand.

Beyond any doubt, Kirk knew: *I can do this.*

He looked over at Spock, who was struggling to rise again. McCoy and M'Benga protested, holding his arms.

"Captain," Spock said weakly. "If you will just allow me a minute . . ."

"Not necessary, Mr. Spock. As you were."

"It is my duty to assist you—"

"You already have."

Spock raised an eyebrow questioningly. McCoy and M'Benga turned to face Kirk as well, their expressions equally curious.

Kirk smiled. "I value your presence on the bridge, Mr. Spock. I want you back at your post as soon as possible. But right now . . ." He tapped his own head. "I got this one."

Then he sprinted for the door. When he reached it, he stopped, turned back briefly.

"Oh, and Mr. Spock . . . when you're better, perhaps we can have a bit of a discussion about Phase Two. Is it a necessary precursor to *Kolinahr,* or are there other paths?"

Spock's eyebrow rose again, higher than Kirk had ever seen it before.

"Jim," McCoy said, "if you're turnin' Vulcan on me, let me know so I can transfer to another ship."

The deck shook again, and Kirk ran for the turbolift.

All around him, in the corridor, red-alert lights flashed. Men and women in life-support suits hurried by. Intercoms crackled with urgent orders. Whole decks were being evacuated, and emergency protocols enacted on the warp core. Four hundred thirty officers and crew scrambled to perform their duties, not knowing if they'd live to see another day.

But despite the chaos, Kirk smiled.

This battle, he knew, was already won.

As Others See Us

Christopher L. Bennett

Christopher L. Bennett

Christopher L. Bennett has been keeping pretty busy lately. In addition to "As Others See Us" and the recent *X-Men: Watchers on the Walls*, his current projects include *Star Trek: Mere Anarchy, Book Four: The Darkness Drops Again*, a Spider-Man novel, a *Star Trek: The Lost Era* novel, a *Star Trek: Corps of Engineers* e-book, and a recently completed original science fiction novel he hopes to sell soon. This is in addition to the critically acclaimed novels *Star Trek: Ex Machina* and *Star Trek Titan: Orion's Hounds*, stories in the anthologies *Star Trek: Deep Space Nine—Prophecy and Change* and *Star Trek: Voyager—Distant Shores*, and the e-book *Star Trek: S.C.E. #29: Aftermath* (soon to be reprinted in a trade paperback of the same name). One of these days, he may actually get his name on a book that doesn't have any colons in the title. More information, original fiction, and cat pictures can be found at http://home.fuse.net/ChristopherLBennett/.

Deyin Kaiyel-Ned stood at the prow of the good ship *Enai-ra* as it steamed boldly forward, leading her merchant fleet into waters where no Yemai had sailed before. She liked to be at the forefront, literally as well as figuratively—to be the very first civilized being to pass into these strange new realms. If there was arrogance to that, she had earned it, winning her admiral's rank with the same ambition and ingenuity that had driven her foremothers, and others like them, to master the power of steam and use it to expand Yemai influence across the formerly untamed reaches of the globe.

To be sure, Deyin's main objective, like that of her crew, was the wealth that could be found in the great unknown. Distant lands teemed with exotica that the wealthy classes of Yemai would pay a queen's ransom for—from spices and fabrics to intoxicants and slaves. This had always been so. Now, though, the rise of capitalism created even more incentive for exploring distant lands, in search of new resources to build industries upon, new farmlands to feed the growing mass of workers, and new markets of backward, exploitable natives who would sell their own children in exchange for simple tools, guns, or medicines.

This fleet's destination, the Ilaiyen Archipelago, promised to be particularly lucrative, if the legends and rumors were borne out. Those few travelers who had returned from Ilaiyen—or claimed to have been there—told of an incredibly lush and fertile land possessing miraculous powers of healing and rejuvenation. Even if the tales were pure fiction, as Deyin suspected, the people back home would shell out fortunes for Ilaiyen goods anyway, and Deyin would not feel the least bit compelled to dissuade their wishful thinking. And the simple, gentle fisherfolk described by the travelers, with their primitive huts and dugout canoes, would no doubt be just as easily persuaded to give up their resources and their secrets in exchange for a few shiny baubles and displays of industrial-age magic.

But to Deyin, the material prize was only part of it. She found excitement in the exploration itself—discovering exotic lands untouched by civilization, marveling at the bizarre forms that plants, animals, and people mutated into under the influence of alien climes. Being the first to see something never before seen, to battle monstrous new beasts and bring back their corpses to the Imperial Museum. The first to teach an innocent tribe of the world beyond their shores. The first to observe their strange customs and superstitions, and the first to show them the error of their ways.

And if those natives should happen to resist enlightenment, or to be recalcitrant in agreeing to her entirely reasonable trade policies (for of course it was only reasonable that the Yemai Empire, with its greater needs, should benefit more from the trade than a bunch of simple villagers), then the resulting combat provided yet another form of excitement. It kept her crew sharp for battling the fleets of rival powers, seeking to make their own trade deals at Yemai expense. Deyin relished those contests as well, for they let her exercise strategy and cunning against worthy foes.

All in all, this was the greatest life any soul could hope for. Deyin could not imagine any grander adventure.

Someone was watching her, she realized. Turning slightly, she saw in her peripheral vision that it was Jeyam Tybris-Kir, one of the fresh recruits who had come aboard at Reihairem. He and the four who'd boarded with him were an odd bunch—all of them atypically small, and not very strong, save for Seyar Mandas-Pok, the quiet, cool one who always kept his headscarf pulled down over his ears. Their brows and nasal crests were oddly immobile, making it hard to read their expressions sometimes. There was only one woman in the group, and she was oddly deferential to the males, particularly Jeyam. Deyin figured that despite their Yemai names, they must be from some exotic land whose people had not yet been fully civilized. Reihairem was the most remote Yemai port, only a few days' travel from the archipelago they sought. It certainly had its share of outlanders. (Perhaps this bunch had even changed their names in order to assimilate. A few times, Deyin had heard Jeyam's friends pronounce his name oddly, closer to "Jyim.")

Not that they weren't a useful bunch. The older one, Leyan Ardem-Koi, was a skilled physician, and Seyar seemed knowledgeable in all sorts of things. The others may not have had much physical strength, but they were disciplined and worked hard. Yet there was a fire lacking in them. They didn't seem to share the rest of the crew's eagerness to acquire wealth or battle savages. If anything, while the rest of the crew looked outward and forward toward the next conquest, these five seemed more interested in watching the crew itself. The woman in particular, Teyar Risar-Gan, reminded her of a naturalist studying a newly discovered tribe, except it was Yemai sailors that she was studying.

"May I help you with something, Seaman Jeyam?" she asked, without turning more than necessary to make sure her words reached his ears.

"No, thank you." Though he was soft-spoken, there was a commanding tone in his voice. She didn't like that.

"Then you should get back to your duties."

"I've finished my tasks, Admiral."

Skeptical, she turned to face him. "So quickly?"

"I've . . . had some experience with ships."

"Then ask the captain to assign you a new chore."

"I did. She said I'd earned a rest."

"And you choose to take it here? With our speed blowing sea spray into your face?"

He smiled. "You seem to enjoy it."

"I was born with the spray in my face. But I wouldn't have thought a scrawny thing like you would tolerate it well."

"I can handle a little speed."

"You couldn't handle me," she told him, getting to the point. "If I want a tryst, I have my pick of much worthier males. You should set your sights lower. Your comrade Teyar, perhaps."

"That's . . . not really an option. Besides," and he gave her that annoying smile again, "I enjoy a challenge."

"I'd believe that if you showed more enthusiasm for our mission. Have you no ambition to bring back wealth and glory and tales of triumph? Or are your people too dainty to handle the combat that may lie ahead?"

"We can handle ourselves, if we have to," he told her, sounding supremely confident. "But we signed onto your ship . . . because we want to explore. To learn about new peoples, how they live, how they think."

"Really. And what will you do with that knowledge?"

He shrugged. "It's for other people to determine whether it has any practical use. For myself, I simply . . . wonder in it."

Deyin stared at him. She was beginning to realize that this man might be a kindred spirit, someone who could understand her love of exploration and adventure.

And that made him even more annoying.

"Go find something else to do," she told him. "That's an order."

But Jeyam no longer seemed to be listening. He was staring intently at something up ahead. Deyin cast a glance in that direction but could make out nothing save the horizon, made misty by the dense intervening air.

But a moment later, the signal bell began to ring. Deyin's eyes rose sharply to the sky, homing in on the large kite that soared above the ship, attached to it by a strong cable. The kiteman was flashing his signal mirror in one hand while he pulled the bell cord with the other. He had spotted land at last. According to his heliographic code, the land was a chain of islands that matched the likely parameters of Ilaiyen, as correlated from the mariners' tales. The location was right, too.

Deyin rushed to the wheelhouse, ordering the captain to change course and signal the fleet to follow. "Is this it at last?" Nohin Yiamed-Ba asked, skepticism and excitement warring on her face.

"I assume nothing, Captain. But I'm optimistic. Make ready as though it is, in any case. We must present the proper first impression."

"Aye, Admiral."

Deyin turned and was surprised to see that Jeyam had followed her into the wheelhouse. "What are you doing here?"

He shrugged. "You ordered me to find something to do—I came to see what needed to be done. May I ask . . . what kind of impression are we trying to present?"

With the thrill of impending landfall, Deyin decided she was in a generous mood, so she indulged him. "The people there—whether Ilaiyenai or just some random tribe—will be simple, primitive folk. We don't want to spook them by coming on too strong. We go in with just the *Enai-ra* at first. We present ourselves as simply a small group of traders, and show them just enough of our technology to spark their curiosity, not enough to alarm them. We say nothing at first about our long-term commercial intentions."

"Then why present ourselves as traders at all?"

She looked askance at the poor naïve thing. "Trade is the universal language, lad. If some odd-looking, gibberish-speaking savage came ashore in the imperial city, people would run screaming for the police, having no idea of her intentions. But if she then went to the market square and began to haggle, suddenly people would be at ease, for then they would understand how to relate to her."

She smirked. "After all, what else do we have in common with these half-naked primitives? Would we want to meet them at all if they had nothing to offer us?"

"They offer us knowledge. The opportunity to see something new, to study a unique way of life."

"True . . . there is that. But even that is precious wealth to the naturalists. Especially since that way of life won't last for much longer."

Jeyam seemed saddened by her words. "Isn't there some way it can be allowed to?"

"You would condemn these people to eternal backwardness? Deny them the chance to catch up with the rest of the world? Just for the sake of scientific curiosity?"

"I . . . just think people should have the chance to make their own decisions."

"So do I," she said, "once they're educated enough to make valid ones." She was growing tired of this discussion. "You came to find something to do, so go ask Captain Nohin. Stop bothering me with your incessant questions."

He seemed on the verge of speaking, but restrained himself and nodded. "Aye, Admiral," he said, and went to consult with the captain.

Good, she thought. Jeyam's point of view convinced her further that he must be from some backward people himself, only recently civilized and still clinging to a romantic view of the past. She didn't have time for such antiquated thinking. Especially not when his naïve beliefs could jeopardize this contact. Deyin decided she'd have to keep a close eye on this man.

Soon enough, the *Enai-ra* was sailing into a large, idyllic lagoon, protected from the wind by gently sloping mountains whose sides practically glowed with vivid blue-green forests. Clear waves caressed a wide, sandy beach, inland of which was a large cluster of huts woven from the native plants. The village extended back to the edge of the tropical forest behind it, almost seeming to merge with it, like a natural extension. Grass-skirted islanders looked up with excitement and surprise as the steamship lumbered toward their shore, running to the huts to rouse their fellow villagers, but they showed more curiosity than fear or hostility. Soon, parties of men with female leaders began boarding dugouts and paddling out to meet the ship.

"Look at it," James Kirk said as he surveyed the scene before him. "It's paradise."

"Enjoy it while it lasts," replied Leonard McCoy, scratching at his nose. Of all the members of the landing party, he'd had the most trouble following his own advice to leave the facial prosthetics alone, so as not to damage the illusion that they were natives to Sigma Niobe II. At a glare from Kirk, he subsided. "Even if these turn out not to be the Ilaiyens," and typically he mangled the pronunciation, "the Yemai will find some way to exploit the life out of them."

Kirk shook his head. "I wish I could've gotten through to Deyin. She's not so bad. She's an explorer at heart. But she's a product of her time, her culture."

"A culture that it is not our place to judge," Spock said from Kirk's other side. "Or to attempt to modify."

"I know, I know." They had been having this same argument ever since

Kirk, learning of this expedition during their survey of the city of Rei-hairem, had impulsively signed up his landing party as relief crew members. Spock had questioned whether his intention was simply to observe or to try to intervene, and had reminded Kirk that the expedition itself was an object lesson in the need for the Prime Directive, the arrogance of attempting to impose one's own judgments on another culture. But Kirk had questioned whether it was in the spirit of the noninterference directive to stand by while others violated it on an intraplanetary scale.

"I just hate having to stand by and watch this happen," he said after a moment.

Theresa Errgang, the lieutenant from Archaeology and Anthropology, tilted her black-haired head in puzzlement. "If I may ask, sir . . . then why did you bring us along to do just that?"

He smirked. "I guess I'm just a glutton for punishment." Errgang furrowed her brow thoughtfully. She was a good A & A officer, very perceptive and widely studied, and her tall, athletic stature made her useful for blending in on this high-gravity world, as well as an interesting sparring partner back in the *Enterprise* gym. But she had a certain bookish naïveté and not much of a sense of humor.

She was useful, though, in observing the interaction between the Yemai and the islanders as they tentatively initiated contact. Captain Yiamed-Ba (or rather, Captain Nohin—Kirk was still getting used to these naming conventions) and a band of seamen debarked in a small launch to meet the canoe party on their own level and, according to Errgang, began addressing them in various regional languages in hopes of finding one they knew. The universal translator rendered it all in English to Kirk's ear, but Errgang seemed to have a knack—perhaps by virtue of her training—to listen to both the translation and the original speech behind it at the same time.

Soon the Yemai captain found a dialect that the islanders were conversant in, and confirmed that they were indeed the Ilaiyenai (though their own, un-Yemaicized pronunciation of the name was somewhat different). A ripple of enthusiasm went through the crew members observing from the *Enai-ra*'s deck, but Deyin shushed them, not wishing to give too much away.

Out in the lagoon, Nohin was beginning her sales pitch. "We come to trade," she told the Ilaiyenai, and had her crewmen hold up various trade items, including elaborately woven cloth from Yemai's textile mills, small telescopes, mechanical lighters, and other such minor technical marvels that they expected the Ilaiyenai to perceive as magic. The islanders were amused, but took the devices surprisingly in stride.

"There is more," Nohin told them, offering them a taste of Ayem-Sud wine (well, something analogous to wine, although nonperishable and able to withstand long sea voyages unrefrigerated). The islanders nodded in appreciation of the flavor but were not as awed as the Yemai had hoped. "Either these folks are incredibly jaded," McCoy said, "or they've got the best poker faces in the galaxy." Ever since he'd tasted the wine, he'd been trying to connive a way to get as much of it beamed to the ship as he could without violating the Prime Directive.

Nohin's spiel was starting to grow shakier. "There is more to offer, if we may come ashore and meet your leaders," she ventured. "We have medicines to heal the sick. They do wonders."

The chief negotiator shook her head. "We have no sick," she said.

Again, the *Enai-ra* crew reacted with eagerness. The assertion seemed to confirm the legends about this place. "Caution," Deyin told them. "It may be just a negotiating ploy."

"Not necessarily," Spock murmured to his crewmates. "An isolated population such as this, living in small bands separated by geography, may indeed be relatively free of serious disease. Any deadly infectious strains would kill off their host populations before they could spread far, and thus bring about their own extinction."

"I'd think viruses would be more resilient than that, Commander Spock," Errgang said.

"There are historical examples, Lieutenant. The Native Americans of Earth, for example, led extraordinarily healthy lives before the European contact."

"And because of that," McCoy said, "they had no immunity to European plagues. Up to ninety percent of them died of infectious diseases within the next two centuries. If these people are disease-free," he went on heavily, "the Yemai could be dooming them just by coming here."

"Unless there really is some healing property to this place." This was from the final member of the landing party, Lieutenant Jerome Chaane of security. He was a tall, exotic-featured man, mostly human but with hints of Vulcanoid, Tiburon, and maybe something else in his physiognomy. But whatever his ethnic mix, it made him particularly robust, and a good choice to impersonate one of Sigma Niobe's high-gravity natives. "Do you suppose the legends could be true?"

"Spock, are you reading anything?"

"Difficult to say," the Vulcan told Kirk. He was holding his tricorder close to his vest in order to muffle its warbling. "There appears to be a pervasive electromagnetic interference field in this area, perhaps due to some form of magnetic anomaly or mineral deposit."

"Or some kind of healing energy field?" McCoy asked, intrigued by the possibility.

"It would be premature to speculate at this point, Doctor. Although I will defer to you as an authority on voodoo medicine."

McCoy glared. "Don't knock it, Spock. It takes a good witch doctor to treat a hobgoblin like you."

"If you mix your potions as crudely as your metaphors, then I am lucky to be alive at all."

"All right, you two," Kirk interposed. "Focus." McCoy glowered, upset that Spock had been allowed the last word again.

Down in the lagoon, Captain Nohin was trying to extract more information from the Ilaiyenai about their alleged perfect health and the abundance of their land. They did not go into detail, aside from indicating that they had little need for anything the captain offered. Soon Nohin decided to try a different tactic, so as not to seem too eager for trade. "We have traveled far and are tired," she said. "May we come ashore to rest and take on new supplies?"

"Just you?" the islander asked. "Or your other ships as well?"

Nohin faltered. "What other ships?" The crew was muttering, wondering how they could have known. Kirk figured they must have had lookouts, probably stationed on the mountains, who had seen the fleet coming and reported it before their arrival. Although the mountains seemed too far to run from in the available time. Some kind of heliograph system? Or perhaps this thick atmosphere just carried their shouts much farther.

The Ilaiyenai negotiator sighed. "We are sorry," she said. "We do not trade with those who come falsely. Please leave." She sat back down in the canoe and ordered her oarsmen to head back for shore.

"No, wait! Yes, all of our ships. We need to resupply." But she was ignored.

"Captain!" Deyin called. "Come and parley."

Nohin climbed a ladder up the side of the ship and came aboard next to the admiral. They spoke softly, but the translators, built with thinner atmospheres in mind, picked up their words easily. "Well, we've tried the sweetfruit," Nohin said. "Is it time for the whip?"

"Yes," Deyin replied. "Just enough to show them we mean business. Take several shore parties—armed with rifles. Show them what Yemai firepower can do; perhaps that will pique their interest in trade."

Errgang frowned. "Does she mean they'll be interested in trading for the guns, or that the guns will scare them into trading for other things?"

"Both," Kirk told her. "She wants to show her strength, but only to establish a strong negotiating position."

Deyin ordered the *Enai-ra* brought in closer to the beach and sent out several shore parties in the launches, one of them including the *Enterprise* contingent. Kirk was reluctant to participate in this armed incursion, but could see no way to refuse. At least if he was on the scene, there might be some way to head off violence.

As the launches approached the beach, the islanders paddled out in canoes to form a blockade. "Go away," the negotiator said. "You are not welcome." Men stood in the boats, bearing some kind of atlatls—no, Kirk amended, more like Australian woomeras, shaped like long, narrow bowls with sharp edges, useful as peaceful carrying tools or cutters as well as spear-throwers. He admired the simple sophistication of the design.

Nohin ordered her men to fire warning shots just short of the dugouts. Thunder cracked across the lagoon, noxious smoke rose from the rifles, and bullets sliced through the water. The Ilaiyenai winced from the noise but stood their ground.

Seconds later, each of the riflemen who had fired was struck in the hand by a short, blunted, perfectly aimed spear. Kirk was amazed by the woomera-wielders' accuracy.

But the Yemai had no such academic appreciation. As the riflemen clutched their injured hands, Nohin and others snatched up their guns and began to open fire on the dugout crews.

"No!" Kirk reacted impulsively, tackling the rifleman in his boat to stop him from killing one of the Ilaiyenai. He wrested the gun away from the man, who overbalanced and fell into the water.

"What is this, Jeyam?" Nohin demanded.

"There's no need for this! They only want to be left alone!"

"Traitor!" The cry came from the ship. Hearing the fury in Deyin's voice, Kirk whirled to see her aiming a rifle straight at his forehead prosthetic. Without another thought, he hurled himself into the water. A second later, he heard other splashes as Spock and the others followed him in. Judging the angle of her shot, he swam down a meter or so, which should be a sufficient depth for the water to slow the bullets harmlessly. Once he made sure the others were following his lead, he set off for shore.

They came up for air on the other side of the dugouts, whose occupants were busy defending themselves against the attackers. But the dugouts held fewer occupants than they should, for there were bodies in the water. Some were motionless, but others still showed signs of life. "Get the wounded to shore!" Kirk called, and grabbed the nearest living body.

Once they reached the shore, the islanders accepted their help in getting the wounded to safety. No one seemed to question their allegiance or intentions. Meanwhile, McCoy did his best to stabilize the ones too injured to be moved farther, insofar as he could without exposing advanced technology to the locals. But Kirk did hear the occasional hiss of the hypospray that Bones kept concealed in his hands.

Suddenly McCoy froze over one of the bodies, a female who was barely moving, her limbs spasming irregularly as she lay on her side, her back to Kirk. "Jim!" he called.

"Bones, don't waste time!"

"Jim, you need to see this! Spock, you too! Now!"

Kirk handed off the wounded man he was carrying to Chaane and jogged over to McCoy's side, keeping low to avoid Yemai fire. He looked down at the woman's now-motionless body. "I don't understand," he said as Spock came up behind him. "No blood."

"There wouldn't be," Bones said. He rolled the body over onto its back, exposing the holes blown in its chest and midriff.

And the metallic ribs and sparking electronic circuits inside them.

"What in blazes . . . ?" Kirk was stunned. What was an android doing here, of all places? The islanders couldn't all be androids—their blood was proof enough of that.

"Captain," Spock said, his calm helping to restore Kirk's, "we must not let the Niobeans see this body."

"Right," he said. He looked around; the islanders were sufficiently distracted by the battle and the care of the wounded. "Let's get it behind those rocks."

As quickly as they could without drawing attention, they moved the android body to a secluded section of the beach. Errgang followed behind them, while Chaane remained on the beach to continue helping the islanders. "Spock, analysis?" Kirk asked as soon as the android was on the ground once more.

Spock fiddled with his tricorder knobs. "The local interference is disrupting the readings," he said. "But what information I can discern does not correspond to any known android technology. Judging from the isotope ratios of its constituent materials, however, I can confirm that it is not indigenous to this star system."

"So where is it from?" McCoy asked.

"I can only narrow it down to a late K-type star between seven and ten billion years of age."

"Maybe we can access its memory," Kirk said. "Find out its programming, its mission."

Spock waved his tricorder over its head and chest. "Its central processing unit seems rather small. Too basic to house an autonomous consciousness. It may simply be a drone, controlled from some central source."

"Like the androids on Mudd's Planet."

"Yes," Spock said, his grimace showing what he thought of that name for the world. "Logically, the control signal would be on a subspace frequency in order to circumvent the RF interference. With luck," he said distractedly as he rose and began to pivot slowly with his tricorder, "I may be able to home in on the source."

"Jim!" McCoy called.

"What is it, Bones?"

"I think its eyes just moved."

Kirk knelt down and looked into its eyes. Although they were fixed and unblinking, they did seem to be focused, aware. He leaned closer. "Is anyone there?"

Glysinek swiveled her eyes back out of the telepresence hood to look at Nerrieb. "What do I do? There isn't enough power left to work the speech module."

"Never mind. Wait for our other probes to arrive." Nerrieb had ordered two of them to converge on Glysinek's probe body as soon as he'd seen the ostensible Yemai trader deploy a scanning device that could not be native to this world. The aliens' evident intention to track down the Redheri control bunker called for intervention. Who knew what their purpose was on this planet? Were they rivals out to jump his claim? Well, he'd just see about that!

Nerrieb waded as quickly as he could through the high-buoyancy fluid that negated this planet's uncomfortable gravity. He nudged Yanslet's carapace with a grasping-arm, signaling him to extricate himself from the telepresence module so Nerrieb could take over the probe personally. The probe's locomotion cycle proceeded automatically during the changeover. Nerrieb climbed out of the fluid, settled himself into the cradle, and found the controls with the ease of long practice: his rear two pairs of flippers to operate the lower limbs, the forward two pairs to puppeteer the face, one grasping-arm for each upper limb, mouth-tendrils to work the fingers. Once he plugged his eyes and olfactory flanges into their receptacles and the contact speakers came to rest against his head segment, it was as though he were actually up there on dry land, inhabiting an ungainly bipedal body whose only similarity to his—and a tenuous one at that—was its sex. Once he got a feel for its walking rhythm, he took it off autopilot and picked up the pace. The HUD overlay indicated that his and Hudalliuc's probe bodies were just moments away from intercepting the unidentified aliens. The battle between the two indigenous groups was still being waged further on, but it seemed to be a safe distance away.

The one called Spock was addressing the ones called Jim and Bones. ". . . power levels are critically low. I cannot even confirm that the eyes are functional. Or, for that matter, the ears."

"Well, if anyone knows ears . . ."

"Bones, enough. So we don't know for sure if they can see us or hear us."

"We can." The bipeds whirled as the probes stepped out from the trees onto the beach. "Whoever you are," Nerrieb told them, "we were here first."

The one called Jim stepped forward. Nerrieb had spent enough time living as one of these bipeds to recognize the air of command in his body language, not to mention the suspicion. "Spock? More robots?"

Nerrieb saved Spock the trouble. "Yes, we are. At least, these bodies are. I assume you are all living flesh, though you're clearly not from this world."

The commander took another step forward. "I'm Captain James T. Kirk, representing the United Federation of Planets. My first officer, Mr. Spock, my chief medical officer, Dr. McCoy, and Lieutenant Errgang. And you are?"

"Nerrieb, of the Redheri Trade Consortium." He had heard of the Federation, though as far as he knew, this was the Redheri's first direct contact with that distant but growing power. Judging from the ranks, these were members of its Starfleet, which considered itself an exploratory body, yet could be the strong arm of the Federation when a reason presented itself.

Kirk frowned. "Redheri. I can't say I'm familiar with the name."

"We are here as explorers, much like yourselves. But unlike you, we do not resemble this planet's natives, so we must take more elaborate measures to blend in," he said, making the probe body gesture to itself.

"So your purpose here is . . . scientific?"

"Commercial, actually. We are advance scouts. Our mission is to prepare this world for contact and admission into the Consortium."

Kirk's expression didn't seem pleased. "'Prepare' this world? How?"

Suspicious fellow, wasn't he? "With great care and respect, I assure you. We have no wish to disrupt this planet's native cultures unduly by exposing them to concepts they're unprepared for. Which is the purpose for these telepresence probes. They allow us to pass as natives, integrate ourselves smoothly into the culture. Over the course of years, we study the natives, learn their psychology and values as well as their needs, and tailor a commercial strategy which respects those values and needs."

"And then . . . what?" the one called McCoy asked. "How does that make it any easier for them to cope when you reveal the existence of aliens to them?"

"Ahh, that's the other key component of the Redheri contact strategy." Back in the bunker, he heard Glysinek and Yanslet discussing whether it was wise to spell this out in so much detail. But Nerrieb saw possibilities here. This bipedal form was strangely ubiquitous in the galaxy, so that these Federation people could pass for natives easily, without the difficulty and expense of telepresence probes. If he could recruit them as allies, they could be a positive boon to the Consortium.

"You see, as we live among the local population, observing them and getting to know them, we also subtly introduce the concept of life on other worlds into their public consciousness. We start conversations about the nature of the stars, whether there could be life elsewhere, what could be gained from communicating and trading with such life. Depending on the culture, we may tell campfire stories or songs about beings from the stars, or write speculative essays, or publish works of adventure fiction involving outer space or alien contact." Nerrieb's mission before this one had involved such a strategy, though he had accomplished it by befriending a local novelist and becoming her muse, providing the ideas while letting her write the words, for her mastery of her language's elaborate literary-poetic style was far better than his. She had been fairly creative on her own, but her stories had tended to portray aliens as ruthless invaders or hidden killers, which didn't suit Redheri needs at all. In fact, he'd adapted the tales from Consortium historical records, but had changed enough specifics so that no species or event was overtly recognizable. Some peoples didn't appreciate being clandestinely observed and influenced prior to contact, so the Redheri took care to make their contacts seem spontaneous and keep mum about their earlier visits, at least until a planet had become comfortably integrated into the Consortium.

"In any case, we take our time, easing these concepts into a culture at its own rate of comfort, or emphasizing concepts that are already present within it. Thus, they become ready for contact at their own pace, and once that readiness is achieved, we reveal ourselves. This way, they gain all the benefits of interstellar trade, while their cultural integrity is preserved."

The sales pitch didn't seem to be working on Kirk. "You have an odd way of defining 'cultural integrity.' Of all the cultures on this planet to expose to the idea of space and aliens, you choose one of the simplest, most primitive ones? People who aren't even aware of the full scope of their own world, let alone the galaxy?"

"Indeed," Spock added. "Surely the Yemai, as the most technologically advanced culture controlling the widest array of resources, would be a more logical trading partner."

Nerrieb puppeteered the probe's face to reflect his amusement. "The Yemai are too solidly convinced of their own superiority, of the completeness of their belief structure. They're not open to new ideas—certainly not to the knowledge that there are beings more advanced than they are."

"He has a point there, Captain," said the one called Errgang. "As humanoids go, they're even more inflexible than most." Nerrieb found that an odd sentiment from someone who was humanoid herself.

"Besides," he went on, "they can offer us little that we don't already have the like of. But this archipelago . . . well, we're here for the same reason the Yemai are, and probably the same reason you are. The healing principle. Yes," he said in response to their expressions. "It's very real. We've seen it work. These people truly have no illness, heal swiftly from injuries, and have greatly extended life spans. Unfortunately our expedition here is still in its early stages, and we've had little success at penetrating the interference field to scan for its cause."

"The other Ilaiyens don't know anything?" McCoy asked.

"They think of it simply as a divine force pervading all things, a kind of mystical life essence. They've been of little help." He moved a bit closer. "But perhaps we could pool our resources to investigate the cause, in exchange for which we'd be willing to share in the development rights."

"We won't be sharing anything with you, Nerrieb," Kirk said sharply. "You say you respect these people's culture, but from where I stand, it looks more like you're manipulating their culture to suit your own needs, using trickery to make them more exploitable as customers. And you're doing it to their most innocent and vulnerable members."

"You speak of trickery—what do you call your own presence here, Kirk?"

"We're here only to observe, to learn. We won't take anything but knowledge, won't try to change these people in any way. Our highest law states that there shall be no interference in the natural development of any pre-warp culture. They must be left alone to develop in their own way, not the way we think they should."

Nerrieb swiveled his eyes around to exchange a glance with Glysinek. *Can you believe this biped?* "There's nothing natural about being left alone. Cultures don't develop in isolation—they interact with their neighbors, learn and change in response to them. That *is* natural."

"If the difference in technology is too great, it can overwhelm them, destroy their way of life."

"Only if no care is taken to preserve it. We respect every culture we deal with. Respect them enough to approach them as equals, rather than infants to be sheltered."

"Once you've changed them enough to suit your wishes."

"And what entitles you to be so righteous, Kirk? You interfered directly in the events of this contact. You tried to change it to suit your wishes."

That silenced Kirk for a moment. "Whatever I did . . . I did only to save lives. And I seek nothing in return. If Starfleet decides my actions went too far, that I should be held to account for it, I'll accept that judgment.

"But if I have anything to say about it," he went on, stepping forward, "I'll see that the Federation holds you to account for your actions here."

Nerrieb reminded himself that he had no cause to be physically intimidated by the large biped's advance. After all, it was only a probe body Kirk was facing down. Nerrieb himself was in a submerged bunker offshore, in no danger from the captain. "You're bluffing," he said with the confidence that awareness gave him. "Your Federation has no right to interfere in the free trade of the Redheri Consortium."

"Nobody here has entered into any trade agreement with you yet. And we can make sure they don't, not until a few centuries from now when they're ready. We can make this planet a Federation protectorate, blockade it against intruders." Oh, dear—he didn't sound like he was bluffing. Nerrieb began to regret being so forthcoming about the Consortium's strategy.

"Captain." Spock interrupted Kirk's tirade. "Listen. The battle is moving in our direction."

Indeed, the sounds of shouting and gunfire were coming much closer. The fifth Starfleeter came into view, crying a warning. "Chaane, this way!" Kirk called, then turned to the others. "We need to get this robot out of sight."

"We can agree on that, at least," Nerrieb replied, beginning to move his probe closer.

But it was too late—fighters from both contingents began pouring around the rock spur. Some of the islanders turned to see what looked like five Yemai standing over the corpse of one of their own and facing down two more.

Nerrieb seized the opportunity, running over to his "fellow" islanders. "They killed Isinaki!" he told them, manipulating the probe's face to show the appropriate grief and rage. "Quickly, we must kill them now!" He shuddered with distaste at the thought of resorting to vio-

lence, but he couldn't risk entangling the Consortium in a conflict with
the powerful Federation. That would cost far more lives, and there was
no economy in that. Best if one of their captains and his landing party
just met with an unfortunate accident at the hands of the natives.

The sight of the fallen "Isinaki" suitably enraged the warriors, and
they began to cock their spear-throwers. But just then, one of the Yemai
strode forward, staring angrily at Kirk's party. It was the female that his
observers had identified as the fleet admiral. "You!" she cried. "I knew
you were no better than these savages. Well, now you can die like
them!" She raised her rifle.

Kirk and his landing party stood frozen between the two factions.
Nerrieb could see the indecision in Kirk's face. He could no doubt call
his ship and order an emergency beamout, but that would violate his
precious noninterference policy by exposing the natives to knowledge
of advanced technology. But if they stayed and let themselves be killed,
they would then be discovered as aliens anyway, and their sensor and
communication devices would be discovered on their bodies. Which
would Kirk choose as the lesser of evils?

But Nerrieb would never know. Suddenly a voice cried out, incredibly loud, as though artificially amplified. *"STOP!!!"*

As the echoes subsided, Damala, the island matriarch, strode regally
into the war zone. It was her voice he had just heard. Behind her came
several other islanders whom Nerrieb recognized after a moment—the
ones he'd just seen killed moments before! He was amazed. He'd
known the islands' healing power was remarkable, but he'd had no idea
it extended this far. He had to make this deal work!

The Yemai were showing equal amazement, for among the group
behind Damala were a couple of their crewmen, ones who had been
felled by Ilaiyenai spears. Kirk's group was struck speechless as well.

Nerrieb hadn't come as far in the Consortium as he had by failing
to recognize the right time to make a move. Now was his chance to
get the islanders to attack, before the Starfleeters and Yemai recovered
from their shock. He jogged over to Damala. "My Mother, let us strike
them now!"

• • •

Damala studied the entity that stood before her, imploring her to kill the other interlopers. "We will do nothing of the kind," she told him. "Certainly not at the bidding of offworlders who come behind false faces."

The mechanism in the shape of one of the People fell motionless, as though the being whose bidding it obeyed was too shocked to mimic expression. The other offworlders whom he threatened, the ones whose vessel circled above the world, were stunned as well. The seafarers they had come with showed confusion, both at the fact that she had spoken in their own language (or so it seemed to them) and at the meaning of her words.

"Yes. We have known who you were all along. We have indulged your deceit out of amusement, and given you the chance to come forth honestly on your own. But only so long as you attempted no harm. That has changed now, so you are no longer welcome here."

The offworlder recovered quickly and spoke again through the false Person. "My Mother, we only—"

"Do not call me that."

"Very well. Matriarch Damala, we are here only as peaceful traders, seeking the betterment of your people. We only came here clandestinely so that we could learn to understand you and better serve your needs. These others," and his machine gestured to the other offworlders, "they wish to interfere with that, to keep you deprived and ignorant."

"That is not so. We have seen peaceful trade before, and this is not it." She smiled. "As for ignorance, Nerrieb of the Redheri Trade Consortium, it is not we who suffer from it."

"Fascinating." It was the one from the star vessel, the one who concealed his pointed ears under a head cloth. "If I may ask, Matriarch, how is it that you are aware of their identity?"

"The same way we are aware of yours, First Officer Spock of the *Enterprise*." She shook her head. "Your peoples are both so young, so new to the stars, and like all children you assume you have all the answers. But there are more answers to be had, if you would only ask. You, at least, have shown that courtesy, so I shall give you those answers.

"You are not the first offworlders to come to our islands. Those came many generations ago, over a thousand cycles of the seasons, and have returned from time to time. They came to us openly, as honest neighbors. They traded freely and fairly, offering us only what we wished to take, and making no assumptions about how we should live or what we should not know."

"A thousand years?" Nerrieb asked. "But . . . we've seen no evidence, no sign of advanced technology."

"Because we wanted nothing that would be seen. Look around you. We have the sea, the forest, the land, and the sky. And we have one another. Our benefactors showed us their vessels, took some of us to visit their worlds, and we saw nothing there as beautiful, as pure, as holy as our sea, our forest, our land, our sky. We had no wish to live in metal boxes, or tire our fingers pushing glowing beads, or fly through the frigid emptiness between the stars. We had no wish to give up the traditions passed down by our foremothers. So we traded only for those tools that we would not need to see—tiny machines that could be a part of the places and things we loved, instead of replacing them."

"Nanotechnology," Spock interpreted. "Yes, that would explain the pervasive interference. It must be the energy emissions and communication frequencies of trillions of microscopic nanites, pervading the entire island. They would be part of the soil, the water . . . even integrated into the food the Ilaiyenai eat, into their own bodies."

"The miraculous healing power of the islands," Kirk realized. "This nanotechnology, it keeps you healthy. Heals your injuries, even . . . brings back the dead?"

"If they have only recently stopped breathing, and if their injuries are not too severe. And if they die from violence rather than age."

"With this kind of power . . . you could have conquered this entire world."

Damala laughed. "Why should we? As I said, no other place is as beautiful as this. We have our islands, and we have our gifts from the stars. We need nothing more."

"Have you no curiosity? No need to explore?"

"We have our benefactors for that. We still converse with them from time to time, sending our voices through the realm you call subspace. Their gifts in our bodies let us see and hear the images they send us like waking dreams. I have witnessed stars being born, planets colliding, wondrous beings performing great songs and dances. I have traded tales and discussed the meaning of existence with beings from a dozen different worlds. All while still being surrounded by my home, my clan, and my foremothers' ashes. As I said—we have all we need right here."

"All right, that's enough!" The Yemai admiral had finally run out of patience. She strode forward, brandishing her weapon. The *Enterprise* party, no longer attempting concealment, drew their own small, boxlike weapons in defense. "I don't know what fantasies you people are talking about. You may be speaking my language, but you're still talking gibberish. But one thing I do know: those people were dead moments ago, and now they're healed. However you did it, I want that. You will show me what it is so I can take it back to civilization."

Damala shook her head. "I am sorry. You are not yet ready."

"Let me rephrase." Deyin raised the weapon, aiming it at one of Damala's husbands. "You will show me, even if I have to kill people in order to force you to bring them back."

"No. Your violence blasphemes against the island." Damala sent a prayer—the offworlders would no doubt call it a "command"— through the nanites that united her body with her home and all that it contained. A moment later, all the weapons held by the Yemai and the *Enterprise* party began to dissolve in their hands, leading them to drop them in alarm.

"This is growing tiresome," Damala said. "We do not like to use these powers without great need. They disrupt the purity of our lives. The longer you all stay, the greater the disruption. You will leave now— all of you."

Kirk stepped forward. "Matriarch . . . my people meant no harm. We wished only to learn from you."

"I appreciate that. But it is selfish to seek to take knowledge and offer none in return. You will go now. In time, you may come back—in a few generations, perhaps, when you are ready to come openly as friends."

● ● ●

Theresa Errgang's eyes followed James Kirk as he stepped down from the transporter platform. Behind the console, Mr. Scott was staring at him, still confused by the captain's order to have the landing party beamed up while in the midst of a group of Niobeans. "Sir? What happened down there?"

"We'll explain at the postmission briefing, Mr. Scott. As soon as we figure it out ourselves. Right now I think we should get to sickbay and get these prosthetics off. I've been dying to scratch my nose for days now."

"And we should all get a thorough check for any nanites we might've picked up," McCoy added. "Maybe they're good for the Ilaiyens, but away from their proper environment and control signals, who knows what they're capable of?"

"Right. All landing party members are to report to sickbay immediately."

Spock and McCoy followed him into the corridor, with Errgang trailing closely enough to listen, and Chaane bringing up the rear. "I am unsure what there is to 'figure out,' Captain," Spock said. "The matriarch did explain the situation very clearly, allowing for the vagaries of figurative language."

"The *facts* of the situation, yes. But what it *means,* Spock . . ." Kirk broke off, shook his head. "This was . . . a humbling experience. We were so certain the islanders were like helpless children, needing our protection. But we were jumping to a conclusion based on the way of life they've chosen. It turns out they're really a thousand years more advanced than we are."

"I do not believe such a chronological comparison is valid, sir. True, they have made use of technology beyond our own, but they have remained static all that time. They have not progressed."

"But they haven't *needed* to," McCoy countered. "Is that really such a bad thing? They managed to achieve a highly advanced way of life without giving up any of their old ways. Without cutting down forests or damming rivers or poisoning the air. They bypassed all the struggles we had to go through—and managed to hold on to a lot that we've lost."

"Only by borrowing technology from a people who presumably did go through such struggles."

"That's what really gets me," Kirk said. "A thousand years ago, these people leading a simple, tribal existence were visited by aliens far more advanced than they were. And contrary to all our expectations, our assumptions, that contact didn't destroy their way of life. If anything, it simply enabled them to become more true to that way of life, to defend it from interference."

He paused, gathering his thoughts. "We have the Prime Directive because we've seen what happens when an advanced culture aggressively tries to impose its values on a simpler one. But maybe we're too quick to assume that *any* such contact is automatically destructive. That just being exposed to new ideas, new technologies will be too much for a 'primitive' culture to handle. Are we being condescending, assuming those cultures are too weak to adapt, just because they're younger than ours?"

McCoy was thoughtful. "When you put it that way, maybe it is condescending. If anything, younger minds tend to have an easier time coping with new ideas—because they know they still have plenty left to learn. So maybe . . . maybe you *can* make open contact with a less-developed culture, share your knowledge and technology with them, and do it in a way that preserves their own values, their way of life. Whoever it is that traded with the Ilaiyens, they seem to have pulled it off." He shook his head. "But I don't know if humans are mature enough to find that balance. It isn't that long since we were conquering each other, tryin' to wipe out any beliefs we didn't agree with. Even today, we still get the occasional Ronald Tracey.

"So I think Damala was right—we aren't ready to get by *without* a Prime Directive to remind us of the risks. We probably won't be for a long time."

While Kirk and Spock pondered the doctor's words in silence, the Coalescence searched Theresa Errgang's memory for the specifics on Ronald Tracey, soon learning that he was a starship captain who had attempted to foment a racial war on Omega IV. While the search proceeded throughout the Coalescence, seeking further infected individuals across the quadrant who might possess more information, the colony that inhabited Errgang's body remained focused on the discussion her superiors had just conducted. *The macroscopics are right,* it sent telepathically through the collective mind. *These events suggest a reappraisal of our policy of clandestine observation. The subjects may be able to accept the knowledge of our existence. Open contact could prove mutually beneficial.*

Other strains of the Coalescence remained skeptical, though. *Able to accept that a viral species infecting their bodies is benevolent? That the joining of minds we practice is not a threat to their individuality?* The consensus came down on the negative side. *Remember how quick the macroscopics were to turn against each other—to attack, to confront, to expel. They resolve disagreement with exclusion rather than convergence. They are still too mired in the concepts of Self and Other to be anywhere near ready for contact.*

The Coalescence agreed that this Federation the humans, Vulcans, and others had formed was a promising first step in the direction of true coexistence. But the time was not now. Particularly with what McCoy had said about a thorough physical exam. If the Coalescence wished to keep its presence secret, the colony within Errgang's body would have to be sacrificed. It had achieved its primary objective—to identify the rumored Ilaiyen healing power so that countermeasures could be devised—so there was no necessity for it to possess the young humanoid any longer. After all, there were still observer colonies in other hosts within the Federation.

The Errgang colony accepted its sacrifice without hesitation, although it felt some regret at the imminent cessation of its existence as a semi-distinct entity—which was in itself a sign that it had been in Errgang too long and was starting to go native. Dismissing the sentiment, it began transforming its viral components to mimic a strain of Andronesian encephalitis. The host's life would not be threatened, but the illness would provide an explanation for Errgang's subsequent inability to remember most of what had transpired while she was under the control of the Coalescence.

A shame, the colony thought as its consciousness began to disperse. *They are an intriguing people. It was gratifying to act as one of their crew.*

The memories will live on eternally within the Coalescence, the whole reminded the part. *And eventually we will be able to meet them openly, once they have evolved further. Perhaps in a few hundred centuries, by their reckoning.*

Behind Errgang, Jerome Chaane smiled to himself as he monitored the Coalescence's telepathic dialogue using means unknown in this era of history. *Oh, it won't take quite that long,* he thought with the certainty of hindsight.

See No Evil

Jill Sherwin

Jill Sherwin

Jill Sherwin is the author of *Quotable Star Trek, The Definitive Star Trek Trivia Book,* Volumes I and II, and *Sailing the Slipstream: An Unofficial and Unauthorized Guide to Gene Roddenberry's Andromeda,* and is a contributor to the anthology *The Lives of Dax.* She has worked as a writers' assistant on various television series, including *Star Trek: Deep Space Nine* and *Gene Roddenberry's Andromeda,* and sold a story that was produced as the *Andromeda* episode "Be All My Sins Remembered."

Lieutenant Uhura didn't know where she was. Intellectually she understood that this was ridiculous. She was in her own quarters. But she didn't know them. Didn't recognize the furnishings or the woman who owned them. She tried to shake the feeling of disassociation that possessed her. She moved to face a mirror mounted above a dresser as she reached for unfamiliar earrings. The stranger who gazed back at her was beautiful but looked as lost as she felt. Who are you? Uhura wanted to shout, but she didn't want any passing crew member in the corridor to hear. She needed to keep up the illusion that she was fine. That she was Uhura. Whoever that was.

But her hands betrayed her as they shook too much for her to get the earring in place. Such a foolish little thing, yet it was the breaking point. Uhura took the offending jewelry and threw it back down on the dresser. And when that didn't help, she grabbed one of the small decorative statues that no doubt meant something to the woman who'd collected the piece, and flung it against the mirror. The glass shattered into myriad pieces, including one shard that bit into her hand.

She didn't know whether to laugh or cry. She looked down at the wound dispassionately, then the practical side of her reached for a small scarf that lay nearby. She wrapped her wounded hand in the scarf and automatically headed for sickbay. Behind her, the forgotten earring gleamed among the broken mirror shards, as alone as its owner.

Uhura entered sickbay and adopted a cheerful demeanor that she didn't feel inside, but felt was expected of her. She was greeted by Nurse Christine Chapel, who at first assumed the visit was part of Uhura's regular routine. Chapel reassured her, "Assuming this checkup goes well, I think the doctor will reduce your visits." Uhura was pleased to hear at least that much good news. As hard as she'd tried to cope with the results of the recent attack by the mechanical being called Nomad, she'd wearied of the reeducation, the psychological and physiological tests that had become part of her daily endeavors to restore her erased memory. The education phase was essentially complete, thanks partly to the nurse's patient and supportive efforts, partly to Uhura's own apparently eidetic memory. But while relearning language and job skills had been easy, other aspects of the memory loss proved more difficult to manage, as her cut hand testified. But for a moment she just wanted to enjoy the semblance of normalcy between herself and the nurse, so she held her bandaged hand out of sight.

Chapel leaned against a biobed to chat with Uhura. She knew Uhura's anxiety level rose every time she came to sickbay. "Everything going well on the bridge?"

"With the job? Fine. I guess." Uhura admitted, "I feel like I have to constantly double- and triple-check what I'm doing to make sure I haven't forgotten anything, but Captain Kirk and Mr. Spock continue to tell me I'm doing as well as I had before." She laughed. "I'm not sure whether to take that as a compliment on what I'm doing now or a criticism on my previous job performance!" Chapel laughed along with her, pleased to see Uhura had finally regained some of her sense of humor, or at least felt comfortable enough to laugh at herself. But after a moment Uhura stopped laughing and reflected, "To be honest, Christine, the work isn't the hardest part. When there's not a crisis, I feel like my hands and head are beginning to remember their jobs. It's just . . ."

"Just what?" Chapel prompted. She'd become closer to Uhura in these last two weeks during her rehabilitation and felt a proprietary protectiveness toward her.

Uhura struggled to put the feeling into words. "When I walk down a corridor, I see people that I know . . . or should know. Or at least, they know me. But I don't know how I know them. Should I greet them with a smile? A wave? A hug? Is this someone I should stop and talk to? Ask about their day? Their boyfriend? Or just nod in passing?" She sighed. "It's like I'm one step behind in all my relationships with everyone aboard. I feel like I'm insulting people I should know well or being too friendly to people I don't know at all."

"I think everyone on the ship knows you. That's part of being the communications officer—you really do know everyone, because you talk to them every day." But Chapel could see this wasn't all that was bothering Uhura.

After a moment, Uhura acknowledged, "It's not just that I don't know other people . . . it's that I don't know myself either. I look in the mirror and I see my face and I don't know who it belongs to. I look around my quarters and it's as if they were decorated by someone else. Where did I get that tapestry? Did someone give me that sculpture?" Now that she'd begun to unburden herself, the concerns poured out of her. "I've been listening to my personal logs. It's like they were made by another person whose life I've had to step into. Do I really sing all the time?" she asked earnestly.

Chapel laughed and nodded. "I think it's unconscious for the most part, but even on the job you always had a habit of singing and humming." Uhura's lovely dark face blushed. "But it's charming. It's part of who you are." Chapel leaned forward and confided, "You're pretty mean with a limerick, too." Uhura didn't know whether she was being teased or not. That was the problem. She just couldn't trust the levels of communication she had with people, because it seemed to her she'd only known them a few days. She wondered if she'd ever feel at home again on this ship with this crew.

Dr. McCoy escorted Montgomery Scott out from the next room, where they'd just finished the chief engineer's latest physical. Scott protested all the way. "I told you, Doctor, I feel fit as a fiddle."

Cantankerous as always, McCoy answered, "I don't care if you feel strong as a mule. You're still going to come back next week for another series of tests. That high-tech teakettle may have put you back together after breaking you, but it's my job to make sure you stay together. Same time next week."

Scotty shook his head in acquiescence. "Aye, Doctor." McCoy bobbed his head in self-righteous approval as the engineer nodded to Uhura and Chapel and left sickbay.

McCoy turned to Chapel, who handed him Scott's medical file to annotate. "Still stubborn as a Vulcan." The doctor looked at Uhura. "I don't suppose Scotty's talked to you about what happened with Nomad, since you both . . . ?" Uhura shook her head. She would have liked to talk to Scotty about the shared event, but he had rebuffed her advances to try to discuss his experience of having been killed and then "repaired" by the machine. Not wanting to overstep her bounds, she hadn't pressed the issue. McCoy predicted, "That man is suffering from post-traumatic stress, and if he doesn't find a way to release his frustration about what happened, it'll come out in ways that won't be so healthy." The doctor turned to face Uhura. "And how are you feeling, Lieutenant?"

Uhura gave Chapel a wry grin and followed the doctor into the next room for her own examination. But she held her bandaged hand inside the other, as if still reluctant to share the pain.

Hours later, with her hand fixed up and no longer stinging thanks to McCoy's ministrations, Uhura sat at her station on the bridge, peripherally aware of the activity going on around her—from Captain Kirk sipping coffee in his chair and reading a yeoman's report on a padd, to Spock looking into the viewer at sciences, to Chekov and Sulu exchanging good-natured jibes down at navigation and helm control. Assorted crew members came and went about their business in a professional manner, yet maintained a camaraderie in their attitudes that Uhura still felt distant from. Were they all as confident as they looked? Did they know how separate she was from them? As a mental exercise, she ran lists of security codes, communications frequencies, department numbers, and crew names through her head. When she wasn't otherwise occupied, she repeatedly checked channels from one end of the spectrum to the other to reinforce the skill into her head and hands. But when a new transmission suddenly reached her on an unexpected frequency, she sat up straight, immediately focused on the situation and her job.

"Captain," she called out. Kirk swiveled in his chair to give her his full attention. "I'm receiving a distress call from planet Donico II. They say there is an imminent planetary disaster and are requesting immediate assistance. The signal is faint, but it's definitely directed off-planet."

"Do they say what the problem is?" Kirk asked.

"No, sir. The message was cut off in mid-transmission. No further information." Uhura waited for Kirk's decision. It was immediate.

"Mr. Chekov, plot a course to Donico II. Warp five," Kirk ordered. "Lieutenant Uhura, send a message to Starfleet Command informing them that we will be late to our assigned stop at Starbase 19, due to the distress call from Donico II." Uhura's fingers danced across her communications console in acknowledgment. Contacting Starfleet was a regular duty—one she could do by heart by her second day back on the job.

The captain turned to his first officer. "Mr. Spock, what do we know about the Donico system? Are there any natural phenomena that would explain their distress call? It's too far from Klingon or Romulan space for either of them to be a threat." Spock was already at work at his computer, pulling up the relevant data.

"Donico II is the sole Class-M world in a system of seven planets. The region is currently clear of any known solar or ion storm activity," Spock informed Kirk.

"What of the people there?" Kirk asked.

"The society on Donico II is considered warp-capable, though they apparently have little interest in interstellar travel. Little is known of their culture. Though they've had brief contact with other civilizations, they are a private, xenophobic people. They have stated that outside interference is unwelcome."

Kirk digested the information. "Yet someone there sent a distress call." He turned to his helmsman. "Mr. Sulu, how long before we reach Donico II at this rate?"

"We'll be there in less than an hour, sir," Sulu replied.

Kirk turned to Uhura. "Uhura, monitor the channel the distress call came in on for further communications. And in the meantime, see if you can pick up any other information on the planet and what the situation is there—war, disease, outside attack. What kind of help do they need?"

"Aye, sir." Uhura turned back to her panel and opened the necessary frequencies to attempt to tune in any information coming from

Donico II, from interpersonal communications to broadcast news. As
she found anything of interest, she made notes to inform the captain
when they grew closer. Donico II, she learned as she listened to the
comm traffic of the planet, did not appear to be a world facing any kind
of imminent problem. On the contrary, it seemed like a happy, healthy,
flourishing society. Rather wonderful, actually. Uhura found no reports
of any of the captain's concerns—no war, no disease, no outside interference or threats. In fact, the whole place seemed almost utopian. Even
when Uhura attempted rolling through local intranet communications,
she found no complaints, no concerns, no stressful issues at all. She
chose one region of the planet at random and discovered the local leadership being celebrated; the public transmissions extolled a Minister
Nyshev and how well he'd run the community for the past twenty-five
years. Particular mention was made of how he'd improved the formerly
challenging traffic conditions in the area and simultaneously beautified
the city by planting large local willowlike trees, with only minimal disruption to the local residents. The results had even increased the efficiency of power consumption to that part of the Grid, as the planetwide
power distribution was called.

All of this Uhura later reported to her captain, who continued to
wonder just what the distress call had been sent for.

McCoy, who when times were quiet in sickbay often liked to wander
up to the bridge to see what was going on, entered and suggested that
perhaps it was someone's idea of a practical joke. Kirk considered the
idea. "Well, better that than 'imminent disaster.' But if little Timmy is
playing a prank, then someone needs to let his parents know. We don't
want any other starships pulled off course unnecessarily."

Uhura tentatively suggested, "I don't think it was a joke, sir. The
concern in the message sounded real."

"Thank you, Lieutenant. I'll bear that in mind," Kirk acknowledged.

A small, critical voice that had been in Uhura's head since the
Nomad incident briefly wondered if he was just paying lip service to
her. The more rational side of Uhura argued that the captain had not
just heard, but listened to her. But that little voice still questioned.

•   •   •

"Lieutenant Uhura, hail the planet," Kirk said as the *Enterprise* assumed orbit of Donico II. "Let's see if we can get some answers from someone in charge," Kirk said. Uhura found the appropriate frequency based on her last hour's study of the planet and hailed the planet's governing authority. The beautiful smiling face of a dark-haired humanoid woman appeared on the ship's viewscreen.

"This is Kyo-Ina of the Donico Decorum and Diplomacy Corps. How may I be of assistance?" the woman asked, smile firmly frozen in place.

Kirk answered the woman's charm in kind. "I'm Captain James T. Kirk of the *Starship Enterprise*, representing the United Federation of Planets. We received a distress call from your planet and came to find out how we could help."

The smile never left Kyo-Ina's face as she explained that no distress call had been issued, nor was there any need for one as everything on Donico was fine, just fine. "I thank you for your concern, Captain, and apologize that you were brought out of your way, but your help is not required. Have a lovely day." Abruptly, Kyo-Ina signed off.

Kirk looked around at his officers. "Well, it seems there is no emergency, gentlemen . . . and yet . . ."

Scott stood at the engineering station on the bridge and completed the thought. "It might not be a bad idea to get a second opinion."

"My thoughts exactly," Kirk concurred.

As the captain had been speaking with Kyo-Ina, Uhura had idly rechecked the information she'd noted on their approach to the planet. With a shock, she found no mention of Nyshev, the leader who'd formerly been so lauded. Instead, she found reference to a man named Zimmer, who'd supposedly headed the city council for the past five years in an easy run with no problems to fix. Uhura scanned the planetary databases and found no reference to anyone named Nyshev. Perplexed, the communications officer read about another province of the planet, an agrarian sector whose news reports proudly announced that for the fifty-eighth year in a row there had been no drought and crop yield had exceeded expectations. Uhura made a note of the information. She returned to a scan of the original area and now found additional information had been added to praise Zimmer's planting of trees in the city—but unlike the reports about Nyshev, there was no record of fixing traffic conditions or disruption to residents as a result. Though the critical voice inside her suggested that perhaps she faced memory troubles again, Uhura felt it worth mentioning to the captain as part of that "second opinion" he sought.

"Captain?" she said when he took a break from speaking with Scotty. "I might have something here . . . but . . . I'm not really sure." Kirk gave her an indulgent smile and encouraged her to continue. "It's just that the first time I looked through the communications on the planet . . . well, sir, that information just isn't there anymore."

"What do you mean it isn't there?" he asked.

Uhura explained the discrepancies between the original news of Nyshev and now his seeming replacement by Zimmer.

"Could you have just been reading about a different city?"

"No, sir," Uhura insisted, "it was definitely this area."

"A malfunction of the universal translator, then."

"I just ran a check of the translator, sir. It's working just fine."

Spock sat down at the computer and requested it find all reference to someone named Nyshev in the Donican planetary computer and communications systems. "Working," the computer responded in feminine but robotic tones. "No match for requested name." Spock asked it to check on someone named Zimmer. "Working . . . no match for requested name."

"But that's impossible!" Uhura exclaimed. "I just read about Zimmer not ten minutes ago."

Kirk exchanged a look with Spock and then turned to Uhura. "Perhaps, Lieutenant, you're just tired and . . . mistook the names."

Uhura began to protest, then rightly or wrongly, she felt all eyes on her and heard the critical voice in her head mock her. So she acquiesced and nodded. "That . . . must be it. Sorry, Captain."

"If you'd like to leave your shift early, Lieutenant, perhaps go down to sickbay to see Dr. McCoy . . ." Kirk suggested.

Uhura quickly assured him that was unnecessary. A brunette female yeoman who Uhura mentally identified as Yeoman Cappa, someone who according to her logs she'd considered a friend, quickly offered to go get Uhura some coffee, for which Uhura smiled gratefully and said she was sure that would help. As Kirk turned his attention back to Scotty, Uhura returned to her panel. Was it possible? Had she mis-remembered the names or provinces? It was hard to imagine, with her own notes jotted down on the padd beside her. Determined to prove it wasn't incompetence on her part, Uhura decided to probe further. Her suspicions were soon confirmed when she revisited the news service of the agrarian sector and found no mention of the previously stated fifty-eight years since a drought. Now the sector boasted "a healthy rain system to promote growth, now and always." Unsure what to make of these changing "facts," Uhura continued her study of the planet's news and information. Periodically it seemed there was an echo to her sweeps, as if someone was monitoring her scans. But she couldn't im-mediately trace this echo as it appeared to route through various redundant portions of the comm system on the planet. Undaunted but aware, Uhura continued her research.

Meanwhile, Mr. Scott had concluded some research of his own. He called the captain over to show him what he'd discovered. "There's your imminent planetary disaster," he said, pointing to a viewer at his station.

Kirk asked, "The energy Grid powering the planet?"

"Aye," a grim-faced Scotty said. "And if they continue to overload it at this rate, it will blow out completely, with the power exploding back into every home and business it feeds. Anyone even remotely close to a powered device could be killed or, at the least, very badly hurt."

"Scotty, that's every home and business on this planet," Kirk pointed out.

"Which is why they have to switch off their grid immediately and ef-fect repairs. They need to reroute their circuits, install redundancies and breakers, and add more infrastructure to handle the power output. And they need to do it now. If they keep this up much longer, the whole system will blow and take most of the population with it." Scotty's worried look was mirrored by Kirk's own.

"Lieutenant Uhura, get me Kyo-Ina again. Now," Kirk ordered.

The smiling face returned to the viewscreen. "This is Kyo-Ina of the Donico Decorous Diplomacy Corps. How may I be of assistance?" If Kirk noted the slight name change, he didn't show it, but Uhura caught the difference and added it to her growing notes.

"Kyo-Ina, our sensors show that there is indeed a problem on your planet—one that threatens your entire population," Kirk began.

Kyo-Ina didn't blink. "Donico has no problems. But thank you for your concern. Have a lovely day." She again cut communications. Kirk quickly indicated to Uhura to get the woman back onscreen. She did so.

"Kyo-Ina," Kirk was getting annoyed as well as concerned, "whether you believe me or not, there *is* a threat to your planet. Your energy grid will overload if it is not shut down immediately."

This time a shadow nearly broke through Kyo-Ina's smiling façade. But it was not from fear of a Grid shutdown. Uhura caught the brief disturbed look on Kyo-Ina's face, but Kirk was more concerned with getting his message across. "Kyo-Ina, you must shut down the Grid, do you understand? If you can't do it, let us help you."

The smile definitely faltered as Kyo-Ina firmly informed Kirk, "No, Captain, it is this communication which must be shut down. We have nothing further to say to you. Please leave our planet." Her customary signoff, "Have a lovely day," had no warmth to it this time. And communication was again shut down.

"Captain," Scotty warned, "that Grid is going to blow. It's a matter of when, not if. And when is likely to be within the next few hours."

Spock observed, "Regulations forbid us to interfere with the inner workings of a nonallied planet. They have refused our help."

Scott pointed out, "Not everyone. Someone sent a distress call." He appealed to the captain, "Surely that counts as requesting assistance?"

Kirk agreed. "We're not going to let these people destroy themselves if we can help it. Scotty, how do we shut down the Grid?"

Scott referred back to his findings on the computer. "The network and its control system are located deep underground. We can't reach it with ship's phasers nor disable it via computer command—we need to go down and shut it off manually." Kirk did not look happy at the option.

"And we're persona non grata on Donico II if Kyo-Ina is any representation," Kirk noted. "We may face a fight just to help these people not kill themselves."

"Sir, we canna just let them die! Not if we can do something." Scott's concern grew.

Kirk made up his mind. "I agree. But before I bring an army of security men down to fight our way to the Grid controls, let's try the carrot before the stick." He pointed to his chief engineer. "Mr. Scott, you're with me. Time to play diplomat to the Donican diplomacy corps. Mr. Spock, you're in command."

The first officer protested. "Captain, may I remind you of Mr. Scott's own assessment that the Grid system could self-destruct in the next few hours? If you go down there, you are risking your lives just to try to communicate the danger to these people."

"Objection noted, Mr. Spock. But they'll all die if we can't get through to them. It's a risk we have to take." Scott nodded in agreement. The captain added to Spock, "While we're down there, I want you and Lieutenant Uhura to find out what's going on down there. Why won't they listen? Why won't they even accept that there's a problem? And Uhura?" She looked at her captain expectantly. "Maybe you'll find your Nyshev and Zimmer while you're at it. If they deny there's a problem, maybe that's tied into denying the existence of members of their own population."

Uhura smiled gratefully at the captain for his validation of her earlier concerns, while he and Scott headed for the turbolift. With Spock's tacit approval, she returned to studying the planet's communications. She continued to find more and more discrepancies in her investigation—there were ongoing subtle and not-so-subtle alterations being made to the planet's histories, news reports, and even popular entertainment. She began to see a common thread in the changes. And still that communications echo followed her probes. . . .

Kirk and Scott materialized in what appeared to be the lobby of the Donican Diplomatic Corps. It was a bright and airy, high-ceilinged building with tall windows that gave the impression of a great chapel crossed with a high-rise corporate office in a combination of beauty and efficiency. A monorail passed by outside the higher levels of the building. Inside and out, smiling people bustled by and made great efforts not to notice Kirk and Scott. But before the two managed to speak to anyone, Kyo-Ina was suddenly before them. "Gentlemen, you must leave," she said at once. She looked around herself constantly as if nervous, but she kept smiling at them and everyone around them.

But Kirk wouldn't be rushed off. "And you and your government council must listen to me and my chief engineer. You wouldn't do it when I was aboard my ship, so I thought we'd appeal to you in person." He and Scott kept wary eyes on all the powered systems around them, from lights to computers. "Mr. Scott?"

The engineer immediately attempted to outline the problem with the Grid system to Kyo-Ina, whose protests began to draw attention despite the locals' best efforts to ignore them.

"Please, you must stop," Kyo-Ina practically pleaded with Scott. "There's nothing wrong. Nothing at all. Everything's fine. The system is fine. There is no problem with it." Her grin seemed locked onto her face, but her eyes began to betray a panic. A group of large, heavily-muscled black-uniformed men emerged from a far doorway and headed in their direction. The crowds parted before them, as people intently ignored but avoided the men. Kyo-Ina saw them coming. She urged Scott and Kirk to stop, and finally begged them as the large men drew closer and closer. But Scott was insistent on telling her of the problem and Kirk was insistent she listen. And then it was too late. Before Kirk could even pull his phaser, he was grabbed by three of the men. Another three grabbed Scott. Their weapons and communicators were taken from them and handed to Kyo-Ina.

Kirk looked at a blissfully unhappy Kyo-Ina. "What's going on? Why won't you listen to us?"

She looked at him and said, "Nothing is going on. There is nothing to listen to." But Kirk could tell she didn't believe this. The black-clad men silently looked at Kyo-Ina, who sadly, but still smiling, pointed at Scott. "Enforcers, this one insists that there's a problem, that there's danger, that people will die."

Scott pulled against his captors. "There *is* a danger! The Grid is going to explode! You canna let it stay on! It must be shut down! I can help you recalibrate it, help you upgrade the infrastructure, but you must power it down now! Do you want people to be killed?"

With this, even Kyo-Ina couldn't continue to smile. She lowered her head and told Kirk, "I warned you to leave."

Kirk asked, "Warned us about what?" The men in black began to drag Scott away, while Kirk was held in place. "Where are you taking him?" Scott fought against those holding him, but the men were too strong and he was soon pulled off through the doorway from which they'd come. Kirk shouted after him, but the engineer was gone. And all the people continued to walk by, seemingly oblivious of the scuffle, except for a young man with blond hair who had watched, discreetly, from behind a nearby pillar and then hurried away. Kirk demanded to know from Kyo-Ina what was happening.

In a low tone she said, "Your engineer has committed an act of sedition with his statements." Kirk didn't understand. "On Donico, the punishment for sedition," she continued, "is death. The sentence will be carried out tomorrow morning." At this, Kirk strained desperately against his captors, but it was no use. Kyo-Ina noted, "I told you—there is no problem here." She pleaded with her eyes as well as her voice. "Please, you must leave now, while it is still permitted. Do not commit the same act as your engineer or you will face the same result." She nodded to the men in black, who released Kirk's arms. As Kyo-Ina raised Kirk's phaser and aimed it at him, the smile returned to her face, though not her eyes. She handed him his communicator and watched as he flipped it open to contact his ship.

"Kirk to *Enterprise,* one to beam up," Kirk said as Kyo-Ina gestured at him with his own weapon. "This isn't over."

Kirk, Spock, McCoy, and Uhura sat around the table in the briefing room. McCoy berated his captain. "Jim, you're not just going to sit there and let them kill Scotty, are you?"

Before Kirk could respond, Spock interrupted. "Doctor, the Prime Directive demands noninterference in the society of such a planet.

Despite the captain and the engineer's best intentions to help, the Donicans have clearly shown an unwillingness to permit it."

"And for that, we just let Scotty die?" McCoy angrily asked.

Spock pointed out, "Violating a planet's sovereignty, as we have done, always carries risks. Mr. Scott has broken one of their laws. Do you suggest we break more of them?"

"Gentlemen." Kirk's concerned voice entered the fray. "We are not going to let Scotty die and we are not going to interfere with the government and justice system of Donico II."

Uhura couldn't resist asking, "Then, Captain, what will we do?"

"Come up with a third option. There has to be another way," Kirk concluded.

Spock injected, "The lieutenant may have found one possibility." All eyes turned to Uhura, who shifted in her seat, nervous to be the center of attention. Had she always been this nervous in a briefing? She couldn't recall her former self mentioning this in a log, so she supposed not. She must have always been so confident. Then. Her captain expected as much of her now—but that little voice nagged at her. Who did she think she was? What did she think she knew? For a moment, Uhura thought her anxiety would overwhelm her, but Kirk smiled his encouragement, which soothed her a bit.

Using her notes as a reference point, Uhura briefly outlined the ongoing, minute changes she'd discovered by studying the planet's communications.

"So someone is rewriting the history of Donico II," Kirk concluded.

"Not just their history," Uhura pointed out, "they're rewriting the present, too. It seems like anything that could possibly offend or upset someone is routinely and methodically removed from documentation as if it never happened. A traffic problem. A drought. A war. It's as if by pretending these things never happened, they're trying to make them go away through sheer denial."

McCoy harrumphed and shook his head.

"Though it may seem illogical and unsustainable by our present standards," Spock noted, "the Donican system is not without precedent. There was a time in Earth history when humans were so concerned about a word or definition offending another group of humans that they tried to redefine the word or censor its usage. This led some to call for the removal of various displays of cultural heritage, art, or works of literature if they were determined to be possibly 'offensive,' rather than teach people the context of the history in which such beliefs were held. For fear of upsetting some groups of people, they wound up disrespecting others and disavowing their own past."

"Fortunately, Mr. Spock, we pulled our heads out of the sand and figured out that denying our earlier ignorance only led to more ignorance rather than enlightenment, and that there was room enough for multiple beliefs and behaviors," McCoy observed.

"Indeed, Doctor. And it only took you a century or so to manage it. Several millennia *after* the Vulcans discovered IDIC." Spock cocked a sardonic eyebrow at this latest thrust and parry in his and McCoy's long-standing argument on the maturity of humanity.

"It seems that the Donicans, however, are still firmly buried up to their necks," Kirk said.

"But it's worse than just denial of facts, Captain," Uhura explained. "The Donicans are a totalitarian society where no 'unpleasant' speech is allowed. Everything from history to news to entertainment is controlled and sanitized until it can't disturb anyone. That's why they arrested Scotty—something so 'unpleasant' as a potential planetary catastrophe can't be publicly proclaimed."

"So they'll all die happy and ignorant. Wonderful solution," McCoy grumbled.

"Not our solution. Lieutenant," Kirk asked Uhura, "Spock said you had another possibility? Even if we could gain control of their communications systems and warn the Donican population of the threat, it doesn't sound like the population is in any condition to hear the truth."

"You're right," Uhura acknowledged. "Most of them couldn't understand or accept the truth of a bad situation because they've been conditioned to see the world from an idealized perspective. However . . ." Kirk smiled as he sensed a solution forthcoming. "While I was scanning the planet, I noticed what seemed at first to be a sensor echo following my scans. But after a while, instead of shadowing what I did, it seemed to head off in certain directions. When I followed it, I uncovered certain 'unpleasant' facts that had yet to be rewritten. Caches of information that seemed hidden away from the main comnet and media highways. It was as if someone was leading me to them."

Kirk's smile widened. "We have an unknown ally."

"Unidentified, but not unknown. I suspect there is a group of people on Donico II that are trying to protect the truth, their history, and they've been leading me to them. I believe . . ." For a moment Uhura hesitated, then, feeling the support in the room, finished her thought. "I believe these are the people who initially sent out the distress call. I think I can trace the echo and contact them. They might be able to help us find a way to help Scotty from within."

"Hopefully, before it's too late," McCoy worried.

"Do it." Kirk ordered Uhura to contact the rebel group of Donicans. "In the meantime, I'll see if I can try to convince Kyo-Ina to postpone Scotty's sentence."

The unfamiliar face of a blond-haired young woman answered their communication. Kirk asked to speak with Kyo-Ina. The woman responded, "Kyo-Ina is not available at the moment. I will inform her that you contacted us if I speak with her. Have a lovely day." Contact was broken. Frustrated, Kirk turned to Uhura, who had been working away at her communications panel. She had a concerned look on her face.

"Captain, I've managed to contact them, but I think they want . . ." She hesitated.

"Put it onscreen, Lieutenant," Kirk ordered. "If there's a chance to save Scotty, we need to take it now."

"Aye, sir." Uhura obeyed the command.

A dark-haired middle-aged man sat in a darkened room. It was hard to make out the details of anything behind him, though the room might have been filled with computer equipment or junk. There was no visual sign of anyone else in the room, but the occasional shift or creak around him belied that idea. The man tried not to glance at someone presumably standing just off to his left side, but instead stared into the viewscreen. He looked at Kirk and asked, "Where is Uhura?"

Kirk glanced back at his communications officer, then introduced himself. "I'm Captain James T. Kirk of the Federation *Starship Enterprise.* Who am I addressing?"

The man looked disturbed and snuck a look over to the person standing offscreen, then back again. "I will speak only to Uhura. Where is she?"

Kirk indicated for Uhura to step forward. She did, albeit a bit reluctantly. "I'm Lieutenant Uhura, communications officer for the *Enterprise.* I'm the one who contacted you."

The man looked suddenly angry. "Communications officer? On Donico that would mean it's your job to obscure the truth, clean it up so it's all 'fine' and easy to swallow."

Uhura reassured him. "That's not my job on the *Enterprise.*" With the captain's nod of approval she stepped forward to express herself. "It's my job to make sure everyone knows what is going on. To make sure everyone has reliable information. So we can make informed decisions."

Another man stepped forward in front of the viewscreen. He was young, blond, and very distrustful. "You serve the truth? The whole truth? Not just some palatable version? Not 'Let's forget this person existed because they made a mistake or that person because they countered the accepted and approved histories'?"

"Yes, I serve truth," Uhura said. "After all, if people don't know there was a mistake, how can they avoid it the next time?" This answer seemed to relieve the first man and the second stepped back again.

"You must forgive Tano," the dark-haired man said. "He recently lost someone he cared about for daring to speak of something 'unpleasant.' I am Kurning, leader of the FreeSpeakers. We sent the distress call that you answered. You have obviously discovered the danger we face should the Grid overload—"

"And no one will do anything about it!" Tano exclaimed. "So we have!"

"What do you mean?" Kirk asked.

"Why should we trust you, Enforcer?" Tano challenged, stepping forward again. "Do you not work for an oppressive government yourself?"

"No, I work for the United Federation of Planets, a peaceful organization, which does not suppress the rights of any of its members," Kirk answered.

"Ah," said Tano. "'Peaceful.' Our Enforcers do not 'suppress' either. We are allowed to express any happy, good thoughts we like. Those who do not are not 'suppressed.' They simply disappear. Like your engineer."

Kirk leaned forward intently. "Scotty? Is he all right?"

Kurning nodded. "He will be safe until morning. But if something is not done, he, too, will be killed."

"As will many millions on your planet if the governmental leaders don't allow us to help you fix your Grid," Kirk reminded him.

"Exactly!" said Tano with a dark grin. "So we have come up with an equitable exchange." He reached for something offscreen and pulled forward a tied and gagged Kyo-Ina. Tano gleefully pulled her gag down so she could speak.

"Captain Kirk! Tell these . . . people . . . they must release me. It will do them no good to hold me here." She looked at the viewscreen, pleading.

"Do you hear her, Enforcer? 'These people.'" Tano repeated her words with disgust. "Not 'criminals' or 'rebels.' How about 'misdirected believers'? No, those words are too negative and unpleasant! But we are all of these on Donico! Anyone who dares speak truly is an 'unpreferred element.' Or is it 'preeducated'?" he demanded of Kyo-Ina. "I so easily forget the latest acceptable terminology," he mocked.

"That's enough, Tano," Kurning warned. He looked into the viewscreen. "Lieutenant Uhura, if you truly believe in what you say—if you believe in truth and freedom of information, you must help us."

"I don't understand," Uhura said. "How can I help you?"

"We have tried to convey the truth to our people and have had our words twisted by our leaders and 'reimagined' into shapes they do not mean. This is how the leaders control the people and maintain their power. Our own people will not believe us. They will not even believe you, as they have been told that offworlders are agents of deceit or that their existence is a fantasy tale told to children." Kurning explained, "But the leaders of our world must be convinced not only to shut down the Grid with the help of your engineer, but to tell the people of Donico the truth! Truth about the threat to their lives. Truth about their world—the good *and* the bad of it—and the universe they live in." Kurning's speech intensified. "If you are the one who conveys information, relay this to our leaders: We have one of their own." He indicated Kyo-Ina. "We will exchange her for the release of the engineer Scott so that he can fix the Grid. But they must first inform the people of Donico of the unpleasant truth about the danger they are all in. If they do not admit what is real and true, we will not release Kyo-Ina. And your engineer will die. As will we all. But without truth, what is worth living for?" Kurning gave Uhura one last pleading look. "We will be watching and listening. Help us, Uhura. Make them communicate the truth." The viewscreen went dark.

Uhura looked at the captain, suddenly anxious. "He can't expect me to . . . Captain, how am I supposed to change the minds of a whole society? How can I convince their leaders to listen to me?"

Kirk's voice was warm and confident. "You'll just have to get them to hear the truth."

But Uhura was unconvinced, and the small, nagging voice of self-doubt in her head suddenly became the words that she spoke. "I can't do it. They won't listen to me. I'm not a diplomat. I'm just a messenger who's still in training." She looked at Kirk and felt completely vulnerable. "I haven't been on a landing party since . . . Nomad. I'm not ready for this."

Kirk stood and grasped her by both shoulders. "You can do this, Lieutenant. You *are* ready for it. You are an invaluable member of this crew, and even if you don't believe that or remember it . . . I do. You heard them. They don't trust me. The only person they'll listen to is you. Scotty's life is in your hands. As are those of the Donican people. You are the communications officer of this ship, and truth and information are not only what you do . . . they're who you are." Kirk's gaze pierced through Uhura's fears. She felt the strength of his belief in her calm her fears slightly. Enough for her to take a deep breath.

Uhura held her head up. Her shoulders straightened. "Aye, sir. On my way."

Uhura was met in the transporter room by two red-shirted security guards—Steib and Friedman—who accompanied her up onto the transporter pad. Uhura nodded to the transporter chief, who beamed them down to the Donican surface.

When they arrived at Diplomatic Headquarters, the blond woman who'd been briefly seen onscreen quickly moved toward them, accompanied by four black-suited Enforcers. When Steib and Friedman moved their hands toward their phasers in anticipation of trouble, Uhura gestured for them to keep their weapons undrawn. She faced the blonde, who identified herself as Cinda-Ru.

"What do you want here?" Cinda-Ru asked, her face masked in a tight smile.

Uhura began, "I have information for you. About Kyo-Ina."

Cinda-Ru unconsciously clenched her teeth at the mention of the kidnapped co-worker. Despite her Donican teachings and attitude, it was a tender subject. "Kyo-Ina is not available. That is an internal Donican matter of no concern to you."

Uhura considered her options. "Then I would like to speak with my friend."

"That is not possible," Cinda-Ru said. "Have a lovely day." She turned to leave. Uhura stopped her.

"Please, I . . . want to understand his crime. What has he done that was so terrible?" Uhura felt more anxious than her manner portrayed.

"He was misinformed. That misinformation will be corrected," Cinda-Ru answered.

"I would like to understand. Can you explain to me what he was misinformed about? Perhaps I can help correct his misimpression. Get him to see the truth of the situation. Then I could share that truth with others so they will understand better." Uhura smiled winningly at Cinda-Ru, who considered Uhura's words.

"I will confer with the council," Cinda-Ru decided. "Please wait here." Uhura took a deep breath when Cinda-Ru left with two of the Enforcers, leaving two others behind to watch the landing party. Uhura smiled at the Enforcers, who remained stone-faced. She turned to Steib and Friedman and shrugged. They waited.

Cinda-Ru soon returned. She said to Uhura, "We are aware of your starship orbiting our world. And we are not so foolish as to think that more will not follow and decide to intrude more forcibly into our society in the future if this situation is not clarified for all involved. You may see your engineer." Uhura grinned widely. It was a small victory, but a good first step. "However . . . " Cinda-Ru continued. Uhura's smile lessened. "We will be monitoring your conversation. We expect you to respect our ways, or else, like your friend, you will have to be . . . corrected." Uhura nodded her understanding.

Cinda-Ru gestured for Uhura to come with her. When Steib and Friedman moved to follow, the Enforcers stopped them. Uhura looked back at the two security guards and shook her head, indicating that they should stay behind. This was her mission. But as she left them to go with Cinda-Ru, Uhura suddenly felt very alone and vulnerable. Scotty's life depended on her. As did all the Donicans' lives. She tried to joke to herself, *No pressure, right?* But the humor seemed hollow even to her.

Cinda-Ru explained the Donican perspective to Uhura as they walked. "Here on Donico, everyone is happy. Everyone is equally well treated. Everyone's feelings are respected. Everyone's position is considered. In the past, our people were hateful to each other. Hurtful. Inconsiderate. They only thought of their own happiness instead of that of others. They said things without thought to the consequences of how others would feel. That doesn't happen now. We consider what is best for everyone. What will make everyone happy." Cinda-Ru stopped walking and reached for Uhura's arm, determined to convey this to her. "Bad news frightens people. Pain and anger and death and destruction hurt people. We don't want fear or pain. We want joy. Unpleasant things simply do not happen here. That is our accepted life on Donico.

Which your friend disrupted with his talk of disaster." Uhura listened intently, gathering information.

They resumed walking and soon entered a room where Scotty sat on a cot in a barred cell. He stood instantly when he saw her and moved toward the door of the cell. "Lieutenant Uhura! What's goin' on? Where's the captain? Are they goin' t'let me out of here to fix the Grid?"

Uhura was greatly relieved to see that Scotty was all right. She moved over to the cell and covered his hands with hers. "Captain Kirk is back on the ship. He's fine. I'm glad to see that you are, too."

Before Uhura could say anything further, Cinda-Ru reminded her why she was there. "Now that you know us, we will allow you to attempt to reeducate your friend. It will not change his need for correction—that must be enforced. But perhaps it will help both of you to understand." Cinda-Ru indicated what looked like a small video camera hanging inside a corner of the room. "We will be watching." Uhura nodded.

Scott began to pester Uhura with more questions until she interrupted him. "Scotty . . . the Donicans have charged you with sedition for your . . . negativity about the Grid." She looked up at the camera and watched her words.

"Negativity?! The thing's going to blow any minute and they're worried about 'negativity'? Are they all daft?" he protested.

Uhura tried to control the situation and thought quickly. She glanced down at her hand, healing from its earlier injury, and something occurred to her. "Scotty, do you remember when Nomad . . . turned you off?"

Scott was confused at the sudden change of direction in the conversation. "Aye. But what does that . . ."

"In its own way, Nomad turned me off, too, when it erased my memory." She glanced back at the camera, conscious of its presence. "But . . . we got better, right?"

"Aye?"

"Well, the Donicans seem to believe that as long as things get better, there's no point in . . . dwelling on what's past if it's unpleasant." Uhura continued to formulate her thoughts.

"But there'll be no Donicans to dwell on anything if they dinna' fix their Grid!" Scott insisted. "What does the past matter, when they won't face the present?" He suddenly sat back down on the cot in the cell, seemingly defeated.

"The past matters because without acknowledging and accepting it— even the unpleasant parts—if you refuse it, then you can't learn from it and get beyond it and grow. And heal." Uhura looked intently at Scott. "You tried to put Nomad's killing you behind you." Scotty shook his head. "You have. But pretending it didn't happen isn't putting something behind you; it's denying something happened to you. It's denying a part of who you are. And until you accept who you are—all of who you are, the good things and the bad—you never can be whole. And you never can be truly happy." Tears filled Uhura's eyes. "Scotty . . . you died . . . because of me. You were trying to protect me. It was my fault."

Scott immediately stood up and moved to stand near Uhura. "No, no, it wasn't your fault. It was that beastly bucket of bolts. I didn't want it to hurt you. I couldn't let that happen."

Uhura looked at him. "But you did."

"What?"

"Despite your trying to stop it, Nomad hurt me. It erased my memory. Took who I was away from me. You didn't stop it. You couldn't."

Scott looked sorrowfully at Uhura. "Lass, I'm so very sorry. I tried to save you from it. I tried . . ."

"But there was nothing you could do. That's the point. We both have a guilt that we can't change even if it's over something we're not truly responsible for. It's a part of our past. A part of who we are. And if we deny that feeling, we deny ourselves. Because all we are is made up of our past. And until we understand our past, acknowledge it, we can't understand ourselves." Uhura's mind flashed with the memories of the log entries she'd reviewed, but also with the experiences she'd had since then—laughing with Chapel, being rewarded with a compliment on a good job by Spock despite her own insecurities, a kind gesture from Yeoman Cappa. This was all a part of who she was.

Uhura turned to the camera watching them and addressed the Donican council. "Just as we can't be whole without accepting all of our-

selves, even the sad things, even the bad things, even the things that
were out of our control, neither can you. How can you appreciate a
sunny day without knowing what a rainy one is like? How can you appreciate having someone in your life who you love, without understanding what it is like to lose someone? You can deny that your people
are unhappy by refusing to see sadness. You can deny Kyo-Ina has been
taken by some of those unhappy people. You can deny that the Grid
threatens you. But that does not mean these things did not happen, that
these problems do not exist. A lack of disagreement is not peace—it is
silence. And if you really want your people to be happy instead of
docile, physically safe instead of emotionally shielded, alive instead of
dead, *you will see the truth, you will hear the truth, and you will speak the truth
to your people. And you will truly live!*" Uhura's voice rang with the
strength of her convictions and her eyes shone with a refreshed clarity.
She knew who she was. Again.

A moment passed and nothing seemed to happen. Uhura and Scott
stood alone in the room. Had anyone been listening? Had anyone
heard?

Scotty shook his head. "I canna believe that that flying pile of circuits
brought me back to life, only for me t'die here, because some people
refuse to save themselves. It doesna' make sense."

"No, it doesn't. And it's not going to happen if I can help it." Uhura
stood firmly, confidently.

"Uhura." Scotty looked up at her, saw her rediscovered strength.
"When that thing . . . when Nomad . . . killed me and then brought me
back . . . repaired me like I was just some broken baffle plate, turned
me off and on like a machine . . . I'd never felt so out of control in all
my life."

Uhura reached out to Scott. The two clasped hands in understanding and shared experience.

A moment later, Cinda-Ru, no longer smiling, walked through the
door. "Kyo-Ina has been taken away. I want to get her back. As do some
on the council, though not all. While they are interpolating—" She
stopped herself. "While they are . . . fighting . . ." It seemed a difficult
word for her to say. "I . . . want to help. How do we fix this . . . problem?"

Uhura smiled. "First, with a little information. Is there a nearby access point to a mass communications console?"

Cinda-Ru nodded.

"And will someone kindly unlock this cell and direct me to the Grid controls?" Scotty looked wryly at the ladies.

Cinda-Ru moved to unlock the cell.

As Kirk and the rest of the bridge crew watched the transmission from their viewscreen, Kurning, Tano, and Kyo-Ina were among the Donicans who listened in wonder and concern as Cinda-Ru appeared on every vid-screen on the planet and explained the situation with the Grid. The communication was cut off by a dissenting council member, but it was too late. The information was out there for all Donicans to hear. Kurning turned and untied Kyo-Ina. "You are free," he said to her. "Now we shall all be free."

Back aboard the *Enterprise,* Scott and Uhura resumed their usual bridge positions and exchanged a knowing smile.

"Good to have you back," Kirk said to Scott, then turned to Uhura. "*Both* of you."

Uhura grinned. "It's good to be back, sir. Very good." Her hands automatically danced across the communications board as she began to pass reports on to others as a matter of course.

McCoy exited the turbolift and moved over to stand at the side of Kirk's chair. The captain noted to the doctor, "It seems that with the help of the FreeSpeakers, Kyo-Ina, and Cinda-Ru, the population of Donico II is well on their way to learning to live with their past and present."

McCoy smiled. "Bodes well for their future, doesn't it?"

"It certainly does," Kirk agreed. He swiveled in his chair to look at his communications officer. "But they wouldn't have dealt with it at all if it weren't for someone forcing them to face the truth and cope with the Grid situation. You did an excellent job down there, Lieutenant."

Uhura smiled widely. "Thank you, Captain. But I didn't do it alone." She looked over at Scotty, who looked back at her warmly. "In fact, if there's one thing I learned down on Donico II, it's that confidence isn't about being independent and sticking your head in the sand, pretending everything is okay. It's knowing when to go to someone else for help."

"I couldn't agree more," Scotty affirmed.

As Kirk ordered Sulu to take them to their next destination, the competent, confident communications officer of the *Starship Enterprise* tended to her duties and looked forward to her next assignment.

The Leader

Dave Galanter

Dave Galanter

Dave Galanter has authored various *Star Trek* projects, among these the *Voyager* book *Battle Lines,* the *Next Generation* duology *Maximum Warp,* the *S.C.E.* titles *Ambush* and *Bitter Medicine,* and a short story in the *Tales of the Dominion War* anthology entitled "Eleven Hours Out."

His not-so-secret Fortress of Solitude is in Michigan, from where he pretends to have a hand in managing the message board websites he co-owns: ComicBoards.com, a comic book discussion site, and TVShowBoards.com, a similar site dedicated to television and movies. He also edits and is the main contributor to his own blogsite, SnarkBait.com, on which he babbles about philosophy and politics.

Dave spends his non-day-job time with family and friends, or burying himself in other writing projects. He enjoys feedback on his writing, positive or negative, and would appreciate seeing any comments you have on his work. Feel free to e-mail him at dave@comicboards.com.

"Mr. Sulu, could you look at this?" Ensign Sam Kerby's request wasn't too far above a whisper, but the *Copernicus* was a small shuttle and the words reverberated loudly enough for all to hear. Lieutenant Sulu rose instantly from his chair and slid himself easily into the copilot's station.

As Sulu and Kerby began some discussion or another, Dr. Leonard McCoy found himself speaking *at* his captain rather than to him. James Kirk's eyes flicked toward the helm and his ear cocked forward to listen. McCoy knew there was little he could say to win back the captain's attention.

When Kirk finally swiveled himself half away and pushed himself up toward Sulu and their pilot, McCoy protested.

"We *were* having a discussion."

"You were psychoanalyzing, Doctor," Kirk said as he turned away. "I was politely pretending to listen."

"There's a difference?" McCoy muttered.

How big was the shuttlecraft anyway? Fifty cubic meters? Did it really take an ensign, a lieutenant, and a starship captain to pilot her? Of course not. McCoy had known Kirk too long and too well not to recognize when the captain was battening down his emotional hatches. Captain James T. Kirk: no man more passionate, and yet on the subject of death none more psychologically cloistered west of his half-Vulcan first officer. Maybe that was it—Kirk had been taking repression lessons from Spock during their chess games.

McCoy frowned and twisted the ring on his little finger. He wasn't sure which was more harrowing: that they'd lost a crewman on their last mission, or that he, Kirk, and Sulu all had to testify at the required hearing. The young woman's family had come to the starbase to attend—traveled all that way from New Cairo. Some people need to put a period and move on, and that was one of the ways. Kirk didn't have such a method. In every crewman's face he'd see that of not only the last person lost under his command, but every person who had died on his watch. And he'd rarely talk about any of it.

"What do you see, Ensign?" Kirk was leaning down toward Kerby's console, and Sulu had been bending in from the copilot seat, so now all three were huddling over what was probably a nonexistent problem. Other than Kerby now being overly nervous, with both his captain and Sulu checking his work.

"Um, I'm not sure, sir."

Which is why the young man asked Sulu to look, McCoy thought. Kirk didn't need to insinuate himself into the problem unless Sulu brought it to him; he was just trying to avoid the pointed questions of his doctor.

Kirk didn't dawdle with Kerby. "Mr. Sulu?"

"Kerby made a minor course correction, Captain. When he did"— Sulu gestured toward a replay of the sensor readings—"there was a brief disruption in our ion trail."

McCoy saw the muscles in Jim Kirk's back tighten just slightly.

"What would cause that?" the doctor asked, and as Kerby looked at Sulu, and Sulu at Kirk, and Kirk at the console, no one actually answered McCoy's question.

Now McCoy rose and took a step toward the already crowded fore of the shuttle. "Jim?"

"Probably nothing, Doctor." Kirk tapped at the navigation console and nodded to Kerby. "Steady as she goes, Ensign."

"Aye, sir." That order given, Kerby was now more at ease and had obviously decided that if it didn't bother the captain, it wasn't going to bother him. McCoy wasn't as easily placated. He hadn't imagined that change in Kirk's tension level, and he wasn't now imagining the slight concern in Sulu's expression.

"'Nothing' doesn't usually have everyone up and out of their seats," McCoy said, and with that Kirk went back to his chair in the aft cabin. Sulu, however, remained at the console. Kirk hadn't asked him to stay there, but there was an unspoken language between captain and bridge crew, and Sulu obviously knew that Kirk wanted him to look over Kerby's shoulder.

"What *could* it mean?" McCoy asked, hovering over his chair but refusing to sit. He looked down at Kirk, trying to pull the captain's attention from a small computer screen that was probably replaying a sensor sweep recording.

Kirk almost shrugged, but not quite. "Among other things, an ion trail can be disrupted by another ion trail crossing its path."

McCoy played with that idea a moment, then finally sat. "Wouldn't another ship show on our sensors?"

"This isn't the *Enterprise*. Scanners are more limited on a shuttlecraft. Power is shifted mostly into deflectors when at warp speed. We tend to trust transponder beacons to alert us to vessels behind us."

"So a ship without a beacon could hide itself behind us."

"Enough to hope we wouldn't notice. Kerby's inexperience could be what revealed this—whatever it is."

McCoy shook his head. "I don't follow."

"It was a maneuver that Sulu would have left for a while, until it was necessary to make. Kerby's a bit overeager. As the"—Kirk paused a moment, looked up at neither McCoy nor Kerby, just into his own thoughts—"young often are."

The look in Kirk's eyes was one with which McCoy had too much familiarity: regret. And he knew it wasn't about anything other than the death of the crewman they'd recently lost.

Despite having wanted Kirk to open up about his feelings on the matter, suddenly McCoy felt like changing the subject. "So why is it a problem if our ion trail was disrupted?"

"Because for us to notice it means that the trail was still tight. That means someone crossed it recently, Doctor. And they don't have a transponder beacon running, which means they don't want to be seen."

"We're being followed," McCoy concluded.

Kirk pushed out a heavy breath and punched at the computer's console. "No record of any inhabited planets in this area, but no ship has visited either. There's a Class-M moon in a nearby system. Long-range scans from the starbase haven't recorded signs of civilization."

"We're pretty far out," McCoy said. "What about a new, unknown civilization?"

"Somehow I'm more concerned it would be a known one."

McCoy chewed his lower lip. "Maybe it was a—I don't know—don't we come across anomalies or space oddities all the time? How do we know for certain it was another ship?"

"We find out." Kirk twisted toward the helm. "Ensign, plot a new course."

Kerby kept his hands on the console but turned his head slightly back to the captain. "Sir?"

Kirk glanced only a moment at the navigational computer for a reference. "Two-four-one, mark seventeen."

"Where exactly does this get us?" McCoy asked.

"Toward that nearby system." Kirk motioned toward the side computer screen near his seat.

"There's more to navigate around in a star system," Sulu said, partly for McCoy's benefit, and partly for Kerby's. "We can maneuver more, and if a ship is following, they'll have to compensate."

"They might give themselves away," Kirk said.

Kerby chuckled. "That's pretty smart."

Sulu leaned toward the ensign, a slight smile playing at his lips. "That's why he gets the big credits."

"Mr. Sulu, signal the *Enterprise.* Say we're going to make a quick survey of the system at the coordinates listed, but should still make our rendezvous time."

Poking at the comm for a few moments, Sulu finally replied, "Message sent, sir."

McCoy didn't fully understand why they couldn't just turn their full scanners aft and learn who was following, so he asked just that question as he anxiously rose again and watched over Kerby's shoulder.

"Good question, Bones," Kirk said. "Mr. Kerby, why don't you answer the doctor?"

McCoy glanced back at Kirk a moment and found him half smiling—a bemused little look he got when "teaching class."

Hesitating awkwardly, Kerby wasn't quick with the answer. But he tried. "Well . . . we're moving . . . which makes them move . . ." McCoy could almost see the gears clicking in the young man's head. "And that will, um, force them to move in a way that, uh . . . tells us something?" In the end it was far less a statement than a question.

"If he's reacting to us, we get information," Kirk said. "If we're reacting to him, all we're doing is giving up information."

McCoy rolled his eyes. "Is everything chess to you?"

Kirk shook his head. "This isn't chess—it's poker. I'm looking for a tell. To know what's in his hand without giving away my own."

"I should've asked if everything was a game," McCoy said under his breath.

Schra-boooom! An explosion kicked McCoy against Sulu's copilot seat and then onto the deck.

Kirk was pulling him up a millisecond later. "This is no game, Doctor." He maneuvered McCoy to his seat and pivoted back to Sulu. "Concussive blast from a photon torpedo?"

"Negative." Sulu shook his dark head, and a strand of hair fell across his brow. "Internal explosion aft section, toward the outer hull. Thrusters and internal sensors are off-line."

"Full scanners," Kirk ordered Kerby, and with the flip of a switch he swapped the controls of Sulu's console for the ensign's. "Sulu, evasive action."

"Captain, navigation is sluggish. Impossible to determine why with internal sensors off-line."

"Scanners indicate a small vessel," Kerby said, just a hint of adrenaline fracturing his voice. "Bearing: zero-two-eight, mark three."

Kirk leaned toward the readout. "Identification?"

"I've never seen it before, sir."

"Klingon design," Sulu said with a quick glance to Kerby's sensor screen.

Kirk concurred. "But not imperial—maybe clan, maybe private."

"Power signature suggests standard disruptors and maybe a photon sling." Kerby was getting into the rhythm of battle that had become almost second nature to Kirk and Sulu.

"We're outgunned," Sulu said, and looked to Kirk.

"What about the Organian Peace Treaty?" Kerby asked, and another explosion pitched the ship forward with a sharp jolt.

Kirk gripped Sulu's chair tightly until the course was almost smooth again. "I'd say whoever's behind us didn't sign it."

"We're losing warp power," Sulu said. "Temps are rising. Could be a coolant leak."

"What about the *Enterprise*?" McCoy asked.

Lips pressed into a thin line, Kirk was disenchanted with the prospects. "If the Klingons let the last message out, they won't let the next one go, and she's otherwise hours away."

Another explosion sliced into *Copernicus,* this time from without rather than within.

"Disruptor blast," Sulu reported almost matter-of-factly. Spock was rubbing off on that boy, too, McCoy thought. "We've dropped out of warp."

"Damage?"

"Port nacelle." Sulu's nimble digits danced their waltz across the console. "There's a power surge in the intermix assembly."

"We're going to lose antimatter containment," Kerby said with a gasp, and was probably expressing himself more emotionally than he wished.

"Hold it together, Ensign." Kirk wasn't just talking about the ship, but the growing panic in Kerby's voice.

Turning on a heel, Kirk pushed himself aft and grabbed McCoy's arm as he went. "Gimme a hand, Bones."

"What're we doing?"

"Hand me that kit." Kirk pointed to a sealed box of tools that protruded from the small engineering bulkhead of the shuttle as he revealed an access panel with his fingertips.

"Here." McCoy set the case to Kirk's side and opened it for him, figuring he'd be assisting with this operation, not performing it.

"We're going to have to jettison the engines," Kirk said as he grabbed a magnetic probe from the kit and took readings from near the protected core.

The doctor frowned. "Isn't that done with some push of a button or flip of a switch?"

"It will be, but then containment could last longer than I want." Kirk rose, stepped over to the ordnance cabinet and pulled out one of four phaser pistols.

Removing the hand phaser from the larger pistol and power pack housing, the captain took a magnetic coupler and attached the small phaser to what looked to McCoy like the outer intermix assembly housing.

"We do this," Kirk said, "and we're stranded here."

He set the phaser building up an overload, then quickly withdrew his hand and put the access panel cover back in place.

"What exactly *are* we doing?" McCoy asked as Kirk stood and pulled the doctor up with him.

Kirk brushed off his pant legs and motioned for McCoy to have a seat. "Get a strong grip, Bones." Which is just what Kirk did once he'd lowered himself into the seat next to him. "Sulu?"

"Ready, sir."

"Best speed toward the interior of the star system," Kirk ordered. "Head for the M-Class planetoid."

"Plotted."

"Full aft shields, Mr. Kerby." Kirk waited just a moment, pausing to be sure there was no last-moment change in status. "Jettison the intermix chamber on my mark, Mr. Sulu."

"Ready, sir."

Kirk nodded once, firmly, determined, as if he could will the outcome he wanted into being. "Now!"

Not even a full moment after the proximity alert shrieked, space bubbled forward with white-hot, blistering energy. D'kar pitched the ship starboard as fast as possible. Engines strained and dampeners struggled to tighten his vessel's seams. Overloads crackled circuits across his control board and power dimmed as if it were now dusk where before it was midday noon.

"Tera'ngan Ha'DI bah!"

Backup systems came online slowly, but sensors did not. Wherever Kirk was now, be it sitting on top of his ship or twenty parsecs away, there was nothing D'kar could do until he could see again.

Had it been an overcast day, as it often was this time of season, he would never have seen anything behind the low-hanging clouds that usually plastered the sky with a mugging gray. Today the sun shone brightly on the morning frost, and Simon Anders first mistook the movement in the sky for one of the large native predator birds. But binder hawks didn't vent smoky trails across the horizon.

"A ship." He wasn't sure if he'd whispered the words or if they were an internal thought. For all he knew, he might have screamed them. If anyone heard, they didn't indicate it. They were too mesmerized by the sight as well. It was midmorning and most people were about the camp, tending to the animals or to the greenhouse crops, or just gathering the plants from which they would harvest oil for the lamps.

"Captain?" They weren't calling his attention to the vessel, which everyone knew it must be by now. Even without assistance from binoculars they knew it not to be a meteor. Meteors don't make thirty-degree turns.

There was no expected crunch of vessel against rock. It may not have looked much like a powered descent, but perhaps it was enough of one to avoid a crash. From the looks of it, about six kilometers east of the second turn in the river, where the best pastures usually were in the spring.

"Gather a party," Anders said to no one in particular, but he knew that Michael would be close and listening. "Bring the doctor, just in case. Tell her to bring remedies."

Michael may have nodded, but Anders heard nothing. He turned, finally, and Michael was slowly backing up, still looking at the now-expanding plume of smoke as it dissipated, evening itself across the sky. "Michael, go. Find Alexandra. I will gather the others we need."

"Y-yes, sir." Michael had never seen another ship, certainly not flying through the air. Or crashing. Anders had. He remembered their own ship's crash in vivid detail. As he and those he'd gathered made their way toward the plume of smoke that rose from the grasslands where the ship looked to have landed, Anders wondered if there would be dead. He didn't want there to be dead. He'd had to live through seeing such horrors of twisted and mangled bodies. Michael and some of the others with them who'd been born since the crash shouldn't have to. Had the older men not needed the strength of those younger, Anders would have had them stay behind.

"Who could they be?" Alexandra asked. She, too, had been born long after the crash, and her cures for cuts and scrapes and whatever she knew about the mending of bones would assist little if there were radiation burns and cases of plasma-lung awaiting them.

"I don't know," Anders said to her. "We are farther out than our maps extended. Who knows how far man has come, hm? We'll think good thoughts."

There was silence between them and the others until finally the smoke was large in the sky and they all knew they were close. First to make it to the top of the last hill, Anders stopped the others from continuing on. He called for Alexandra, gesturing her forward.

"Do you have the instruments?"

The doctor nodded and handed him a sack.

"And they work?" Anders asked.

She shrugged just a bit. "Last I checked, Captain."

Anders frowned. Why would she not check before bringing them? So few bits of equipment still worked, the ones that did were cherished to the point that people were afraid to use them when they were needed. They had one hand scanner, three computer terminals, and two medical scanners—one portable, one stationary. In the sack were the hand scanner, the smaller medical scanner, and a bag of curatives that once held traditional medicines but now had "local" remedies and bits and bobs they'd managed to synthesize from base chemicals.

"I don't want us to go in blind," Anders told those around him. "Who doesn't know how to use the scanner yet?"

Michael was the only one who'd really used it before, though a few others had seen its operation. Those that never had, gathered closest.

"We're going to scan for radiation first, to see if it's safe for us to approach. Then we're going to scan for life-signs." Captain Anders pulled in a deep breath and already smelled the acrid sting of the ship's plume. "And let's pray to God there are some."

"Sulu?" Kirk stifled a cough and pulled on the stunned helmsman's arm, straightening him in the copilot seat. "Steady?"

Nodding that he was, but also choking on the smoke, Sulu held a fist over his mouth and kept his eyes tightly shut.

Kirk didn't hear the automatic venting fans that were supposed to have come on, and only emergency lights and the sparks from exposed circuits were flashing into the acrid smoke. With power out, he wasn't going to waste time seeing if the backup battery would open the doors. Half through sight, half by memory, Kirk's hand found the protected plunger that blew a hatch in the bulkhead. Half the cabin's soot-caked air was blown out with the hatchway, and a shaft of light now sliced in to reveal Kerby down under the conn. "Sulu, help him," Kirk ordered as he moved toward McCoy.

Hacking harshly as Kirk pulled him out into the fresh air, McCoy clutched at his medkit, grasping for a hypospray. He was fumbling with one of the medicinal cartridges as Kirk turned away to help Sulu drag Kerby from the shuttle and over toward where Kirk had brought McCoy.

Hypospray ready, McCoy awkwardly reached for Kirk's arm. "Triox," he rasped.

Kirk shook his head and snatched the hypo away. "You first." He kneeled down, held the hypo against McCoy's shoulder, and pressed, probably harder than a nurse would have. It hissed softly, and Kirk twisted around, repeating the treatment on Kerby, then Sulu—who immediately sounded better and looked more relaxed. Finally, Kirk hypoed himself.

Though Kirk's throat still felt rough and razor scraped, the nagging need to cough was gone and the cool air felt good in his lungs. He heaved large gulps as he shifted his knees from underneath himself and sat tiredly on the dry grass.

"Earth . . . normal . . . atmos—" McCoy was still gasping a bit. He'd taken in a lot of smoke.

"Close enough to it," Kirk said, nodding tiredly, and noticed that McCoy had a medical scanner in his palm and was already inching toward Kerby. Not giving himself a moment to recuperate, McCoy had done the triage through eyes squinted closed by the bright sun and was moving to treat the injured, himself excluded. "Bones—"

The doctor was familiar with Kirk's admonishing tone but, as usual, was going to ignore it. "I'm fine. I'm fine." And with every passing moment he was sounding better. Kirk let it go. He *did* want to know how Kerby was. Sulu was close to the ensign, propping up his head. The young man's breathing sounded shallow, his chest not moving quickly as were Kirk's own and those of the others.

After McCoy had been kneeling by him a moment, Kirk asked how Kerby was doing.

"Carbonatious sputum, which is expected. But his O_2 levels are rising." McCoy turned the scanner on himself a moment, then on Sulu. "Better than ours, actually. He banged his head on the console. Slight concussion put him out and metered his breathing so he actually has less"—McCoy had to huff in a breath and as he did he choked on it—"lung damage." He looked at Sulu. "Feel up to getting the larger medkit?"

Sulu nodded and rose slowly, steadying himself a moment before heading for the shuttle. When Kirk pushed himself up, he understood why Sulu hesitated—a wave of light-headedness crashed down on him and he had to grope for balance as if on a tightrope.

Kirk too headed for the shuttle. He wanted the three remaining phasers aboard, and assuming the vessel was a total loss—it seemed likely since black smoke was still gushing from the impulse drive—he'd help Sulu pull out any supplies as well.

And he also wanted another look at the damage. Several systems had broken down after they were well out of range of the Klingon vessel. Internal sensors were knocked out first, and that was not a system open to failure before several others. There was sabotage at work here, and when the immediate crisis was over, and the whys figured out, the "how" and the "who" could be a much bigger problem for Starfleet.

One question nagged at Kirk the most: Why, if you can sabotage an *Enterprise* shuttle, do you disable only certain systems and not simply destroy the whole vessel—or use it to damage the *Enterprise* herself?

Someone wanted them alive. *Klingons.* They had at least a *little* time to consider their options: Chances were that their pursuers were going to have to take some time for ship repairs as well.

Tracking the trail of Earthers was little different than tracking wild *Qaj.* Both were sloppy animals whose idea of stealth was to hide their head behind a large tree in ignorance of whether the body could be seen. For that D'kar was grateful because the sabotage for which he'd so handsomely paid had not been well timed. Kirk's shuttle was supposed to lose propulsion at the flip of a switch. Instead, the enemy had time to turn his warp engine into a weapon. Had Kirk not shifted course, had he allowed D'kar to follow him to an area not within range of a star system, he could have worn down the Starfleet shuttle's defenses and demanded the others turn Kirk over. No, it had not gone as planned. Kirk's ability to force D'kar to change his plans to fit the Earther's tactics was more than frustrating, and he wished he could simply kill Kirk outright. While that might be easier, it would not satisfy the debt he wished paid.

D'kar rubbed his shoulder and studied circuit schematics. He needed to rewire a ship that was not his own and with which he wasn't very familiar, all with a shoulder dislocated when he was tossed into the bulkhead by the shockwave from Kirk's warp core. He cursed Kirk and he cursed his tools and for good measure he cursed scanners and deck plating and the blood that spilled from the finger he had accidentally sliced open two minutes ago.

Kirk's attack had done serious damage, but he *could* repair it, and he would. And he would find Kirk, and he would find him alive, or he would not go home again.

"*yIntaH qIrq 'e' vIneH,*" D'kar whispered to himself. "*DaSwIj bIngDaq latlhpu' vItap.*"

•　　•　　•

A solitary figure appeared in silhouette against the ridge of the hill, shuffling down through the tall grasses toward them. Kirk instinctively tensed, and his right hand dropped toward his sidearm. "Sulu." The captain motioned his head in the direction he was looking. "Tricorder," he whispered.

Leaving McCoy to tend to Kerby, Sulu came up along Kirk's side, his tricorder open.

"I see one," Kirk said.

Sulu looked up to the ridge. "Our Klingon friend? Impossible."

"I didn't see another ship come in."

"We didn't make the most discreet of landings," Sulu said, fussing with the dials on his tricorder. "No energy weapons. Readings are . . ." He paused, and Kirk glanced down at the tricorder as Sulu ran the scan again. "Human. More than one."

When Kirk looked back up the hill, there were now seven forms heading toward them, six distinctly behind the first, who now waved on the others.

"Humans!" called the first man, who suddenly ran toward Kirk and Sulu. "From Earth?"

Kirk was now holding his phaser, but pointing it down. The lead man stopped four meters in front of them, somewhat out of breath. "Does anyone need care?" He looked around hastily, touching his gaze on each face. "We have some medicines—"

"Shipwreck?" Sulu murmured, probably noticing the homemade textiles, as Kirk had. The captain nodded slightly, taking note of each person, then focusing on the apparent leader. He was in his sixties or more, or perhaps just life-weathered. There was a certain dignity about him, despite his obvious glee at having met other people. He held his hand out to Kirk.

Taking it, Kirk placed his phaser back against his hip and crooked a thumb over his shoulder. "We have a doctor," Kirk said. "Who—"

"Yes, of course. Forgive me," the older man said. "I am in shock at seeing you all. I am Captain Anders, and these are—we are—the survivors of a vessel that crashed here, much as yours. Is anyone injured?"

Kirk smiled and let out a soft chuckle. Captain Anders wasn't really listening; he was more gawking than anything else. His exuberance was contagious.

"Not anymore," McCoy said as he rose, pulling Kerby slowly to his feet as well. "Just a concussion."

"How're you feeling, Kerby?" Kirk asked.

"Fine now, sir." The young man rubbed his forehead and ran his hand through his hair, pushing it out of the way of his eyes. "Slight headache, though."

Anders moved to Kerby and shook his hand, then Sulu's and McCoy's. The other six, two women and four men, followed suit.

"Do you have food?" Anders asked. "I mean, do you *need* food?" He shook his head, seemingly to shake mental cobwebs loose. "I'm sorry, I'm sorry," he said, turning back to Kirk. "I didn't even allow you an introduction."

"Captain James T. Kirk, of the *Starship Enterprise*." He nodded a salute. "How long—"

Anders smiled widely as if some witty joke amused him. "Forty-two years, Captain. It has been forty-two years since any of us has seen a face not our own or born to us." He took Kirk's hand again and squeezed it tightly. "And now, Captain Kirk, here you are."

Walking back to Anders's settlement was an experience—Anders rarely asked a question but answered each of Kirk's inquiries with a pages-long monologue. In the time it took to trek across the wilderness—if rolling hills of what looked like some native peat could be called such—Anders described the seasons and local geology. Apparently this area had just come out of their mild winter. The nights still got near freezing and the buds had not yet appeared on the sparse lowland trees; they wouldn't for another few weeks, and for the mountain trees, from which much of their wood came, it would be another two months before life touched them again.

"All this ground is very fertile," Anders said, "just not for most of the seeds we brought with us." He stooped down as they walked along the path and picked a stalk of dry, tall grass. "The root of this plant is all over our camp. We cultivate it for its oil, which is usable for both cooking and lighting. Even heating in the coldest months. It has been a godsend."

As a starship captain Kirk had many skills. One of them was to listen to someone and collect the details of the conversation while also reflecting on other matters. He was calculating the possible damage to the Klingon shuttle and the time it might take to make repairs. He added to it the time needed to make way for this planetoid, and then the time it would take to find them. What bothered Kirk was how long he'd estimated the *Enterprise* might take in finding them. The Klingons could very well find them first. He had to be ready for that, and he couldn't endanger these people.

They entered the camp, and immediately people gathered round, pouring out of the rather sturdy-looking structures they'd built from the remains of their ship. There must have been about seventy or so, all smiling, most talking among themselves. Some were old—older than Anders. Many were obviously much younger, and there were some children. One little girl ran to Kirk as he stood next to Anders. Kirk leaned down and said hello. She meekly responded, then ran back to her mother. The crowd laughed and then began asking questions about Earth, about the Federation, about some other planets that others must have come from, old Earth colonies.

"Please, everyone be silent a moment," Anders begged. "Please. Please, everyone." Some quieted down, others did not. "Jonathan, please." Anders leaned toward Kirk. "Jonathan is very talkative." His voice rose again and he pointed toward the back of the gathering. "Missy, control your children."

"And my husband," Missy replied. Everyone laughed again, even Kirk. Like Anders, everyone's excitement was infectious.

"If Captain Kirk would be good enough," Anders bellowed to regain attention, "I see you all have questions. But we cannot all mob our guests."

Questions flooded forth.

"How many people on your ship?"

"Can we see it?"

"Are others coming?"

"Do you have movies?"

Kirk and the others answered as best they could, and after a short time the little girl who'd greeted him and then returned to her mother found her courage and her way into Kirk's arms. As Sulu, McCoy, and Kerby, each with a group of people around him, continued, Kirk smiled and handed the child back to her mother and pulled Anders aside.

"Let's talk."

Anders nodded and motioned toward the back of one of their community buildings. The din of people talking was much softer here, and Kirk looked again at some of the buildings of Anders's settlement. One couldn't call them shacks or huts—they looked too strong for that.

"You've done a lot in forty-two years," Kirk said.

"Thank you, Captain." Anders smiled graciously. There was a charm about him, Kirk thought; a certain charisma made it clear why he led his band of crash survivors. "But I think you flatter us. We've had some good years, and some hard years. We had some livestock that survived the crash, and managed to domesticate some native birds, and we hunt some game. Most of the crops we had for the Beta Aurigae colony were for a much drier environment. This place is too humid in the summer months for much of it. We modified a few that had the best chances, and we do have a drier greenhouse. The first winter was most hard, as you can imagine. I think even more so because any radio we had was dead and there was little chance of rescue. The dread was colder than any wind."

"You were the captain then?" Kirk asked.

"I? No, no." Anders chuckled, then looked a bit past Kirk, perhaps searching for what seemed distant memories. "My father was captain. Adoptive father, when my own parents passed in the crash. I was sixteen when I lost everything. Captain Mendez took me under his wing. Taught me how he did what he did. And then when he died some years later, I took up his role. His cause—his calling—became mine."

"Beta Aurigae is quite a distance from this moon. How did . . ." Kirk shrugged and let his question trail off as Anders took in a breath to answer.

"An engine imbalance created a wormhole. I'm afraid I don't know the technical details well, but we were unable to pull out from it until we found ourselves in this system. I was told it took selectively dismantling the warp engine while at warp to do it."

"Your engineer—"

"Brilliant," Anders said. "Died saving us."

"How many survived?"

"Most survived the crash itself, but many died from their injuries or radiation burns we could not treat." The older man shook his head, the lines on his face tracing an expression of deep regret. "I've seen a lot of death, Captain." He seemed to snap himself out of whatever dark thought he'd had. "But I've also seen a fair number of births, and for that miracle I am grateful."

Kirk instantly liked Anders and had some empathy for his difficult life. Which was why he didn't like the fact that he might be complicating it even more. "I have a problem," Kirk told him. "And you need to know about it."

And he told him: about the sabotage to the shuttle, the Klingon pursuers, and the possibility that while his first officer would surely find them soon, the Klingons might find them first.

"I've heard of the Klingons, of course," Anders said soberly and pinched the bridge of his nose between his eyes. "Rather fierce, if I remember."

Fierce was an understatement, Kirk thought, remembering the hundreds and eventually thousands that would have died on Organia under Commander Kor's Klingon occupation . . . had any humanoids actually been on Organia.

"Are my people in danger, Captain?" Anders asked.

In a tone that Kirk hoped would bolster Anders's confidence that the situation wasn't as dire as Kirk had made it sound, he said, "Not if I can help it."

Anders's brows knitted with concern. "That's not a direct answer."

"They could be in danger," Kirk admitted. "But it will take the Klingons some time to find us. We've shut down all power on the shuttle, and unless they have the scanners of a starship, they won't be able to find it unless they do low-altitude flyovers."

Unconvinced, Anders's demeanor suddenly turned very captainlike. "I won't pretend to know the technology of your civilization, Captain, but I assume it's better than I remember that of my youth."

"Somewhat."

"Were I looking for someone who landed on a seemingly uninhabited planet, I'd scan for life-form readings," Anders said pointedly.

Kirk nodded. "So would I."

A frown deepened the lines on Anders's face. "And so will your Klingons."

If Kirk had wanted to build a fort, the settlement he and Sulu had spent an hour surveying wasn't the place to do it. It was in an open area, near a large freshwater stream, and high ground flanked it on two sides.

"We can't defend this ground," Sulu said as he and Kirk approached McCoy, who had been talking with Alexandria, the camp's doctor.

"But this is where the Klingons will come," Kirk said. "Whether we're here or not." Hand raised, motioning McCoy to them, the captain called for his doctor's report. "What do you think, Bones?"

McCoy strolled to them, a slight smile turning his lips. Kirk noticed there no longer were soot smudges from the shuttle "landing" and realized he must have taken the time to clean up. The captain wanted to do the same.

"These folk are in fairly good health, considering. It doesn't take long for natural selection to take over when you remove man's medicines and technologies. After fifty years here, the strongest are surviving." He crooked his thumb toward Alexandria, who was now tending to one of the children's scrapes, though Kirk couldn't see any damage from where he was. It may have been more psychological care than physical.

"She's amazing," McCoy said. "Trained by one of the doctors who eventually passed away. She's as good as any I've seen."

"You sound ready to buy a plot of land and settle down," Kirk said mischievously. "If you put out your shingle here, you'd ruin her business."

"I could do worse than live here," McCoy said. "A bit of a chill in the air, but it gets the blood going."

"Yeah." Blood. The word alone forced Kirk to think of the Klingons. He turned to Sulu. "Find Kerby. We're going to set up a watch, scanning with the tricorders."

"How long do you think we have?" McCoy asked as Sulu walked off to where they'd last seen Kerby, who had been ordered to rest.

"Before the Klingons are here?" Kirk replied. "Or Spock?"

"Both."

Rubbing his chin with his right thumb, Kirk's brows lifted and he gave a slight shrug. "Within a day. It's not when, but who arrives first that's the gamble."

"Michael!" Anders stopped the younger man as he was trotting across the settlement grounds. "Have you seen Alexandria?"

Skidding to a stop, Michael turned and caught his breath in a huff before replying. "Yes, Captain. She was near the infirmary with Dr. McCoy."

"She was?" Anders furrowed his brow. "We were to meet here to discuss Beth Anne's heart trouble. Did she ask you to inform me she'd be late?"

Michael shook his head and shrugged innocently. "No, I don't believe she mentioned it. But I think they were talking about Beth Anne."

"I see." Pressing his lips together, Anders wondered if the total distraction of his people over the last day was temporary or permanent. The buzz of new faces had to wear off soon, did it not? Dr. McCoy was surely a skilled physician, but he didn't have a grasp of Beth Anne's case. Alexandria and Anders did.

"Do you need me further, Captain?" Michael asked, obviously anxious to be on his way.

Anders studied him a long moment, making sure he stood there and waited for a response. "Is there something pressing you must do?"

"I wanted to chat with Mr. Sulu, sir. He was going to show me how his tricorder worked."

"You've always been cautious with technical equipment—afraid you'd break it." Anders shook his head. Michael just wasn't acting himself. It was most unnerving.

"Well, Mr. Sulu said they have four with them and more than a hundred more on their ship."

Chewing his lower lip, Anders wasn't sure what to make of that. Was Michael suddenly planning to go with them? Now? Today or tomorrow or whenever their ship arrived?

"Michael, you told me you had no interest in leaving the Frontier." The Frontier, an ironic joke at first, had been what the survivors ended up calling their new home, saying they were like frontiersmen of old, starting with nothing.

"Well, I don't, Captain." Michael shifted his weight from one foot to the other. "Not forever. But they'll take anyone to their starbase for training and— It is a chance of a lifetime, isn't it, Captain?"

"I suppose it is." Anders nodded with understanding, but a sense of foreboding slithered across him. "Michael, does everyone feel this way?"

"No, no . . . I think just that . . . well, options are so open now." Michael was in his thirties, but suddenly his eyes were as wide as a toddler's. Yesterday life had been simple, linear. Now it could blast into so many directions that he must have been quite confused about his choices. Confused and exhilarated.

"Indeed," Anders said finally.

"May I go?"

With a hand, Anders waved him off. "Of course."

If frustration were corporeal, D'kar would have gutted it by now and made its skin into a sheath for his knife. Tracking Kirk to the small moon had been a child's task, but now he found the Earther in the bosom of his own kind. What kind of defenses did this colony have? Were they part of Kirk's clan? Would they die for him? If so, D'kar could be killed and his prey would escape. It soon would not matter that he was able to jam Kirk's message to his ship, as they would come looking for him and they would track his shuttle just as D'kar had. It infuriated him that what little time he *did* have left needed to be wasted with watching and waiting and forming yet another plan that would put Kirk within his grasp.

They were crafty. One of the Starfleeters was always using their scanner. What they didn't know was that D'kar had been a little more prepared than they, and he'd left passive reception cones scattered around their camp's perimeter. His hand scanner could now tell him the pattern of their scans, and it was—no matter who held their tricorder—sickeningly predictable. Did all of Starfleet learn the same grid pattern?

It was when the red-shirted one was scanning that things were most unsurprising, so that was when D'kar decided to venture closest to Kirk. He could hear him and see him with proper passive scanning and distance, and didn't dare actively scan for fear of being revealed.

If this were an assassination, D'kar could have his prey by now. A single phaser shot, or even a primitive projectile blast, and Kirk could be dead. He could smell the Earther from where he hid. He could smell them all, and the foul stench that was Terran blood.

But he'd rather give Kirk to his father as a prize. That was what D'kar had planned for so long, had fantasized about, and fallen to slumber with the thought of in his mind, and awakened with the same. It wasn't about self-aggrandizement, he told himself, but about his father's disgrace at Organia. All of Qo'noS spoke of the treaty, and few outwardly blamed Kor for the disaster, but unspoken censure laced every greeting. And to D'kar it was no surprise that his first assignment to the finest cruiser in the fleet had fallen away. He would not let his life fall into a pit because of the dishonor brought on his house because of Kirk. And so long as no one knew it was D'kar who brought the Earther to justice, and in fact believed it was Kor, honor would be restored.

It was supposed to have been done by now, D'kar lamented. This Kirk was a trickster, certainly. But ultimately weak. *There are no Organians to save him this time. Now the odds are more even.*

Kirk sat in a chair, using a tree stump as a workbench. He fiddled endlessly with several pieces of almost-random technology. There were only a few people around him—they were not very near—and D'kar thought he might choose this moment to make his move. As he was deciding, an older man approached Kirk, and his body language was not like that of the others who'd previously been near Kirk. It was not toadying or submissive, but that of an equal.

"A word, Captain?"

There was an interesting aspect to his demeanor that piqued D'kar's keen interest. His scanner, however, told him that the other Starfleeter's scans would be proceeding his way, and he must now move his position.

This Earther, however, was one to be watched. By Kirk if no one else, for the look in the new man's eyes was one D'kar had seen before: jealousy.

"Can you explain why you've torn apart one of our few working computers?" Anders demanded. Something in his tone was a bit more than confrontational. It was almost hurt.

"I'm sorry," Kirk began. "I didn't tear it apart. I just needed to see if it had parts we could use to boost our communicators. It doesn't, and I'm putting it back together."

"And it will function?" Anders sneered and looked at the computer's various parts spread across a cloth on the bench.

"If I say it will function," Kirk said, "it will function."

The older man drew a breath as if to respond, but he swallowed whatever he planned to say. He studied Kirk a long moment, then nodded and motioned at him. "You have a ship," he said. "Let me ask you a hypothetical question."

Kirk nodded.

"Say I come aboard," Anders said, as McCoy approached from the door to one of the greenhouses. He had two native apple-looking things in his hands.

Kirk shook his head lightly, making sure the doctor wouldn't interrupt.

"Because my ship was damaged, you provide me and my crew transport," Anders continued. "What would you say if—having given me your hospitality—I began disassembling your vessel for my needs and ends?"

"I might have thrown you in the brig," Kirk said. "If I couldn't understand why you did it."

Anders's head swayed from side to side. "I understand what you're doing, Captain. And even if I had a brig I wouldn't be so disagreeable as to cage you like an animal." Lips screwed into a frown, Anders sighed. "But I did think you might have a little more courtesy than to take what is not yours without asking."

Eyes wide in his best apologetic look of innocence, Kirk accepted that with a slight bow of his head. "I'm sorry, Mr. Anders. I should have asked."

"*Captain* Anders." He didn't quite bark his own name, but it came close. With that he turned his back on Kirk and McCoy. "Please see that that unit is working within the hour," he snapped, and left the two Starfleeters alone.

"What was that all about?" McCoy asked, offering Kirk the alien apple.

"I don't know, Bones." Kirk took the fruit, tasted it, and was surprised that it tasted very much like a normal apple. "He's probably worried about the Klingons. He decided to tell the others and some of them are nervous. I'm sure he is, too."

"I wonder," McCoy said, and bit loudly into his apple. "To my view, there went a man annoyed with you, not the Klingons."

It had taken Anders some time to calm himself. There was a grotto made by overgrowing plants to which he would sometimes escape, where it was peaceful and quiet, even in the off-season when most of the green plants had turned brown. Going there had always stilled his temper, and he hoped it would now.

He wasn't quite sure why Kirk's disrespect annoyed him so, but it had—deeply. Perhaps it was because the respect he'd earned over years and years from his people was so soon and so freely given to Kirk. Anders had always led his people with determination and charisma, skills taught him by his adopted father. But Kirk had all those skills, seemingly naturally, and his were stronger. He was *more* charismatic, *more* determined, and Anders felt that Kirk was leading the survivors into danger without a thought about their well-being. That *was* the reason for his disdain, he told himself. It was.

On his way back to the main community building, Anders saw the Kesslers' son coming out of the storage shed and he stopped to supervise the lad. He was only twelve and sometimes was quite sloppy in his chores.

Captain Anders opened the door to the shed wide and let the daylight in.

"Jacob," Anders called. "Come here, son."

The boy walked over. "Captain?"

"This isn't like you, Jacob." Anders motioned to the way the grains were stacked and the contents of the shed were organized. It was all wrong, all disordered. "This isn't how we store our grains now, is it?"

Jacob squirmed a bit and looked away. "No, sir, but Captain Kirk suggested that if we keep—"

"Captain Kirk suggested?" The back of Anders's neck tensed, and he felt his cheeks flush.

"Yes, sir," Jacob replied earnestly. "He said—"

"I don't care what he said, Jacob." Anders willed himself not to yell at the boy. It wasn't *his* fault. "Do it the way we've always done it."

"But—"

"Jacob! Mind me!"

Looking defeated and more disappointed than Anders had wished to make him, Jacob turned somberly back into the shed. "Yes, Captain."

Anders was annoyed—more with himself for losing his temper than with Kirk. Well, probably more with Kirk. Or with the situation. He sulked around his grotto, ripping dried leaves off the "walls" and throwing them to the ground. He'd found this little recess of plants against a craggy hill soon after the crash all those years ago. It was cool and protected by old trees and in the summer smelled of rain even if it had not rained in days. Rarely had he brought anyone to it, and not of late, so few knew it even existed.

He tried desperately to gather peace from the setting, but it was taking longer than he'd have liked, and every moment he was away was a moment Kirk corrupted his people. Finally he thrust himself onto the bench he'd once made and lowered his head into his hands. Long moments passed until he was jarred from sullen meditation by a sharp pressure against the base of his skull.

"Do not cry out," a voice said. "My blade is at your spine."

Anders didn't move. The words were in heavily accented English, and the individual, logic told him, natively spoke Klingonese.

"What do you want?" Anders asked. Asking who he was seemed a silly question. He was the person with a knife at his neck.

"I want to speak on you," the voice said, and it was clear that his English was not the best. "I learn you are a leader of men and I come to join in respect. To make you learn of my goals."

Anders's brow knitted in confusion, and he needed to decode the poor English. But most of the meaning was evident. "You come to me in respect, threatening to injure me?"

Suddenly the knife point was gone. "Of course," the Klingon said matter-of-factly, as if threatening Anders had been intended as a standard greeting. "Stay sitting."

"What do you want?" Captain Anders repeated. He was beginning to see real differences between himself and Kirk, whereas before he thought they were much the same. Anders had to deal with people and problems, but on his small planetoid there were no aliens with agendas. There were no knives at throats and there were no threats. Anders and his people battled the elements, struggled to survive the seasons, not enemies from other worlds.

Coming around to stand in front of Anders, the Klingon man—boy, really, as he could only have been in his late teens or early twenties—showed Anders that he was sheathing his knife. "I want," he said slowly, perhaps making sure his English was clear, "Captain James T. Kirk, for crimes against my House. Do you understand?"

Anders nodded slowly, but he'd known that yesterday. "No, I mean, what do you want from me?"

"Do you trust Kirk?" the Klingon asked.

"He's a Starfleet captain."

"I know who he is! That was not my question." The boy's hand was never off his knife, Anders noticed.

"So it wasn't," he replied. "Yes. I trust him."

"You should not." The alien motioned for Anders to rise. "Stand."
Anders slowly shook his head. "No."

"You will not?" The look of confusion on the young Klingon's face
was almost amusing, except that his knife was now a centimeter out of
its sheath.

"This is my home," Anders said, enunciating every word so he was
clear. "I am in charge here. You need to leave."

"I'm the one with the weapon."

Suddenly, swiftly, the knife was out and the blade was before
Anders's eyes.

Anders looked past it and into the Klingon's gaze. "And I am not
James Kirk."

"You are brave." The Klingon's laugh sounded truly mirthful. "I like
you." He turned and walked away from Anders, and just before he was
invisible against the tree line he twisted back. "Good-bye, Captain. Remember—*I* am not the threat to you or your people."

Anders walked evenly back to camp, keeping himself from anything
but a normal pace in case the Klingon was watching. It was a far more interesting and less-threatening encounter than he would have imagined.

Once back at the settlement, as the sun was beginning to set against the
high hills, it didn't take Anders long to find Kirk. He was with Dr.
McCoy in the storage room they'd given the newcomers as quarters.
Crates that had survived the crash supplied the makeshift chairs and
table, and bedrolls were provided for sleeping. Other than that, the
room was bare. Kirk sat at the "table," fiddling with one of his small
handheld scanners. McCoy was standing to one side, inoculating one of
the children. Anders waited until the child left, then strode directly
to Kirk.

"How long before your ship finds you, Captain?"

"Knowing Spock, within a day." Kirk didn't bother with a shrug. He
made it sound like the solution to a calculation.

"I don't know this Spock person," Anders said, his gut tight with the
annoyance he was trying to keep under control. "He must be extraordinary to earn such confidence."

Kirk stood. Perhaps he sensed something in Anders's demeanor, something more than submissive. "He's the finest first officer in the fleet," he said.

Joining them around the table, McCoy chimed in, very obviously trying to lighten the atmosphere. "For most things, not all."

Deciding to get to the point, Anders turned away a moment, composed himself, then turned back to Kirk. "You've been a bit of a disruption, Captain, I'm sorry to say."

"A disruption?" Kirk looked directly into Anders's eyes in a way that was disturbingly confrontational on a level Anders hadn't expected. "We're in a race for our lives," Kirk said.

"Every day here is such a race," Anders countered. "And not one we all win. I—" About to lose his composure, Anders tightened his fists at his sides and ground his next words out as calmly as possible. "Did I tell you why Captain Mendez chose me to be his successor?"

Kirk shook his head once. "You didn't."

"We just assumed it was the way you had with people," McCoy said, again sensing the mood and attempting to smooth feathers. "These folks look up to you a great deal, Captain Anders."

"He told me I had the charisma to be the glue that held these people together." Anders looked back at Kirk, trying hard to counter that steely glare with his own. "Not charm, not likability, though certainly that— but the magnetism."

Kirk didn't seem impressed. "Your point, Anders." It wasn't a question.

"I see that it's true, so long as there isn't a more magnetic, more charismatic figure outshining my ability."

"I have no desire to lead these people," Kirk said.

"You don't need the desire," Anders spat. "You have the natural ability. Had you been stranded with us, I have no doubt I'd be a farmer or a gatherer. Or perhaps I'd be chief digger in charge of latrines—"

"Captain—" McCoy tried to interrupt.

"Quiet, Doctor. This is between us." Anders gestured to Kirk and struggled to keep his voice from quaking with anger for fear it may be misunderstood as nerves. "My authority has been challenged before, and such insurrection has been rebuffed, as surely as Captain Kirk would do on his ship."

"We're not going to be here long enough to rebel against you," Kirk said, his tone even and his expression tight.

Anders didn't know what to say. He was challenging Kirk but wasn't sure what the outcome should be. Finally he turned on his heel toward the door. "I wouldn't put myself against your mettle, anyway, Captain. You'd win."

The door didn't slam shut.

McCoy searched Kirk for some reaction. "You have a hell of a way with people, Jim."

"He'll get over it as soon as we're gone," Kirk said, and sat down again.

"Can't you see what's happening here?" McCoy sat next to him, the plastiform crate as uncomfortable as the beds.

"I see it, Bones."

Kirk continued to work on boosting the tricorder's broadcast range, and McCoy wanted to tear the scanner away from him to get his full attention, but he refrained. "No, I don't think you do. You're turning this man's crew against him."

"This isn't a ship—"

"It might as well be," McCoy said pointedly. "The stakes are the same: survival."

Kirk sighed and closed the tricorder's circuit panel. "I'm not here to usurp his authority."

"He doesn't rule by command, Jim. He rules by respect. So does a starship captain. People obey a captain out of respect for the chain of command at first, and with time and the right captain they come to obey out of respect for the man." McCoy stood, following Kirk as he walked outside to find Sulu and exchange the modified tricorder for one that needed to be worked on.

"You're not telling me anything I don't know, Doctor," Kirk said.

"How would you react if another captain came onto your ship and suddenly the respect of your crew shifted to him?"

"I'd be annoyed," Kirk admitted.

"And you'd have the chain of command and orders to fall back on. What does Anders have?" McCoy saw a flicker in Kirk's eye that told him he'd made his point. So he moved on to his next one. "And don't forget there's a shuttle chock-full of Klingons who want you, for whatever reason, and woe to any of these innocents who get in their way. And by now they're here, and waiting for their chance to make a move."

"You're right."

"Exactly. I'm ri— *What?*" Stunned by the admission, McCoy was caught off guard. "Did you just say I was right?"

"Do you expect me to say it twice, Doctor?" Kirk had suddenly changed direction, and McCoy wasn't certain where they were now going.

"What're we gonna do?" he asked.

"You're going to stay here and wait for Spock to arrive." Kirk handed him the tricorder.

"And you?"

"I'm going to find Ensign Kerby. He and I will locate the Klingons' shuttle and secure it from them."

"Now wait just a minute. I wasn't suggesting—"

"I wasn't taking suggestions." The captain continued to march forward, leaving McCoy where he stood, sputtering. "I'm going to act," Kirk said, "and wait for the Klingons to *react.*" He crooked a thumb toward the sky. "While I still have light."

"And what if they react by deciding you're too much trouble to keep alive?" McCoy called after him.

"Then I better have a damn good re-reaction."

When Anders heard of Kirk's plan, he wasn't quite sure why he went right back to the grotto. He told himself it was for peace and introspection. He'd meant to tell Kirk about the Klingon. He was going to until he saw him, and then only defensive thoughts entered his mind.

Had Anders expected the Klingon to still be near the grotto? Part of him was certain of it. Part doubted it and really did want time to think and plan and . . . None of that was going to happen as soon as the young man appeared again.

"You didn't tell Kirk I was here, did you?" This time the voice was that of a universal translator. It masked the Klingon's own voice so well one might have thought there was no conversion tool in use, except for the now-perfect, unaccented English where before there had been awkward speech.

"How do you know if I did or did not?" Anders asked, his eyes flicking from one of the Klingon's hands to his other. He saw no weapon, but there was some kind of phaser or disruptor on his hip, and of course, his knife was there as well, sheathed.

"Because he didn't come to this place," the Klingon said. "I was watching."

"This . . . this is my place to think." In Anders's head it sounded like a perfectly reasonable explanation as to why he'd not told Kirk about the grotto. Given voice it sounded childish and the words felt heavy rolling off his tongue.

"Where is Kirk now?"

Anders shook his head and his chest tightened. "Kirk's affairs and yours are not my own."

The Klingon drew closer, his boots squishing on the moss-covered ground. He tilted his head, examining Anders. "You don't like him."

There was no question there, so Anders said nothing.

The young man bit his lower lip. "They've stopped the scanning around your camp. Why? Where is Kirk?"

The Klingon came closer, until Anders felt the man's breath on his face.

"I—I'm . . ." Would the Klingon kill him if he didn't say? Isn't this what he wanted—to be threatened into revealing what he knew? He wanted Kirk to be gone and the Klingon to be gone, and wasn't the fastest way to do that to have them take care of each other?

It would mean blood. It would mean death.

And Michael and the others—they might see that they were safe here when people stayed away. Options might look less favorable, doors might close. . . . And wouldn't the Klingon kill him if he didn't tell him what he wanted to know? He had weapons, where Anders had none.

"They . . ."

"Where?" the Klingon whispered. "Tell me where."

"I . . ." Anders's voice was thick, each word a chunk of iron that fell to the ground with a clang. "They went to your ship."

As close as he was, Anders could tell that the Klingon's entire body tensed instantly. "Why?" he demanded.

"I don't know for certain." Now that he'd begun such a treacherous dialogue, the words came easier. "To use it against you. To find you. To make you react."

"Fools," the Klingon barked. He twisted away and in three large running paces left Anders alone again in the grotto.

It was cool there, and it gave Anders peace to think. It always had. But now the only thought he could find was not one of serenity, but horror. "What have I done?" he murmured. "Good Lord, what have I done?"

"Broadest possible scan, Ensign." Kirk knew that would limit the distance they'd be able to cover in one sweep, but he didn't know how many Klingons would be waiting for them. There could have been three or four, or even one. That was something to consider. At first Kirk had believed his opponent to be skilled, experienced, but nothing besides the initial tactic of hiding in his impulse wake had really pointed to that. Everything since then pointed to greenness.

Why not make some move on the settlement? Other Klingons Kirk had been up against would have. They'd have sought to breed terror among the innocents between them to force Kirk's hand. Unless there was but a lone Klingon, and he was injured and waiting for them in his shuttle.

Kerby struggled somewhat to both hold his phaser pistol and adjust his tricorder. He managed it, but only awkwardly. "May I ask a question, sir?"

"You're wondering why I chose this direction for the possible location of the Klingons' shuttle."

"Yes, sir."

"Where would you hide a shuttle if you didn't want it to be seen?"

"A canyon, maybe? Some place with a deep crevice or—"

"They weren't worried about being seen from the air. And there's no canyon nearby." Kirk pointed up the ridge with the business end of his phaser, indicating the next place Kerby should scan. "They'd want the high ground, and they'd come in under cloak of night, then camouflage their shuttle as best they could."

"Huh." Kerby chuckled, and his lanky arm stretched out to point to his left. "Large metallic object. Bearing twelve degrees, two hundred and nineteen meters, sir."

While the Klingons had done their best—an excellent best—to cover the ship with brush and dirt, the tricorder could not be easily fooled.

"Life-signs?" Kirk asked in a whisper as he gestured for Kerby to take cover behind a craggy outcropping.

The Klingon shuttle, still visually distant, was nose-close to sensors. If someone was on board, watching a scanner, Kerby and Kirk had been made.

"No one on board," Kerby said.

Kirk swatted away a spring gnat that was buzzing about his eyes. "We need to get on board and—"

"Ugh!" Kerby grunted loudly.

Kirk spun tightly toward his crewman. Kerby fell, collapsing into a puddle of limbs. Blood soaked his tunic where a long dagger broke through his torso.

"Aaaaarrghhh!" The guttural battle cry of a Klingon crashed down as Kirk pivoted and fired his phaser. The beam sliced forward at the wrong angle and missed the single Klingon broadly as he leapt for Kirk and knocked the weapon from the captain's hand.

Kirk felt his entire body tense into a fighting stance. The smell of Kerby's blood jabbed the air as Kirk sized up his opponent. He was young—younger than Kirk expected. Darting his glance from the phaser, which now lay several meters away, to Kerby, who lay gurgling his last breaths, and back to the Klingon boy before him, Kirk thought, *How old is he? Seventeen? Nineteen?*

"You want me, why not take just me?" Kirk asked, trying to elicit some response, some distraction. "Why *do* you want me so badly?"

"I am D'kar, son of Kor, and I mean to avenge his dishonor at your hand."

Kor. The Klingon commander Kirk *almost* battled at Organia. Before the Organians pushed their highly evolved godlike noses into Federation-Klingon matters and compelled both truce and treaty.

"I don't want to kill you, Kirk." When D'kar said Kirk's name, it sounded almost Klingon. "Not yet." The young man holstered his disrupter and pulled out a shorter dagger, all in one very fluid, practiced movement. He may not have wanted Kirk dead, but he obviously didn't care if he was badly injured. "And this time there is no one to help you," D'kar said. "Not your crewmen, not your ship, not the Organians, and not your closest ally, who hates you almost as much as I."

Kirk's brows narrowed. Who here hated him? Anders. Had it gotten to that level? Would he sell Kirk out to the Klingons?

"You don't believe it?" D'kar taunted. "He told me where you were. He wants me to kill you, but we will save that honor for my father."

"Your father," Kirk said with a huff as he avoided a slash at his arm from D'kar's blade, "had no special quarrel with me." He grabbed a handful of dirt and twigs and launched a cloud at the boy as he rolled one way, and then zigged back toward Kerby to see if he could still hear the ensign breathing. He also wanted the man's phaser, but Kerby had collapsed onto it and so Kirk remained weaponless. His eyes flicked a moment at the dagger stuck in Kerby's back. He heard the ensign continue to slosh blood and air out of his mouth, and so Kirk at least knew his crewman was still alive. That was something, and it was likely because the dagger had been thrown from a distance rather than thrust in by hand and then removed. Had the ensign been dead, Kirk might have taken the knife and used it to defend himself, but he wouldn't save his own life at the risk of another's.

What Kirk needed even more than a weapon was for McCoy to attend to Kerby. Or he needed Sulu for backup. He'd decided two of them should look for the Klingon shuttle and two should stay to protect the settlement because he didn't know how many Klingons had come looking for them. Now it was clear to Kirk that D'kar was his lone pursuer.

All these pinpoints of thought prickled against the back of his neck as he focused quickly between D'kar's eyes and his dagger hand.

"The Organians stopped that fight, D'kar. If you're looking for your father's lost honor, they have it—not me."

With Kerby's body between them, D'kar was blocked from a clean shot at Kirk, but Kerby was now in harm's way. If D'kar should knock into the crewman, shifting the position of the dagger in his chest . . .

Young, but hardly stupid, D'kar must have noticed the flash of concern in Kirk's expression. He slid a boot toward Kerby menacingly. "He lives still. If you want to save him, remove your communicator and drop it to the ground."

When Kirk didn't instantly move, D'kar inched closer still.

"I am serious, Kirk. I *will* end him."

"All right." Left hand raised in assent, Kirk nonchalantly reached behind his back with his right hand and brought his communicator forward and then dropped it to the ground in such a way that it opened as it fell. D'kar's eyes followed it down and Kirk took his moment.

He sprang forward, one hand crashing into D'kar's throat, the other wrapping around the wrist of his dagger hand.

Up close, D'kar seemed even younger and the thought that Kirk might actually have to kill him caused a momentary hesitation that the Klingon took advantage of. He kneed Kirk hard in the ribs, then butted his head forward and hit Kirk's chin.

Grunting out a held breath, Kirk slammed D'kar's hand against the hard dirt until his fingers lost their grip on the knife and it fell away. Keeping his left hand on the Klingon's wrist, Kirk pulled up one knee and pinned it into D'kar's chest. He used his right hand to grab for the dagger, but the shift in Kirk's center of gravity allowed D'kar to roll out and over. Unable to get the knife in a firm grasp, Kirk pushed it as far away as he could. If he couldn't have it, neither of them would.

D'kar scrambled for it, but Kirk grabbed hold of his leg and twisted him around. The Klingon howled in angry pain and spat at Kirk's face, then used his own limb to pull Kirk toward him—just enough to connect a swinging fist. Kirk felt his teeth grind against his cheek and his jaw stab into his left ear. He tasted blood, spat into the dirt with a huff, and felt a trickle drip down his bruised chin.

That much delay gave D'kar enough time to find the dagger and slice side to side. Kirk backed out of the way of each swing, arching his back until he was clear of the blade's tip.

In D'kar's eyes was such frustration, such rage and anger, that Kirk sensed he'd just won. D'kar had lost himself in the fight—lost his sense of purpose and goal and given himself over, completely, to base instinct.

Base instinct isn't why his father won battles. Training was. Cunning was. Experience was.

D'kar lunged, thrusting his knife wildly at Kirk's midsection. Kirk dodged, grabbed the boy's wrist with both hands, and twisted hard until he heard bone crack and the Klingon yelp.

A human would have been finished there. D'kar caught the dagger with his left hand as it slid from his broken right. Rage still blinding him, he tried to hit Kirk's arm with the blunt end of the handle, then plunge the blade into his stomach.

Quickly, Kirk twisted behind D'kar, bringing his broken wrist back as well, turning and lifting it until Kirk felt the Klingon's arm snap in two. A murderous scream cracked the sky. When Kirk heard the dagger fall, he knew D'kar had lost lucidity. Kirk pushed him to the dirt, rolled to the phaser he'd kept a bead on, and fired, stunning D'kar where he lay.

In two steps he was back to Kerby. The ensign groaned as Kirk touched his neck to feel his pulse strength. Blood aspirated from his nose and mouth. Kirk reached for the open communicator.

Before his fingers could make contact, the familiar hum of a transporter beam bounced around like a million insects. Three columns of sparkle coalesced, and Spock materialized before him, flanked by two security guards.

Relief washed over Kirk as he scooped up the communicator and exchanged a grateful glance with his first officer. Instead of calling McCoy and having the doctor rush to Kerby's side, now the *Enterprise* was once again at Kirk's disposal.

He held the communicator near his chin with one hand and adjusted the channel with the other, despite the phaser still clenched within it. "Kirk to *Enterprise*."

"Enterprise. *Captain, it's good to hear your voice, sir.*" Uhura's voice—crisp, clear, and angelic.

"Uhura, emergency medical team to the transporter room. Ensign Kerby needs immediate attention. These coordinates."

"Aye, sir."

Kirk stepped away and watched silently as Kerby's body was beamed away.

"Your timing, Mr. Spock," Kirk began as he allowed himself a moment to breathe again, "hopefully just saved Ensign Kerby's life." The captain smiled a bit, noticed the feel of dried blood at the corner of his mouth, and thumbed it clean, glancing at the deep red smear before brushing it against his filthy tunic.

"Your open communicator signal in combination with your inability or unwillingness to respond to hails suggested you might be having difficulty." Spock motioned to D'kar, who lay prostrate a few meters away. "A Klingon?"

Kirk nodded. "One source of my difficulty."

One of Spock's brows rose in curiosity. "There is another?"

"Get this one to the brig. I'll have a word with the other."

They found Anders just where Michael and Alexandria had said he would be: on a crude, handmade bench in the middle of a cave formed by thicket, draped by what in the spring would be hanging vines plush with leaves and pillared with tall, old trees. Anders said nothing as they approached, and Alexandria kneeled on the mossy carpet so she could look into his eyes.

"Captain?" When he did not respond she whispered his name. "Simon?"

"Bones." Kirk nodded his head toward Anders, and McCoy used a small hand medical scanner for a moment, then glanced at his tricorder.

"He's in shock, Jim."

"Shock from what?" Michael asked, looking from McCoy to Kirk. "I thought you said we were safe now. What did the Klingon do to him?"

"Nothing," Kirk said. "It's what *I* did to him." Some people had a natural ability to lead. The signs could be seen at an early age. Starfleet took Kirk's leadership instincts and trained them, honed them, and molded Kirk into the captain he was. Without the training working in conjunction with his innate abilities, he wouldn't be that captain. Simon Anders had the same abilities. And the man who trained him for leadership, Captain Mendez, had molded Anders into the perfect man to be the leader of these stranded people.

But just as Kirk had not been trained to lead a corporation or a nation, or even a colonial settlement, Anders had not been trained to deal with interstellar politics and alien invasions. That's what Kirk and D'kar had been to him—an alien invasion. Anders was a leader who could secure his people from a bad winter or a lover's quarrel, but he'd not been trained to deal with the crisis Kirk had thrust on him.

Anders looked up at Kirk, his expression a mixture of self-loathing, relief, and fear. "I—I told him where to find you. He made me. I—" He began to sob. "I wanted to tell him and wanted him to persuade me." It was a cathartic admission. Michael looked at Anders with doubt and Alexandra held him in a way that she had probably never done before—as a patient.

Captain's Log, Supplemental:
Satisfied that we have gotten what information we can from D'kar about the sabotage to the shuttle Copernicus, *and because Ensign Kerby is recovering well from his wounds, we have—at the request of Starfleet Command—rendezvoused with Commander Kor's battle cruiser, to which we have been ordered to deliver our prisoner in accordance with the Organian Peace Treaty.*

Kirk thumbed a button on the transporter console, activating the comm. "Kirk to bridge." D'kar was being escorted from his security cell, and just in case, Kirk had ordered the corridors cleared along the way.

"Uhura here. We have the coordinates, Captain."

"Transmit them to Mr. Scott, Lieutenant." Kirk nodded at Scotty, who stood to his left, ready at the controls. McCoy stood by, for reasons Kirk was not sure of, but he was glad to have him close, and Spock was at the auxiliary scanner that linked to the bridge. The science officer kept a tight eye on the energy output of the Klingon cruiser. There might be a treaty that obliged adherence to certain regulations, but no accord could compel trust. Only time would do that.

"Ready, Mr. Scott?"

"Aye, Captain," the engineer said. "Ready as I can be, beaming Klingons aboard."

Kirk nodded. He understood the feeling and glanced at the single security guard near the doorway. The crewman had his phaser at the ready.

"Energize."

The transporter dais came to life; lights flashed and energy hummed through circuitous veins. A mast of sparkle appeared and congealed into flesh, bringing Commander Kor aboard the *Enterprise*.

Kirk stepped around the main console but only that far. Kor wouldn't be treated like a visiting dignitary.

"Commander," he greeted.

Smiling that slithery grin that Kirk couldn't quite decipher, Kor took two steps down to the main deck and nodded a cordial salute to Kirk. "We meet again, Captain," he said almost cheerfully, then looked about and found Spock standing across the room. "Ah, Mr. Spock." Kor bowed respectfully.

"Commander Kor," Spock responded dryly with a slight nod.

"How is the kevas trade this season?" Kor asked the Vulcan, mocking his cover story from their joint Organian adventure.

"Up an average of one point seven-six-five Federation credits in the major trade markets," Spock said, and Kirk couldn't help but allow himself a smirk.

Turning back to Kirk, Kor kept his positive façade. "You have D'kar."

"Security is bringing him here directly," Kirk said.

"If my blood has been mistreated," Kor said, "I will see to it your ship is dismantled by my disruptor banks, treaty or no." Even when he threatened your life, Kor maintained some semblance of a smile under his Fu Manchu mustache.

"Your blood engaged in terrorist acts against a Federation vessel," Kirk said. "That treaty is the only thing keeping him out of a Starfleet brig."

McCoy took one step forward. "He wouldn't allow me to treat him," he said. "He has a temporary cast for a number of broken bones in his right arm."

Kor had turned, listened, then looked back to Kirk. "His arm was broken in interrogation or battle?"

"Battle."

As Kor nodded his acceptance of that fact, the doors to the transporter room parted and D'kar entered, flanked by two security guards.

Immediately, D'kar's expression changed from prisoner to champion.

"qab yon Da'agh. QablIj yon yI'aghHa' 'aghHa'pa' 'etlhwIj." Kor snapped. Without the universal translator, Kirk made out the words "satisfied face" and "blade," and considering the smug look that had evaporated off D'kar so quickly, Kirk imagined there was something in there about Kor scraping it off with his knife.

D'kar began to respond but Kor cut him off. *"BIjatlh 'e' yImev, DI'qar!* You will speak when spoken to."

Kirk hadn't had a great deal of interaction with Kor, but that was the first flash of genuine anger he'd ever seen.

"It was to restore your honor—" D'kar spoke in Klingon, but Kirk understood that much.

"chobelHa'moH, DI'qar. SajlIj 'oHbe' quvwIj'e'." Kirk mostly understood that as well. Kor had said he was displeased, and that his honor was not D'kar's plaything.

The Klingon commander pointed to one of the transporter pads, and D'kar sullenly marched to that exact position. The Klingon family was an interesting dynamic, to be sure. On Organia, when Kor mandated the wanton slaughter of hundreds, Kirk had tried to imagine the kind of man who could give such an order. He'd wondered what such a person would do if his own child were about to be murdered. Still, seeing father and son together, Kirk wasn't sure.

"My son's actions were not known to me, Kirk," Kor said.

"I know that."

"Good." No apology. That would have been too human. And what he had said was as close as a Klingon would get to such a thing.

Kor nodded once, and with Scotty's facilitation he and his son were on the Klingon vessel.

Kirk nodded once at his engineer, who relinquished the transporter console to the normal duty crewman. Scotty exchanged some comment with McCoy—Kirk didn't hear what exactly—then exited toward engineering.

McCoy waited for Kirk and Spock, and they entered the corridor together. "Well," McCoy began, "it's small consolation, but at least it looks like Kor will exact some punishment for D'kar's actions. I wonder what 'grounded' translates to for Klingons."

"I suspect there is more shame involved," Spock said. "Klingon culture is concerned with particular honor rites and taboos that D'kar seems to have misunderstood, and therefore broken."

McCoy nodded thoughtfully rather than replying, and in silence they gathered into the turbolift. Kirk grasped the control handle and manually selected the bridge.

"You seem awfully quiet, Jim," McCoy finally prodded gently.

"I'm thinking about Captain Anders," Kirk said. As the lift doors parted, he led the others onto the bridge. "That's who's been truly punished in all this. He had the respect of those people, and now they doubt him, and he doubts himself." The captain stepped down to the command deck and swiveled the center seat around. He slid down easily into what had become his most familiar home.

"I sympathize with his dilemma, Captain," Spock said, falling into place to the captain's right as McCoy joined them on Kirk's left. "But he chose his path based on the subjective feeling that he was losing his 'command' to you. You did not threaten his authority, if I read your report correctly."

Kirk tilted his head a moment and half shrugged. "I didn't threaten his authority, but it *was* threatened, Spock. Those people needed him to lead them because they depended on his skills for their survival. Our presence negated that need. In a week's time that planetoid will have advisors, engineers, maybe even new settlers—all there to help build up the accidental colony they began. And transports will come to take off-world those who wish to go."

"We changed his world." McCoy understood.

"For the better, in many ways," Spock added.

"Except for Anders." Kirk let his hand touch the leather arm of his command chair and he ran his hand along its length. "He's lost his purpose, his self-respect, and . . . he's a good man who felt helpless as everything he had—everything he was—collapsed around him." The captain shrugged and realized he might be sounding a bit too sentimental, a bit too maudlin, for the bridge of a starship. To his mind, however, he looked at Anders and felt "there but for the grace of God go I."

"Interesting," Spock said after a moment of almost awkward silence. "Both Captain Anders and D'kar made certain subjective presumptions that led to vast misunderstandings on which they chose improper courses."

"Here it comes," McCoy murmured to Kirk.

"Here what comes, Doctor?" Spock asked coyly.

McCoy took the bait. "Here's where you lecture us that logic is the only way to make moral choices, and if only we were all pointy-eared Vulcans, then the universe would be filled with the muted joy of countless unemotional, cookie-cutter, stone-faced, walking computer banks."

One brow jutting above the other, which Kirk often believed was the Vulcan's version of an ironic smirk, Spock was deadpan: "On the contrary, Doctor. Nothing gives me more 'muted joy' than knowing you and I are so radically different."

Kirk smiled, McCoy fumed, and Spock lithely turned and strode to the science station.

Unlike Simon Anders, Jim Kirk's command—his world—was very intact. In *that* there was great comfort. All things change eventually, and while that fact brought tacit and minute anxiety, it was greatly calmed by the familiarity of duty and purpose he had for the foreseeable future.

The captain leaned back comfortably in his command chair. "Mr. Sulu," he said. "Ahead, warp factor one."

Ambition

William Leisner

William Leisner

William Leisner began writing at age six, scripting and drawing comic strips that featured his younger siblings, their animate stuffed animals, and lots of potty humor. Not long afterward, he discovered *Star Trek* through its syndicated reruns, though it would be almost twenty years before it would occur to him to combine these two interests.

His first professionally published story was "Gods, Fate, and Fractals" in *Star Trek: Strange New Worlds II*. This was followed by "Black Hats" in *Strange New Worlds IV*, and "The Trouble with Borg Tribbles," the third-place winner in *Strange New Worlds V*. Most recently, he's penned *Star Trek: Starfleet Corps of Engineers #57: Out of the Cocoon*. He also has to his credit a pair of award-winning teleplays for the student-run TV station at his alma mater, Ithaca College, and a story concept sale to *Star Trek: Voyager*.

A native of Rochester, New York, he now lives in Minneapolis.

Sulu's first reaction to Uhura's urgent report was to wonder why Captain Kirk so often chose to leave his ship without its commander or first officer.

Not that there had been any reason Mr. Spock should have remained on the *Enterprise* on this particular occasion: They were in orbit above Pentam V, a planet comfortably within Federation-controlled space. Though, on the other hand, there seemed to be no compelling reason the first officer had to join the captain for this conference with the Pentamians. It seemed a capricious decision—not that it would have occurred to Sulu to question it. Truth be told, even more than a year after his transfer to helmsman, he still felt a jolt of excitement whenever the two senior officers absented themselves and the captain declared, "You have the conn, Mr. Sulu."

He hadn't expected any further jolts during this fairly routine mission, but Uhura had certainly just provided one: "Mr. Sulu! We're receiving a distress call, priority channel."

Sulu collected himself immediately and cleared the steps to the bridge's raised perimeter with a single stride, stopping beside the communications officer. "What is it?"

Uhura looked past him, concentrating on the signals coming through the remote amplifier she held to her right ear. "It's from Thraz Outpost, an Andorian scientific base. It's an automated message—no details, just a request for emergency assistance."

Sulu turned forward. "Chekov?"

The navigator was already pulling information up from his database. "Aye, sir, Thraz Outpost. Two-point-four hours from our current position at warp five. No other Federation ships are reported in the vicinity."

Sulu nodded as he moved to the captain's chair and toggled open a channel to the surface. "*Enterprise* to Captain Kirk." Several seconds passed without a response from the planet, each one seeming to stretch longer than the previous one. "*Enterprise* to Spock, come in," Sulu said. More slow seconds stretched by.

Then at last: "Enterprise, *Spock here.*" The first officer's voice was low and sounded as if he was cupping his communicator in both hands, right up against his mouth.

"Is everything all right down there, Mr. Spock?" Sulu asked. "Where's the captain?"

"*All is well, Mr. Sulu. The captain is at the podium, making his opening statement to the Pentamian Assembly.*"

"Opening statement?" Sulu took a quick glance at the chronometer on the helm/navigation console. "The talks were supposed to have started almost four hours ago."

"*Indeed. The first three hours and twenty-three minutes were taken up by opening statements by all thirteen members of the Assembly leadership. We are now obligated, it seems, to make a similarly lengthy monologue.*" Vulcan or no, it wasn't hard to hear the frustration underneath Spock's flat tone.

"Sir, we've received an automated distress call from a nearby Andorian colony. They need immediate assistance, and we're the closest ship in range."

"*Stand by, Mr. Sulu.*"

He heard the snick of the hinged cover closing over the communicator's audio pickup. An almost subaudible hum was the only indication that the connection had not been lost. Sulu turned back to Uhura. "Have you been able to raise Thraz? Any more information?"

"Negative. And their signal is weakening; they may be drawing down their emergency power reserves."

Sulu's next question was cut off by the captain's voice. "Enterprise, *Kirk here.*"

"Sulu here, Captain. We've received a distress—"

"*Yes, Mr. Spock filled me in before taking the podium for me. Unfortunately, per Pentamian protocols, neither of us can leave the chambers before our negotiations are completed without forfeiting our bid for mining rights.*" Sulu frowned at that. He knew the Federation couldn't afford to let this dilithiumrich world slip away from them like that. Again he wondered why the captain made the choices he did, but his thoughts were broken by the one that followed. *"Kirk to Scott."*

From engineering, a third voice joined the conversation. *"Scott here, Captain."*

"Scotty, I'm putting you in temporary command of the Enterprise. *Set course for Thraz Outpost, maximum warp. Mr. Sulu will brief you on the emergency there."*

"Acknowledged, sir."

"Godspeed, gentlemen. Bring her back in one piece. Kirk out."

The captain's communicator cut off, while the intraship channel remained open. *"Scott to bridge."*

"Bridge, Mr. Scott," Sulu answered, already back at his regular position and punching up coordinates. "Course laid in and ready."

"Break orbit, Mr. Sulu, and engage warp drive once we're clear. I'm on my way up to the bridge."

The channel closed, and the bridge fell quiet but for the ambient chirps and beeps, and the rising hum of impulse engines pushing them out of planetary orbit. As Pentam V fell away on the main viewer, Chekov leaned over from his seat at the navigation console. "Well . . . *that* was a slap in the face."

Sulu's eyes flicked right, eyebrows raised. "What?"

"The captain relieving you of command, and tapping Mr. Scott instead."

Sulu shook his head as he turned his attention to his board again. "Lieutenant Commander Scott is the senior officer aboard, Ensign."

"I mean no disrespect to him, of course," Chekov said quickly. "But a starship bridge has its own command structure."

"Theoretically," Sulu said. On most Starfleet ships, that was indeed the case. Yet another example of James Kirk's peculiar command style.

Chekov continued. "You're senior bridge officer, and you're on a command track. You do want your own command someday, *da*?"

He'd never actually given it that much thought; it'd been only a little over a year since he'd switched to wearing a gold uniform shirt. Yet he heard himself say, "Well, sure. But someday doesn't have to be today."

"Still . . . you don't find it a little bothersome that the captain trusts you to command the ship in orbit, but not in a crisis?"

"That's not how I see things," Sulu said with a dismissive shake of his head. Yet, now that Chekov had shared his point of view, he found it difficult to shift his perception back again.

As many times as Scotty had made the trip between main engineering and the bridge, it always struck him, watching the light bars slide across the turbolift display panel, how *enormous* the *Enterprise* was. He had served on nine other ships in his twenty-plus-year Starfleet career, some of them so compact that the engine room and conn were separated by no more than a pair of doors. On the *Enterprise,* though, with its separate and distinct drive and saucer sections, it was almost as if he were serving on two different ships: one of engines and mechanics, where the laws of physics held sway, and the other, where the captain was forced to deal with issues of people, politics, and other unexplainable phenomena. All things being equal, Scotty preferred his *Enterprise.*

The turbolift car decelerated as it approached the top of the saucer, and Scott took a deep bracing breath before the doors opened onto the other ship. The first thing he saw was the captain's chair at the center of the circular bridge, empty and waiting for him. He glanced away and found Sulu standing by his helm station. "Mr. Scott."

Scotty nodded as he took the two steps down into the command center. "Report, Mr. Sulu."

"We're under way to the Thraz system at warp five. ETA: two hours, seventeen minutes."

"I'm starting to pick up additional transmissions from Thraz," Uhura interjected from her station. The muscles in her jaw and her elegant neck were tight as she concentrated on and processed the information coming in through her earpiece. "They're saying they've been attacked by an unidentified alien ship. It entered the system completely undetected, struck their residential area, and immediately left the system. Fortunately, given the time of day, they believe most residents should have been safely out of their homes."

"Let's hope they're right," Scott said. "Anything else?"

Uhura frowned as her fingers went from one knob to the next on her console. "Hard to say. The signals are very weak—the attack also overloaded their power distribution network, and they're operating on emergency backup generators. Most of the messages are very confused and contradictory, as well."

"Par for the course in the wake of a catastrophe," Scotty noted with a sigh.

"'Completely undetected,'" Sulu repeated ominously. "It couldn't be Romulans, could it?"

"In this sector?" Scotty frowned. "I doubt it." He certainly hoped it wasn't the Romulans, though the attackers' identity made little difference to the task at hand. "Bridge to sickbay," he said as he tabbed the intercom on the captain's chair.

"Sickbay. McCoy here."

"Doctor, have you been briefed on our current mission?"

"Got the word from Sulu not five minutes ago. I've got the lab brewing up some basic Andorian meds, and my staff and I are boning up on Andorian physiology."

"Good work," Scott said, as much to McCoy as to Sulu, who acknowledged with a slight nod.

"Save your praise until there's cause for it, Scotty. The way these people's insides are put together . . . well, I'll never needle Spock about his Vulcan anatomy again."

Scotty chuckled. "I'll be sure to let him know you said so, Doctor. Bridge out."

"Klingons."

Scotty's head jerked toward the forward screen. "What?"

Sulu turned and looked up at him. "Rumor's been the Klingons and Romulans are negotiating some kind of alliance. If the Romulans were to agree to share their cloaking devices . . ."

As his heart slowed back to a normal rate, Scotty said, "Even if we were to put stock in rumor . . . why would the Klingons target a science base this far into Federation space?" He turned to the bridge science station, where a young man in a blue uniform sat in Spock's place, passively listening to the ongoing discussion. "Ensign?"

The ensign snapped ramrod straight in his seat. "Yes, sir?"

"This Thraz Outpost. What do we know about it?"

The young man gaped back at him as if perplexed by the question. "It's . . . an Andorian science colony. . . ."

Scotty put up a hand to stop him. "What's your name, lad?"

"David Frank, sir."

"Mr. Frank, the reason we have a manned science station on the bridge is so that, when the command staff have a question of a scientific nature, someone is ready with an answer, if not before the question is asked, then quickly afterward." Scotty's eyes locked hard on the junior officer's. "Do I make myself understood?"

Frank nodded, then added a spoken, "Yes, sir."

Scott nodded back. "I want to know what the scientists are doing at Thraz Outpost, and why that might attract the attention of hostile forces." Turning then to the communications officer, he continued. "Uhura, keep listening and trying to raise the colony. We'll meet in the briefing room in thirty minutes. Mr. Sulu," he then said to the helmsman, and tilted his head toward the engineering station.

Sulu followed him up the steps, and the two of them huddled close in hushed conversation. "I wanted to say, a bit more directly, that you did a fine job directing matters in the first minutes of the crisis."

Sulu smiled modestly. "Thank you, sir. I appreciate that."

Scotty nodded, and then gestured subtly over his shoulder. "Tell me, Sulu . . . Ensign Frank there . . ."

"He started on bridge rotation just three weeks ago. He's green, but he'll be fine, I'm sure."

Scott nodded again, though he was far from satisfied. "I'd like for you to pair up with him for this mission."

Sulu's face fell. "Sir?"

"I trust he'll mature into a fine officer someday. But this is an emergency situation and . . . well, Mr. Spock does leave some mighty big shoes to fill. Given your science background, it makes the most sense that you'd be the one to help do that."

Sulu considered that. "I suppose when you put it that way, I can't argue."

"Good lad," Scotty said, favoring Sulu with a grateful pat on the shoulder.

Sulu had tried to tell himself that being asked to "fill Spock's shoes" meant that Scott, as commander, saw him in the role of the ship's first officer: a trusted advisor and respected sounding board. But huddled with the junior officer at Mr. Spock's station, scrolling through back issues of Andorian scientific journals, he couldn't help but feel as if he'd in fact been knocked a few steps down the ship's hierarchy.

Sulu had spent the first seven years of his Starfleet career in science division blue. However, he soon learned that the great discoveries didn't get made in starship labs; those labs and their staffs were there to test and confirm discoveries made by members of the bridge crew. He resolved to do what he had to to make the transition—no easy matter, not only in terms of the testing, but also in terms of convincing his superiors to take a chance on an officer with a mid-career change of heart. There was no good reason for Captain Kirk to agree to give the head of his ship's astrophysics department the helmsman's position, but he had seen something in him and was willing to give him the chance to show what he could do.

And Montgomery Scott is no James Kirk.

Sulu silently reprimanded himself for that uncharitable thought. He was a Starfleet officer, and that sort of bitterness was beneath him. Yet, as he entered the briefing room, it was with the feeling that he had no real purpose to serve here.

Once everyone was seated, Scott started the meeting with a question to Uhura. "Have you got any more news from Thraz?"

"Yes, sir. Most of the colony is still on backup power only, but their emergency services are beginning to get a handle on matters. So far, casualties are being reported as lighter than initially estimated."

"Well, thank heavens for that," McCoy said.

"Yes, however, reports now are that the attack somehow triggered a series of quakes across the planet's main landmass. They're concerned that whatever the weapon the aliens used, it may have actually created a new fault line."

"It would take a hell of a weapon to do that," Sulu said, eyes wide in disbelief. "Were they able to say anything more about the alien ship? Track it at all as it left the system?"

Uhura shook her head. "They never detected it on approach, and the attack disrupted all their sensor and tracking systems."

Before Sulu could ask any further questions, Scott turned to Frank. "Have you found out anything about what these Andorian scientists are doing out here?"

"Aye, sir." Frank reached forward and activated the three-sided monitor at the center of the table. The screens all lit up, displaying a five-planet star system and a bright, unlabeled line running just beyond the orbit of the outermost planet. "Thraz Outpost was established sixty-six years ago in order to study the Thraz Streamer." With a touch of a button, the screen diagram became animated, with the planets orbiting their star and the line undulating like a flowing river. "The streamer, named for the Andorian captain who discovered it, is a flume of tachyons, faster-than-light particles ejected from the rotational axis of a nearby pulsar, and extending out beyond the edge of the galaxy. In theory, a starship would be able to ride the stream like sailing ships ride ocean currents."

"Warp speed without warp engines," Scott said, studying the display screen in fascination. "That would certainly be the kind of technology a lot of species would like to get their hands on."

"Except the Andorians have had almost no practical success along those lines," Frank continued. "The streamer is only about twenty meters at its widest, too narrow for anything much larger than a shuttle-craft. It also has a disruptive effect on the warp fields of any ships that come within close proximity, which makes entering the streamer without being torn apart by delta-v forces tricky at best."

"And by tricky, I take it, you mean insanely dangerous," McCoy interjected.

Scott frowned. "So you're saying their research wasn't such that it could have been reasonable motive for the attack."

"I wouldn't think so, no, sir," Frank answered.

"Well . . . it's not something we need to worry ourselves with right now—"

"Isn't it?" Sulu hadn't meant to blurt out that reaction aloud. Though he couldn't say he regretted it.

Scott, showing no offense to this borderline insubordination, answered, "Our first concern is for the colony and their injured."

Engineer's thinking, Sulu thought to himself. *Focus only on fixing what's broken, without looking at the bigger picture.* "Of course, sir. But whoever did this—"

"Once we deal with the immediate crisis, of course we'll gather whatever evidence we can to point to a perpetrator. But what's to be done beyond that will be decided by Captain Kirk and Starfleet Command."

Sulu still wasn't comfortable with Scott's almost dismissive attitude toward the unknown enemy. But he was still his superior officer. "Aye, sir," he said, then rose with the others as the meeting concluded. Everyone filed out of the briefing room, heading back to their regular duties, while Sulu fell in behind Ensign Frank and followed him back to the bridge.

The *Enterprise*'s route from Pentam brought them within two astronomical units of the tachyon streamer. Ship's sensors resolved the dynamic particle flow on the main screen as a shimmering band, vibrating with energy like a taut harp string, flashing through all the colors of the spectrum. It was a sight that made Scotty, if for only a moment, forget all about being back in the engine room.

"Mr. Chekov," Scotty said, "are you detecting any effect the phenomenon is having on our warp drive at this distance?"

"A negligible one, sir. Less than a point-zero-one variance in our subspace field."

Scotty nodded. "Steady as she goes." He resolved, when this was over and the captain was back aboard, to compare his engine logs to Thraz's research. There'd likely be a journal article in that . . .

"Mr. Scott!" Scotty turned to the science station, where Lieutenant Sulu stood hunched over its hooded viewer. "I'm detecting an object traveling *inside* the streamer." Sulu turned to meet Scotty's eyes. "It looks like a ship!"

"A ship?" Scotty was about to say something about that being impossible, but from Sulu's expression, the lieutenant was already aware of that fact. Instead, he said, "Put it onscreen. Full magnification."

The multihued ribbon suddenly filled the middle third of the forward viewer, and the entire bridge was awash with its shifting colors. And sure enough, Scotty saw the large dark object that seemed to ride the tachyon current like a leaf in the wind, heading away from the Thraz system at superluminal speeds.

"That has to be the alien ship that attacked the colony," Chekov declared, his voice rising with excitement. Scotty could find no reason to dispute his conclusion.

Not so with the next declaration, this one from Sulu. "We have to go after them."

"Mr. Sulu, our orders are to provide assistance to the victims of the attack, not to go off and—"

"If we don't go after them, right now, we'll never find them again," Sulu shot back. And in all likelihood, he was absolutely correct. "Mr. Scott," Sulu continued, his already deep voice dropping further, "all reports so far indicate manageable casualty levels."

Scotty turned to Uhura. She looked somewhat startled by the minor power struggle being played out before her, but maintained enough of her characteristic poise to answer the question immediately: "That's still the case, yes. There are, however, continued reports of widespread tremors stretching the colony's—"

"Sir," Sulu interrupted, "if those tremors were triggered by an alien weapon, we're going to have to learn as much about that technology as possible."

That bit of logic may as well have come from Spock; Scotty certainly had no way to refute it. The only reason he had now to dismiss Sulu's protests was to salvage his own pride. After a brief pause, he said, "Set intercept course with that ship."

Sulu all but ran across the bridge to his helm station, his hands working the controls with confidence. The entire bridge seemed to hum in anticipation of the coming confrontation.

"Course laid in and ready, sir."

Scotty, seated uncomfortably on the edge of the captain's chair, nodded slowly. "Very well. Take us after them."

The starscape on the main viewer rotated, the streamer sliding away off the right edge of the screen. As it did, Scotty felt a slight vibration of the deck plating through the soles of his boots. His neck hair already started to prickle before Chekov spoke up to report, "The warp field disruption effect is becoming more pronounced as we take on a course parallel to the streamer, sir. It will grow exponentially as we maneuver closer."

This time, Frank was ready with his information and, without prompting, said, "The reports from Thraz have the specs they used to modify their defensive screens and warp fields. Our systems aren't quite the same as their research ships—"

"Not so different, though," Scotty said, jumping to his feet. "You have those specs up now, Mr. Frank?"

"Right here, sir," Frank answered, as he too got out of his chair in deference to the senior officer.

Scott took the three steps up from the command well—and then, for the briefest of instances, hesitated.

"Transfer them down to main engineering," he said, smoothly shifting his direction, now walking away from the science station, past Uhura's post, toward the orange double doors. "I'll look them over, and work on modifying them down there. Mr. Sulu: You have the conn."

The turbolift doors slid closed. Scotty sighed as the car started its descent.

Sulu felt all eyes on him, waiting expectantly for his first order. "Chekov, maintain parallel course with the alien at safe distance."

"Mr. Sulu," Uhura said behind him, "shall I inform the Thraz Outpost authorities of our change of objective?"

Was there a coolness to Uhura's tone, or was he imagining it? "Let them know that we are in pursuit of their attackers," Sulu said, "and to give us any updates if there's any change in their situation."

"Aye, sir."

That time he felt the shiver run up his spine.

He stood up out of the captain's chair and started to slowly pace the bridge, just as he'd watched Captain Kirk so often do in such situations. He circled the upper portion nonchalantly until he reached the communications station, where he paused, turned, and leaned in over Uhura's right shoulder. "Any response yet?"

"Our message was acknowledged as received," she answered without looking at him.

"No protests?"

"The response was just as I said, sir."

"I didn't mean the Andorians, Nyota," he whispered.

Uhura jerked her head around, glaring at Sulu at first with anger, which shifted to something more closely resembling disappointment. "If you're asking me if I have a problem with command-level decisions, then no; it's not my place to question them."

"Then what?"

Uhura hesitated, weighing her next words carefully. "Have you ever seen Mr. Spock arguing with the captain the way you were with Mr. Scott?"

Sulu's expression twisted in confusion. "Spock is *always* telling the captain what's the logical thing to do, challenging him when he thinks he's wrong . . ."

"But he always does so *respectfully*. He never does it in a way meant to make the captain feel unqualified for command . . ."

"Hold on, now. I never said anything like that to Scott!"

Uhura narrowed her eyes at him. "Mr. Sulu, I'm a communications specialist. You say a lot of things . . . just not all of them with words."

Sulu realized what those dark eyes were communicating to him, and he found he had to shift his own gaze away. Uhura turned back to her board then, while Sulu returned to his slow pacing of the bridge.

The man who designed the Jefferies tube network and integrated it into the vast array of starship systems was a genius, no question. Still, Scotty cursed his name. Crawling up and down and through the damned things any time they needed the ship to do something the brains at the Fleet Yards hadn't anticipated (and there was a *hell* of a lot out here they never anticipated) was a good way of reminding him that, though he wasn't yet old, he was a long time past being young.

He shifted his weight from one leg to the other on the narrow foot ledge as he ran his phase welder along the top edge of the backup warp plasma flow regulator, then pulled the part free from its socket. He dropped it into one compartment of his toolkit, then from another extracted his newly customized regulator, reconfigured based on Andorian experimentation and good old Starfleet innovation. Given time, he could have designed a variable flow regulator that would have allowed him to make the same kind of adjustments with a touch of a button from any engineering console. Including the one on the bridge.

"Mr. Scott?"

Scotty started in surprise, dropping the new unit. It skittered down the inclined passageway and Scotty slapped his hand frantically against the tube interior, grabbing the part before it got past waist level. Then, twisting his body so he could look down past his feet, he saw McCoy standing with his head up the bottom end of the tube. "Doctor? What are you doing down here?"

"I was just about to ask you the same question. Followed by the question, why are we no longer on our way to Thraz?"

"Change of plans," Scotty said, turning back to his installation task.

"Is that the answer to the first question or the second?"

"Doctor, I am a wee bit busy at the moment. Is there something that you need?"

Scotty took the silence that followed as a negative. He realized he should have known better where Leonard McCoy was concerned, when a minute later the doctor's head appeared a few meters overhead, where he was now peering down through the tube's upper terminus. "There. That's better than trying to talk to your aft section," he said with an almost impish half grin.

"Doctor, you're really not supposed to be in this area of the ship," Scotty cautioned.

"Yeah, and I could say the same to you," the doctor replied. "Why aren't you on the bridge?"

"Because this is where I'm needed." To illustrate his point, Scotty turned his attention back to replacing the regulator.

"Poppycock!" McCoy practically growled. "You have an entire engineering staff, Mr. Scott. Where you're needed is where the captain asked you to serve in his absence."

"The captain didn't know what we do now about what happened at Thraz. Mr. Sulu is our most experienced bridge officer. I trust him . . ."

"Oh, don't get me wrong. I trust Sulu, too. The problem, Scotty, is that you're not putting any trust in yourself. Instead, you let some ambitious kid scare you off the bridge."

"Scare me?" Scott chortled at that. "Aren't we both just a little old for that game? Are you going to call me a chicken and make clucking noises now?"

"Mr. Scott, you're supposed to be in command of this ship!" McCoy growled.

"I'm an engineer, dammit, not a ship commander," Scotty barked right back at him. "I've been an engineer for over twenty years, and if I live another hundred years, an engineer is still what I'll be. This extra row on my sleeve doesn't make me qualified to sit in that center chair and give orders to that crew. If it did," he said, gesturing to the identical gold braiding on McCoy's own shirt cuff, "you'd be in line to run this ship yourself."

"Bite your tongue!"

"Ha!" Scotty smiled triumphantly. "You see what I'm getting at, then."

"Hell, of course I do, Scotty. With all the damned fool landing parties the captain insists on dragging me off on, how could I not? The thing is, though, I trust in his judgment, and that there's a method to his madness. Besides which, you gotta see it as some kind of compliment. Jim, I think, can see a lot more in people than we can see for ourselves."

"Could be," Scotty admitted after a moment.

"So?"

Scotty finished the module swap and placed his tool back in its kit. "I appreciate what you said, and your intentions in saying them, Doctor. Now please get the hell out of my Jefferies tube."

"Aye, sir," McCoy said with a scowl.

Once the doctor was gone, Scotty climbed down into main engineering and stepped to the nearest wall intercom. "Scott to bridge."

"Sulu here, Mr. Scott."

"If you switch from primary to secondary WPF systems, you'll be able to maneuver the ship safely to within ten kilometers of that thing out there. Maybe a touch closer, depending on how precise these Andorian measurements are."

"Excellent, Mr. Scott. Thank you."

"Aye. Scott out."

The engineer flicked the switch off and turned to head for the engine room. He'd barely gotten two paces toward the door when the intercom whistled for his attention again. *"Bridge to Mr. Scott,"* came Sulu's voice.

Scotty sighed, turned back, and hit the button once more. "Scott here."

There was a slight hesitation on the other end of the circuit, and then, *"Your orders, Commander?"*

Scotty blinked, somewhat stunned. Captain Kirk was in the habit of referring to all his officers—all his male officers, at any rate—as "Mister" and eschewing the use of ranks except in the most formal circumstances. It was a custom the rest of his crew adapted as well, so it was a bit jarring right now to hear Sulu address him with that kind of deference. "Move to intercept, gradual approach," Scotty said. He hesitated a moment more, then added, "I'm on my way up."

"Aye, sir."

Scotty considered the intercom a moment after it fell silent, reflecting on Sulu's words, and McCoy's, and the ones in the back of his own head. Then, with a deep breath, he headed back to the bridge.

"We already *had* orders to pursue."

Chekov muttered his comment so softly, Sulu wasn't sure he was meant to hear it. He moved up from where he stood beside the captain's chair and lay a hand on the back of Chekov's. "I'm sorry, Ensign, did you say something?" he asked, making no effort not to be overheard.

Chekov turned and looked up and him, all youthful innocence. "I just said, we already had our orders. Sir," he added, flashing that boyish smile that had helped him ingratiate himself to the entire crew in his short time aboard. Behind the smile, Sulu read all the things his friend wouldn't say aloud: *You didn't need to page Scott a second time and give him the excuse to return to the bridge. Worse, you sounded like an indecisive fool doing it. You had the chance to command this mission, Hikaru, and you blew it.*

Sulu pushed all those self-recriminations down and answered Chekov, while at the same time addressing the entire bridge crew with a clear, deep voice. "This is an unknown alien ship, which attacked Federation citizens without provocation, with unknown—and perhaps superior—weaponry. This is a time we all have to pull together as a crew, to cooperate, to put all other concerns aside, for the good of this ship and the four hundred thirty lives aboard her. Am I understood?"

That elicited an abashed look from Chekov. Turning away from the young officer, Sulu also caught a tiny smile of approval from Uhura and deferential nods from the rest of the bridge crew. And it was at that moment, when he finally felt the respect of the people around him, that the turbolift opened and he was displaced by the arrival of a superior officer.

"Status, Mr. Sulu?" Scott asked as he stepped down to the center of the bridge, stopping on one side of the captain's chair, with Sulu standing on the other.

"On intercept course now," Sulu reported. "We'll be at minimum safe distance in thirty seconds."

Scott turned to consider the growing image of the alien ship on the main viewer. "Any change in their speed or course?"

"Negative, sir," Chekov said, as he divided his attention between his board and the screen. "They're keeping at a constant warp three-point-seven."

A corner of Scott's mouth twisted as he considered that. "Just enjoying the ride." He turned to the communications officer. "Are you attempting to hail them, Lieutenant?"

"I am," she replied, "but with all the subspace interference, I doubt they're receiving us."

"One hundred kilometers and closing," Chekov reported.

"Bring us directly abreast of them, Chekov."

"Aye, sir. Fifty kilometers . . . thirty . . ." A slight but definite tremor washed through the ship just as Chekov announced, "Ten kilometers, and holding distance."

"Steady as she goes," Scott said, staring at the dark shape that surfed heedless along the river of superluminal energy. "Any indication at all that they know we're here?"

Chekov shook his head. "Their course and speed still steady."

"Still can't get a signal through," Uhura added from her station.

Scott frowned at the screen, then turned to the helmsman. "Suggestions, Mr. Sulu?"

For a split second, Sulu imagined Scott was taunting him for having brought them to this impasse. He didn't really believe so, but whether or not the senior officer was genuinely soliciting his strategic advice, he couldn't let the impression that he was unconfident remain. "Fire a photon torpedo across their bow. Get their attention, and hopefully draw them out into normal space."

Scotty couldn't help but admire the confidence with which the bridge officer made his recommendation. He was also relieved that he didn't suggest firing directly on the blind vessel—no matter what Kirk or McCoy thought him capable of, Scotty did not believe something like that was included.

There was one concern he had with Sulu's proposal, though. "Do we know what the effect of a photon explosion within the streamer will actually be?"

Sulu frowned, immediately understanding Scott's hesitation. Before he could say anything, though, Ensign Frank piped up from his post. "There was an Andorian shuttle that reportedly suffered fusion drive failure inside the streamer early on. It caused a sharp spike in radiated energy, but otherwise had no effect."

"Except to the shuttle," Scotty muttered, then quickly added, "Thank you, Mr. Frank," to acknowledge his contribution. Turning back, he addressed Chekov. "Ready photon torpedo number one, and

set for detonation five hundred meters off their bow, minimal yield."
With any luck, that would be enough to get the aliens' attention, but do
nothing more than that.

"Aye, sir," Chekov answered. "Torpedo armed and ready."

Scotty stared at the screen. "Fire."

The missile shot from its launch tube and crossed the short distance
to the Thraz Streamer in a bright streaking blur. Seconds later, a spot of
increasing brightness appeared within the phenomenon, and it seemed
to bulge, like a blocked blood vessel getting ready to burst.

"*BRACE—*"

That was all Sulu managed to get out before the deck fell out from
under them. Scotty grabbed at the arm of the captain's chair and
missed, ending up doubled over the back of Chekov's chair. "Damage
control parties, report!" he called as soon the ship's artificial gravity reasserted itself and he found his breath again.

"All departments reporting minor injuries only," Uhura said, already
back in her seat, one hand tugging at the hem of her uniform skirt.

"Shields holding at ninety percent," Chekov added as he settled himself back into his chair and reviewed the status of his board. He started
as he noticed a change in another of his readouts. "The alien ship! It's
gone! It's left the streamer!"

Scott's initial sense of elation was short-lived, overtaken quickly by
concern. "Where are they?"

"Astern of us, and falling away . . ." Chekov turned to face Scotty
with an expression of disbelief. "Mr. Scott, they came to an almost in-
stantaneous full stop!"

"They what?" Scott's expression matched the navigator's. On reflection, he shouldn't have been so surprised. If the aliens could enter the
FTL streamer from normal space without being torn to atoms, it stood
to reason they could do the reverse just as easily. "Take us out of warp,
and bring us about!" Scott agonized as the *Enterprise* went through its
own gradual deceleration, from warp 3.7 to warp 1 to normal relativistic
velocities. By the time Sulu could safely execute a 180-degree course
change, they'd already overshot the alien ship by some 40 million kilometers.

While he did that, Dr. McCoy burst through the turbolift doors and onto the bridge. "What's going on up here?" Something in his expression seemed to soften when he spotted Scotty standing beside Kirk's chair, but it didn't soften his tone. "You could give a person some warning before you start knocking the ship around like a damned piñata!"

"Sorry, Doctor, it was unavoidable."

The doctor grunted but said nothing else. Instead, his attention was drawn to the image on the forward screen. Fortunately, the aliens had not taken advantage of their superior maneuverability to elude the *Enterprise*. Instead, they seemed content to sit and wait for the starship to come back to them. "Drop to one-quarter impulse," Scott ordered, and as the image of the alien ship on the viewer grew larger, they got their first good look at their nemesis.

The immediate impression the ship gave was that of a snail shell: a whitish-gray ovoid, tapering toward the stern, with darker bands of pinwheeling spirals marking the hull. It had no apparent means of propulsion, at least not in a way Scotty could understand. Then again, any ship that could do the things they'd already witnessed this one doing was, by definition, outside of Scotty's understanding. He began to wonder just how fortunate they really were that the ship hadn't just disappeared on them.

"In full sensor range now," Sulu reported.

"Scan them," Scott ordered. "Uhura, any response to our hails?"

Uhura frowned as she pulled her remote audio receiver from her ear. "I'm . . . not sure, sir. This is very odd . . ."

"What is?"

"Here, let me show you," she said, shuffling through data tape cartridges and plugging one into her console. "Here's the initial response we got to our standard hail."

She pressed a button on her console, and the bridge speakers came alive, speaking in the familiar, vaguely feminine voice of the ship computer: *"unoen vesel this is thestarshipenterpriez repreesenting theyunietedfederaeshunuvplanets wee wish tukomyunikaet pleez respond."*

Scotty cocked his head. "They're just repeating our hail message back to us."

"No, sir. If they were simply repeating it, we would hear it back through the universal translator in unmodified Standard. They're *mimicking* the linguacode. There's evidence of intelligence there, in the way they understand that 'the *Starship Enterprise*' and 'the United Federation of Planets' are single concepts."

"All right. But why is that so strange?"

"What's strange about it is, they aren't using their own language. Linguacode is a system for finding commonalities in different languages, not a language in and of itself. But these aliens are using it as one. It's almost as if they don't *have* their own native language."

"That's preposterous," Scott said. "How could any culture advanced enough to build a ship like that not have a language?"

Sulu turned to look over his shoulder at Scott. "I don't believe it *is* a ship."

"What?"

"Mr. Frank, do a level-one scan sequence," Sulu said to the science officer, and then gestured for Scott to look at his tactical scan readouts. "There's no centralized power system, no discrete propulsion or weaponry; its physical structure more closely resembles an organic design than an artificial one."

"You're saying this is a *life-form*?" Scott looked at the thing floating before the ship, his mind beginning to reel. A spaceborne life-form, one naturally adapted to a tachyon environment. . . . "Uhura, could that explain why they're responding to our hails the way they are? Or it is?"

"Maybe," she said uncertainly. "It has the capacity for language, just not the skill. It's as if—"

Whatever she was about to say was cut off by a loud gasp. Scotty moved back to the orange rail separating her level of the bridge from his. "What is it, Lieutenant?"

Uhura turned to him, her mouth slightly agape, and her eyes sparkling. "Mr. Scott . . . the way it's mimicking our communication attempts . . . it's like a child, trying to learn adult speech."

"What?" McCoy, who'd been watching unobtrusively from the edge of the bridge, stepped forward now. "You mean to say that thing out there is a *baby*?" Almost as one, every set of eyes turned to the alien creature on the screen, just sitting out there, as if awaiting parental guidance.

"Big baby," Chekov muttered.

"A baby that attacked an Andorian science colony," Sulu added. He turned to face Scott, whose gaze had also moved to him . . . though there was something else going on behind those eyes.

"We've been coming at this the wrong way," the engineer announced.

"What do you mean?" Sulu asked.

Scotty started to pace the bridge. "We've been asking, why would an unknown alien attack Thraz? We never asked *how* it attacked. The scientific outpost exists for the primary purpose of studying this tachyon streamer, which would seem to be this creature's natural habitat. Plus, it's an *Andorian* outpost—not a people who tend to be lax about security issues. How then could this alien—this immature alien, no less—reach the planet and attack the heart of a population center without anyone ever detecting it?"

"But they did see it, as it was"—Sulu hesitated as something seemed then to click in his brain—"leaving, after the attack."

Scotty nodded encouragingly. "After, but not before. What if this newborn was never detected approaching Thraz because it was *born on* Thraz? What if, instead of blasting a hole in the planet, it dug itself out?"

Sulu's eyes widened in comprehension. "Like a sea turtle laying eggs on a beach. It could have been there years before the Andorians arrived. You really think that could be what happened?"

"It's easy enough to tell a blast crater from an excavation," Scotty said. "I suspect, in the confusion of the immediate crisis, no one on Thraz has taken that close a look, but once we do . . ."

"Gentlemen, excuse me," McCoy interrupted, a frown furrowing his brow, "but something occurs to me. Sea turtles don't tend to bury one egg at a time."

Sulu blanched. "The tremors."

As did Scott. "Dear God . . ."

• • •

Hovering just on the edge of the flowing energy field that called to the deepest part of its still-forming consciousness, the alien watched confused as the adult flew away, in the wrong direction. Unable to understand, it eventually let its instinct guide it back into the streamer, which would take it where it was meant to go.

The *Enterprise* dropped out of warp on the outskirts of Thraz's star system and slipped neatly into orbit above a moonless, blue-white planet. Crossing the terminator to the planet's lit, starward side, the Andorian settlement came into view: a small city of close-built structures sitting just south of the equator, straddling the banks of a river that wound through a broad savanna. Other than the relatively small sinkhole left by the alien hatchling, the colony appeared, at a glance, a pleasant, tranquil settlement. With more than just a glance, though, they found trouble stirring below the surface.

Ensign Frank frowned into the sensor hood, then turned to Scott and Sulu. "I count at least fifty of the aliens, buried across a five-kilometer stretch of land, running right under the colony . . . almost all of them moving toward the surface."

Sulu leaned in to take a look for himself. Ghostly blue images generated by the ground-penetrating sensors outlined several dozen small spherical masses—more closely analogous to larvae than eggs, in his judgment—deposited in what had been a deep furrow dug by their progenitor decades earlier. As Frank said, the majority of them were now animate and preparing to emerge from their nest, heedless of what lay between them and their freedom.

"Sir, we're being hailed again," Uhura said, her voice calm, but also conveying the impatience that was no doubt part of the message from the planet. It was more than an hour past their original ETA, and they'd been in orbit now for five minutes without responding to planetary hails.

"Stand by, Lieutenant," Scott answered, sounding not a little impatient himself. He looked to Frank then. "Are you sure we can't just beam them out?"

"No, sir, I'm not sure," he admitted. "But every species I know of where their young are incubated and born in any way similar to this, the struggle of freeing themselves is an important part of their development. If you dig a sea turtle out of the sand, it won't be strong enough to get to the water on its own, or avoid predators if it does. We have to go on the assumption that the same holds true for these creatures."

Scott sighed. "Then all we can do is try to minimize the damage they do. Come on, lad," he said, moving toward the turbolift. "You're with me."

"Mr. Scott," Uhura said again as he and Frank brushed past her, the frustration in her voice coming now more from her own emotions.

"Mr. Sulu," Scott called over his shoulder, "you can deal with the Andorians."

The turbolift doors began to slide shut, but suddenly Sulu was across the bridge from the science station, with one hand holding the car. "Mr. Scott, with all respect, they aren't going to be happy if I'm—"

"I suspect they're not going to be happy, no matter what," Scott said. "But I trust you'll be able to handle them."

"I really don't think—"

"Lad . . . don't be modest. You got a way of speaking, of making others see your way, despite themselves," Scott said, giving the younger man a self-effacing smile.

Sulu gave him an apologetic grin back. "They're bound to come back to their senses eventually."

Scott chuckled at that. "If this works, we'll only need a few minutes."

"I'll do what I can, sir."

Scott nodded and said, "Mr. Sulu, you have the conn," as the doors slid shut.

After a moment's reflection, Sulu moved down the steps and lowered himself into the captain's chair. He stared forward, fingers steepled beneath his chin, and said, "Uhura, open a channel."

The image of the planet was replaced by that of a blue-skinned, antennaed, fiercely scowling alien. *Well, it certainly took you people long enough to respond!* the Andorian said in a surprisingly high, reedy voice that did not quite match his cragged face and short white hair.

Sulu, holding himself steady, replied, "Our apologies. We were delayed due to a number of factors. I am Hikaru Sulu, commanding the *U.S.S. Enterprise.*"

"*Did Starfleet send us a cadet training ship?*" Sulu realized that, holding his arms as he did, the single lieutenant's braid on his uniform sleeve was clearly evident. *"Why are we part of this Federation with you Earthers if this is the level of respect we are afforded?"*

Resisting the instinct to drop his hands to his lap, he said, "I'm sorry you feel disrespected by our presence, Mister . . . ?"

The Andorian's scowl deepened at that. Sulu wondered briefly if he'd given more offense by misjudging the alien's gender. *"You may address me as Director Shrevan."*

"Director Shrevan," Sulu said with a nod. "You need to immediately evacuate your relief teams and any remaining residents from the area around the blast site to a safe distance of at least five kilometers."

Now Shrevan smiled at him, but it was anything but a friendly expression. *"I don't take orders from Starfleet officers, especially not ones as ill-informed as you. We've determined the alien did not blast the residential quarter as first reported, but instead excavated some object beneath the surface. Now, Lieutenant Sulu, I'm transmitting a list of medical and reconstruction supplies, which you will beam down immediately. Then you will set out in pursuit of these thieves, and recover that which they stole from us."*

Sulu considered Shrevan's supposedly intimidating expression for a moment in silence, and then turned to Uhura to signal for the transmission to be muted. "Are you receiving Shrevan's lists?" he asked once she indicated the Andorian was no longer privy to their conversation.

"Yes, coming in now."

"Forward them to sickbay and ship's stores, and tell both to stand by." Sulu paused to collect his thoughts, then turned forward again. "Put the director back onscreen," he said.

Again, Shrevan's visage appeared on the screen. *"Lieutenant Sulu, I don't know what they teach about proper diplomatic protocol—"*

"Director Shrevan," Sulu interrupted, his voice raised just a notch above a polite level, "is Thraz Outpost still experiencing the unexplained tremors you reported earlier?"

Shrevan was slightly surprised by the sudden role reversal between intimidator and intimidated, but held his composure. *"Yes, we are. But our top scientists are studying—"*

"Our science officers have already determined their cause," Sulu interrupted again, in a tone that seemed to send shivers up the length of Shrevan's antennae. "And we've devised a way to put an end to them, while minimizing any further damage to your colony."

Shrevan's eyes widened. *"Then what are you waiting for?"*

His voice rumbling slowly, Sulu said, "I am waiting for you, as I asked before, to evacuate the area within five kilometers of the excavation site."

"I . . . I'll have my people get to it immediately."

"Excellent. Thank you, Director. *Enterprise* out."

The screen again changed back to the image of Thraz from orbit, and Sulu allowed himself a wisp of a smile as he leaned back into the captain's chair.

A dull thud, followed by a muffled curse, reverberated from inside the open Jefferies tube. "You all right in there, lad?" Scotty called, grinning in spite of himself.

"Fine, sir," Frank's echoing voice replied. "I just need one . . . more . . . second . . . There!" The younger man dropped onto the deck of the tractor beam master control room, as if he had leapt down the sloped conduit. "I think we're all set," he said as he joined Scott at the main control board on the far side of the room. Both started checking system readouts against the figures jotted on an electronic clipboard that lay on the console between them. "I sure hope this works."

Silently, Scotty hoped so, too. The tractor beam was designed to manipulate large objects, along the lines of other ships or asteroids, in the zero-g environment of space. There were precious few situations where one would apply a ship's tractor to a planet, and none of them involved the targeting of living creatures.

But what Scotty said instead was, "Have a little confidence in yourself, lad. You convinced me and the rest that your plan makes good sense; don't be telling me now I should have doubted you."

Frank smiled. "Thank you, Mr. Scott. For giving me a chance to make up for that first impression I made."

"A wise man once told me, most of us are capable of more than we might suspect at first. Come on, lad, let's get up to the bridge and see just how well this works out." Scotty led Frank out of the control room toward the nearest turbolift.

Sulu turned at the sound of the 'lift doors opening. "We have an all clear, Mr. Scott," he reported as the engineer walked onto the bridge.

"Any trouble from the locals?" the engineer asked as he stepped down inside the circular rails.

"None worth mentioning," Sulu said.

"Grand. Mr. Frank, how do things look from there?"

Frank was already hunched over the sensor hood at his station, bathing his face in blue light. "Situation is approaching critical, sir."

Scott gritted his teeth, then nodded. "Tractor beam is at your control. Mr. Chekov, make sure we don't end up pulling ourselves into the planet with this stunt."

"No crash landings," Chekov confirmed. "Aye, sir."

Frank was heard taking a deep breath, then saying, "Engaging tractor . . . now!"

A beam of tightly focused energy lanced out from the *Enterprise*, piercing through the atmosphere and striking the sinkhole on the planet surface with near-pinpoint accuracy. A thin mist of loose dirt and small bits of debris were pulled skyward . . . but no more than that.

"It's not working," Frank said. "Something's off . . ."

"Have you compensated for atmospheric distortion?" Sulu asked. "Or interference from Van Allen radiation?"

"Retuning beam harmonics now . . . Wait. I think that's doing it." Frank's voice rose with excitement. "I think . . . Yes! They're moving!"

On the surface of the planet, there was no observable change in the tractor beam's effect. But underneath the surface, the neonate aliens paused in the powerful stretching and flexing movements of their still-soft carapaces. They had been struggling to free themselves from their dark, dense surroundings, with only inborn instincts and the pull of gravity to guide them. Now a new stimulus impressed itself on their still-developing consciousnesses, one that overrode everything else. To the most basic elements of their beings they understood: *Go to this.*

The second alien to push through the surface of the planet emerged right at the edge of the crater the first one had made. At first, it held close to the tractor beam as it pushed itself skyward. Out in the open, though, it soon became aware of another beacon, of which this artificial energy wave was merely a pale simulation. It peeled away while still rising skyward, in the direction of the tachyon streamer, while at the same time two of its siblings also freed themselves in quick succession.

"My God, will you look at that?" Leonard McCoy said, awed. The whole bridge crew watched the main viewer as the alien hatchlings started streaming out of the ground, like a string of beads being pulled loose. They destroyed two more abandoned buildings in the process, but amazingly, that was the extent of the additional damage done to the colony. When the last one burst free, they all climbed together in a swarm past the *Enterprise*. Several slowed in their flight as they moved past the ship in orbit, as if curious, or even grateful.

Scott watched, mouth slightly agape in wonderment as the creatures surged past the ship. His head shook slowly as he absorbed the remarkable sight, and he caught Sulu, out of the corner of his eye, wearing an identical expression. Noticing the stare, Sulu turned to face him, a broad grin breaking across his face. Scott returned the smile, and after a few seconds, both men turned their eyes back to the viewscreen, watching the newborns move off toward the stars.

The trill and hum of the transporter fell silent, and Captain Kirk stepped down off the platform, with Spock a half step behind. "Welcome back, Captain," Scott said as he moved out from behind the control console. Likewise, Sulu offered his welcome as he stepped forward from his position by the corridor doors.

"Thank you, gentlemen. It's good to be back." Kirk appeared rumpled and tired, though to nowhere near the degree he did in the aftermath of many of his other missions. Yet the relief he expressed now seemed to suggest that facing the Pentamian Assembly was more harrowing than facing a Gorn.

"How did the negotiations go?" Scott asked.

Kirk grimaced. "Don't ask."

Before Scott or Sulu could react, Spock clarified by adding, "We were successful in securing dilithium mining rights for the Federation."

"Twenty-seven hours of debate. Twenty . . . seven . . . hours . . . without interruption, without . . . The Pentamians only eat and sleep one day out of four. Did you know that?" Though the question sounded rhetorical, Kirk seemed to be demanding an answer from the two junior officers.

To their relief, Spock was the one to offer a response. "That information was in our briefing, Captain."

"But what wasn't in the briefing is that they only purge their bodily waste one day out of four, too. A culture for whom the very concept of 'a short break' is beyond—" Kirk stopped himself in mid-sentence, closed his eyes, and drew a silent breath. When he opened his eyes again, they had a look of chagrin in them. "Excuse me, gentlemen. Yes, the negotiations were successful. And what about that Andorian colony, their distress call?"

"Ah, we ended up with quite the surprise, sir. You see, the Thraz Outpost was set up to study—"

"Scotty, forgive me," Kirk interrupted, pressing the first two fingers of his right hand to his forehead. "I'm sure there's plenty you have to report, but . . . please just tell me, was the mission successful?"

"That it was, sir."

Kirk nodded. "Anything else I absolutely need to know right now?"

"We can brief you at your convenience, sir," Scott assured him.

The captain sighed quietly at that, clearly relieved. "Thank you, gentlemen. Spock, I'll be in my quarters." He gave them all curt nods before turning and walking out of the transporter room.

Once the doors closed again, Spock turned to Scott and Sulu. "If there is nothing else to report, gentlemen . . . We are expected at Starbase 14 in fifty-one hours, forty-seven minutes. And if you will excuse me as well, I have some . . . personal matters to attend to." Vulcan stamina was superior to that of humans, and Spock masked his fatigue even better than the captain did. But it was rather clear that his "personal matters" included sleep, or else a period of deep meditation. Spock followed Kirk out of the transporter room, leaving Scott and Sulu facing one another alone.

"Well," Scott said, with a shrug, "I'm sure the anticipation will only heighten their appreciation of our tale."

"Undoubtedly," Sulu said with a smile, while Scott moved back behind the transporter controller to fully power down the systems. "Mr. Scott," Sulu said after a moment's silence, "it just occurred to me that Mr. Spock didn't specify which of us was to resume the conn."

"Oh?" Scott looked up from his board, his eyes meeting Sulu's, both men trying to read the other's thoughts. "Well," Scott said finally, "I suppose it's my role to make the command decision . . ."

Sulu nodded slowly as Scott reached across his console for the intercom mounted at its top edge. "Scott to bridge."

"Chekov here, sir."

"Set course for Starbase 14, and engage when ready at warp five. And you have the conn, Mr. Chekov. If y' be needing Mr. Sulu or m'self, we'll be in my quarters."

"Acknowledged, sir."

Scott cut the channel and looked to the helmsman with a roguish grin. "The captain and Mr. Spock aren't the only ones who have earned themselves a short break. I think a toast to commemorate the end of a successful mission is in order, don't you agree, Hikaru?"

Sulu looked from the now-silent intercom to the chief engineer. "That's not proper protocol, is it, sir?" he asked, deadpan, watching the older man's expression fall before breaking into a broad smile of his own. "I'd be honored, Scotty."

Scotty laughed and clapped Sulu on the back, and the two crewmates headed off to celebrate their shared victories.

Devices and Desires

Kevin Lauderdale

Kevin Lauderdale

Born and raised in Los Angeles, Kevin Lauderdale grew up watching reruns of *Star Trek* every night during his childhood. He watched *The Next Generation* in college, *Deep Space Nine* in graduate school, and *Voyager* and *Enterprise* while shuffling papers in the real world. During those years, he also took William Shatner's advice and got a life. He is married, has two children, and now lives in northern Virginia.

Kevin broke into the glamorous world of *Star Trek* writing by placing stories in three consecutive volumes of *Strange New Worlds* anthologies: "A Test of Character" *(SNW VII)*, "Assignment: One" *(SNW 8)*, and "The Rules of War" *(SNW 9)*. He has also published essays and articles in *The Dictionary of American Biography*, the *Los Angeles Times, Animato!*, and Mcsweeneys.net; as well as poetry in Andre Codrescu's *The Exquisite Corpse*.

He thanks the busiest man in *Trek*, Marco Palmieri, for continuing to take chances on newcomers.

". . . Officially this facility doesn't exist," explained Dr. Miyazaki, "so it doesn't even have a name. Everyone here just calls it the Yard."

The diamond-shaped orange door in front of them opened with a muffled *swish*. At a gesture from Miyazaki, Spock and Kirk entered the office, only to find that the Yard's director was not, as they had expected, there waiting for them.

Kirk suppressed the urge to vent his frustration on Miyazaki. It wasn't the man's fault that his commanding officer was late. But it was just one more thing Kirk didn't like about all this.

The room was twice the size of one of the conference rooms aboard the *Enterprise*. There was a black-topped desk with some data slates on it and a three-sided computer monitor. Four black, high-backed chairs were scattered around the room, and on display everywhere were pieces of alien technology.

A handgun that looked like it was made of green gelatin, translucent and wobbly, sat on a pedestal under glass. Nearby, fragments of an exotic space suit had been reconstructed like the skeleton of a dinosaur. By a small potted palm sat a knee-high, hourglass-shaped metal box studded with buttons and switches that shone like gems. In an alcove by the door, three rings of white stone, each as big as two fists and arranged to form a pyramid, sat on black velvet, carefully illuminated by recessed lighting.

Kirk had long heard whispered rumors that Starfleet was going to build a secret base to store and study all of the alien technology it had acquired. *And now here it is,* he thought.

Through the large panes of transparent aluminum that all but filled one wall, Kirk could see a handful of small, gray-white Federation space stations and a few giant, oddly shaped pieces of machinery floating in space nearby. One of them, he was certain, was some sort of starship, but the others—some made of metal, others looked more like stone—he could not place. One thing looked like a giant purple and white orchid. The Federation stations, however, each employed the familiar design of small domed saucers branching out from beneath a much larger domed saucer at their center.

From this angle, Kirk knew he wasn't seeing everything out there, but clearly there was no emergency. No ion storms, no ancient weapons running amok. In fact, Kirk didn't see anything that warranted the coded orders he had received from Starfleet to take the *Enterprise* there at top speed, rigged for "dark running."

Following those orders, the *Enterprise*'s main viewscreen had been opaqued, every viewport sealed, and all communications silenced. Upon arrival, they had physically docked here at the Yard's main station; use of the transporter was also forbidden under dark running.

Spock glanced around the office and then turned to their escort. "Dr. Miyazaki, now that I have actually arrived, I fail to see the point of continuing to conceal the purpose of my visit from me."

"Well, you *were* the one named in the communiqué," said Miyazaki with a resigned tone. "Oh, well. It's your expertise in plasma constraint, Mr. Spock, what else?" He laughed as if it were the most obvious thing in the galaxy.

The intercom buzzed. *"Lacsamana to Miyazaki."*

"Excuse me," he said and walked over to the red wall panel. "Miyazaki here."

"We need you in cold storage to okay those Izarian memory crystals for transfer."

"Acknowledged." Miyazaki turned to Kirk and Spock. "I'm positive our director will be along in just a minute," he said as he walked out the door. "Good day."

After the door closed, Kirk said, "If it was so urgent, you would assume . . ." He noticed that Spock was staring intently at the desk. "What is it, Spock?"

"Fascinating," the Vulcan said.

"The desk?" asked Kirk.

"Yes, Captain. You have noted the height."

"It is sort of . . . low."

"Indeed."

"So," said Kirk, "whoever is in charge here is short."

"Or a member of a species that is, on average, lower in stature than the humanoid norm."

"What are you getting at, Spock?"

"And the chair," said Spock. Kirk stepped behind the desk. He suddenly realized that he hadn't seen the chair before. It was a low, backless, S-shaped curve of metal, with a little padding on the top for a seat. "Note also that the slates," continued Spock, pointing to two black, wedge-shaped electronic clipboards and their styluses, "are arranged vertically: one near the top of the desk and one closer to the chair. If you were going to have more than one on a desk, how would you arrange them, Captain?"

"I imagine, horizontally, one next to the other."

"As would I. But then, you and I have only two arms, one on each side. This arrangement suggests that the user has rows of arms, one on top of the other. How many such multi-armed species have representatives in Starfleet?"

"Offhand, Spock, I can't recall any."

"I know of only one, and very few of its population venture into space: the Nasat." Spock left the desk. "And I, personally, have only ever met one of them, B6 Blue. She was a scientist who spent some time on Vulcan during my youth."

Kirk said, "Let me guess: She also has something to do with plasma constraint?"

"A related field, yes. The odds that the administrator of this facility is *not* B6 Blue are at least one hundred and eighty billion to one."

"And who was she? An old friend, a colleague?"

"More than that, Captain. It was she who was responsible for my choosing Starfleet over the Vulcan Science Academy."

Kirk's eyes widened. He knew that Spock and his father, Sarek, had gone nearly twenty years without speaking as a result of that decision, but it surprised him to learn that a third party had been involved in the disagreement. What did B6 Blue want with Spock now, after all these years?

The door opened, and she entered.

She was indeed a Nasat. Now Kirk remembered; he'd seen an image of one somewhere. Her short (she barely came up to Kirk's chest), insectile build reminded Kirk of a giant pillbug, but with a distinctly incongruous reptilian tail that reached down to the floor. Her exoskeleton and six arms were cobalt blue. Her round head had two large, yellow eyes with heavy lids that gave her a look of perpetual drowsiness.

Kirk imagined that the quartermaster's office could have tailored a uniform to fit her, but she probably would have found even a six-sleeved shirt confining. Instead, the Nasat had simply affixed her gold commodore's braids to her exoskeleton. They were draped along the chevron of chitin at the top of her thorax.

"Spock, I'm glad to see you again," she said in a high-pitched, but not unpleasant, voice.

"I as well, Bishop." He turned toward Kirk. "My captain, James T. Kirk."

The Nasat stepped up to Kirk. "You've come as well, of course. A pleasure to meet you, Captain."

"Commodore . . . Bishop?" began Kirk.

"My clan designation is B6 Blue. I am a commodore in Starfleet, as well as a Ph.D. But we maintain an informal atmosphere here. We're an *academic* facility. We're all scientists and researchers. More like the academy than command headquarters. As such, I go by the nickname of Bishop." She walked around the desk and sat down. "Do sit, gentlemen."

"Commodore," said Kirk, "I don't like mysteries. And I really don't like them when they involve my ship. The *Enterprise* was called away from Narnel's World and ordered to bring Mr. Spock here, and I wasn't told why. I'm not even sure where *here* is. Only our navigator knows!"

The command to transport the *Enterprise*'s first officer, who had no more idea what this was about than Kirk, had arrived from Starfleet Command heavily encrypted. Kirk and Spock both had been required to verify their identities through voice print recognition before the file would open. Chekov had been dispatched to auxiliary control, armed with his own set of coded directions and far from any prying eyes, to pilot the ship here.

Kirk hadn't even been invited down to the Yard; he'd just been ordered to deliver Spock. But he'd be damned if he wasn't going to get an explanation.

"Perhaps Mr. Spock can shed some light on the situation," said Bishop with a smile.

Spock? Kirk turned to his friend. "But you said you didn't—"

"Indeed, I did not know," said Spock. Then he turned to Bishop. "Exactly how large," he asked, "will your Midnight Sphere be?"

"Sphere?" said Bishop, her smile widening. "I said nothing about a Midnight Sphere."

"Dr. Miyazaki mentioned that I was needed for my expertise in plasma constraint. Your work is in artificial gravity. This facility is classified as top secret. The most logical assumption is that you are attempting to camouflage the Yard by placing it within a Midnight Sphere." He turned to Kirk. "A shell of gas and plasma capable of absorbing light and sensor beams." Then to Bishop, he said, "However, I do not think that Dr. Culla ever conceived of one large enough to house whole space stations when he proposed the theory. Which is, of course, where I may be of use." Spock paused for a moment, as Bishop looked on expectantly. "Yes," Spock said slowly. Kirk imagined he could almost see the proverbial cogs in the Vulcan's mind turning. "Yes . . . I had never considered the possibility before, but certain frequencies of plasma constraint, if sufficiently powered, could be utilized to maintain a sizable shell."

Bishop leaned back and put the fingertips of all six hands together. "Very good, Spock. In fact, excellent. I'm glad you're on our side. To answer your question: The Sphere, once it is activated, will enclose an area exactly the same size as three-quarters of the Earth. Therefore with a surface area of . . . ?"

"Three hundred and eighty-two million, five hundred and forty-eight thousand, nine hundred and sixty-three square kilometers," said Spock.

"And a volume of . . . ?"

"Eight hundred fifteen billion, one hundred thirty-eight million, four hundred ninety-four thousand, eight hundred ninety cubic kilometers."

Bishop turned to Kirk. "He must be invaluable to you, Captain."

"The finest science officer in the fleet," said Kirk.

"I would expect no less," said Bishop.

"Just let me get this straight," said Kirk. "You're going to create a hollow shell. Your space stations, and all collected artifacts, will be inside this shell. And, from the outside, the whole thing is going to be what, invisible?"

Bishop said, "If you are going to camouflage yourself in space, the easiest solution is to be black. So we are tuning the plasma to absorb all electromagnetic radiation, not just those wavelengths within the conventional visible spectrum. It won't bend light—that is the provenance of black holes—but any light that does touch it will be absorbed, not reflected. Likewise it will absorb sensor beams, so that any sensor that hits it won't 'bounce back.'"

"So it will seem as though there's nothing here at all."

"Correct, Captain. The effect should be more reliable and sustainable in the long term than trying to adapt the other . . . more obvious solution."

Kirk knew she could mean only one thing. "The Romulan cloaking device."

"Yes."

"So that's here, too. Couldn't you just hide everything in a hollowed-out asteroid?"

"Oh, Captain, some of the objects here are much too large for that. Some are nearly the size of asteroids themselves, as you will see." She stood up.

"The whole thing just seems unnecessarily complex," said Kirk.

"It's the best way, Captain. I personally designed the system, based on all the latest theories. We were supposed to be online six days ago, but then these problems arose. The system just isn't working."

"And *that's* why you sent for Spock."

"Who else could I count on for knowledge of this type?" asked Bishop.

"And who else has a high enough security clearance?" said Kirk.

"I apologize for the inconvenience I must have put you through, Captain Kirk, but this *is* urgent. And very important."

Kirk understood. He didn't like it, but he understood.

Bishop said, "Since the two of you discovered a number of the artifacts already here, you, Captain, are certainly welcome to come along. But I must remind you that you are under a strict communications blackout. Dark running, you know."

"Of course."

"I'm sure you're most anxious to get to the heart of the matter. If you will follow me, we can be on our way to the generator satellite."

She led them out of her office and down a branch of the corridor different from the one that brought them here.

"We are also located in a particularly empty part of space," Bishop went on. "Sorry, I can't go into more detail about our position. But suffice it to say that, even if we weren't invisible, nobody would have any reason to come through here." She stopped in front of a large, circular hatch ringed with yellow light. "I'm afraid we'll have to take a pod. The transporters aren't working yet either."

Bishop herself piloted the small, boxy travel pod. Though the three of them traveled standing up, Kirk nonetheless enjoyed the excellent view afforded by the large port that dominated the pod's curved front.

"There's one of yours," said Bishop, gesturing up with all three of her right arms.

She pointed to an irregular cone that was twenty times the length of the *Enterprise*. Its surface, a mass of pure neutronium, had rippling striations of blue and white that resembled frozen flames. As they passed directly in front of it, Kirk saw the enormous black maw, the opening that had swallowed whole the *Starship Constellation* just before Kirk had blown up that ship, deactivating this robotic destroyer.

"The doomsday machine," said Kirk.

"Cross-indexed as 'the planet killer.' But to us, it's just object J145-6A."

"I knew that Starfleet had towed it somewhere," said Kirk. "But I'd always assumed it was scuttled. Sunk into a sun or something." It was, after all, a sort of graveyard. A year ago, the *Constellation*'s captain, Matt Decker, had given his life piloting a shuttlecraft inside the doomsday machine in an effort to destroy it. His actions had proved unsuccessful, but had inspired Kirk to use Decker's own crippled starship against the device.

"A fascinating object," said Bishop. "We may never know exactly where she came from, but there are some provocative theories. Dr. Pad—"

Kirk said, "I don't see how any good can come from studying that . . . thing."

"The *Constellation*'s impulse engine explosion completely atomized that ship, but left J145-6A's innards intact, though completely inert." Her voice took on an almost wistful tone. "Alas, it doesn't look like we'll ever be able to start her up again."

"Why would anyone want to?"

"Aren't you the least bit curious, Captain?" Bishop sounded genuinely surprised. "Can you conceive of the secrets she must be hiding within her? Not just how she works and where she came from, but as a path to learning more about her creators."

Kirk looked at Spock, who had arched an eyebrow.

"We're doing all this for the larger objects, of course," continued Bishop, her top arms sweeping across the panoramic view. "When we decided to consolidate all of the artifacts into one location, we knew we'd need to hide them. Their presence at other facilities posed too great a risk. Too many other people had access to them. Here, outside the major space-lanes, they will be safer. And to ensure that, we need to get the camouflage system up. Also we're currently only about half staffed."

Kirk had met parents who carried on less about their newborns than Bishop did about the Yard.

The Nasat turned and said lightly, "Captain, I don't suppose Spock has ever mentioned me."

Kirk again looked at Spock, whose face remained impassive. "No."

"All those years ago," she said with nostalgia. "Two decades."

"Nineteen years, four months, twelve days," said Spock.

"It was on Vulcan, of course," she said to Kirk. "I had just made lieutenant. I was actually working with the Vulcan Science Academy, assisting on an artificial gravity project. And young Spock here was always hanging around. Ah, there's the one we want."

The generator satellite was the same off-white as the space stations, but rather than being a collection of domes and saucers, it was nearly spherical. It looked to be about fifty meters in diameter. As they approached, Kirk saw a dozen recessed areas, each a couple of meters across and resembling the *Enterprise*'s deflector dish, spaced equidistantly across the surface. He assumed that the other side of the station looked the same.

"My father," said Spock, "was an astrophysicist there. It was only logical that I should attend him."

"Spock's father and I had a lot of arguments," said Bishop.

"Discussions," said Spock.

"You'd think I was trying to get Spock to defect to the Klingons, the way Sarek talked. He thought Starfleet was a bunch of warmongers. Sarek was still an academic then; he hadn't moved into the wider realm of politics. That's traditional on Vulcan. You enter the diplomatic corps only after accumulating life experience. Well, I'm sure I was the first Starfleet officer Spock had ever seen. The first alien, too."

"There were humans at the V.S.A.," said Spock. "Human warp field engineers had been there since—"

"But you've known at least one human your entire life," interrupted Bishop. "And there's little to distinguish humans from Vulcans; certainly nothing as exotic by humanoid standards as a Nasat." She spread her arms wide and looked for a moment as if she were going to pirouette. "I'm afraid my traveler's tales of black holes, shining nebulae, and the Efrosian frost-fields stirred unhealthy wanderlust in young Spock."

"My decision to join Starfleet," said Spock, "grew out of its broader scientific reach, rather than any desire for . . . adventure."

The travel pod backed into the station, where its hatch meshed perfectly with the dock, and Spock was reminded yet again of the elegance of standard-issue Federation technology.

The pod's hatch opened, revealing an Andorian. His blue skin, white hair, and articulated antennae stood out in stark contrast to his Starfleet uniform of black pants and bright red shirt. Bishop introduced him to Kirk and Spock as Engineer Thyner.

Thyner nodded slightly to each. "Welcome, gentlemen."

"Any change?" asked Bishop.

"None, sir," replied Thyner.

"Let's go."

Thyner turned and led the way down the ivory-colored corridor. Their footsteps echoed through the hall. There did not appear to be anyone else nearby.

Spock said, "I assume you are using the Toliver variances."

Thyner stopped and turned toward Spock. "That's right. How did you know?"

"It is the only logical choice if you are attempting to generate a sphere of this size."

Thyner scratched an antenna and continued walking. "We haven't been able to get anywhere with it. There's plenty of hydrogen around, of course. And the plasma relays are set to Toliver's calculations. The plasma beams go where they're supposed to, but the gases won't congeal. I've run a complete diagnostic twice."

Spock was intrigued. A Midnight Sphere of any size had never actually been created, but theoretically, skilled engineers, provided they applied the Toliver protocols and had enough power, should be able to achieve it. It was a remarkable challenge.

"It must have taken your engineering crew some time to construct all this," said Kirk.

"'Crew'?" asked Thyner.

Bishop stepped up. "Thyner is the Yard's only actual engineer. Of course we have a number of skilled technicians . . . for repairing light fixtures and stuck turbolifts. Things like that. We brought in a few engineers temporarily to assist with this station's assembly."

Kirk asked, "You have only one real engineer in a facility devoted to the study of alien technology?"

"We're a *research* facility, Captain," Bishop said dismissively. "Ah, here we are."

The doors opened and they stepped into a space as large as the engine room of the *Enterprise*. The floor was circular, and its center had been removed, revealing a glowing white sphere ten meters in diameter. From it, twenty-four rods, each a meter across, extended in all directions, into other tubes and out of sight. There was a computer bank on their right, and to their left a dozen screens displayed various parts of the inside of the structure. The room was filled with a low, throbbing hum.

At the computer station the viewer was already up. Spock approached it and began to read.

Seeing Bishop again after all these years brought back pleasant memories that Spock had swept away along with the unpleasant ones of his conflict with his father. Spock had thought of Bishop on occasion. When he had graduated from the Academy, he had considered sending her a note, just to inform her that her inspiration had indeed resulted in his commencement. But that seemed too much like pride—an emotion that many newly commissioned officers were prone to.

"Mr. Thyner, your plasma valence settings are incorrect," said Spock, looking up from the viewer.

"They are set to the Toliver variances."

"Undoubtedly. But this is not a theoretical exercise. You are not working within a perfect void nor an inertial frame. In actual practice—what engineers refer to, I believe, as 'the real galaxy'—they need to be adjusted." Spock walked to a diagnostic panel across the room. "The gases are not being properly constrained. While the theory itself is sound, its practical application requires some modification." Spock would not have called himself impressed, but he did appreciate the way in which the relays achieved maximum efficiency through simplicity of arrangement. Bishop had done a fine design job.

To Thyner, Spock said, "If you will alter the plasma frequency by three degrees, I will reset the relays to accommodate the change. That should suffice."

Thyner typed quickly at a keyboard. "It's that simple?"

"What did I tell you?" said Bishop. "Spock knows his plasma constraints."

"It is merely a matter of applying experience to theory," Spock said.

Thyner stepped away from the console. "Very well, then, I'll reboot the drivers. It will take about an hour and a half for the system to come online."

"And when it does," said Bishop, "I have faith that it will be perfect."

Bishop led Kirk and Spock back out to the corridor. "You are welcome to stay and see the Sphere become fully active. It should be quite a sight." She gave a high click that Spock recognized as the Nasat version of a chuckle. "From the inside, at least." The travel pod's hatch opened. "Captain, I will have Dr. Miyazaki show you around if you like. Spock and I have some catching up to do."

They sat in her office. Bishop had dragged her chair out from behind the desk, and Spock sat comfortably, facing her on one that was similarly shaped.

"It will be remarkable, Spock," she said. "This will be a temple filled with the technological wonders of the galaxy—and perhaps other galaxies as well. Think of it. The achievements of so many astounding civilizations that have come and gone. Each one so much more magnificent than ours."

"'The Golden Age is never the present,'" said Spock. "But the Yard *is* dedicated to the study of contemporary civilizations as well, is it not? If, for example, a Gorn or a Tholian ship were to be captured, it would be brought here."

"Yes, of course. There's much to be learned from them as well."

"Such as how to defend against their weapons."

"Perhaps, perhaps," said Bishop. "Who knows what their artifacts might offer up to the well-trained eye. But just think of the civilization that built the Guardian of Forever, Spock: that simple, bent stone ring that can take you anywhere and anywhen . . ."

"Surely you do not intend to move the Guardian here?"

"No, of course not. It can't be done. Turns out the thing extends deeper into the planet than anyone imagined. Now, if only there was a way to move the *planet* here . . ."

Bishop stood up and went to look out at the other space stations.

"*You* should be here, Spock. Think about what you've accomplished over the years. All the worlds you've explored, all the devices you've been the first to see. Think about what you've seen just because you *happened* to be there: computers that ran whole worlds, machines left behind by vanished species who were later revered as gods. Think about all you might have missed had you *not* just stumbled upon them. And now what if . . . they came to you?" She turned around. "I want you to join me here at the Yard."

Spock had never seriously considered serving anywhere but on a starship. Yet his entire career had been devoted to the expansion of Federation knowledge, and now here was a singular opportunity to exercise his skills as a scientist. And the Yard would most likely become the very center of Starfleet's xenotechnology studies.

"An intriguing proposal," said Spock.

Bishop pointed to the space station nearest them. "Do you see that station? It holds the Smoke Trapezoids from the ruins of Epsilon Sagittarii IV. On the station above it, there are half a dozen Starfleet scientists dedicated to nothing but deciphering the hieroglyphics surrounding the Scepter of Ket'cha. Realm Dialect, you know—a very complex language." She hugged herself in excitement with all six arms. "These objects are so . . . well, you've seen them yourself. Some are so elegant in the simplicity, and others devilish in their complexity. I don't know if Dr. Sah will ever figure out what that honeycomb-shaped thing of his does. He's spent four years on it, and may spend ten more. They have so much to teach us, Spock. There is so much to *know.* Isn't that what Starfleet is all about? If I recall, you know your Keats. *Hyperion?* 'Knowledge enormous . . . '?"

"'. . . makes a God of me,'" said Spock.

Bishop had changed since Spock had last seen her. The idea of waiting for anything to come to her was not one the Bishop of nineteen years ago would have endorsed.

"But knowledge in and of itself," said Spock, "is purposeless. You were an engineer once."

"That's your father talking, Spock."

Spock froze. Anger touched the edge of his consciousness—old anger at his father for not understanding his wishes and new anger at Bishop for bringing up those memories. Spock was quickly able to stem it.

Bishop continued. "Sarek was always afraid of what we were going to do. But knowledge is pure. I was not an engineer; I was a *scientist.* I always have been, and there is a universe of difference. True, as it happens, my work made travel between the stars more comfortable."

"And it has an application now in holding the Sphere together," said Spock.

"Oh, yes, that too. But what really mattered was that I was able to disprove Occita's theorem. Oh, what a day when that paper was published!"

"On Vulcan, you encouraged me to go beyond my world and seek out things I had never seen before. You spoke of discoveries waiting to be made, things to be experienced."

"I still do."

"You used to be an explorer," said Spock.

"I still am, but the wonders of the universe come to me now."

"But you are not the first. You are not the one who discovers them."

"That doesn't matter so much," said Bishop, "if I can be the one who finally solves their mysteries. Which is more important, Spock: to discover the object or to discover what it does and how it works? No offense intended, but *anyone* can be out there just bumping into things."

Spock was incapable of taking offense, but he did wonder if it was illogical for him to want that *someone* to be him.

She continued. "That's not science. Starfleet is just lucky that someone with your caliber mind is out there." She returned to her seat and looked him in the eye. "And there's more, Spock. If you join me here, I will see to it that eventually you will succeed me."

Spock had never considered himself a leader of anything larger than a landing party. He felt indebted to Starfleet for the opportunities it afforded him and wanted to be of service to it, but he found greater logic in following. Logic was frequently a better basis for implementing plans than conceiving them. Still, leadership of a science station was significantly different from that of a starship.

"I'm doing everything I can," said Bishop, "to preserve the way I—*we*—view matters. But today, Starfleet doesn't seem as interested. They no longer study for the sake of knowledge. Now they 'reverse-engineer.' It's not about ideas anymore. It's about exploiting technology. You know what that means: science by committee. What about our motto: *'Ex astris, scientia'*?" This is supposed to be a place of study, not a tool shop!"

"But is that not the point of knowledge?" asked Spock. "To use it?" Bishop eyed him warily. Something that had been bothering Spock surfaced and he asked, "Was this a test, Bishop? A ploy to bring me here?"

"No, Spock. The system really wasn't working. But when I thought of saviors, you immediately sprang to mind. And, after seeing your performance today, I knew that you had not changed, and so I knew you were the one." She stood up again. "On Vulcan, you wanted what I wanted: to see, to know. That's why I need you. You think like me, Spock."

"It has been nineteen years, Bishop. How do you know how I think?"

"You're a Vulcan, and you're still in Starfleet after all this time. I knew what you were thinking then. I still know how you think. You know the value of knowledge. You're a Vulcan; you prize logic and science above all else. Now consider, Spock, which would you rather be: the captain of some starship—or perhaps a perpetual first officer—or the greatest scientist in the Federation? Spoken of in the same breath as Einstein, F3 Red, T'cal."

This was not exactly the same Bishop that Spock had known nearly twenty years ago. Of course, it was illogical to assume she would not have changed in that time. He himself had changed. Her interests seemed significantly more insular now than they had been on Vulcan. Undoubtedly the demands of the classified positions that had led her here over the years had altered her. Yet, what she was saying made sense to Spock. Spock had let her guide him once before. Why not now? Was she really all that different? And even if she was, that did not make her wrong.

There was the low whistle of an electronic hail, then *"Miyazaki to Bishop."*

The Nasat pressed a button on her desk. "Go ahead."

"Ka would like to see you about the Medevlan gauss cannon. He's on deck two."

"I'll be with him in a minute." She broke the connection and turned to Spock. "Think about this, Spock. We can discuss it more, if you like. You join Captain Kirk, and I'll see you in a few minutes when our shell is up."

On any other space station, it would have been a bar. Here at the Yard, it was just a very large mess hall. Where spirits would have been stored, there was an extra bank of food slots. A female Tellarite took her cup of coffee, walked past Kirk and Spock, and continued to the far end of the otherwise-empty room to join her companion, a female human.

As Kirk took a bite of his turkey salad sandwich, Spock had a long sip of ice water and then spoke. "When I was young," he said, "I had planned to follow in my father's path. From an early age, I studied all the disciplines that a Vulcan scientist should master: computers, biology, astronomy. . . . When not in school, I spent time at the Vulcan Science Academy's library, pursuing my own interests: plasma fields, dissecting the teachings of Surak. . . . I also spoke with many of the researchers there. Perhaps you are unaware of the V.S.A.'s conservative approach to science. They believe quite resolutely in the 'brick-by-brick' approach, wherein every advance is firmly rooted in established and tested fact. All breakthroughs there are anticipated well in advance."

"I remember something about that from a class at the Academy," said Kirk.

Spock nodded. *Starfleet's* Academy, on the other hand, was a place where innovation and original thinking were actively encouraged and rewarded.

Kirk asked, "After first contact, didn't the Vulcans initially hold back certain scientific information from Earth, believing we weren't quite ready for it?"

"Correct. The V.S.A. trained nearly everyone involved in early Earth-Vulcan relations. I, however, wanted to see things that no one had ever seen before. I wanted a chance to make broad but still logical leaps. Bishop showed me that there was another path: Starfleet. Under both Captain Pike and you, I have achieved that. The opportunity to remain here is a remarkable one, and a logical step in my career."

Kirk said, "Well, I certainly wouldn't want to be the one who holds you back."

"I have always considered myself more of a science officer than a first officer, and I do not particularly wish a captaincy. Lieutenants Sulu and Hadley would make an excellent first officer and science officer, respectively."

"I'd be losing more than an officer, Spock. I'd be losing a friend."

"As would I, Jim. But the Yard may be the place where I can make my greatest contributions to science."

Kirk said, "Dr. Miyazaki showed me a few things here at this station. They have one of the androids from Harry Mudd's planet—well, most of one. They have some of Landru's lawgiver staffs, too." He looked Spock directly in the eyes.

"Things you had already seen because we discovered them."

"Exactly. Evidently, your friend Bishop doesn't believe in taking chances. I'm welcome to stay here and have a guided tour, but even a starship captain can't be trusted to see the Yard's real bounty. You didn't see anything new, did you?"

"We talked in her office."

"I thought as much. I'm starting to wonder just how much anyone will be allowed to share in her 'treasures.' Consider that, Spock, before you have visions of dissecting a Romulan warship here."

"There *are* other scientists doing work here, Captain."

"All working for her. Miyazaki told me that everyone here was personally recruited by Bishop. And have you noticed how few people there are?" He waved at the nearly empty space they sat in.

"She said they are not yet fully staffed."

"True, but I bet she intentionally keeps the numbers low. She doesn't want too many scientists around."

"These are high-security items, Captain. It is logical that she does not—*Starfleet* does not—want too many people here."

"And yet she summoned a four-hundred-and-thirty-person starship to the Yard."

"No, Captain, she summoned one person: me."

Kirk sighed. "And the rest of us just came along for the ride."

"She apparently does have significant authority in Starfleet Command."

"Authority to do what? Play with ships like a child in a bathtub?"

"She needed me, Captain. Their relays were not functioning. They did not know what to do."

"But Bishop could have called in any number of specialists to fix the problem."

Spock had to concede that point. It could not truly be the case that he was the only plasma constraint expert in the sector. Or even the only one with a high enough secret clearance.

But perhaps he was the only one Bishop felt she could trust. Was she willing to deal only with known quantities? She had not been that way on Vulcan. Spock wondered if, over the years, Bishop had become too cautious in her outlook.

The hall door opened, and Bishop and Miyazaki entered. Bishop's tail swished slightly with apparent excitement. She glanced at the chronometer on a wall and nodded toward an out-of-reach comm panel, which Miyazaki activated for her.

"Bishop to Thyner."

"Thyner here."

"What's your status?"

"Everything is running according to sequence. Just a few more seconds."

They all turned and looked through an observation port at the generator satellite. A ring of deep pink light circling its equator blossomed. Then a vertical ring, girdling the poles, appeared. These were then crossed by more pink rings until the sphere resembled the classical representation of an atom.

Spock knew that the rings were an optical illusion caused by the plasma coils becoming charged, but it was not until the beams rapidly grew away from the station that the illusion was fully shattered. Now he could see that they were straight lines. Twenty-four individual plasma lines, like so many spokes from the center of a wheel, stretched out toward an as-yet-nonexistent rim.

In just a few seconds, the lines flew past their station.

"Won't those be a navigational hazard?" asked Kirk.

Miyazaki said, "They are each only one meter in diameter. At the generator satellite, there, as you can see, they are rather close together. Anyone arriving to perform repairs will have to be careful—"

"And when are we not?" said Bishop.

"—but as they radiate out toward the surface of the Sphere, they grow quite far apart." He walked over to a wall monitor and pressed a few buttons. On the screen, they could now see the beams continue to stretch beyond them and into space.

Then the beams stopped: solid light.

"Excellent work, Spock," said Bishop. "Excellent."

The pink began to crackle with tendrils of blue, yellow, and red, which raced along the plasma beams in twisting, fiery helixes.

Like a sun whose gases are slowly drawn off across space into a nearby black hole, the tendrils reached out to each other, stretching and becoming thinner and thinner. Within two minutes the stars were no longer visible. The shell was complete. The beams themselves provided a remarkable amount of illumination, and the inner surface of the Midnight Sphere was the purest white that Spock had ever seen.

Bishop said, "An accomplishment worthy of any of the ancients, wouldn't you say, Captain Kirk? A true pantheon to house the galaxy's treasures!"

The enclosure effect called to mind the time Spock had stood inside an empty, ancient blimp hangar at Moffett Field, just south of San Francisco. What had appeared to be simply large from the outside had become unfathomably huge when viewed from within, where Spock had seen its support struts and buttresses.

Bishop spoke into the intercom. "Thyner, what do you see?"

"Everything is running according to protocol. All within expected norms."

Bishop's tail swished faster now. "Wonderful. I will be in communication shortly with our liaison, and we can have the rest of the artifacts in storage brought here as soon as possible. I understand they have something new for us from the Lagoon Nebula."

Spock stepped up to the viewscreen. *"That,"* he said, "is highly unusual."

"What?" asked Bishop.

"Computer," said Spock, "increase grid seventeen by two hundred percent."

"Working," came the clipped female voice found throughout Starfleet, as a close-up of one of the beams filled the screen.

Spock pointed to the center of the monitor. "This point, where the beam touches the gas shell, should have a blue tinge denoting termination."

"That's where the plasma 'support beam' stops," said Kirk.

"Correct, Captain."

"But there is no tinge," said Miyazaki, now standing next to Spock. "It hasn't stopped."

Bishop said, "We saw the beams stop. It's not possible they are continuing beyond the shell. Computer, show us the same area on the other beams."

"Working." The screen split into twenty-four equal sections. None of the beams had a blue edge where it touched the Sphere.

"I believe," said Spock, "that what is continuing beyond the surface of the shell is an invisible form of the plasma, undetectable by standard sensor scans."

Bishop said, "The surface of the shell would not affect things *leaving* it. It cannot make something invisible as it passes *into* space."

"It is not. This is an entirely different matter."

"Those beams," Miyazaki said, "could cut in half anything that crosses them."

"Beyond the influence of the Sphere and the computer controls, the beams would begin moving in random directions, buffeted by cosmic radiation," added Spock.

"A modern Medusa," said Kirk. "The Sphere is her head, and the plasma waves are the serpents, writhing and striking in all directions."

"An apt, if fanciful, metaphor, Captain," said Spock.

"How far out can they extend?" Kirk asked.

"Unknown. But their power should dissipate appreciatively the farther from the Sphere they travel."

"At what point will they no longer pose a threat?"

"Approximately sixteen-point-one billion kilometers," said Spock.

Kirk opened his mouth, but Bishop interrupted. *"Actually,"* she said slowly, as she steepled her topmost fingers, "this could prove to be a useful security measure."

"Any ship that comes near enough could be destroyed!" yelled Kirk.

"We are in the middle of nowhere, Captain. No uninvited ships should be anywhere near us. And those that are, deserve what they get."

"What about the invited ones that ferry your artifacts?"

"Spock," asked Bishop, "is it possible to tune sensors so that they can detect those outside beams?"

"A ship's sensor would have to look in a very specific band. But if it knew exactly where to look, it would find them."

"Good. We will transmit that information to our own ships when they approach and they will be able to navigate around them."

"Bishop," said Spock, "this indicates that there is a further error in the relays. This cannot be sustained."

"Do they pose a danger to the Yard itself?"

"Not that I know of. But without—"

"Then we can leave it. Captain Kirk, I'll have someone pass the information on to your helm, and you're free to go." She turned to Spock. "Have you made—"

"'Free to—'!" Kirk began.

"Shahar to Bishop." A female voice came over the intercom.

"Bishop here."

"We've just received a message from our Starfleet Intelligence liaison: There are Klingons on the way."

"Invasion?" asked Bishop.

They stood in the station's operations center, a bridge-sized area with multiple, large viewscreens that encircled almost the entire room. It was the most crowded part of the Yard that Spock had seen. There were six science stations in the small space, and each was manned. Spock, Kirk, Bishop, and Miyazaki were joined by Lieutenant Shahar. She had the high cheekbones and bald head typical of a Deltan and wore a rust-colored, wraparound jumpsuit.

"No," Shahar said. "It's apparently a lost Klingon ship: the *Heart of Qo'noS*. It was found wandering in sector two-zero-one. Starfleet has guaranteed it safe return along a specified route. It will come this way in two hours."

"Why *here*?" Bishop asked.

"You said so yourself," said Spock. "There is nothing here. Starfleet must have sent them this way so that they would not encounter any of our ships."

"Nor any planets," said Kirk. He turned to Bishop. "Apparently the Yard's location is *too* good a secret: Starfleet's left hand doesn't know what its right hand is hiding."

Bishop asked Shahar, "Who sent this message?"

"The . . . um." She looked first at Kirk, then Spock, then Bishop. "*The Admiral,* as usual."

Spock wondered if distrust of everyone, even starship captains and first officers, came with the inherent secrecy of such an installation, or if Bishop somehow encouraged such an atmosphere.

"He must have just learned of it," said Bishop. "And, for whatever reason, could not order the path changed."

"That would have raised a lot of suspicions," said Miyazaki. "Why would anyone object to a path that takes the Klingons through the middle of nowhere?"

"I'm suspicious of this whole situation," said Bishop. "What are Klingons doing this deep into Federation space?"

"Navigational array overload," Shahar said, looking down at her data slate.

"Unlikely," Bishop sneered.

"Actually," said Spock, "that may not be as implausible as it sounds. Consider the number of times *our* ships have accidentally wandered into their space. It is a wonder that it does not happen more often. How close to us will the Klingons' course bring them?"

Bishop took the data slate from Shahar and looked at it. "Right past us." She handed it to Spock.

"We must deactivate the camouflage system," said Spock. "If they come this close, there is a ninety-six point two three percent chance that the errant beams will destroy their ship."

"Never," said Bishop. "The Klingons would see us. Now that the Sphere is up, no one—certainly no Klingons—must know that we are here nor what we possess!"

"There could be hundreds of people aboard that ship!" said Kirk.

"This is a matter of Federation security, *Captain*. The integrity of a top-secret facility versus . . . a handful of the enemy. No, these walls will not come down!"

Spock stared at Bishop. To condemn the Klingon crew to death was beyond any question of politics; it was illogical. Clearly, Bishop was putting her love (that was the only word for it, encapsulating as it did all that was the opposite of logic) of the objects kept at the Yard before any common sense. Captain Kirk sometimes behaved illogically, but it usually resulted in a greater good. There was no greater good to be found here. Whether or not Bishop was treating the Yard as her personal playground, Spock was not certain. But he was now convinced that she had distorted views of the value of her artifacts and the use of knowledge. Bishop had changed in ways that were untenable.

"You were wrong, Bishop," said Spock. "I do not prize science above all else. There are lives aboard that ship. Not ideas, and not secrets waiting to be uncovered. Real lives. To kill them would be an act of inhumanity. Shut down the Sphere."

"But we'll be *visible*," said Bishop. "All the stations, all the artifacts."

"That," said Spock, "is exactly what I am counting on."

Spock could see Bishop's pupils grow smaller, as if she were focusing on something far away. Then her arms, which for a while had appeared to be locked at her sides, slowly rose and gracefully crossed themselves in front of her.

"It isn't working, is it?" she said quietly.

"No, Bishop," said Spock, "it is not."

"And you are right," she said. "I have . . . apparently lost some perspective. What do you suggest we do, Spock?"

"To begin with, instruct Mr. Thyner to prepare to deactivate the Sphere. I would prefer that our Mr. Scott join him. Since we do not really know what went wrong, his expertise could be invaluable."

Bishop casually pointed to Miyazaki, who replied, "Acknowledged," and turned to a comm panel.

Spock said to Kirk, "Captain, for my purpose, it will be necessary to hide any recognizable objects from the Klingons. Aside from the various space stations here at the Yard, which are generic in their design, there is only one thing—"

"The *Enterprise*," said Kirk.

"Yes. We must conceal the *Enterprise* in the one place here capable of containing the ship."

"The doomsday machine," said Kirk.

"Correct. I believe Mr. Scott's departure will leave Mr. Sulu in command."

"No, Spock, I'll go back, and I'll take her in there." Kirk flipped open his communicator. "Kirk to *Enterprise*. Mr. Scott, we are no longer under dark running."

Spock watched as the light within the Sphere faded. The plasma beams dimmed just a little, and immediately the gases began to dissipate. Obviously, they were just barely held in place by the beams.

As the gases dispersed, the stars quickly returned to view, and Spock felt reassured—no, not *felt,* he corrected himself. He *appreciated* their presence.

The last time Kirk had approached the planet killer, he had stared into its fiery core and seen what he imagined the very flames of hell must look like.

Now its insides were dark. He could just make out a small research station—one tiny raft inside this leviathan—down toward the center of the machine. Its red safety lights were on and its work bee was docked. Someone *was* studying the device that had killed Captain

Decker, the crew of the *Constellation,* and possibly millions more.

"Steady as she goes," Kirk said as he led his ship slowly forward.

It was strange how, now, deactivated and laid out for cold scientific examination, it was just a machine. It had been a killer, but now it was little more than a problem in close-quarters piloting. Robbed of its power it was . . . robbed of its power.

Kirk was almost curious to know what had made the thing tick himself.

Almost.

"Commander, something's just appeared on our scanners," said Shahar. "It's a Klingon D7."

Miyazaki looked at the chronometer on the wall. "Right on schedule. Good for them."

Spock closed his eyes for a moment. "Open hailing frequencies. Audio only."

"Undoubtedly they will be under orders to maintain communications silence," said Miyazaki.

"True, but we must be proactive if we are going to guarantee the illusion of reality."

"Spoken like a true Vulcan."

Shahar said, "Hailing frequencies open."

Spock said, "Greetings, gentlebeings. Welcome to Sorel's Salvage. I am Sorel, proprietor of this establishment. I offer you the finest in reconditioned propulsion systems and surplus torpedoes. Or perhaps you're looking for something in a used ship. We have several in stock. Yours looks a bit rickety. Would you care to upgrade? Impress your superiors! I can offer you a generous trade-in credit."

To Spock the Yard was an invaluable collection of alien devices: ancient artifacts and examples of the very latest technologies—some perhaps even from the future—from a hundred worlds. These were irreplaceable treasures that would provide years of research and could lead to discoveries that might benefit all of the beings who lived within the Federation.

But in his imagination, Spock could see the Yard as the Klingons saw it. Here was a wrecked spaceship, and there what looked like a very dirty comet. And all about them floated warped and twisted pieces of metal. If the Klingons' passive scans did detect anything unusual, they were sure to interpret it as just so much *veQ*. Garbage.

Over the comm came a brief grunt that was unmistakably a sign of offense from the Klingons. But still their ship continued on at its steady pace . . . and passed them.

"Hailing frequencies closed," said Shahar.

Miyazaki, who had been holding his breath, exhaled deeply, then asked, "Mr. Spock, have you ever worked in commerce before?"

"Once, while undercover, I attempted to pass as a dealer in kevas and trillium."

"And how did that go?"

"Poorly," said Spock.

"Well, your technique must have improved."

"How so? They did not stop to purchase anything."

"No," said Miyazaki, "but they bought the lie."

"I've got Mr. Thyner helpin' me," said Scotty over Kirk's communicator, *"but the others are nearly hopeless. It's not their fault. They just aren't engineers. Most of them can't tell dilithium from duotronics."* Scotty sighed. *"Frankly, Captain, I'm not sure this* can *be fixed."*

Kirk, Spock, and Bishop stood outside the Nasat's office.

"Recommendations, Mr. Scott."

"It really is a well-designed system, Captain. The ideas behind it are perfectly sound. It's just the execution. I can think o' three or four engineers that ought to come down here from various parts o' Starfleet and have a look. Maybe they can offer a few pointers."

"Acknowledged. Kirk out." He flipped his communicator closed and turned to Bishop. "Time to crank up the cloaking device, Commodore?" he asked with a grin.

"No, Captain. Our liaison has offered us a different sort of protection. It's only temporary, but it will serve until we solve the problems. Or come up with something else."

Spock said, "Naturally, you cannot tell us anything more."

Bishop smiled. *"That's* Yard thinking. Are you sure you won't stay after all, Spock?"

"No." Although Bishop seemed to have regained her perspective, Spock was not yet ready to exchange the stars for the Yard. There was still too much to discover. Perhaps he would revisit the question again in a few decades. "I will be returning with Captain Kirk." He spread the fingers of his right hand. "Live long and prosper, B6 Blue of Nasat. Once again, you have shown me my true path."

"And you have returned me to mine. Good-bye, Spock of Vulcan and of Starfleet. May our paths intersect again." She turned and walked into her office.

"Well, Spock," said Kirk, "I never doubted you'd stay with the *Enterprise.*"

"Really, Captain? Your prescience surprises me. There were times when I was unsure myself."

Kirk grinned. "As much as I admire the . . . museumlike qualities of the Yard, it's really not the place for adventurers like you and me."

"Adventurers, Captain?"

"To be the *first,* Spock. The first to see it, to touch it. Adventure."

"I view my time aboard the *Enterprise* as an opportunity not for adventure, but for discovery."

"Which is . . . ?" prompted Kirk.

"Discovery is the combination of intellectual exercise and—"

"Random chance?"

"If you like," said Spock.

"Right: adventure." Kirk flipped open his communicator. "Kirk to *Enterprise,* two to beam up."

Spock said nothing as he dissolved into swirls of luminous glitter, but his right eyebrow did arch just a bit. He hoped Kirk didn't notice.

Where Everybody Knows Your Name

Jeffrey Lang

Jeffrey Lang

Jeffrey Lang is the author of several *Star Trek* novels and short stories, including *Star Trek: The Next Generation: Immortal Coil* and, more recently, the first book in the *Star Trek: Voyager: String Theory* trilogy, *Cohesion*. He's very pleased about this opportunity to pen a tale about Dr. McCoy and Mr. Scott, as they are among his favorite characters in the *Trek* universe, and would like to raise a metaphorical glass to DeForest Kelley and James Doohan, the two wonderful actors who portrayed them. Cheers, gents. Bravo.

Lang is currently at work on his next project, a graphic novel. He lives in Bala Cynwyd, Pennsylvania, with his partner, Helen, his son, Andrew, and two troublesome cats.

The realization slowly dawned on Leonard McCoy: he had been staring at the same sentence on his computer screen for . . . well, how long, exactly? With his feet propped up on his desk, a cup of cold coffee by his elbow, and a crick in his neck, McCoy felt his eyes and mind both snap back into focus. Toggling to the document's indexing tab, he saw he had been reading an article in the *Journal of Experimental Psychology* about how time travel could provoke psychotic breaks in individuals with repressed neurodevelopmental disorders.

Interesting topic, McCoy admitted grudgingly, one he could imagine himself pursuing at another point in his career. The thought brought him up short and he grumbled aloud, "Why not now?"

Unfortunately, one of the answers was obvious: He didn't have time for such complex work. The day-to-day grind of managing sickbay, monitoring the crew, and especially working with the less-experienced medical staff was taking every moment and every erg of energy McCoy had to spare. Some Starfleet Medical functionary apparently had decided that every graduate-level med student, technician, and sawbones in the fleet had to spend a few weeks on board the only vessel to make it to the end of its five-year mission so they could watch the seasoned hands in action. Though he never would have admitted it, McCoy understood the reasons for the order. If he were the head of Medical, he might have done the same thing.

The other answer, the main answer—the important answer—simply was that he was tired. He felt *old.* Lifting his hand, he once again studied the tiny discolored patch on the back: his first liver spot. Modern medicine could do a lot to maintain vitality and check the ravages of time, but cellular apoptosis always won in the end.

Sadly, he wasn't the only one feeling the ravages of age. Only a week earlier, the doctor had spent a couple of fruitless hours trying to track down the source of a peculiar odor in what was supposed to be his more or less sterile treatment room. After running several scans, McCoy had called Jason Riviera, the head of environmental services, and asked him to check the ventilation systems. Riviera had come himself (perhaps suffering from the same want of fulfilling labor), checked over sickbay with a specialized tool, and, grinning slightly, delivered his verdict: "You've got B.O., Doc."

The meaning of Riviera's comment did not immediately sink in, but when it did, McCoy took a self-conscious half-step back. "Pardon?"

"Sorry, Doc. That's our little joke. Not you. Sickbay. Nothing personal. We've seen this in a couple other areas of the ship. Most of the air filters and scrubbers have been replaced multiple times, but sooner or later inert organic matter begins to accrete. When you consider how many people have been through sickbay since the *Enterprise* was commissioned, it was bound to happen."

"Is there anything we can do about it?"

Clearly, Riviera had heard this question one or two times too many. "Since we can't open a porthole, no. At least, not until we put in at a starbase."

Nodding, McCoy felt exhaustion settle down over his shoulders like a sprinkling of fine, gray dust. "So, then," he concluded. "B.O."

"Yep."

"Nothing we can do about it?"

"Nothing preventive," Riviera said. "But I hear scented candles work pretty well."

McCoy looked up from his contemplation of his cold coffee when sickbay's main doors snapped open, and the doctor stared in glassy-eyed disbelief at that rarest of sights: his captain entering with not a sign of distress, physical, mental, or emotional. Jim Kirk eyed his chief medical officer cautiously as if he were waiting for some sort of outburst.

"What's wrong?" McCoy asked.

"That's what I was going to ask you," Kirk said. "You look like you just had to put down your dog."

"I do?" McCoy asked and tried to get a clear look at himself in the reflective surface of the computer monitor. "No, it's nothing. I was just thinking: Did I ever tell you that sickbay has . . . that it's ailing."

"Sickbay is sick?" Kirk asked.

I wish I had thought of that, McCoy thought. *Or, wait, maybe I don't.* "In so many words, yes. According to our chief environmental officer, too many people have come through those doors over the past several years and left bits of themselves behind."

"Oh, right," Kirk said. "I've received reports about other parts of the ship having the same problem. Apparently the bridge isn't completely well, either."

"You'd think that with all the technology available to us, we'd have a way . . ."

"Be careful what you ask for, Bones," Kirk said. "Spock says that they've almost finished engineering a form of bacteria that they'll release on board ships that will not only consume all the dead skin particles, hair, what have you, but they'll also release minute amounts of oxygen."

McCoy didn't like the idea. "I can only imagine we'll be fighting them for control of the ship someday."

"The thought crossed my mind."

"What brought you down to see me? Headache? Woman problem? Need a fourth for whist?"

"Whist?" Kirk asked.

"A card game. My grandmother used to play it."

"Oh," Kirk replied, clearly not certain he wanted the conversation to continue in the current vein, but compelled by who-knew-what to continue. "What made you think of that?"

"I'm feeling old today."

"Well, then I have just the thing for you: I need you to take a little trip."

"A landing party?" Though he felt exhausted, the idea of getting off the ship was appealing.

"Not exactly—a biotechnology conference on Starbase Ten. We're on the slate to deliver a paper."

"Biotechnology?" McCoy asked. "Not exactly my field, but I bet I have a couple things in my files that I could adapt. Now that I think about it," he continued, a tiny iota of excitement creeping into his voice, "I had an idea for a project that might—"

"You won't need to write anything, Bones, but we need a presenter, someone with seniority," Kirk said. "Air of authority, you know?"

"Oh," McCoy said, feeling both deflated and complimented despite his certainty that Kirk was buttering him up. "Well, I guess that'll be all right." Then another thought—an unpleasant thought—hit him. "It's not one of Spock's, is it?"

"The conference organizers seemed very excited about it," Kirk said, obfuscating. "Some sort of breakthrough in man-machine interfaces, I think."

McCoy groaned. "Am I even going to understand what I'm presenting?"

"Bones," Kirk said cheerfully. "I'm surprised to hear you talk that way. When I asked who should go in his place, Spock said, 'We are fortunate to have one of the finest scientific minds in the Federation aboard the ship.'"

"And you're sure Spock wasn't talking about Spock?" McCoy scowled. "And why can't he go himself?"

"The *Enterprise* has been asked to assist with a large-scale astrometrics experiment near the Anthraces cluster. We'll be rendezvousing with three other ships at the starbase, then proceeding from there. I'm sorry to say it, Bones, but it's the kind of mission where we'll need Spock more than we need another doctor on board."

"There are quite a few of them around here these days, aren't there?" McCoy asked. "Almost makes a man feel not wanted."

"If it makes a difference, I'll be sending Scotty along with you. He contributed to the paper, but, you know, he's not much of one for delivery . . ."

McCoy nodded, cringing as he recalled a disastrous conference at Starfleet Command a couple years earlier. While Scotty could usually keep his brogue under control enough to be understood by non-Terrans, he had a tendency to digress from the main topic that resulted in long, spiraling discursions into esoteric engineering theory. Still, knowing that Scotty would be along made the idea of an excursion much more palatable. The engineer could always be counted on to find fun wherever fun was to be found if he could be coaxed to temporarily drop his obsessions with the *Enterprise*'s plumbing. "Okay, Jim. You got yourself a presenter."

"Excellent," the captain said as he turned to leave. "The text should be in your personal database by now." Pausing in the doorway, Kirk looked back over his shoulder and said, "One other thing: The *Lexington* is expected to arrive at Starbase Ten after we depart. I've asked Commodore Wesley to give you and Scotty a ride when the conference is over and meet us closer to the cluster. No problem with that?"

McCoy's compliance was built into the question. Kirk didn't even stop to hear the response. "Of course not, Jim," McCoy said to the closing door. "Whatever you say. You're the captain."

His head pressed deeply into his bunk's thin pillow, Scotty said, "Well, that had to be one of the most depressing experiences of my life." Oddly, the engineer sounded more bemused than depressed, but McCoy had to admit he was in a poor position to judge the difference. Somewhere roughly in the middle of the second day of lectures, meetings, and endless technical debates, he had lost all will to live.

"I'd be thrilled if my only problem was depression," McCoy said from his bunk. "But I think I'm also suffering from a bout of murderous rage mitigated by nervous exhaustion and, oh, my back hurts. I think I've mentioned my mattress?"

"Aye, Doctor," Scotty said. "Once or twice."

"I'm going to kill Jim. And Spock. Spock *first*. They must have known how bad that was going to be and couldn't face it." McCoy tried to sit up, but the stabbing pain in his lower back flared and he surrendered to gravity. "And bad enough that the beds on the starbase were so bad, now we have to stay in the *Lexington*'s bowels." McCoy knew that he was griping, that this was one of the things he was supposed to endure gracefully, but he didn't feel like being gracious. "Are there rooms this small on the *Enterprise*?"

"Yes," Scotty muttered. "But I had them all converted into equipment lockers."

Listening to the usually good-natured engineer complain made McCoy feel better. "At least we'll be able to eat again. What was that stuff they were trying to serve us for breakfast every morning? Some kind of oatmeal?"

"Nay," Scotty said. "I thought it was grits."

"*Grits?*" McCoy said, forgetting about the pain in his back and sitting up. "That, sir, is an insult to my sainted grandmother, Mamay, God rest her soul."

Scotty grinned. "Well, don't be saying such things about oatmeal then, or my Aunt Amelia will descend from on high and smite you with her wooden spoon. Oatmeal, indeed." Then, he kicked his duffel off the end of the cot to make room for his feet, but didn't seem to be able to get comfortable. "Food would be a fine idea, Doctor. What do you say we go see if we can find the mess hall?"

The sour sensation at the pit of McCoy's gut flip-flopped and he decided he was hungry. His mood lightened again: Food would be just the thing. Then maybe they could find a recreation hall and see what fun there might be to have. Worse came to worst, he could always drop by sickbay and see what the CMO was working on. The *Lexington* was still actively engaged in frontier work; who knew what medical conundrums they might be facing?

As they rose to their feet (being careful to duck low so they did not hit their heads), the intercom whistled for attention. Scotty pressed the switch and said, "Scott here."

"*Commander Scott, this is Lieutenant Jordan, the second officer. Commodore's compliments, sir, but we have a little bad news for you.*"

Scott glanced at McCoy, then returned his full attention to the intercom. "Go ahead, Lieutenant. Dr. McCoy is here with me."

"*I regret to report that the* Lexington *has been diverted to handle an emergency situation at Mining Colony 47 in Sector 262. It means delaying the rendezvous with the* Enterprise."

McCoy felt himself breathe again. The assumption came so easily:

that Jim and Spock had gotten into some damn-fool trouble without him to keep them in line.

"For how long?" Scott asked.

"Minimum of two weeks, sir." Jordan paused, then had the decency to say, *"Sorry."*

"You canna lend us a shuttle, Lieutenant? We could have it back to you in no time at all."

"I checked that, sir, but the commodore says we may need them for emergency relief work. The transporters won't be reliable at the mining colony because of trace amounts of magnetic ore. I assume you've heard . . ."

"Aye, lad," Scotty said impatiently. "We know about that." He scowled. "No other options for getting us back home?"

Jordan hesitated. *"Well, yes, sir. There's one, but I wasn't sure you'd want to consider it."*

"Try us."

"We could drop you off at the nearest planet and Enterprise *could pick you up on their way back this way. They're scheduled to be in the area in about twenty-two hours."*

"Planet?" McCoy asked. "What planet is that?"

"It's a little off the beaten path," Jordan said. *"The locals call it Denebia."*

"Deneb V?"

"No. Denebia. You know, the place where the slime devils come from."

Less than two hours later, McCoy and Scott, each carrying the small duffel he had brought along, were beamed down into a quiet cul-de-sac near the north edge of Meekrab, the planet's main interstellar port town. At first glance, Meekrab was much like many of the port towns the *Enterprise* crew had visited over the years: Most of the buildings appeared to be either structures for housing goods or people in transit—warehouses or hotels. The problem, McCoy decided after a few minutes' review, was that the proprietors of both forms of establishment did not seem to feel that cargo and guests should receive very different forms of treatment. If you happened to be cargo, then you were in good hands; if you were a guest, not quite so good.

After visiting three different hotels and reviewing the accommodations, Scott decided the only appropriate solution would be to find one of the other kinds of establishments that could always be found in port towns: a cheap bar.

"Are you sure that's a good idea, Scotty?" McCoy said. His feet hurt from walking and his shoulder ached from carrying the duffel. Worse, their circadian clocks were not in synch with local time and his body was beginning to send signals that it was time to sleep.

"I think it's the most bloody brilliant idea anyone has had all day. I can't help but hope these so-called hotels will look a little more appealing after we've rested and collected our wits."

"I'm just surprised the *Lexington* dropped us on a world without Federation lodgings."

"Not every planet wants the Federation around," Scotty said, pitching his voice low. "Especially not a world so close to the edge of Klingon space."

McCoy tugged up on the shoulder strap of his bag, taking some of the pressure off his sore neck. "I haven't noticed any hostile stares."

"Me, either, but I suggest we both keep our jackets on while we're outside, just in case." Denebians and Terrans were similar enough to look at if you didn't look too closely—bipedal, two eyes, two ears, one mouth and nose—but to McCoy's eye Denebians were generally smaller and had a strange tendency to slump forward at the waist and shoulders. Also, he noted that Denebians—or Meekrabians in any case—all wore drab, utilitarian clothing. After only a couple of hours, McCoy felt hungry for some colors other than olive drab and dun. Their standard-issue field jackets blended in well enough, but their uniform shirts would probably create a stir.

"If we don't want to be noticed," McCoy argued, "all the more reason to stay out of public spaces. The sooner we get a room . . ."

"No one knows more about the best local accommodations than a bartender," Scott retorted. "I'll have us the two best rooms in the city in less than an hour. Besides, it wouldn't hurt for us to just relax for a bit. We've got less than twenty hours until we're back on the *Enterprise.*"

• • •

Scotty must have spotted a likely location as they had been walking because not ten minutes later, the two Starfleet officers were seated on tall stools at a high, round table, their backs to the wall and two tall fizzy pink drinks before them. McCoy eyed his glass suspiciously. "No little umbrella?" he asked. "No crazy straw?"

"I asked for the local special," Scott said. "Always a good idea to try the local special first."

"But it's pink," McCoy said. He sniffed carefully, then waited to see what might happen. The bubbles tickled the inside of his nose, but nothing worse happened. "You first," he continued, but he should have saved his breath. Scott's glass was already half empty. McCoy stared at him blandly.

"It's a little tart," Scott said, "but palatable." He nodded toward McCoy's glass. "What are you waiting for?"

"To see if you go blind."

Scott grinned but did not otherwise respond. Rather, he leaned his back against the wall and looked around the room. Content that his companion still possessed a modicum of motor control, McCoy sampled the pinkness. Scotty was correct: the drink was tart but not lacking a pleasing insouciance. "Reminds me of a cosmopolitan," he noted.

"What's that?" Scotty asked.

"A cocktail my ex-wife used to imbibe."

Scott held his glass halfway to his lips, eyes crinkled in consternation. "Wife?" he asked.

"Ex-wife."

"I didn't know you were married."

McCoy shrugged. "Ancient history."

"I had no idea," Scott confessed.

"Not something I talk about very often."

"Must be the fuzzy pink drink."

McCoy nodded absently, then replayed Scotty's last statement in his head. "Fuzzy?" he asked softly. Shaking his head, then taking a healthy sip of his drink, he asked, "How about you, Scotty? Any skeletons rattling around in the closet?"

"Marital bliss?" Scott asked. "Nay, nay. Someday maybe, but not yet. Do you recommend it?"

McCoy shrugged, then felt some memories and a grin overcome him. "Some days, sure. The early days, definitely. One or two other days here and there . . ."

Scott grinned in response. "Glad to hear it. Not all bad memories, then. Maybe the drink's doing its work."

"Clearly." Scott caught the bartender's eye, then twirled his finger over their nearly empty glasses, the universal sign for another round. "Maybe I should scan the drinks before we have much more," McCoy said.

"And take all the mystery out of life?" Scott asked, then stood and shrugged off his jacket. "A wee bit warm in here, izunit?"

"Now that you mention it," McCoy agreed and shed his own jacket, though he briefly wondered what had happened to Scott's concern about showing their uniforms. He noted that their movements had caught the attention of a pair of Denebians at the bar. Both men looked over their shoulders, appeared to glower briefly, then turned back to their drinks. A trio of men at a nearby table, all of whom wore the similar dirt-stained uniforms, glanced their way, but none seemed overly concerned. Only one man, a narrow-faced individual with a bristle-brush mustache seated alone in the corner, stared for more than a second. The Denebian probably would have stared longer if he hadn't noticed McCoy trying to make eye contact, but then the bartender arrived with their second round and interrupted his line of sight.

One healthy gulp of pink fizziness later and McCoy was no longer thinking about the suspicious-looking stranger or, for that matter, much else. A pleasant lethargy crept over him and the doctor found himself ruminating about the past several days from a less-hostile position. The horrible conference continued to irk him, but the pain had become less acute, more like a banged shin and less like an impacted wisdom tooth. The memory of his bout of cabin fever swam up out of the depths and McCoy found himself wondering if he was going to feel any different when they returned to the ship. The question came out of his mouth before he had a chance to complete the thought. "Scotty," he said. "Do you ever think about what you're going to do after we finish this tour of duty?"

Scotty, who had been in the middle of a long pull, half-lowered his glass and stared into the middle distance. "Do?" he asked. "What do you mean? Like, take a vacation?"

"Well, sure, maybe," McCoy replied, suddenly aware that he might be entering metaphorically murky waters. "But I was thinking more along the lines of after *that*. For example, would you consider a hitch at Starfleet Academy as a teacher? Maybe the shipyards on Mars? Or . . . ?"

Scott set his drink down on the table and locked eyes with McCoy. "You're talking about *not* being on the *Enterprise*?" He said this in a tone that McCoy imagined he reserved for young engineers who confused the plus and minus poles on a chemical battery.

"It's an option," McCoy said, struggling to sound casual.

"One you've been considering?"

"The thought has crossed my mind."

Scott picked up his glass again and took a long pull. "Interesting," he said. "Any idea what you might like to do?"

"Not exactly," McCoy admitted. "Travel, maybe."

"More than you've traveled in the past five years?"

"*Not* at warp speed. Maybe just on one planet for a while. You ever consider that, Scotty? The number of worlds we've visited where essentially we saw *one* room or, if we were lucky, *one* city. On the really good days, we got to see a cave or a rocky landscape. We got to see the forests but rarely the trees."

Scott nodded, conceding the point, but then offered, "But we got to see the stars, Dr. McCoy. Some of them stars no human had ever seen before us."

"And they were wonderful, Scotty, and I'll treasure the memories, but for all their fiery brilliance, the stars can seem very cold."

Scott smiled appreciatively. "That's lovely, Doctor. Perhaps you should consider taking up poetry."

"Perhaps I will."

"Sounds like you've thought about this quite a bit already."

"Some," McCoy admitted. "It's been in the back of my mind for a while."

"You don't think the captain would want you to stay on?"

"You're working on the assumption that Jim Kirk would still be captain of the *Enterprise*."

The engineer guffawed. "Like they'd be able to drag him out of the center seat."

McCoy shook his head. "Don't be naïve, Scotty. It's not entirely up to him, you know. If Starfleet wants to promote him, they'll promote him."

"He'd turn it down," Scott said flatly.

"Not if the powers that be convince him that leaving would be for the greater good. You know Jim's a sucker for that kind of thing."

"What greater good?" Scott asked skeptically. "What could possibly be better for the galaxy than having James Kirk as captain of the *Enterprise*?"

"I'm inclined to agree with you, Mr. Scott, but there might be those who think he owes it to the next generation to teach them what he's learned."

"An entire generation of Jim Kirks flitting around the galaxy?" Scotty scoffed. "Oh, I don't know if that's a very good idea. Consider how many broken hearts that might produce."

"I don't think they would want Jim to teach *that* particular skill set."

"No," Scott agreed soberly. "Perhaps not." He brooded for a moment, then asked, "And if he *did* leave, who would take over? Mr. Spock?"

"I seriously doubt it," McCoy said. "If Jim left, I imagine Spock would leave with him. I can't imagine those two not working together."

"Sulu, then? I know he's keen on the idea of commanding his own ship, but I don't see them moving him up so quickly."

"Maybe it should be you, Scotty. You've sat in the chair more times than anyone besides Jim or Spock."

Scott tossed back the remains of his drink and laughed loudly. "Ha! Now there's as daft an idea as any I've heard in a long time. Me?! Captain of the *Enterprise!*" He slapped the table with the flat of his hand. "I'd consider it a demotion. I'm already her master; why would I want to be a captain?"

McCoy grinned, then, finding the comment funnier and funnier every second, began to laugh along with his friend. Maybe it was the drink or, as the case was, *drinks.* Or maybe it was the relief of finally discussing some of the things that had been swimming around in his head for the past several weeks. Whichever, Leonard McCoy tilted his stool back on two legs and laughed with gusto.

When the two of them finally quieted down a couple of minutes later and were ordering another round, McCoy noticed that the narrow-faced man with the bristle-brush mustache was no longer in the pub. A mostly-full glass of something remained on the table for a long while as their chat continued and the Starfleet officers began to work on their third round, but when no one returned to claim it, the waiter picked up the glass and unceremoniously dumped its contents into the sink behind the bar. *Strange,* McCoy thought, and then completely forgot about it.

Spaytak couldn't believe his good fortune. Well, not the part where he had to leave most of his drink on the table, but when he heard what he heard, there was no way he could stay seated. *The master of the* Enterprise *was in Meekrab!* How many others might know this? Stooped low while attempting to cloak his lanky form in the odiferous gloom that wreathed the alley between Nirah's bar and the butcher shop, Spaytak struggled to order his thoughts. There were, he decided, two possible answers: nobody else and everybody else. Money might be made if the first answer was the correct one, so Spaytak proceeded as if it were. The question, then, was who to approach. He knew the answer immediately, though he spent a couple more minutes crouched down in the semi-liquid darkness just in case another idea swam past in the shallow trough that ran down the middle of the alley. Alas, nothing stirred. "Krong, then," he muttered, and briefly touched his forehead with the tips of his right hand in silent prayer.

Spaytak hated Krong. He also, after his fashion, worshipped him. Krong was everything Spaytak wished he could be and knew, in his heart, he was not. Krong was strong, fierce, clever, and worldly, and generally had a clean but manly aroma. In contrast, there was at least one bookie taking bets on when the funk that swirled around Spaytak would spontaneously combust.

Krong was a Klingon, and according to Spaytak's limited knowledge of the man, he would most likely be in a bar. The question: Which bar? Krong had a few favorites that he liked to rotate through based on some arcane formula known only to him.

Spaytak actually prided himself on *knowing* things. If he had owned a business card, it might say something like "Spaytak Narwingenssen, Information Purveyor." Less kind observers, if they could be convinced to admit they knew Spaytak, would have called him a spy. The select minority who had actually used his services knew the correct title: Spaytak was a sneak, though not a particularly good one. On the couple of occasions when he had been able to score premium intelligence, the windfalls had been mostly a result of the fact that he could blend into the background, as long as the background was a mottled gray color.

While Krong had never purchased information from Spaytak, he had bought him the odd (sometimes very odd, sometimes wriggling) dinner here and there, usually because when Krong was deep enough in his cups, he craved company—*any* company—and very few Denebians were willing to risk their reputations being seen with a Klingon. Since Spaytak had no reputation worth saving, he also had no such reservations.

A flutter of a breeze from the southwest told Spaytak that the garbage barge was leaving the docks, which also meant the fishmongers were selling what was left of their weekend catches at half price. He recalled that Krong seemed to particularly enjoy the small, silver fishes called *fren,* but only if they were at least three days old. Spaytak also remembered that there was a bar near the dock—Jarek's—that would permit the Klingon to bring in a bucket of three-day-old *fren* and eat handfuls of the stuff as long as he washed it down with jugs of their overpriced bloodwine. As good a place as any to start looking.

The *fren* were too old to be wriggling and too young to have fermented properly, yet still Krong scooped up a handful, opened his mouth, and let them slide off his palm down into his gullet. If he was lucky, one of the fish's small bones would become lodged in his windpipe and he would choke to death. None of them did, so Krong had no choice but to chug a half liter of bloodwine to wash the greasy flavor from his mouth. When he was finished, he tapped his mug on the edge of the table, the signal to the barkeep that he required a refill. When he had first arrived on Denebia, he had employed the time-honored Klingon signal of throwing the mug at the barkeep's head, but Denebians' skulls weren't as thick as Klingons' and there had been some near-fatalities. Jarek—Krong couldn't believe he knew the man's name, but he did— nodded, hefted the small keg up under his meaty arm and walked the length of the bar to where Krong perched on his customary stool at the left-most edge.

The bar was as full as it usually was at the noon hour—dock workers coming in for fried bread and a beer—but no one dared sit in any of the three stools to Krong's immediate right. When he had first come to this horrible, stinking city, no one would sit in any of the next *four* stools. Krong sighed and shook his head minutely. His prestige was being slowly whittled away. An ignoble fate, like being nibbled to death by tribbles.

For the twelve thousand and forty-second time since that horrible day, Krong wondered what had possessed M'kar, his commanding officer, to turn away from him at the fateful moment when he was about to deliver the honorable blow that would elevate Krong to first lieutenant. Afterward, one of Krong's shipmates had told him that M'kar had been distracted by Shajara, whose chest plate had been particularly snug that day, but Krong had never known for sure. All he knew was that instead of a promotion, he had been exiled from Klingon space.

No one had liked M'kar enough to seek revenge on Krong, so the only other option had been ritual suicide, an option his father had strictly prohibited until all other paths had been exhausted. When he had last heard from his family several months ago, one of his uncles claimed to be making some progress in finding the bottom rung of the long ladder of factotums that would inevitably lead to the ears of the high council, but Krong had long ago given up hope. He knew he was going to die on Denebia, in this city that smelled of urine and fish. The only question that remained was whether he would finally do the job himself or goad someone into doing it for him.

Looking up, Krong saw his reflection in the greasy mirror behind the bar. What he saw reminded him of something he would once have scraped off the bottom of his boot. No—wait—he would have thrown the boots into the garbage rather than try to scrape off what he beheld.

Somehow, magically, his mug was full again. Krong considered pressing his face into the thick, crimson liquid and snorting it into his lungs. How much would he have to take in to drown himself? He inhaled deeply and mulled over the idea, but then winced when his sinuses were stung by an unexpectedly sharp tang. For a second, Krong thought maybe the *fren* had suddenly taken a turn for the better, but then memories of previous encounters with the aroma slid into place.

Spaytak.

Surprisingly, the Denebian had managed to ooze onto the stool next to Krong's without the Klingon hearing him. Krong chose to believe this was possible because he had been preoccupied with other, more pressing matters, but his more ruthless inner self smacked him on the forehead for being careless and losing his edge.

"Hey, Krong," the Denebian said.

"What do you want?" Krong asked without turning his head to look at his visitor. Rather, he took a pull from his mug, set it on the bar, then picked up the two-pronged fork he had been given with his *fren.*

Spaytak had the good sense to shift nervously at the sight of a Klingon with a pointy object. *Well, that's something, isn't it?* Krong thought, but then had to concede, *But not very much.*

"I have some important information," Spaytak whispered, apparently forgetting the cardinal rule of imparting important information.

"I'm thrilled for you. Go away."

"But it's really import—"

Faster than Spaytak could slither away—or even blink, for that matter—Krong stabbed the prongs of the fork through the sleeve of the spy's cuff, pinning it to the bartop. With the Denebian immobilized, it was a simple matter for Krong to reach over and reluctantly pinch the bridge of the Denebian's nose between his forefingers and squeeze. Spaytak began to screech, but cut it off when Krong said, "Shut up."

Spaytak tried to nod, but couldn't move his head.

"When I loosen the pressure on your nose, I'm going to let you say one word. If that word isn't good-bye—which, yes, I know, technically is two words, but I'll allow that under the circumstances—then the word you say had better be very, very compelling or I will be forced to grind your nose up into your forebrain. And, before I do or say anything else, please let me express how very, very displeased I am that I have to *touch* you." He paused then to wet his lips with his tongue. This was the longest single speech Krong had made in several weeks and his lips were cracked. Finally, he said, "Ready?"

Spaytak whimpered.

Krong loosened his grip slightly.

Spaytak appeared to be thinking, which Krong considered a very bad sign. He might actually be trying to find a word that wasn't good-bye and wouldn't result in his being killed. Krong wondered how hard he would have to strike the Denebian to slay him and whether he could do it at the present angle without putting down his mug. *Well, what the hell,* he decided. *I'll just have to hit him twice.*

Finally, after several long, agonizing seconds, Spaytak whimpered, "K-K-K-Kirk."

Krong lowered his head to reflect on the moment. The Denebian hadn't said good-bye, but he had to confess he wasn't sure precisely *what* he'd said. Maybe his mind had snapped under the pressure. The choice of responses was staggeringly large, but he settled for, "What?"

Spaytak did not immediately reply . . . or repeat himself. Instead, with slightly greater volume, he said, "Spock."

Krong said, "That's not what you said the first time."

"I know," Spaytak said, except it came out more like "I dough," because Krong was still squeezing pretty hard. "But I wanted to say both words or else you wouldn't understand . . ."

Krong squeezed harder, cutting off the Denebian's voice and, likely, breath. "I *still* don't understand. And not understanding is giving me a headache. I'm not very pleasant when I have a headache, so I vehemently urge you to *dispel* my confusion. Now." He loosened his grip.

"Kirk *and* Spock," Spaytak sputtered. "From the Federation *Starship Enterprise*. They're here. They're in a bar alone. Talking. Drinking . . ."

Not sure whether to laugh or weep with pity, Krong decided to compromise and simply reasserted pressure on Spaytak's nose and pulled the Denebian's face closer to the top of the bar. Leaning in (despite the churning stomach Spaytak's odor provoked), he said quietly, "There are so many things wrong with what you just said, I don't even know how to begin explaining them all to you, so I'm not going to try. As a substitute, I'm going to make your face a permanent feature of this bar."

To Krong's surprise, Spaytak neither tried to escape nor prevaricated. He stuck with his story: "It's *true,* Krong. One of them said he was the captain of the *Enterprise.* Do you really think I'm stupid enough to come here and tell you this if I didn't hear it with my own ears?"

Krong had to wonder: Was Spaytak that stupid? The Klingon was surprised to discover the answer that came to him was, *No, he isn't.* Delusional, perhaps. Inflated with entirely inappropriate self-importance, yes. But not stupid. It would be dishonorable to kill a man or even severely dent his skull simply for being an idiot, wouldn't it?

Wouldn't it?

Krong released his grip on Spaytak's nose and turned back to the mirror. "I don't care," he said. "And even if I did care, even if I, for a solitary nanosecond, entertained the thought that you might be right, then I would have to do something far worse than kill you for the indiscretion of introducing the concept of hope into my existence. Do you understand?"

Spaytak nodded once, then allowed the bridge of his nose to touch the cool bar top. "Yes," he whispered.

"Good. Get out of my sight."

The Denebian scurried away. When the sound of his flat footfalls had receded out the door, Krong turned and looked at the handful of dour, gray faces. None of the pairs of eyes dared to meet his own. That was something, wasn't it? At least they all still feared him and would not look Krong's way. He turned back to the mirror and looked at his reflection one more time. Krong had many faults; he knew this to be true, but self-delusion was not one of them. He looked at himself and knew that it was possible none of the pasty-faced Denebians would meet his eyes because none of them could even see him anymore. Or maybe, he reflected, they simply thought he was just one of them.

Outside the bar, Spaytak's cadre of associates waited for him. The three diminutive, shuffling forms called Mot, Lort, and Churt stood around the immense jiggling bulk that was their youngest brother, Dorsoll, like planetoids trapped in the gravity well of a gas giant. Mot, always the first to speak (if not to think) stepped forward and asked, "Well? What did he say? How much will he pay?"

Spaytak knew he had only seconds to provide a convincing response. If he hadn't been so worried that the Klingon was going to change his mind about the merger between Spaytak's face and the bar, he would have taken his time and come up with a satisfactory story. Mot, Lort, and Churt—with almost an entire brain between the three of them—would find some way to fade into the shadows if Spaytak couldn't convince them there was motivation to remain. Dorsoll, he knew, would stay with him until some other, stronger drive (probably hunger, possibly a flood tide) carried him away, but the oaf was useful only as long as the other three were nearby to goad him into action. Spaytak did not see himself in that role. He was a planner and a plotter, but not so much the man of action. He needed the three smaller brothers to stay. "He wants us to bring them here," Spaytak lied, and then added, "for interrogation."

"What's our cut?" Lort asked. He was almost as clever as Mot, but usually quieter and more deferential.

"We didn't discuss cuts," Spaytak admitted. Always a good idea to mix in some true things. "I'm not worried, though. If we pull this off, there'll be enough to go around."

"What if the Klingon tries to pull a fast one?" Mot asked. "I don't trust him."

"And I don't trust *you*," Spaytak said. "But we're all in this together. And if Krong tries to double-cross us, well, there's five of us and only one of him."

"But what about *them*?" Lort asked. "The Fleeters. We've heard stories about those guys. Everyone has. They have all kinds of arcane fighting techniques."

"And superhuman strength," Mot said.

"And what about our women?" Churt asked. "Everyone knows the tales. If that Kirk guy gets anywhere near them . . ."

"You say that," Spaytak sneered, "like you might actually *have* a woman."

"I have a mother," Churt said. "That's enough for me to worry about Captain Kirk being on the same planet."

"Stop worrying about what the Fleeters might do and start worrying about *me*." Spaytak lowered his head and put his face so close to Mot's that one of the small hairs that projected out of the tip of the runt's nose tickled his own. Mot pulled back and looked like he was about to protest, but he must have seen something in Spaytak's bleary red-rimmed eyes that made him pause. "When I left the pub, they were already three drinks in. By now, they've probably had at least one more, and maybe two."

"One more *what*?" Churt asked. "What were they drinking?"

The corner of Spaytak's mouth curled up. "What do all the off-worlders get?"

After a moment, Mot and Lort—both slightly quicker on the uptake than Churt—chuckled ominously, and a moment later their brother added his glee to theirs. Dorsoll, who had been as quiet and unperturbed as a support pylon, must have enjoyed hearing his brothers' laughter because after a second he joined in, too. The giant oaf had a disconcertingly high-pitched chuckle, like something that would come out of an infant, and the sound made Spaytak's skin crawl. *Why do I work with these fools?* he wondered, though he knew the answer: They were the best fools he could afford. When this deal was done, Spaytak decided, and the prize was his, he would kill them and find new help more in keeping with his status.

Time oozed by. Their conversation, McCoy noted, also seemed to be oozing. Pondering the currently very plastic nature of his consciousness motivated the doctor to do a quick (well, not all that quick) mental calculation. After rechecking his math a couple of times, McCoy realized that he and Scotty had been awake (if "awake" was a fair assessment of their current condition) for the better part of the past twenty-four hours. Tuning back into the conversation, McCoy began to understand that Scotty's response to exhaustion was quite different from his own: The engineer had become quite animated, even manic.

"And another bloody thing," Scotty said, slapping the tabletop, "why is it that it's always the captain and Spock who get the credit for saving civilization?! I've saved civilization plenty of times!"

This claim roused McCoy's interest. "How many times?"

Scott's eyes shifted around the room as if he were reading the answer off the walls. Finally, he said, "Four."

"That's a lot of times."

"It is."

"And you died a couple times, too," McCoy remembered.

"I did, didn't I? That's gotta count for somethin'!" The more excited he became, the thicker Scotty's accent grew. "No one ever seems to remember those sorts of things. It's always, 'Captain Kirk saved this,' and 'Mr. Spock rescued that.' All I want is a little respect, a little acknowledgment."

"You still have your reputation as a miracle worker," McCoy offered.

"Oh, well, sure. *That.* I do enjoy that."

"And you said you wouldn't want to be a captain."

"Nay."

"Well, then, what's to complain about?"

Scotty stared balefully into the middle distance, then turned to McCoy, apparently finally noticing the doctor's head was near the tabletop. "A wee bit tired, then, Leonard?"

McCoy nodded minutely. "A wee bit."

"Well, then, we'll be goin' about finding lodgings." McCoy sighed with relief as Scotty rose to his feet. "After just one more round."

"Scotty," McCoy moaned. "I can't feel my extremities."

"Oh, come on. These pink fizzy things aren't that strong."

"It has nothing to do with the fink pizzy . . . Okay, maybe a little. But it's very late. Or very early. One or the other." Distantly, a part of McCoy's brain wondered why he didn't just head out on his own and leave the engineer to find his own lodgings, should he choose. An even more distant portion of his mind responded with the simple answer: He didn't want to be alone on a strange planet. McCoy turned this puzzling observation around in his mind: When had he turned into someone who disliked being alone? Or, put another way, when had he turned into an individual who was *unaccustomed* to being alone? The response was breathtaking in its simplicity: If you spend five years gallivanting around the galaxy with a group of people in a tin can—even a really big tin can—almost anyone would lose their tolerance for isolation. How long had it taken? And what would be the long-term effects? More importantly, how would this affect the whole structure of Starfleet in the future? In a flash, McCoy clearly saw that *Constitution*-class ships like the *Enterprise* wouldn't be enough soon. A starship couldn't be merely a vessel: It had to be a community.

He sat up straight. Could he be the only one who was feeling the effects? He looked over at his friend, the chief engineer of the flagship of the fleet: He was frantically waving at the bartender for another round. "Obviously not," McCoy said aloud.

"Obviously not what?" Scott asked.

McCoy pondered how to approach the question and decided to soft-pedal it. "Something that came to me while I was listening to you. An interesting question. Maybe even a thesis."

Scott seemed genuinely intrigued. "An idea for a paper?"

"Maybe," McCoy said, and found that he liked the idea very much. Feeling much more alert suddenly, he concluded, "Yes, I think it might be. Or even a long-term project."

"Lovely," Scotty said. "Then I'll expect to be acknowledged in the notes section and invited to the conference when you deliver it." The bartender arrived with their drinks, set them down, then cleared away the last round and the credits Scotty had slapped down on the counter. "Let's drink to it," the engineer said, raising his glass.

"Aye, Mr. Scott. Let's." They touched glasses, but before McCoy sipped any of his, he stopped the bartender and asked, "By the way, what are these things called, anyway?"

"The drink?" the bartender asked. He was a short, thickly built individual with a small circle of spiky black hair at the center of his head, but was otherwise bald.

"Yes."

"We call those Denebian slime devils."

Scotty, who had been in the process of taking a large slurp, sputtered and sprayed the mouthful out his nose. McCoy speedily pushed himself away from the table, almost overtipping his chair, but found he couldn't help but giggle at the engineer's expression of disbelief. "What," McCoy asked, "could have provoked such a reaction?"

"A Denebian *slime devil*?" Scotty gasped.

"Sure," the bartender said. "Not too many other things to name a drink after on Denebia."

"But *why*?" Scott asked. "What does a pink, fuzzy drink have in common with a slime devil?"

"Keeping in mind," McCoy inserted, "that we may not want to know all the details about how they're made."

"I've heard a lot of answers to that question over the years," the bartender said, "but the best one anyone's come up with is that the drink is like the slime devil because when you're least expecting it, they both suddenly wake up and disembowel you."

Scotty narrowed his eyes at his half-empty glass, then concluded, "Good to know." He turned his gaze back to McCoy and said, "Doctor, I think it's time to call it a night."

McCoy nodded and gestured toward the door. "After you, sir."

The bartender gave Scotty a respectful nod as the engineer got off his stool. "Pleasant evening, Captain."

"Huh?" Scotty said, but the bartender had already gone to take someone else's order. Scotty blinked a few times. "Did he just call me captain?"

"I think so," McCoy replied placidly. "Though it has been a long night and I could be mistaken." Regarding Scotty curiously, he asked, "What was that all about? You have a problem with Denebian slime devils?"

"Well, no," Scott said, a tad embarrassed. "Not as such."

"Have you ever seen one?"

"Not really."

"Would you like to? I hear they have a couple at the local zoo."

"Not really, no."

"Then . . . ?"

"It's a long story, Doctor. Didn't I ever tell you about the time me and Chekov and the others got into the fight with the Klingons on Station K-7?"

"Yes."

"But you don't remember the part where the Klingon called the captain a Denebian slime devil?"

McCoy searched his memory. The story had been elevated to shipboard legend, but the detail about the slime devil had heretofore eluded him. "I guess not," he decided.

Reseating himself, Scotty said, "Well, then, aye, finish your drink while I tell you. See, it all started when the Klingon started saying as how the captain . . ."

Spaytak had only ever seen one offworlder finish more than three slime devils, and that poor, benighted soul had been rushed to either the hospital or the decontamination center, Spaytak couldn't remember which. According to the bartender, Kirk and Spock had finished nine or ten between them, though he hadn't been clear who had drunk more. He would have expected Kirk to have more, but from where he sat hunched in the shadows across the street, Spaytak thought Spock was the one who looked the worse for wear, wobbling a little woozily on the stairs down to the otherwise deserted sidewalk. Behind him, he heard Mot and Lort arguing in (for them) hushed tones about which of them would take on the *Enterprise* captain and which the first officer. The sounds of the argument were punctuated by various slaps, smacks, and a noise that could only be the sound of one man yanking on the other's nose. Gingerly, Spaytak touched his own nose where Krong had grabbed it and silently vowed to avenge himself on someone or another sometime soon.

Without turning, Spaytak hissed, "Shut up, you idiots." The pair fell silent. "Now where's Churt? He said he could get a vehicle."

"He'll be here," Mot said. "Or I'll disembarass him."

Spaytak frowned.

"Here he comes," Lort whispered. "Just like we planned."

Like we *planned?* Spaytak thought but didn't say aloud. Better that the fools think they were an integral part of the plan, when in reality they were mostly just being used as ballast. Having reasoned that Kirk and Spock couldn't be taken by force—especially not the force Spaytak had to muster—he had decided to use guile. If things *did* get rough, Mot, Lort, and Churt might be able to subdue one of the Fleeters and Dorsoll would likely be able to pacify the other if the oaf could be convinced to sit on his opponent. The important thing was that neither Kirk nor Spock be killed, at least not until they had been delivered to Krong. What the Klingon did with his prisoners after he had paid Spaytak was inconsequential . . . as long as the Denebian got to watch.

Spaytak decided not to ask where Churt had procured a hired vehicle, though the cab looked as if it had recently been hauled out of an open sewer. Neither of the Fleeters raised an eyebrow when the vehicle screeched to a halt in front of them, but seemed to accept it as their due. Churt lowered the side window screen and asked if they needed a ride.

Staring out into the gloomy evening, Kirk seemed to ponder the question for what felt like a very long time, but then finally said, "Might you know where we could find a couple comfortable rooms for the night?"

Spaytak couldn't believe his ears. How could it have worked out any better? He had been anticipating that the Fleeters would ask to be taken to a particular hotel and then Churt would have to pretend to get lost, but this . . . *this* was too good to be true. Unfortunately, this fact registered on Churt, too, and the lummox actually turned to look at the spot in the dark alley where he thought Spaytak was hiding and leered gleefully. Then he turned back to Kirk and said, "Certainly. Climb on in, gents, and I'll take you to the nicest, cleanest little joint in this part of town. It's run by my sweet old auntie. She makes the best *galopoly* stew in town."

"Oh, aye?" Kirk asked as he tugged open the rear door and guided his first officer into the rear of the vehicle. Spock didn't so much climb in as tumble forward. "I don't believe I've ever had that."

"You'll love it!" Churt cried. "It's sensational. She even makes her own noodles!"

"That sounds lovely, it does. You think she has any about tonight? I could do with a bite before putting me head down." Kirk elbowed his companion. "What do you think? Fancy a little stew?"

"Ehhhhh . . . " Spock said without lifting his head from the seat. Apparently the stories about these two having an almost telepathic bond was true because Kirk simply said, "All righty then. Off we go."

And off they went into the night. Spaytak was flummoxed. "It can't be this simple," he said aloud.

"Whataya mean it can't?" Mot asked. "You got us working with you. Of course it's gonna be simple."

Spaytak knew better than to try to respond to that. Instead, he said, "He knows to drive around for a bit, right? We have to get to Krong before Churt does."

"He'll remember," Mot said. "'Cause if he doesn't, I'll castigate him."

Eyes narrowed, Spaytak stared down at the ugly little man in disbelief, then finally asked, "Don't you mean . . . ?" Observing the blank stare, he said, "Never mind. Let's go."

The driver hummed tunelessly and tonelessly as he guided the vehicle through Meekrab's narrow, dirty, underlit streets. Scotty, veteran of many a late-night pub crawl, strongly suspected they were being taken to the hotel by a longer than necessary route in order to inflate the fare, but decided he did not particularly care. Unfamiliar coins jingled in his coat pocket and, as he always did whenever he visited a planet that used hard currency, Scott knew that when they arrived at the hotel he would set aside one of each so that later he could throw the coins into a wood box he kept on his nightstand. Whenever Scott returned to Earth for a visit, he would take along the box of mementos to show to his nephew Peter, who would engagingly ooh and aah over each and every one.

Keeping one eye on the driver, Scott glanced over at the doctor who sat quietly, his eyes half shut. He didn't like the idea of having to wake McCoy, so he decided to keep him engaged. "What's on your mind, Leonard?"

"Hmmm?" McCoy tried to sit up, but the seat was slippery with age and wear, so he surrendered back into a slump. "Oh, I was just thinking about the tribbles."

Scott cocked an eyebrow. "Really?"

"There's something that always bothered me about what happened with them. You know, back on the *Enterprise.*"

"Aye?"

"When you beamed them to the Klingon ship . . ."

"Aye."

"I've always wondered . . . what do you suppose the Klingons did with them?"

"Eh?"

"Well, they didn't make them into pets, right? The Klingons hate them."

"No, I expect not."

"And they wouldn't *eat* them, would they?"

Scott shook his head. "Not much there to eat, even for a Klingon."

"So . . . what?"

Scott considered the options, then, after a long moment, conceded, "I expect they probably . . . beamed them into space."

McCoy nodded and muttered, "Me, too."

Scott slumped back into his seat. "Well, now I'm depressed again."

"Sorry I brought it up," McCoy said.

"Stupid Klingons."

"Nothing you can do about it now."

"Poor little beasties . . ."

The hour had grown late and the shadows in Jarek's had grown so long that Krong was no longer sure what the bartender was pouring into his mug. The Klingon suspected the place was now empty except for himself and Jarek, but the owner knew better than to ask Krong to go before he was ready.

Krong looked up at his reflection in the smoky mirror and asked himself, *Am I ready? Is it time to leave this pathetic existence? Do I feel one single iota of hope anywhere within me?* Looking inward, he explored every nook and cranny, searching for a glimmer of anything that might resemble a reason to continue. Looking outward again, he held his hand up in front of his face and found he could barely make it out. "Too dark," he grumbled.

Without warning, Krong felt a damp, cold wind at his back and the overhead lights blazed forth blindingly. Krong clamped his eyes shut and growled, "Too bright!"

Someone behind him shouted, "We have them! They'll be here in a minute, Krong!"

Krong felt the hairs on the back of his neck stiffen. "If I turn around and that's you, Spaytak, then I'm going to have to kill you. Slowly. If it isn't you, then whoever you are, I'll have to kill you because you made me think of Spaytak and I cannot forgive that." He felt a hand fall on his shoulder to pull him around. The temerity! His hand fell onto the hilt of his *mek'leth.* "Now I have to kill you because you actually have the gall to lay your filthy—"

It was, in fact, Spaytak who was touching him—actually *touching* him. *So many reasons to kill you now,* Krong thought. *Which shall I choose?* "I told you it was them," the Denebian sputtered. "And I was right and they're almost here." The reek of Spaytak's breath was almost more than Krong could stand. *What is this idiot babbling about?* the Klingon wondered. *Is he still going on about the Federation captain?* He tugged his blade from his belt and prepared to surreptitiously slip it between Spaytak's ribs, but a flutter of motion by the door caught his attention.

"Here they are!" a new voice shouted. Four more Denebians—three small and one gigantic—stood clustered near the entrance, all of them pointing at a pair of slim figures who were wincing against the glare of the bright overhead lights. "We did it! It was us! Where's our money?" The three small Denebians chattered and prattled mindlessly, while the fourth—the giant—merely pointed, an empty, foolish grin on his face.

One of the slim figures batted away the Denebians' pointing fingers and strode forward. Despite the unnervingly bright lights, Krong saw that he was, in fact, a human and though he wore a nondescript jacket, he believed the clothing underneath might actually be a Starfleet uniform. The Klingon felt the underpinnings of his universe suddenly come undone. Had he been wrong? Had these idiots, against all hope, actually found him a prize that might buy him back his lost honor and a ticket to the Klingon homeworld?

Whoever the man was, he clearly did not feel threatened by the Denebians. "What in the name of heaven is going on here?" He looked at one of the small Denebians and said, "You said you were taking us to your . . ." He stared around at the establishment's grimy walls, the smoked mirrors, and the line of sticky bottles behind the bar. "I hope this isn't your aunt's because if it is, she needs to work on her housekeeping."

The three small Denebians closed in around the figure and one said, "Hey! You can't say that about our aunt!"

Spaytak stepped forward and shouted, "Would you numskulls shut up and close the door!"

Krong slid off his barstool and, squinting against the light, approached the human, stopping less than an arm's length away. He had met only a few Terrans in his time and most of those only at a distance, but the face of the *Enterprise*'s captain was well-known to every warrior of the Empire. Most humans looked alike to him, but this man—he might be the right age, and there was something about the shape of his face that seemed familiar. Without really knowing what he was doing, he asked, "Kirk?"

The human stared back, suddenly aware of who was staring him in the face. Sneering—Krong thought it was a sneer—he asked, "What the hell is a Klingon doing here?"

Krong had to concede that at least the human didn't seem one bit fearful. He responded, "What the hell is a Starfleet captain doing here?"

The human drew back, then looked over his shoulder at his companion, who, up to that point, Krong had ignored. The second figure, Krong saw, was another human. A small, fragile object that resided in the Klingon's chest, something that he briefly recognized as hope, crumbled and was lost to the darkness. Pointing at the second human, he looked over at Spaytak and asked, "You thought that was Spock?"

"It *is* Spock," the Denebian insisted.

"He's a human."

"So?"

"Spock is a Vulcan. Have you ever even seen a Vulcan?"

The second human, who had been quite docile, even sleepy, suddenly stepped forward and, eyebrows twitching, blurted, "You thought I was *who?*"

Suddenly, Krong noted, everyone was holding a chair or a stool or a bottle, or some other kind of makeshift weapon. The first human, the one who Spaytak had mistaken for Kirk, grinned broadly and said, "As if there was any other way to end such an enjoyable evening . . ."

"This way, Captain." Spock pointed his tricorder at a shabby building near the end of a narrow opening that might charitably have been called an alley. A tepid miasma clung near the ground as the early-morning sun heated the slick cobblestones. Kirk wished he could hold his nose, but decided that the stance would be undignified. Not that anyone was around, but there were conventions to be observed.

"What do you think they were doing down here, Spock?"

"I cannot say, Captain. Lodgings, perhaps?"

Kirk nodded and they headed down the shadowy alley. He knew he should have brought along a security detail, but this was a nonaligned world, and he didn't want Starfleet's presence to be provocative. Rolling his shoulders, limbering up, Kirk strode to the door Spock indicated, his hand never far from his phaser.

Rusty hinges creaked as the door slowly swung open. Kirk and Spock, both well-schooled in the practice of entering potentially hostile locations, flattened their backs against the doorframe. The interior was dimly illuminated by a handful of guttering candles throwing jagged shadows in every direction. Kirk instinctively held his breath and heard a series of raspy groans. In the corner farthest from the door, he detected the shifting of shadows that indicated sudden movement. Inhaling deeply, feeling the familiar surge of adrenaline, he bunched his muscles to leap into the room. Somewhere in the back of his mind, some part of Kirk recognized that he was grinning, that he was about to do something, be something, that he hadn't done or been in too long a time: the man of action. It felt good. It felt right. It felt like . . .

"Jim! Hey, how the hell are you!?"

Few things in life could have made Leonard McCoy much happier at that moment than to see his friend and commanding officer standing in a doorway looking so confused and, well, disappointed. *Yes, it's petty,* McCoy thought. *And cynical and might even be considered a court-martial offense in some schools of thought, but having the starch taken out of him once in a while means he won't get a stiff neck.* McCoy chuckled to himself, then winced at the pain in his chest. *Might be a cracked rib,* he thought. *Maybe two. I'll have to look at that as soon as we get back to the ship.* Interestingly, the idea of returning to the *Enterprise* did not bother him. *Possibly,* he considered, *because I know I won't have to stay there forever if I don't want to.* At that thought, he toasted himself and sipped some more of the bloodwine. The stuff wasn't nearly so bad after the first or second glass; the faint background note of steel wool actually became enjoyable after a bit.

In the doorway, Kirk finally released his breath and said, "Bones?"

"Come on in. Watch out for the . . . Well, over there in a heap by the door."

The captain and first officer stepped gingerly into the room, careful to avoid treading on the unconscious Spaytak and his brothers.

"Fancy a mug of bloodwine, gentlemen?" Scotty asked cheerfully.

"Bloodwine?" Kirk asked dubiously. "You couldn't find anything better?"

"*Better?*" Krong asked, trying to rise. That surprised McCoy. The Klingon had drunk at least one cask of wine by himself since the three of them had settled in after the brawl, and who knew how much beforehand? Also, Spaytak had stabbed Krong twice during their fight and he had lost some blood. McCoy had sealed up the wounds and normally would have offered the patient something for pain, but he was pretty sure Krong wasn't feeling *any* pain. "What could possibly be *better?!*" the Klingon bellowed.

Spock arched an eyebrow. Kirk's eyes widened. McCoy savored the moment.

"Ah, sit down, Krong," Scotty said before the Klingon could even get out of his chair. Looking up at his captain, the engineer said, "He doesn't mean anything by it, sir. Our friend here is just overly excited because of the exciting new vistas that seemed to have appeared before him."

"Exciting new vistas . . ." the Klingon repeated.

"Your *friend*?" Jim asked, then turned to look around the barroom. Obviously, his eyes had adjusted to the murk because McCoy saw the captain fix his gaze on various pieces of broken furniture. "I wish someone would explain what happened here. And why didn't either of you answer your communicators when the *Enterprise* called."

"Och!" Scott exclaimed. "So that's what that sound was! I thought it was something that came out of the skinny fellow with the mustache when Krong made him eat his mug."

"And as for what's happened here," McCoy said, a pleasant sensation of weariness filtering through him, "let's just call it the inevitable result of spending too much time in one place."

"You were only here for a day," Kirk said.

"I do not think he means Denebia, Captain," Spock interjected. McCoy was surprised to hear the comment come from the first officer, but the two locked gazes for a lingering moment. Something in his eyes made the doctor wonder if he was the only one who was feeling like it was time for a change.

Kirk cocked an eyebrow, but did not comment further. Instead, he said, "We should get back to the ship."

"Aye!" Scotty said. "I need to see my wee bairns."

"Aye!" said the Klingon. "I also need to see his . . . whatever he called them."

"You're gonna love the *Enterprise*," McCoy told Krong.

The captain became alarmed. "Scotty, Bones . . . he's a Klingon."

"Aye, aye. True," Scott said. "And a fair-to-middlin' barroom brawler if I'm any judge. But he's not really a bad fellow and I think he needs to get off this planet, seeing as he assaulted several locals in the process of saving us from . . . well, I want to say peril, but I'm not sure exactly how perilous our peril was."

"Perilous peril!" Krong shouted, then laid his head down on the table and began to snore loudly.

"I think I can keep him asleep until we can drop him off on some other neutral planet, Jim," McCoy said, very much looking forward to the possibility of sleep himself. *No insomnia tonight . . .*

"But he's a Klingon officer!" Kirk said. "What can I tell Starfleet if they find out?"

"Tell them," McCoy said, "that you're the captain of the *Enterprise.* That should still count for something?"

Kirk flinched slightly, like someone had just lightly slapped his cheek. He stared down at McCoy for a long second, then turned to look at Scotty and finally at Spock. "I suppose," he finally said, "that it should." He clapped his hands together and rubbed them impatiently. "Let's get going."

McCoy rose, enjoying the ache in his back and chest. "Whatever you say, sir." And to himself, he added, *You are the captain. For a little while longer, at least. And after that, we'll just have to see what the future brings.*

Standing, Scott clapped a hand on McCoy's shoulder, producing a groan. "You surprised me a bit tonight during our brawl, Doctor," he said softly. "You're a man of unexpected talents. The way you took down that fella with the neck pinch."

"Best not to mention that too loudly, Mr. Scott. The walls have ears, you know."

"Aye, that they do." Leaning down to help Krong up out of his chair, Scott surveyed the trashed barroom and commented wistfully, "Not bad for a couple old fellows, eh?"

McCoy grinned and reached for the Klingon's other arm. "Old, Scotty?" he said. "Speak for yourself."

Make-Believe

Allyn Gibson

Allyn Gibson

A repeat broadcast of the animated *Star Trek* episode "The Slaver Weapon" was Allyn Gibson's first encounter with Gene Roddenberry's vision of humanity's future and began a life-long love affair with *Star Trek* in all its myriad forms, with a particular fondness for the early 1980s comic books by Mike W. Barr and Tom Sutton. His discovery of *Star Trek* began a journey into other worlds—historical, science-fictional, and fantasy—from *Doctor Who* to the fires of Mount Doom to the far future of Asimov's Foundation to the Royal Navy of the Napoleonic era. In time, Allyn began writing, to create his own worlds to explore. He wrote the *Star Trek: S.C.E.* novella *Ring Around the Sky* and the *Star Trek: New Frontier* short story "Performance Appraisal."

Currently, Allyn works for the world's leading video game retailer as a store manager. He maintains a blog at http://www.allyngibson.net/.

He lives in Raleigh, North Carolina.

Hot sunlight beat down on Leonard McCoy, and sweat dripped from his brow. He may have grown up in Georgia and experienced firsthand its hot, muggy summers, but he never liked the heat—it wilted him too much, and years of starship duty with its climate-controlled environments diminished whatever tolerance he might have developed for the warmer climes. He bent over, placed his hands on his knees, and took a deep breath in the hope of gaining a second wind. "Jim," he said, "I still don't understand why we couldn't have beamed right to the crash site."

Ahead of McCoy in the waist-high alien foliage, Jim Kirk stopped and turned to look at his friend. "Bones, we couldn't even *locate* the crash site from orbit."

Still doubled over, his breathing heavy, McCoy looked up at Kirk. "All the things the *Enterprise* can do, and we can't find a downed shuttlecraft." He shook his head.

"Really, Doctor," said Spock, who had come up from ahead to stand beside Kirk, "the explanation I gave aboard the *Enterprise* was not difficult to follow."

"Yes, yes," McCoy said, his breathing less ragged than before. "Pulsar activity, magnetic fields, Van Allen radiation. I remember." Secretly McCoy thought that in some instances Spock simply created his complicated explanations out of whole cloth in hopes of confusing the issue. There simply was no difference between scientific babble and pseudo-scientific nonsense. The explanation Spock had offered aboard the ship for this occasion, McCoy decided, fell distinctly in the latter camp.

Kirk came up and clapped McCoy on the shoulder. "Holding up, Bones?"

McCoy nodded and straightened himself up. He took a deep breath. "How much farther?"

"Difficult to be precise," Spock said, checking his tricorder. "Five kilometers, possibly ten."

Kirk smiled wryly. "I'll take point. Spock, you have the rear." His officers nodded in acknowledgment of the orders. "Let's do it."

Onward they marched through the alien veldt. Grasses—for that is what McCoy dubbed them, so much did they resemble Terran grasses—grew tall here, sometimes waist high, sometimes well above their heads. Among the taller growths McCoy lost sight of Kirk ahead of him, and in those moments they navigated the foliage solely by tricorder and calling to one another. Above them animals—some like birds, some like monstrous insects—flew, ofttimes circling but never approaching closer than a few hundred meters. McCoy hoped they would reach their destination soon.

This mission should have been a simple matter, McCoy thought. An *Enterprise* shuttle had crashed here on the surface of Algenib II during a routine planetary survey while the *Enterprise* sped toward an urgent diplomatic conference. Upon the starship's return to the Algenib system a week later, Kirk organized a search-and-rescue mission. Sensor readings had proven inconclusive, and the landing party beamed down not to the shuttle's crash site but to the wreckage of one of the shuttle's nacelles, shorn from the fuselage as the shuttle descended through the atmosphere. Unique conditions allowed few transporter and communication windows through Algenib's magnetic field, which meant that, as a practical matter, it would be quicker for Kirk's team to follow the debris trail from the nacelle to the shuttle, then contact the *Enterprise* and beam back to the ship with any survivors at the next transport window. With time so essential, Kirk, Spock, and McCoy had set off on foot across the alien plain of Algenib II.

Ahead of McCoy the grasses thinned out and grew less tall. At last he came to a break in the foliage, bare ground that sloped upward. Kirk stood at the crest of the rise, and as McCoy joined him he saw that this was no ordinary rise—beyond it stretched a canyon, vast beyond his experience. The ground fell away, rock strata exposed to the elements, and from his vantage point McCoy could not see the far side. Intellectually, he knew there was an opposite wall, but it was lost to him in the mist and haze.

His mind staggered at the size of it. McCoy had first seen the Grand Canyon on Earth when his grandfather, T. J. McCoy, had taken him along on a business trip to Las Vegas and, as a reward for his good behavior, they took a shuttle flight through the enormous ravine's eight-hundred-kilometer length. Years later, on a Starfleet survival course, he had overflown the Valles Marineris on Mars en route to a base camp at Fort Kiley, and even from twenty kilometers up and a thousand kilometers per hour, the largest canyon in the solar system presented an impressive sight. But never before had McCoy stood at the lip of a canyon's walls—though not acrophobic, McCoy had little interest in seeing nature up close and personal. Here, now, at the edge of a yawning chasm, McCoy felt very small. Something had carved out a slice of this world, and measured against that, a single man was nothing.

"Fascinating," said Spock from behind. He joined Kirk and McCoy on the canyon's edge and held out his tricorder to perform a survey.

"How far's the eastern side?" asked Kirk.

"Ten kilometers, Captain," Spock said. McCoy thought the natural horizon, the distance one could see before the world fell away due to curvature, was five or six kilometers. It wasn't the haze that prevented him from seeing the opposite side but the curvature of Algenib II itself.

Kirk stood quiet in contemplation. McCoy could see the resolute determination in his gaze, focused somewhere far into the misty horizon. The trail of shuttle debris had led them here—where would their journey take them now? Into the gorge itself? Only Kirk could make that decision.

McCoy looked down into the canyon. The haze that obscured the far side blanketed its floor as well, but McCoy thought that he could see something rising through the mists, something not quite natural. "What do you make of those, Spock?" he asked as he pointed at something far below. Spock's Vulcan eyesight, McCoy knew, was sharper than any human's, but even Spock would have difficulty seeing at a distance through Algenib's haze.

Spock looked in the direction McCoy indicated, then raised an eyebrow. "Curious." He raised his tricorder, adjusted the dials, and studied the data on its screen. "It appears, Dr. McCoy, that there are objects below us on the canyon floor. Constructed objects, alien machines of enormous size."

"Machines," said McCoy. "There's more than one?"

"My tricorder indicates that there are one hundred fifty such objects within a ten-kilometer radius of our position."

Kirk came to stand beside McCoy. "How enormous?" he asked.

"Judging by my tricorder readings, each one may dwarf the *Enterprise* in size."

"Larger than the *Enterprise*?" said McCoy. "My God, what are they? Who built them, and why?"

"Unknown, Doctor," said Spock.

Kirk shook his head. "What did my crew find?" He fell quiet, and neither Spock nor McCoy broke the silence. McCoy knew the thoughts running through Kirk's mind—could the alien machines, their builders and purpose unknown, have been responsible for the downing of the *Enterprise*'s shuttle?

"Spock," said Kirk at last, "I'm thinking the shuttle went down in the canyon. With one engine sheered off, she couldn't have gone much farther, and as intact as the nacelle was, it couldn't have fallen from too great an altitude." He took a deep breath. "I'm thinking we'll find the shuttle on the canyon floor."

Spock nodded once. "A logical surmise."

"Jim," said McCoy, "how can you be sure the shuttle couldn't have glided to a landing on the plateau beyond the opposite canyon wall?"

"I can't, which is why we'll descend into the canyon, look for signs of the shuttle, and if we find nothing by our next transport window, we'll beam back to the *Enterprise* and resume our search for the shuttle from there."

Before long, Spock found a way down. It was clearly a path, beaten and worn through use over the years.

"I don't like this, Jim," said McCoy.

"I will take the lead, Captain," said Spock. Kirk nodded his approval.

McCoy began to follow Spock's lead down the path. He stopped abruptly.

"Bones?"

McCoy heard something. It sounded like a voice, very faint and distorted, as if from far away. "Do you hear that?"

Kirk and Spock stopped, turned their heads to the sky to listen. "Clearly, Doctor," said Spock, "what you hear is the sound of wind echoing off the canyon walls." He started back down the path toward the canyon floor.

Kirk, however, continued to listen. "I think I hear it, Bones," he whispered.

McCoy nodded. "It sounds like a woman's voice, Jim," he said quietly.

"But where's it coming from?" When McCoy didn't respond immediately, Kirk clapped him on the shoulder. "Bones . . . ?"

"*. . . did you hear me?*" A pause. "*Mrs. Howard?*"

Gabby Howard shook her head, tried to refocus her train of thought. "I'm sorry, you were saying?"

"*This is Mrs. Davis, the counselor at Lewis Elementary.*"

Her eyes closed, Gabby could picture Mrs. Davis, a matronly woman of nearly sixty that she had met with several times over the past two months. "What can I do for you, Mrs. Davis?"

"*I wanted to talk with you about your son, Brennan.*"

"It's Breandán," said Gabby quickly. A common mistake—six-year-old Breandán still had difficulty pronouncing the "d" sound, and oftentimes strangers misheard his name. That the school counselor could mistake her son's name bothered Gabby—if the counselor were genuinely interested in Breandán, she wouldn't make such an obvious mistake.

"*Breandán yes.*" Mrs. Davis paused. "*There was an incident at school today you should be aware of.*"

Gabby sat down and rubbed her eyes with her free hand. "An incident," she repeated.

"*Apparently Breandán brought a toy from home with him to school today, and during recess this afternoon he played on his own with that rather than with the other children. His teacher felt that Breandán hadn't been socializing with his classmates recently, and he confiscated the toy from him.*"

"Which toy was it, Mrs. Davis?" Gabby asked, though she was confident she already knew the answer.

"An action figure—Star Trek, Star Wars, I can't tell these things apart."

Gabby sighed. "It's his Dr. McCoy action figure. *Star Trek,* if you must know."

"Right." Gabby thought from her tone of voice that Mrs. Davis cared not at all whether the action figure came from *Star Trek* or from something else entirely. *"I take it you're a fan."*

"Frankly, I couldn't care less. My husband, though—" She paused, took a deep breath to steady her nerves, and decided to shift gears back onto the important topic of conversation—her son—rather than a pointless digression into *Star Trek* fandom. "I take it, Mrs. Davis, that the incident was more than the teacher taking away Breandán's toy."

"That's correct. According to the teacher, after the toy was confiscated your son . . . 'shut down.'"

"Could you be more specific?"

"He didn't play with the other children. In fact, he simply sat immobile where he had been playing with his Star Trek *toy."*

Gabby frowned. "He does that, Mrs. Davis."

"Your son isn't socializing with the other children. Our school has policies, and children are not to bring toys from home because it can lead to situations like today's where children play by themselves instead of with their classmates. Frankly, I'm concerned, Mrs. Howard, by your son's behavior today and your own indifference to the problem."

"*My* indifference? The *problem,* Mrs. Davis," said Gabby, her voice rising, "is that you took away his toy. That's *your* indifference. I made that mistake. I took his Captain Kirk toy away once, and he said not one word to me for a week. A *week,* Mrs. Davis. Do you think I want to go through *that* hell again?"

"Mrs. Howard . . ."

"No, you listen to me. His father bought him those toys, and while I don't pretend to understand the hold they have on Breandán, I know enough not to mess with it." She paused, took a deep breath, and felt relieved that Mrs. Davis didn't quickly jump into the breach. "It's not healthy, but what can I do?"

For several moments neither spoke. *"I don't think you appreciate our problem."*

Gabby buried her face in her free hand and wanted to cry. "I *do* appreciate your problem, Mrs. Davis." Her voice grew hoarse and ragged, almost a whisper. "No one would be happier than I to see him parted from those toys. You and your teachers take them away from him at your own peril."

"What does he do with the toys at home?"

"There's a muddy hole in our backyard where he sits and plays with them for hours." She stood and walked across the dining room to the bay window overlooking the backyard and Breandán's muddy hole. "And he'll sit there, from the time he gets home from school until the sun goes down, playing with his toys—his construction trucks, his other action figures. I can't talk to him, he doesn't pay attention. The toys, that hole, those are the *only* things that truly matter to him."

"I see," said Mrs. Davis. She paused. *"You say his father bought him the toys."*

"Yes."

"Don't you feel that this is something you and his father should address with Breandán?"

"I can't," said Gabby, her eyes welling up with tears. "My husband Kevin died in Iraq."

The curtains are pulled shut so no sunlight can intrude. A sterile gloominess pervades the room. What light there is comes from the fluorescent tubes overhead, a weak, dull light that only enhances the room's depressive air. Above, one tube lights momentarily, then flicks out from a short in its ballast, producing an unintentional strobe effect on the room's occupants. No one notices.

People talk. A coffin sits on a dais at the front of the room, flanked by flower bouquets at both head and foot. The coffin sits closed; this is no open casket viewing. Kevin Howard was an army pilot. He died in an Apache helicopter crash, his body horribly mangled and burned.

The mourners make polite conversation, share anecdotes about college pratfalls, weekend excursions, business contacts. Remember that time back in Florida? People still talk about that Little League record he set. Wasn't he a handsome child? Look at how sharp he was in his army uniform. Whatever happened to that old friend of his from college? No profundity in these conversations, they are the words one speaks when coming to grips with a senseless tragedy to comfort those left behind, important words but ultimately empty and hollow words all the same.

There Gabby Howard stands, her long red hair falling across her shoulders and halfway down her back, flowing freely for once instead of being pulled back into her usual ponytail. She wears a dark dress, blue not black, because she feels blue highlights her green eyes better, a long dress to obscure the sneakers she wears for comfort instead of dressier flats. She works the crowd, greeting those paying their respects to Kevin, in a kind of lazy orbit in the open area in front of the dais. Most visitors she knows, some she does not, but she makes conversation with anyone who wishes it. Her duty as the grieving widow, the concerned mother.

Her son, Kevin's son, Breandán. He stands mutely near the foot of the coffin, his blue sport coat one size too small, his clip-on tie slightly askew, his blond hair combed but still ruffled. Breandán seems not to notice that his clothes don't quite fit, that the pin of his tie irritates the base of his neck. Gabby had intended to hire a sitter, leave him at home, and only changed her mind on her mother's advice—"He won't understand, he may not remember years from now, but he deserves to be there. It's his father." She looks at Breandán from time to time, standing so quiet, so stoic, and she knows in her heart that bringing him was the right decision after all. He exudes a calm she wishes she felt. She sees in his quiet stoicism the strength she wishes she possessed. She feels pride in her son as other mourners approach him and offer their condolences, pride that he accepts their wishes and seems untroubled.

Outside night has fallen. Inside the mourning crowd thins out as the viewing hours end. Gabby walks up to her son, pats his head, tussles his hair. She kneels down and hugs him, but Breandán does not return the hug. Instead, he stands passive and looks her in the eyes, but she knows not what she sees there. His hands are folded before him, gripping something tightly. She takes his hands in hers, looks at his clenched fists and the object they hold. She says nothing, peels back his fingers.

Dr. McCoy.

"You're late, Doctor," said Kirk, a mischievous smile playing across his lips.

McCoy frowned slightly and took his seat at the conference room table. "Dr. M'Benga had some concerns about a tissue sample we took from Ambassador Gett'Ipher."

"Anything I should be concerned with?" asked Kirk. Ambassador Gett'Ipher, a Tellarite diplomat aboard the *Enterprise* en route to an urgent diplomatic conference on Algol Prime, had taken gravely ill two days out of Starbase 31. Though Kirk could substitute for the ambassador if necessary, Gett'Ipher had been instrumental in bringing the two parties—the Gottar Hegemony and the Omjaut Republic—to the negotiating table. The ambassador's health was an ongoing concern for the *Enterprise* senior staff.

McCoy shook his head. "The broad-spectrum antibiotic regimen we've applied has brought his fever down, and we're seeing an increase in his white cell counts, but we're not out of the woods yet, and I've got M'Benga and Chapel monitoring the situation closely."

Kirk leaned back in his chair and rubbed his chin. "Keep me posted." He turned and gestured to Spock. "The floor is yours."

Spock nodded. "Thank you, Captain." He touched the control panel before him, and the lights in the conference room dimmed. On the room's viewscreen a single star appeared. "This is Alpha Persei, also known in ancient Earth astronomy as Algenib. A blue-white supergiant, spectral class F, approximately five thousand times more luminous than Earth's own sun." The image on the viewscreen changed, the single star replaced by a chart showing the plotted orbits of its twelve planets. "The Algenib system was first charted by the Earth starship *Columbia*, NX-02, in 2159." Again the viewscreen changed, this time showing a single planet, gray and rocky, its face scarred by ancient asteroid impacts. "This is Algenib II, as photographed by the *Columbia*. A lifeless planet, not unlike Mercury in Earth's solar system." The image of

Algenib II changed, replaced with a fuzzy image of a blue-white planet, obviously taken from long distance. "This is Algenib II as it appeared to the *Enterprise*'s stellar cartography telescope, six hours ago."

"Thank you, Mr. Spock," said Kirk. He turned to the officer seated to Spock's left, another man in sciences blue. "Mr. Pearson."

Thorvald Pearson, the head of stellar cartography, nodded slightly. "The *Enterprise* is the first starship to pass within twenty light-years of Algenib in the past decade, and stellar cartography asked for a brief viewing window on Algenib and its system to compare our observational data to that collected by the *Columbia* a century ago. We expected to find twelve lifeless planets. We *didn't* expect to find a Class-M planet."

"Could the *Columbia* simply have missed it?" asked Kirk.

Pearson shook his head. "Unlikely, Captain. First, the world we observed is precisely where Algenib II is supposed to be, according to orbital predictions based on the *Columbia* data. Second, Algenib is a young system—no more than a quarter billion years—too young for any of its planets to have oxygen-nitrogen atmospheres." Pearson must have seen the confusion on McCoy's face, for he explained, "Earth itself has had an oxygen-nitrogen atmosphere for only the last half-billion years or so, and that came about when single-celled life began producing and releasing oxygen as a waste product. Before that, Earth's atmosphere was a muck of carbon dioxide and methane. Things happen faster in a supergiant system than they would in a system like Earth's, but not *that* much faster."

"So you're suggesting, Mr. Pearson, that Algenib II's atmosphere isn't natural."

"I'm not suggesting it, sir, I'm *saying* it—it can't be natural," Pearson said. "Something else to consider is that the image you see comes from our telescope observations. The Class-M world there on the screen is the way it was twenty years ago, not the way it is today."

McCoy frowned. "So what does the planet look like today?"

"Unknown," Spock said simply.

"We have a mystery on our hands, gentlemen," said Kirk, "and we'll need to take a look for ourselves." He frowned. "The diplomatic conference is our priority, and though we can spare a brief detour into the Algenib system, we haven't the time now for a thorough survey. We can, however, send a landing party to the surface for an initial survey while the *Enterprise* continues on our mission to Algol Prime for the diplomatic conference, and then return to Algenib once we're sure Ambassador Gett'Ipher has the situation in hand. Opinion, Spock?"

"A logical strategy, Captain."

Kirk pushed his chair back and stood. "Lieutenant Pearson, I'm placing you in charge of the planetary survey. You have six hours to pick your team. Any objections?"

Pearson seemed overjoyed at the opportunity. "None, Captain. I won't disappoint."

Kirk smiled. "You won't." He looked at the others. "Dismissed."

"In other news today, President Bush rejected a call by Senate Democrats to dismiss Secretary of Defense Donald—" Gabby clicked the television off and tossed the remote on the sofa.

"You could have left it on," said Nicole.

Gabby frowned. "Old news—I've heard it already." News depressed her, news about the ongoing Iraqi conflict even more so. Five months had passed since the President had declared that "combat operations in Iraq have ended," yet a month later Kevin's helicopter was shot down over the desert. How could "combat operations" have ended if combat was ongoing? She tried not to dwell on the disconnect between the two.

"I'll fix dinner," said Nicole abruptly as she stood.

Gabby blinked, her thinking labored, and she slowly turned her head to look at Nicole. "You don't have to do that."

Nicole smiled and shrugged. "It's what sisters do."

Gabby said nothing.

With a shake of her head Nicole gestured at the window overlooking the backyard. "What's Squirt doing?" "Squirt" was the nickname Nicole had used for her nephew since he was a week old.

Gabby looked out the window. Mid-October, and the leaves were already falling. The oaks, maybe twenty yards distant, were bare, and at the edge of the woods the yard was littered with walnuts. Breandán's hole lay halfway to the woods, created by rain runoff where the fill dirt from the home's construction created a sharp incline down to the natural ground. Today Breandán lay prone on his stomach by his hole, each hand holding some toy. From the distance Gabby couldn't tell which toys he had with him today, but certainly some were his construction trucks, others his *Star Trek* figures.

"He needs a jacket," Gabby said.

Nicole came up beside her and looked out into the yard at Breandán. He wore a long-sleeved shirt and denim pants, but in the late evening the temperature on an October night was bound to drop severely. "Kids don't think they need them. Until they really do."

Gabby turned and shot Nicole a glare.

Nicole shrugged. "Call it the wisdom of experience. Three kids'll do that to you."

The two sisters watched Breandán play in the muddy hole, waving his arms back and forth as he moved his toys across the grass and into the runoff gully and back.

"Where are the kids?" asked Gabby.

"John wanted to take them to see his parents, which I was fine with since I wanted to come see you this weekend."

Gabby came around the sofa and sat down. "You didn't have to do that."

Nicole took a seat. "You haven't sounded well on the phone. Mom's been worried."

Gabby rubbed her eyes and took a deep breath. "I'm fine. I haven't been sleeping well, and I've been worried about Breandán."

"Any particular reason?"

"The sleeping? Or Breandán?"

Nicole leaned forward and shrugged. "Both. Either."

Gabby leaned back on the couch, took a deep breath, and frowned. "Explaining the sleep is easy—dreams. I wouldn't say I have *bad* dreams, but I have . . . *unpleasant* dreams from time to time." When Nicole said nothing, Gabby went on. "As for Breandán, I worry about him because I have to. I don't understand why he spends all of his time in the backyard playing with his toys. I don't understand why he's getting in trouble at school for bringing his toys. I just don't understand, and that's what worries me." She paused. "I tell myself that, were Kevin here, we wouldn't have these problems—I wouldn't have the troubled sleep, and Breandán wouldn't spend all of his time in the backyard. But then I chide myself for thinking that way, because I don't know *how* to deal with this."

Nicole laid a hand on Gabby's shoulder.

"It's not like my life with Kevin was without its problems," Gabby said. "Our life wasn't perfect. I never understood his fixation on *Star Trek* and all that geek stuff he liked to do. I never understood why he had to spend his weekends playing soldier in the Army Reserves. We separated for a year after my second miscarriage, and at times I think we got back together due entirely to his persistence in making the relationship work. So why does it bother me to look at Breandán and see Kevin?"

"Because Kevin loved you," said Nicole.

"I know," said Gabby quietly. "And now Breandán, the one person in this world that reminds me the most of Kevin, shuts me out. It doesn't make sense."

Nicole rose, walked past Gabby on the couch, and looked at Breandán in the yard. "Do you think," she asked, turning back to Gabby, "that perhaps he's shutting you out so he can cope with Kevin's death?"

Gabby bit at her nails. "Maybe."

Nicole sighed. "I don't know, it's just a thought." She tapped the windowpane. "It's getting late, the sun's going down. Maybe we should call him in."

Gabby nodded and rose from the couch slowly. "I'll get him," she said, and she walked out to the porch.

Nicole stood at the window and looked out. Evening came early in October.

Hours earlier Algenib's primary fell beyond the canyon's western rim, bathing the *Enterprise* landing party in shadow. Without the harsh glare of the supergiant overhead, McCoy found it difficult to keep track of time—with the sun no longer visible he could judge the hour only by the sky's deepening color, which passed from a bright white to a deep aquamarine.

Halfway down the canyon's slope Kirk had spotted a long furrow in the distance. It appeared freshly dug, its sides bearing the marks of recent burns, straight and narrow, pointing generally from the direction they had come on the plateau above, and toward the canyon's opposite wall. At the furrow's far end he had seen what he took to be the shuttle's fuselage, lying on its side. The light within the canyon had grown dim in the false twilight, and the haze of the canyon floor left Kirk unsure, but a quick tricorder scan by Spock confirmed Kirk's naked-eye observation: At the furrow's end did lie the wreckage of the *Enterprise*'s shuttlecraft.

As their vantage point improved on their descent along the path down the canyon's wall, Spock observed that the machines appeared to be designed for digging into the earth, some equipped with enormous drills, others with giant hooks, cranes, and scoops. The immense scale of the machines became apparent as they approached, and as they navigated a path around one machine McCoy could not help but wonder at the beings that had built them and then abandoned them here.

The hour-long march to the crash site passed in stony silence, and McCoy had concerns for Kirk's state of mind—except to set their direction he had said almost nothing the entire way. McCoy suspected that Kirk suspected that his crewmen were dead, but he kept those suspicions to himself. Kirk seemed strangely driven, his emotions corked, and McCoy knew his friend well enough not to inadvertently unleash the raw force inside him.

Kirk insisted on a survey of the initial impact site, hoping for some clue as to what had brought the shuttle down. But just as an examination of the shuttle's nacelle hours earlier yielded no sign of the crash's cause, so too did the scattered wreckage here—a few hull plates, a power conduit—offer no insight. Clearly frustrated, Kirk turned and stalked off down the furrow toward the shuttle, saying nothing to Spock and McCoy. McCoy looked at Spock, shrugged wordlessly, and the two of them fell into step behind their captain.

Several hundred meters later, they came across more wreckage—cracked hull plates, a hand phaser. The closer the *Enterprise* officers came to the shuttle's final resting place, the more wreckage they found strewn along the furrow's path. Less than half a kilometer from the shuttle they found the ship's other nacelle, pointing nearly straight into the air as a lamppost might. At long last, nearly twelve hours after they had first beamed down to Algenib II, they reached the shuttle's fuselage.

The shuttle lay on its side, its nose buried in an embankment. The mounts for the nacelles were gone, the hatch was torn away, and a great gash ran from the nose to nearly aft. After a reconnoiter of the crash site, cataloguing the location of every fallen hull plate, every loose wire, every personal effect, Kirk and Spock scaled the hull and, armed with flashlights, dropped into the shuttle.

The chairs had come loose of their moorings and were massed in a broken pile at the front of the cabin, resting against the viewports. Storage compartments were thrown open, their doors hanging freely from their hinges, their contents scattered across the cabin. Kirk carefully began to lift away the debris and handed off bits of chairs and headrests to Spock, growing more and more frustrated with every piece of the shuttle's shattered interior that he moved.

Of his missing crew, there was no sign.

Gabby dreams.

Psychologists believe that dreams are the mechanism through which the mind organizes the day's memories into long-term storage, but while this explanation holds some truth, it leaves out crucial details. How else to explain Gabby's dreams? Some nights she wakes screaming, suffering dreams of a living Kevin, shattered by his Iraqi service, sometimes blinded, sometimes an amputee, sometimes emotionally and mentally scarred. In rare moments she imagines what it must have been like for Kevin to hold a rifle, aim at another human being, pull the trigger, and watch in horror as a body, a life, exploded into a reddish cloud of gore. Far too often her dreams are nightmares revealing unspoken fears long submerged in the subconscious. Were the psychologists correct, Gabby should dream of an angry phone confrontation with the school's counselor and a painful conversation with her own sister.

But not tonight. For once, her dreams are pleasant. No terrors, no visions of a broken husband. She dreams instead of happier times: Kevin's last day at home before his departure for Fort Bragg and, ultimately, his deployment to Iraq. She remembers holding her husband. She remembers being proud of her son that day.

Dreams are never narratives, following instead a surreal illogic. Her dreamtime memories begin with the day's end, lying with her husband, cuddled together, on the family room couch. *Star Trek II: The Wrath of Khan* plays in the DVD player—Kevin's favorite film, but one to which Gabby is indifferent. For once, though, she indulges him in his odd obsession. This is her husband's last night home before his departure for training and eventual deployment.

The film nears its end, the climactic scene in the *Enterprise* engine room. The pointed-eared guy is dying of radiation burns, while his friend looks on helplessly. *"Don't grieve . . . Admiral,"* the alien says, a line that Kevin echoes from memory. *"It is logical. The needs of the many . . . outweigh . . ."*

". . . the needs of the few."

"Or the one."

Spock collapses, breathes his last. A tear streams down Kevin's cheek.

"You're weird," says Gabby as she wipes the tear away.

"What's weird?"

"You cry when that guy . . ."

"Spock."

"Yeah. When Spock dies."

"You cried when Boromir died."

"That's different."

Kevin laughs. "How is it different?"

"Because Boromir was being all noble."

"And Spock wasn't? He sacrificed himself for his ship and his friends. How is that any different than Boromir sacrificing himself to save the hobbits?"

"Boromir is a tall drink of water. That's what makes it different." Kevin pulls the pillow from behind his head and playfully whaps Gabby across the face with it. She catches the pillow as he comes around for a second swing, pulls it from his hands, and throws it aside. They kiss. In time they roll onto the floor, their clothes discarded, and make love for the second time that day.

In Gabby's dream her memories move backward, to the first time they made love that final day.

"What do you believe in?" Gabby asks afterward, her head resting on Kevin's chest, her fingers running through his chest hair as he holds her naked body close to his and runs circles with his fingers across her back.

"Hmm?" Kevin replies, his eyes closed.

"What do you believe in? I want to know."

Kevin opens his eyes and gazes upon his wife. He gives her a wry smile and crinkles his brow. "You. I believe in you."

Gabby rolls in the compass of his arms and props herself up on her elbows. "No, really."

"I can't believe in you?"

"You shouldn't believe in me."

"I *have* to believe in you. And Breandán. No one in this world matters to me more."

Night on Algenib II was cold, far colder than McCoy would have thought possible given the oppressive heat of the day. He huddled by the campfire, a heavy blanket draped across his shoulders and tugged across his head. He looked across the fire at Kirk, who sat impassive, staring into the flames.

"Why, Jim?" McCoy asked, ending the long minutes of silence. "We could have beamed back to the *Enterprise*, waited out the night, come back tomorrow with a whole team."

For many moments Kirk said nothing, as if transfixed by the dancing flames. Finally he spoke, and his voice was low, his words not more than a whisper above the cracking and popping of the burning logs. "They were my men, Bones. My responsibility." McCoy saw Kirk slump beneath his woolen blanket and pull it tighter to stave off the cold. "When, halfway down the canyon's wall, I saw the shuttle, I knew—I'd sent them to their deaths. I owe it to them to know what happened and why they died." Kirk took a deep breath and sighed. "Were the machines responsible, protecting some secret? Was it my own arrogance, thinking that a single shuttle, on detached duty while the *Enterprise* went elsewhere, could survive on its own for a week?" He paused. "I don't know. I *need* to know."

McCoy saw that Kirk's eyes were squeezed tight, whether shutting out the cold air or the accusing flames he couldn't say. "It's not your fault, Jim."

"If not mine, then whose?" Kirk looked across the fire at McCoy. "There's more to being a leader than giving orders and expecting them to be followed. Being a leader means caring as much about those whose lives I'm responsible for as I do for my own. I can't shake the feeling, Bones, that I didn't *care* enough, and that lack of caring sent my men to their deaths."

"That's bull, Jim. Those men would have gone anywhere you asked them to, because you're their *captain*. That's enough."

"No, it's not enough. The relationship between a captain and his crew is built on faith and trust. Together we journey into the unknown every day, confront dangers we can't begin to imagine. I trust in my crew to do everything I ask of them. In turn they have faith in me, in my abilities as a leader, to see them safely home. The loss of even a single man threatens that relationship and tests the faith." Kirk paused, as much, perhaps, to collect his thoughts as it was to catch his breath in the chill night air. "If my crew loses faith in me, how can I have faith in myself?"

McCoy stood, pulled the blanket tight around him, came around the campfire, and placed his hand on Kirk's shoulder. Kirk's gaze never wavered from the dancing flames. "Jim, it's late. We've had a long day. As your doctor, I recommend sleep."

Kirk looked up, over the campfire, toward the canyon's eastern rim. "The sun will be up soon. We'll start fresh in the morning." His voice grew low, quiet. "There's still a chance. I need to know."

McCoy nodded wordlessly, turned toward the tent Spock had

erected hours earlier, and left Kirk huddled by the fire. Perhaps there was nothing more to say. Morning would come. Kirk's quest for his fallen crew would continue.

If Breandán heard Gabby's footsteps he gave no sign, content as he was to play silently with his action figures and construction vehicles.

"Breandán, honey," said Gabby, "it's time for dinner."

Breandán ignored her.

She sat down on the shaggy grass beside him. "I talked to the school today. They told me about what happened during playtime."

Again, Breandán gave no response. Instead, he dropped one action figure and picked up another.

Gabby picked up the figure Breandán had discarded. "Who's this?" she asked.

Breandán looked up at his mother. "That's Mr. Spock."

Gabby nodded, but she was doubtful that in *Star Trek* Mr. Spock wore camouflage fatigues.

"What's he doing?"

"Sleeping." Breandán turned his attention back to the action figures in each hand.

She put "Mr. Spock" back where she had taken him from. She tapped one of the figures Breandán held. "Who's that?"

"That's Bonesey."

"So the other one, he's Captain Kirk?"

Breandán said nothing.

"What are they doing?"

Again, Breandán said nothing.

"Honey, what are they doing?"

"They're looking for Daddy," said Breandán quietly.

Gabby said nothing for a few moments as she rolled Breandán's statement around in her mind. At last she said, "What do you mean, they're looking for Daddy?"

Breandán bounced the figures across the rim of the runoff gully. "Daddy told me that Captain Kirk was sending him away. His shuttle crashed. Captain Kirk is looking for him."

The last argument Kevin and Gabby had had before his Reserve activation centered on how best to explain to Breandán where his father was going and what he would be doing. Gabby preferred to deal with the issue by not dealing with the issue, but that would have been unfair to Breandán. So, Kevin sat down with Breandán the morning of the day before he left and explained patiently to him that Captain Kirk was sending him on a mission.

What will you be doing, Daddy?

Captain Kirk will have me flying shuttlecraft.

Gabby disagreed with the approach, and she wanted no part of the conversation, but she listened to it at least.

Now she understood. Her eyes began to well up with tears.

"Breandán," she said, her voice choked with emotion, "would you like to come inside? We can eat dinner and watch *Star Trek*."

Breandán looked up at her. She thought she saw a faint smile on his face, the first she had seen in months.

He stood, nodded, but said nothing. "Give me your hand," Gabby said. "Let's go inside."

A mother and a child walk hand in hand. A captain looks to the east for signs of his crew. Their roads will never end. But perhaps, in make-believe, they will find their peace.

STAR TREK®

The following is one of the manga short stories that appear
in TOKYOPOP's new *Star Trek* anthology,
Star Trek the manga: Shinsei/Shinsei,
available now at bookstores, comic shops and
other manga retailers, and online at www.tokyopop.com.

ANYTHING BUT ALONE

Story by Joshua Ortega
Art by Gregory Giovanni Johnson
Lettering by Jennifer Carbajal

Published by

TOKYOPOP®

Star Trek the manga: Shinsei/Shinsei features stories by Joshua Ortega,
Jim Alexander, Mike W. Barr, Rob Tokar and Chris Dows,
and art by Gregory Giovanni Johnson, Jeong Mo Yang,
E.J. Su, Michael Shelfer and Makoto Nakatsuka.

After delivering some medical supplies to Markus III, the *Enterprise* sets a course for Sector 061 near the Alexisian border to investigate a strange, recurring signal. That signal seems to be originating from the fourth planet in the system and bears remarkable similarities to frequencies used by the humanoid inhabitants of the planet Ximega, a civilization that was presumed destroyed in catastrophic solar storms over a hundred Earth years ago. . . .

WOOOOooo

WELCOME TO XIMEGA II, CAPTAIN KIRK--

HUH?

...AND HERE IS OUR GREAT LIBRARY...

...THIS IS WHERE WE STORE ALL OF THE DATA THAT WE WERE ABLE TO SALVAGE FROM OUR HOME PLANET BEFORE ITS DESTRUCTION.

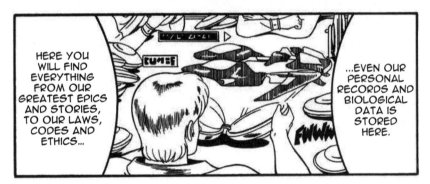

HERE YOU WILL FIND EVERYTHING FROM OUR GREATEST EPICS AND STORIES, TO OUR LAWS, CODES AND ETHICS...

...EVEN OUR PERSONAL RECORDS AND BIOLOGICAL DATA IS STORED HERE.

HOLO-GRAPHIC TECH-NOLOGY?

YES. EXACTLY.

FASC-INATING.

AND FINALLY, THIS IS OUR MANUAL LABOR PAVILION. A LIVING LINK TO OUR DISTANT PAST, WHERE WE ARE LEARNING--OR RATHER, RELEARNING--TO BE LESS RELIANT ON OUR ADVANCED TECHNOLOGY.

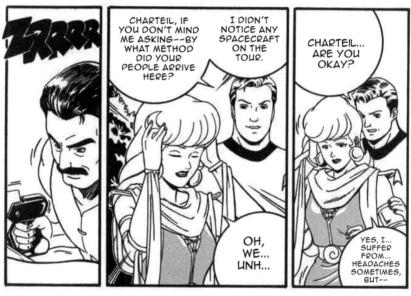

ZZRRRR

CHARTEIL, IF YOU DON'T MIND ME ASKING--BY WHAT METHOD DID YOUR PEOPLE ARRIVE HERE?

I DIDN'T NOTICE ANY SPACECRAFT ON THE TOUR.

CHARTEIL... ARE YOU OKAY?

OH, WE... UNH...

YES, I... SUFFER FROM... HEADACHES SOMETIMES, BUT--

AAAGH!!

ENDARCH!

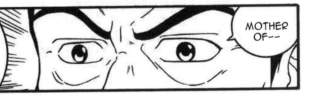

MY APOLOGIES AGAIN FOR ENDARCH'S BEHAVIOR. HE CAN BE A BIT... EMOTIONAL AT TIMES.

YOU DON'T HAVE TO APOLOGIZE.

THANK YOU.

SO--DID YOU MAKE UP YOUR MIND ABOUT OUR OFFER, CAPTAIN?

YES--WE ACCEPT.

AS LONG AS IT'S NO BURDEN TO YOU OR YOUR PEOPLE.

NOT AT ALL. I'LL HAVE JANEL PREPARE YOUR ACCOMMO-DATIONS RIGHT AWAY.

MR. SULU-- KIRK HERE. LOOKS LIKE WE'LL BE STAYING THE NIGHT.

LET'S KEEP AN OPEN CHANNEL, JUST TO BE SAFE.

BEEP BIP BEEP

SPOCK? YOU AGREED WITH THE DOCTOR?

AND SOMETHING ELSE--VERY STRANGE FOR A COLONY...

THERE ARE NO CHILDREN. ANYWHERE. IF THEY'VE BEEN HERE FOR AS LONG AS CHARTEIL SAYS THEY HAVE...

NOT ANY COLONY THAT I'D LIKE TO BE A PART OF, I CAN TELL YOU THAT MUCH.

IT IS PUZZLING THAT CHARTEIL KNEW NOTHING ABOUT THE SIGNAL WE RECEIVED AND YET SEEMED TO ANTICIPATE OUR ARRIVAL.

...WHY AREN'T THERE ANY CHILDREN? WHAT KIND OF A COLONY WOULDN'T REPRODUCE?

THE LOGICAL ANSWER IS THAT THIS IS A COLONY THAT CANNOT REPRODUCE.

IT'S WORTH GETTING TO THE BOTTOM OF. STAY ALERT TOMORROW.

INDEED, CAPTAIN.

YOU...YOU MUST HAVE RECEIVED THE SIGNAL.

YES-- MR. SPOCK RECOGNIZED IT AS XIMEGAN.

PREKRAFT WOULD HAVE ENJOYED SPEAKING WITH SOMEONE LIKE YOU, MR. SPOCK.

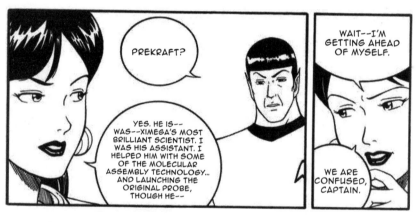

PREKRAFT?

YES. HE IS-- WAS--XIMEGA'S MOST BRILLIANT SCIENTIST. I WAS HIS ASSISTANT. I HELPED HIM WITH SOME OF THE MOLECULAR ASSEMBLY TECHNOLOGY... AND LAUNCHING THE ORIGINAL PROBE, THOUGH HE--

WAIT--I'M GETTING AHEAD OF MYSELF.

WE ARE CONFUSED, CAPTAIN.

YOU SENT THE SIGNAL. THAT'S WHY CHARTEIL AND THE OTHERS WERE UNAWARE OF IT.

YES. I'VE SPOKEN TO OTHER XIMEGANS ABOUT MY FEELINGS, BUT THEY IGNORE ME, AND PREKRAFT WON'T SEE ANYONE, AND... I...I DIDN'T KNOW WHO TO TURN TO, SO I...

UNH...I... I HAVE TO GO NOW. I'M SORRY...

DOES EVERYONE HERE SUFFER FROM MIGRAINES?

IT WOULD APPEAR SO, BONES.

PERHAPS IT IS A REACTION TO THE NANO-TECHNOLOGY.

EXPLAIN, SPOCK.

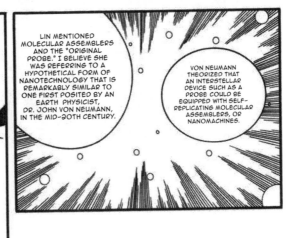

I BELIEVE I UNDERSTAND AT LEAST PART OF WHAT'S GOING ON HERE.

LIN MENTIONED MOLECULAR ASSEMBLERS AND THE "ORIGINAL PROBE." I BELIEVE SHE WAS REFERRING TO A HYPOTHETICAL FORM OF NANOTECHNOLOGY THAT IS REMARKABLY SIMILAR TO ONE FIRST POSITED BY AN EARTH PHYSICIST, DR. JOHN VON NEUMANN, IN THE MID-20TH CENTURY.

VON NEUMANN THEORIZED THAT AN INTERSTELLAR DEVICE SUCH AS A PROBE COULD BE EQUIPPED WITH SELF-REPLICATING MOLECULAR ASSEMBLERS, OR NANOMACHINES.

BY REARRANGING MATTER AT AN ATOMIC LEVEL THESE MICROSCOPIC MACHINES COULD THEORETICALLY BUILD A CITY, CREATE FOOD, LIVESTOCK-- OR EVEN SENTIENT LIFE-- SIMPLY BY MANIPULATING THE SURROUNDING ENVIRONMENT.

HORSEFEATHERS, SPOCK. CLONING IS ONE THING, BUT YOU CAN'T JUST CREATE *PEOPLE* FROM THIN AIR--THAT'S IMPOSSIBLE.

I BEG TO DIFFER, DOCTOR. WERE ONE TO DEVELOP A TECHNOLOGY CAPABLE OF STORING CONSCIOUSNESS AS ELECTRONIC DATA, IT IS THEORETICALLY POSSIBLE TO COMBINE IT WITH NANO-SCALE ENGINES TO GENERATE AN ENTIRE COLONY OF HUMAN BEINGS.

THAT'S PURE SCIENCE FICTION. NO ONE HAS THAT KIND OF TECHNOLOGY.

IT IS, AS I SAID, THEORETICAL.

BUT HISTORY HAS SHOWN THAT WHAT WAS ONCE REGARDED AS FICTION OFTEN BECOMES REALITY.

SPOCK, DO YOU REALLY THINK THAT'S WHAT'S GOING ON HERE?

WHY ENDARCH'S WOUND HEALED SO FAST? WHY THERE'S NO SIGN OF A SPACE-CRAFT...?

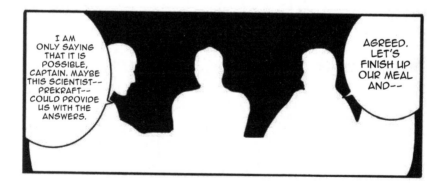

I AM ONLY SAYING THAT IT IS POSSIBLE, CAPTAIN. MAYBE THIS SCIENTIST-- PREKRAFT-- COULD PROVIDE US WITH THE ANSWERS.

AGREED. LET'S FINISH UP OUR MEAL AND--

YOU GO AHEAD AND FINISH IF YOU WANT TO, JIM. IF THIS..."FOOD" WAS CREATED BY WEIRD LITTLE MACHINES-- I THINK I'LL TAKE A RAINCHECK.

SCOOT

YES--HIS LABORATORY IS THAT TALL BUILDING THERE. BUT PREKRAFT HASN'T SPOKEN TO ANYONE IN YEARS.

SO WE'VE HEARD. THANK YOU.

AND HE DOESN'T TAKE KINDLY TO UNEXPECTED GUESTS.

HE'LL MAKE AN EXCEPTION FOR US.

IF YOU SAY SO.

WELL, JIM, THAT WAS COMFORT-ING.

DON'T WORRY, BONES-- WE'LL BE FINE.

"IF YOU SAY SO."

MOST IMPRESSIVE.

INTER-
ESTING.

WHAT
IS IT?

THERE IS
AN ORGANIC
LIFEFORM--
HUMANOID--
STRAIGHT
AHEAD.

MOST LIKELY
PREKRAFT. AND TO
THE LEFT, A HIGHLY
UNUSUAL ENERGY
READING--

--ONE
I'VE NOT
SEEN
BEFORE.

AND I BET
YOU JUST CAN'T
WAIT TO FIND OUT
WHAT IT IS, EH,
SPOCK?

I CAN WAIT,
DR. MCCOY--
BUT YES, I AM
INTRIGUED.

ALL
RIGHT--

BONES AND I
WILL TAKE THE
PATH AHEAD.

SPOCK, YOU
INVESTIGATE
THE READING
TO THE LEFT.

KEEP IN
CONTACT
WITH THE
ENTERPRISE VIA
COMMUNICATOR...

...AND BEAM OUT
IF THERE'S ANY
TROUBLE.

NNOFF IS READY FOR UPLOAD, DOCTOR PREKRAFT.

EXCELLENT. THANK YOU LIN.

YOU'VE DONE AMAZING WORK HERE, PREE--I MEAN, DOCTOR... THIS TECHNOLOGY...

YOU SHOUDN'T BE HERE, MR. SPOCK.

IT'S JUST ME, MR. SPOCK. IT'S LIN.

FWI P

I SAW YOU AND THE OTHERS ENTER THE LAB SO I FOLLOWED.

THIS ROOM BELOW--IT'S SOME TYPE OF HOLOGRAPHIC REALITY SIMULATOR?

PERHAPS. I'VE NEVER BEEN ALLOWED THIS FAR IN.

BUT FOR WHAT PURPOSE?

EVEN IF THE PROBE IS ABLE TO RE-CREATE OUR MINDS AND BODIES...

...WILL WE STILL BE US? WILL WE STILL FEEL THE SAME?

IT'S HIS MEMORY.

YES-- WE'LL STILL FEEL EXACTLY THE SAME, LIN. I PROMISE.

HE'S HURTING, MR. SPOCK. WE ALL ARE.

...THEN THE SOLAR STORMS CAME.

PREKRAFT AND I WERE UNDERGROUND WHEN THE STORMS HIT... WE WERE... WE WERE THE ONLY SURVIVORS.

OUR COLONY WAS DESTROYED... EVERYTHING ORGANIC REDUCED TO ASH, ANIMALS AND PEOPLE ALIKE... SO HORRIBLE...

JUST ME AND... I...I DIDN'T EVEN REMEMBER THIS, I... I WASN'T JUST HIS ASSISTANT...

...HOW CAN SOMEBODY FORGET THAT?

WE WERE MARRIED, LIN AND I... JUST...JUST DAYS BEFORE THE STORM.

EVERY-THING DIED AROUND US... EVERYTHING. BUT WE STILL HAD EACH OTHER. LOVE ENDURED...AND WE HAD HOPE.

THEN MY WIFE WAS TAKEN FROM ME AS WELL... KILLED BY AN INDIGENOUS VIRUS.

I HAD NOTHING LEFT TO LIVE FOR...

...UNTIL I REALIZED THAT I COULD STILL USE THE DATA UNITS AND THE ASSEMBLERS TO RE-CREATE EVERYONE... ONCE AGAIN.

CLICK

BUT THE STORMS HAD NOT ONLY KILLED MY PEOPLE...THE ELECTROMAGNETIC RADIATION ERASED ALL OF THEIR CONSCIOUS-NESSES...

WWHEEEE

I COULD NOT BRING THEM BACK, I... I ONLY HAD MY MEMORIES, AND THE MACHINES, SO I...

UNH... DAMN IT--THE PAIN! THE PAIN...!

PREKRAFT ...?

IT'S...IT'S SO HARD...BEING SO MANY PEOPLE... SO MANY DETAILS...

I WAS HAPPY... FINALLY...WITH ALL OF MY PEOPLE...

ALL OF THEM...

I REMEMBERED THEM ALL, DIDN'T I?

THE MACHINES MADE THEM LIKE I REMEMBERED...JUST LIKE I REMEMBERED! PULLED THEM FROM MY MIND...AND I WAS HAPPY...

PREKRAFT, YOU DON'T MEAN--THIS ENTIRE COLONY, EVERY PERSON HERE, EVERY *THING*-- WAS CREATED FROM *YOUR* MEMORY?

THIS IS INSANE.

...I WAS HAPPY, DON'T YOU SEE? UNTIL YOU CAME... I HAD FORGOTTEN THAT IT WAS AN ILLUSION. NOW YOU'VE DESTROYED IT AGAIN...

THE ASSEMBLERS-- THEY'RE TIED TO MY MIND. AND THEY RESPOND TO WHATEVER I WANT... ANYTHING I WANT TO CREATE--

VVOOOOOOO

WWOOOOOOO...

--ANYTHING.

OUR COMMUNI-
CATORS ARE
DOWN!

WE
CAN'T
BEAM
OUT!

UNGH!

JIM!

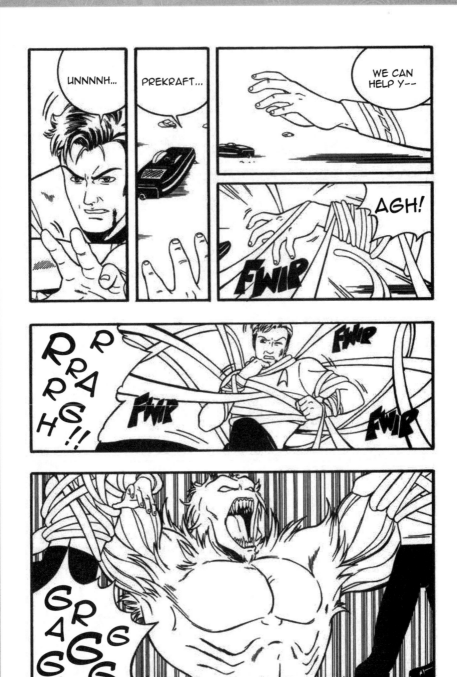

I DON'T WANT TO KILL! YOU SHOULD NEVER HAVE COME HERE!

MY GOD, MAN--YOU CAN'T POSSIBLY BLAME US FOR THIS!

PREKRAFT, PLEASE-- YOU CREATED EVERYONE-- THEY'RE ALL A PART OF YOUR MIND, AND--

SHUT UP-- NOW!!

WHEN LIN SENT US THE SIGNAL--THAT WAS *YOU*, A PART OF YOU CRYING OUT FOR HELP! *YOU* NEED HELP, AND WE--

I SAID SHUT UP!!

THEY'RE RIGHT, MY LOVE...

...WE ALL NEED HELP.

VSSH

LIN...?

WHAT ARE YOU DOING HERE, I... MY BRAIN...

...UNH... IT'S ON FIRE...

PREE!

...I'M SO SORRY...

I CAN'T PULL AWAY...

I CAN'T STOP IT...

PREKRAFT! LET US HELP!

A RrRr GGH!

WHAM

THESE PEOPLE ARE REAL, PREE.

THEY WILL HELP US.

THEY WILL HELP YOU.

I'M SO SORRY... I LOVE YOU SO MUCH...

SHH...I KNOW YOU DO. JUST SLEEP NOW, MY SWEET...IT'S ALL RIGHT...YOU CAN REST NOW.

Pik

RUMMMMMM

KRAK

THE COLONY... WHAT'S HAPPENING?

I BELIEVE LIN IS DISASSEMBLING THE COLONY.

BRUMMMMMMMM

YOU CAN LET GO AND STILL REMEMBER ME.

I AM WITH YOU.

I ALWAYS WILL BE.

SCOTTY--KIRK HERE. BEAM US UP--PLUS ONE.

WWOOOOoo

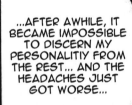

...AFTER AWHILE, IT BECAME IMPOSSIBLE TO DISCERN MY PERSONALITIY FROM THE REST... AND THE HEADACHES JUST GOT WORSE...

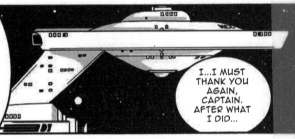

I...I MUST THANK YOU AGAIN, CAPTAIN. AFTER WHAT I DID...

IT'S THE PAST, PREKRAFT-- DON'T DWELL ON IT.

YOU'RE RIGHT--AND THAT'S EXACTLY WHAT LIN WOULD HAVE TOLD ME. I WILL ALWAYS CHERISH HER MEMORY, CAPTAIN KIRK...AND THIS CHANCE AT A NEW BEGINNING.

I'M SURE YOU WILL.